PRAISE FOR WHISPER OF WEAPONS

"*Whisper of Weapons* is a brilliant new addition to the fantasy category. It perfectly weaves together talking animals, cutthroat competitions, and a spark of romance to create a world readers won't want to leave behind."
—Annie Sullivan, author of *A Touch of Gold*

"*Whisper of Weapons* is a thrilling adventure any fantasy fan—and animal lover—will want to go on again and again. Goins paints such vivid worlds with her words, it's impossible not to be immediately transported. I'll definitely be returning for another journey!"
—Cassidy Clarke, author of *The Blood and Water Saga*

"A unique, enthralling concept gorgeously executed, populated with characters you'll want to root for and set in an iridescently enchanting world you won't want to leave. The perfect read for fantasy fans and animal lovers alike!"
—Chelsea Bobulski, author of *The Wood* and *Remember Me*

"*Whisper of Weapons* is the start of a refreshing new fantasy series with unique animal companions and relatable, easy-to-root-for characters. Told from four points-of-view, this story will have you wishing you had your own castling to join you on this sprawling adventure."
—Holly Davis, author of *A Diamond Bright and Broken*

"*Whisper of Weapons* is a Hunger Games-inspired adventure! Heroine Mella must deal with an unorthodox and illegal sidekick, mean girls, palace secrets, and learning to fight with a unique cohort. While she grows in her ability, she gains genuine friends (I loved this cast of characters!) and a sweet love interest. There are still a few unanswered questions, so I can't wait to see where this series goes!"
—**J.M. Hackman, author of** *The Firebrand Chronicles*

"*Whisper of Weapons* is an entertaining multi-POV fantasy with loads of heart, curious secrets, and charming characters. You'll want to join Mella's cohort with your own castling at once!"
—**Julia Simpson, author of** *Ashes Swept*

"*Whisper of Weapons,* a delightfully fun and captivating fantasy, has all the right elements to keep readers turning those pages! This deftly woven tale of found family, loyal animal companions, and courage against all odds will be your new favorite!"
—**Kim Chance, award-winning author of** *Keeper & Seeker*

"Fans of *The Hunger Games* and *Eragon* will love this story of world-changing teens and their talking animal companions! Full of sweet romance, captivating found-family dynamics, and the best character journeys, *Whisper of Weapons* is guaranteed to hook readers of all ages. You won't be able to put this book down!"
—**R. Dugan, author of** *The Starchaser Saga* **and** *Tales of Wonder and Woe*

WHISPER
OF
WEAPONS

WHISPER OF WEAPONS

THE CASTORS OF WRYNFORD BOOK ONE

SAVANNAH J. GOINS

ZURRENBELG

PERLEON SEA

TERRENTHYRS

WRYNFORD

Coliseum

Emberlyn Forest

POLFRYTH CITY

THE CASTORS OF WRYNFORD

LARZANOBYL

Deadland Dunes

MORRENFAYRE

Fossil Gulley

Chapter 1

MELLA

Today, I would cast my future. There would certainly be sharp fangs, broad claws, and a furry hug. At least, the *potential* for a furry hug. The fangs and claws were for sure, though.

Muscles burned in my legs as I pelted for the coliseum.

It was almost time.

And I had to arrive with a few moments to spare or else I'd be walking into the ceremony in a sweaty tunic and trousers.

I pumped my arms, a faded emerald gown bunched up in one hand and my scythe in the other, racing against time.

My boots thunked against the cobblestones as the coliseum loomed before me and smaller ramshackle dwellings cast shadows from either side of the road.

Almost there.

Swerving to one side, I darted around one of the houses and skidded to a halt. I glanced around. No one.

Because all of Terrenthyrs is already inside the coliseum! Princess Selverine and the others will be here any moment.

I tore off the tunic and pulled the gown over my head. Stepping out of my boots, I yanked off the trousers, nearly falling on the ground. "What the muck, you stupid pants!" I hissed, grappling with the ties behind my back. I cinched and bound them quickly—thanks to the last several years without a ladies' maid.

Frowning at the boots, I wished I'd had enough hands to carry my finer pair of shoes. At least the gown would cover them.

I slid the boots back on and peeked around the house.

There were still a few moments left.

A soft breeze cooled my face as I grinned up at the sun.

I'd made it.

The rest of my future was still a mystery. But as I kicked my sweaty street clothes behind a half-dead bush and straightened my gown, I smiled despite the missing pearls around the neckline.

Today I would finally meet the beginning of the rest of my life. The animal companion I'd spent the last six years preparing to cast. The castling who would train and fight and grow to adulthood with me—if we lived that long.

Gliding gracefully back to the road, I scowled at the house—the type of old-fashioned structure Father, his new wife, and I might be exiled to if I failed to perform well today and over the next eight months.

No skunking way I'm going to let that happen.

The sight of their crumbling exteriors and broken beige shutters soured my stomach. But at the far end of the road, the great coliseum rose above it all in its grand, stony glory, covering this outdated side of Polfryth City in its shadow.

In that arena I would meet my castling and join a strong cohort. Then eight months from now, I'd best the other cohorts with my comrades and claim the prize money and all the perks that accompanied becoming one of this year's Grand Castors.

My family's last chance at salvaging our future thanks to Father's rapidly declining fortune.

The heat from my stealthy trek here dissipated, and I shivered in the coliseum's shadow, my pale hands wrapping tighter around my scythe. My castling weapon's blade curved just like a giant claw, and the furry-looking stripes I'd spent countless hours etching into the wooden handle felt familiar and comforting under my fingers.

I'd carved a single word on the handle just under the blade: *Magnificence*. The name that would belong to the casting I was about to meet. The castling who would ensure my place among the better class.

I was *so* close.

Ahead, a group of Princess Selverine's colorfully dressed friends—all daughters of the wealthiest families in Terrenthyrs—rounded the corner opposite the coliseum. The summer breeze tossed their various twists, braids, and ties about their shoulders.

So they'd tied their hair back as well—good. I wouldn't want my chestnut strands flapping around my face today. I smiled as primly as I could and waved. "Hello, Selverine!"

Selverine's amber eyes landed on me, and she smiled back, throwing a carefree wave my way.

Yes!

The invitation to walk with her to the Castling Ceremony was a good sign—the culmination of all my careful attempts to climb past my family's not-quite-ideal social status. I strolled to meet Selverine and her entourage, hoping the other girls' dresses didn't outdo mine by *too* much.

I tried to forget the missing pearls. Father had promised to buy me a gown worthy of a castor for the Grand Castors' ball halfway through the castling year. Something elaborate and gorgeous. I'd look forward to that.

The sun lingered on Selverine's tan skin I so often envied as she tucked a loose brown lock behind her ear. Her emerald humming-avian earrings flashed in the sun. "Are you ready for the ceremony, Mella?"

I beamed as I fell into step beside her, gripping my scythe in both hands. "Very. I can't wait to meet my castling."

An exceptionally tall, pale girl with straw-colored hair strode from a ramshackle house up ahead, a crate of rubbish in her arms.

Yulroe leaned in from behind Selverine and me. Her delicate onyx braids, tamed into a side twist today, tickled my shoulder as she glared across the road. "Look at her. *Cleaning* just before the ceremony. Must be desperate to supplement a lesser-class income. Probably from a musician family." Yulroe snickered.

"Embarrassing," Selverine agreed, glaring at the tall girl. "Or maybe she won't actually be able to cast at all, and she'll be left with no profession. That's more likely than anything, with that plain spear."

I tried to be critical of her too, but I couldn't find anything to comment on. I hoped they were wrong, though. I winced as an image of old Trello and Loryce—musicians by trade who'd sworn off playing music to become castors, and then failed at casting. Trello had finally gotten over the embarrassment and landed an apprenticeship at the mill, despite being in his twenties by then. But Loryce—her torn and dirty beggar's rags flashed through my mind. She'd never gotten past it.

Failing to cast was *not* an option.

Frenna stepped up to my other side as we strode toward the coliseum doors. Her older brother was a member of the cohort who won the last casting competition four months ago. He was guaranteed a place in high society free of financial worries for the rest of his life. I wished that was me.

No, it *would* be me.

Frenna's fingers swept over her bound auburn curls to disentangle one from the fletching of an arrow in her quiver. "I don't know why that girl even bothers trying. She should just stick to what she was born to and leave the casting to those meant for it."

Swallowing, I searched for an appropriate topic change. Probably no one here knew my Momma, Father's first wife, was from a musician family...but if anyone found out...best to keep it to myself as long as possible.

Frenna launched into a debate with another girl about musician families, and I became extremely interested in anything but that conversation.

We were almost to it now. Another breeze rustled something in the rubbish box the tall girl had laid at the street. What was that? A fraying length of twine?

I hung back a step to check, keeping an eye on the others. It wouldn't do to be caught pilfering garbage, but I just might need those strands later. I plucked the fraying cord from the pile without breaking stride and stuffed it in my pocket. It felt like an old bowstring—it was the right length, too.

Holy skunks.

Yes, this would be useful for my illegal little hobby. I'd been worried yesterday when one of my strings had snapped, but now I smiled, giving my new piece of contraband a secret little pat as I looked forward to celebrating alone later today.

Selverine wrenched open the wide doors into the coliseum and grinned back at us. "Ladies, it's time to meet our futures!"

CHAPTER 2

DANE

"**N**ame?" a guard droned as I stepped onto the lower of the two elevated stages suspended over the arena.

"Dane Velowinzinger."

That got a look. His brows drew together as he frowned at my white-blond hair, faded clothes, and too-long last name.

Sweat slicked my grip on my castling weapon.

With a nod and a shrug, he returned his gaze to his scroll and passed me.

Whew. Relieved, I tried to look as haughty and belonging as the others around me who'd be casting today.

Below my view from the elevated lower stage, layers of stone seating wrapped around the inside of the coliseum from one side of the stages to the other. Nobles in draping robes of rich pomegranate and shimmering silks looked on haughtily from the higher rows, their various castlings perched on their shoulders or seated beside them.

Beneath them, paupers in patched breeches and threadbare tunics slouched, peering from the shadows of their lower seats, far fewer castlings among them. Everyone from the most successful merchant of Glenmyre to the poorest Wrynford musician had packed themselves into the coliseum today.

I'd bet a solid month's pay no one in this audience was from the same city I was.

Would I be able to pull this off? If the royals found out I'd actually cast Sprinter over a year ago, my flimsy story would crumble like the weapons of criminals they'd shatter for the worst crimes. An enormous boulder hung suspended with rope well above one side of the arena for just that purpose.

I'd never let them touch Sprinter.

King Jorros and Queen Narellen sat on the upper stage with their castlings—a polar bear and a huge sea eagle—watching this year's new castors chat excitedly on the balcony below.

I winced, fretting again over the unfortunately memorable combination of my strange weapon with my pasty skin and blond hair, as white as the hot popped corn they didn't seem to have on this continent. But the two-span-long tent peg had saved my life many times, so I wouldn't trade it for anything. I slid the weapon into its makeshift leather sheath on my belt.

It was almost time.

The door opened on the ground floor far below, and a rainbow of well-dressed girls poured in. I glanced over their faces out of habit, knowing my search would be as fruitless now as ever. One of them did have her dark mahogany hair, though. And, wait...I focused on her face again, the brilliant sapphire of her eyes visible even from all the way up here.

Blinking, I leaned over the railing to watch her advance. Her pale green dress swished with each step toward the stairs.

It *couldn't* be her. Once she reached this level, I would surely be disappointed again. Which was good. Because finding *her* again on the same day I needed to fake being calm and sixteen and a new castor might be more than I could handle.

The faces and dresses of the other girls blurred as I peered through them, waiting for the one with striking eyes. And there she was, her hair pulled back from her smiling face, her ocean eyes sparkling.

It *was* her.

Her eyes met mine and everything else disappeared. It was *her*. She was *here*. Her gaze skipped over mine—she didn't recognize me.

But today, I would finally learn her name.

Chapter 3

MELLA

We merged with the others on the lower stage. Everyone who had already turned sixteen or would later this year. A few musicians' sons and daughters like that strikingly tall blonde girl mixed with us better-class citizens. Everyone milled about in little clusters, jabbering excitedly.

Willova Calentine—a skinny, pale girl with brilliant scarlet hair parted cleanly down the middle and left to hang loose and cumbersome to her waist—stood right behind me. If my castling chose to manifest as the tiger I wanted, I hoped its fur would be close to her hair's color.

She wore a richly pleated dress with ornate beading and overly long sleeves. The skirt covered her legs all the way to her shoes. Unlike me, she dressed like this all the time, even though it would be completely useless in a fight. But the Calentines were especially prone to showing off. Hadn't they *been* poor, and come into money somehow? They were higher than my family by a lot—even if they hadn't always been that way.

The thick belt resting over her hips made her even more intimidating. That and the sheathed cutlass tapping her leg with each nervous shift of her feet. Her green eyes betrayed no emotion.

Acres Parrianther stood alone with his locs in an untidy bun and a quill pen tucked behind one ear, one throwing star in each hand. Wasn't he of the better class, too? I couldn't remember him ever mentioning what business his family was in when we'd been in the same black-smithing class at the Future Castors' Academy. I still couldn't believe he thought he could cast from two weapons rather than one. Of course only one would work and the other would be useless. Unless he mucked it all up and rendered *both* of them unusable. I really hoped he didn't fail to cast—he was a nice guy.

And really, the double throwing stars were striking, their sharp curved points reflecting sunbeams between his dark fingers. *I wonder what he could possibly hope to cast with a weapon so small?* Between his wiry frame and the minuscule weapons, his castling wouldn't likely manifest as anything of impressive size.

Someone laughed warmly, and I stood on my tiptoes to see that it was Kaido.

Tall, dark, *gorgeous* Kaido.

Kaido threw a glance over his shoulder and winked. My heart soared. *Please be winking at me!* He was too far away to be sure, but maybe I would impress him with my castling.

I rolled my eyes. Who was I kidding? Kaido, the devastatingly attractive son of one of the king's advisors, who would inherit an enormous fortune as the only child of such wealthy better-class parents, would *never* notice me.

I straightened my dress to keep my wits about me while I waited for my heart to calm the skunk down.

Of course everyone knew what *he* would be casting. His whip was coiled on his hip, but we'd all seen the snake head he'd carved into the handle. Not to mention the multiple serpent tattoos winding around his neck and wrists. And maybe other places. I'd heard rumors, but I didn't know for sure myself.

"Making eyes at Kaido Felzane, I see," Frenna whispered, eyeing me through thick lashes. The red fletching of her arrows stood out over her shoulder.

Yulroe grinned from a few specks away. "Ooh!"

I blushed, avoiding their gazes. "I can dream, can't I?"

Appearing at my other side, Selverine threw an arm around my shoulders. "He's just a bit too better-class for you, don't you think?"

I scowled at her. "At least I'm not pining after my grandmother's castling just because he's got wings."

It was definitely the wrong thing to say. Judging by the cold look Selverine gave me as her arm slid off my shoulders, I wondered how much of a blunder I just made. It wasn't hard to put together that Selverine wanted to be the second person ever, after Queen Narellen, to cast an avian instead of the usual woodland or plains animal. But it seemed she was more self-conscious about it than I thought.

"You'd do well to watch your mouth, Mella," Selverine hissed in my ear. "After all, it's perfectly within my power to reveal exactly what your birth mother was."

Blanching, I struggled to control my expression and avoid her eyes. *She knows.*

"Thank you all for joining us today." King Jorros addressed the crowd with open arms. Beside his empty chair, the snow-white polar bear sat on her haunches, her onyx eyes and nose prominent as they followed his every movement.

Queen Narellen's massive sea eagle perched on a stand to her right, looking too big to be real. Selverine's grandmother had the same beautiful tan skin as Selverine, looked younger than she was, and always wore a kind, wise smile. Just like today. It was too bad Selverine couldn't be a bit more like her.

Grimacing at the crowd, I latched on to the first change of topic I could. "I'll never find where my family is sitting in all that."

"Lucky you," Willova mumbled, tucking a rich burgundy strand behind her ear.

I frowned at the back of her head, unsure whether I'd heard her right.

The king raised his arms. "Today is a day of celebration! Today we welcome to adulthood our sixteen-year-olds as they take their place among us and meet their castlings for the first time!"

The crowd cheered, the bright and shining colors of the richest nobles fading to the darker drab rags of the lesser-class peasants in the lower seats.

Seats I will never sit in because I won't muck this up.

The king looked down on us from the upper stage, gesturing to the wall behind him. "Allow me to remind you all to remain in the room behind the stages after the ceremony for your training cohorts to be assigned and your castlings registered. Please do not leave without registering your castling, as harboring an unregistered castling is illegal."

He eyed each of us as if we were under suspicion, then continued.

"From then on, leather protection over the sharp points on your weapons is required during the first month of training. On Wager Day six months from now, you will return and demonstrate how your fighting skills and those of your castlings have progressed, at which time citizens will be allowed to place bets on the winning cohort and best castor and castling pair. Eight months from today, the cohorts will face off in a Grand Castors' Tournament, and the winning cohort will receive the prize money and permanent positions with the Terrenthyrs military, including a manor house and a fine monthly income!"

The crowd cheered again, louder and longer, right along with my heart. My cohort would win. Whoever was assigned with me, I would see to it that we trained harder and longer than anyone else. I would save my family's fortune with my skill and discipline.

"And let's not forget the Grand Castors' Ball, held shortly before Wager Day to celebrate the members of the oldest cohort, who have reached retirement and will be replaced by this year's winners! You'll receive instructions closer to that time."

The king laid a hand on his polar bear's head. "Lastly, please remember that a castling call is sacred. No doubt you'll all know each other's calls like the back of your hand before long, but except in an extreme emergency, it is never acceptable to take someone else's weapon and attempt to cast their castling." His stern glare melted into a smile as he raised his arms. "Now, shall we begin?"

His voice echoed through the now-silent coliseum. It was time. "Beldon Berroman! Please bring your castling weapon to the stage!"

At the front of the line, a tall dark-haired guy who looked far too bulky to be sixteen gripped his mace, swallowed, and took the stairs to the upper stage. He was unfamiliar. Definitely lesser class. Maybe I'd seen him on the drums at a party? Or he could've easily been from a different town.

"Beldon! Welcome!" King Jorros bellowed, clapping his shoulder. "Let's have a look at your weapon of choice, shall we?"

Silence dominated as the king's eyes roved over the sinister mace, its span-long handle, and the chain connecting them.

Then he shouted, "Beldon has forged a mace and chain! The body and spikes of the mace are of a black metal, as is the chain. A light hardwood handle bears the raised appearance of a large animal's teeth, with prominent canines. Well-carved and smooth to the touch. Smart to use the teeth artfully *and* practically, as tread for a strong grip!"

It would be interesting to see how focusing on teeth would suggest what animal his castling manifested as. I'd considered it, but dentition was too similar across species. I hoped the etched stripes would be a clearer suggestion to my castling. It would never be able to change after its first manifestation, so clear and concise indications were the most likely way to cast the tiger I wanted.

King Jorros slapped Beldon's back again and returned his mace. Beldon glanced excitedly at someone else on the lower stage—possibly Yulroe? No way *she* knew this guy—then faced the crowd. Taking a deep breath, he thrust the mace in front of himself, and spoke his casting cry:

"March forth, my Brawler,
An unstoppable force,
Be the tallest, the strongest,
And the greatest, of course!"

A shimmering ebony mist whirlwinded from his mace toward the stage, and a moment later a bright pair of eyes peeked out at him from under a tuft of dark fuzz at his feet.

A baby bear? No...a gorilla?

Grinning like a fool, Beldon stooped to pick up the creature as it raised its arms, almost like a human baby.

Brawler was an interesting name choice.

Selverine smirked and whispered, "Brawler? What a dumb name."

Relieved that she was acting like we were friends again, I shot a knowing look at her and then watched what he'd do next.

He held the gorilla in one arm and brandished his mace with the other, facing the crowd.

They cheered and clapped—an excellent start to the ceremony. It must've been a long time since Terrenthyrs had seen a gorilla castling. I'd never seen a live one myself and couldn't remember reading about them in my research.

King Jorros placed a friendly hand on Beldon's shoulder and bellowed, "Congratulations on your successful casting, Mister Beldon Berroman!" He released Beldon and pointed toward the door at the back of the stage. "I think we can safely assume he got what he was hoping for!"

Beldon left the stage cradling his gorilla castling, and King Jorros gestured toward the lower stage again. "Miss Willova Calentine, please come forward and present your weapon!"

Willova hesitated, breathing deeply, her face expressionless between the curtains of her red hair.

"Good luck, Willova," I whispered.

She gulped and stepped toward the stairs. Sweat darkened the armpits of her fine dress. She stumbled but quickly righted herself. Someone scoffed in the crowd and...was I mistaken, or did her fingers roll into fists?

Willova reached the stage and faced the crowd, her cheeks now as red as her hair. Her face remained impassive as she regarded the hundreds of people and their castlings, her fingers now a little too straight at her sides.

King Jorros greeted her. "Willova, welcome."

She faced him, her eyes downcast, and laid her sheathed cutlass across his open hands.

The king took up the handle and admired the blade, drawing it partially from its sheath. "Beautifully etched fur stripes, I see. And a handle with a similar teeth-shaped grip to that of Mister Beldon's mace. Well-smithed, Willova. You should be proud."

Furry *stripes?* A pang of fear shot through me. Surely she couldn't be trying for a tiger too. Multiple castlings of the same species were, of course, allowed. But it always looked bad for the person who cast the second in the same ceremony. *Of course her last name is alphabetically before mine. Ugh!*

She held out her hand toward King Jorros. Why couldn't he just hurry up and give it back so we could get this over with? I needed to know what she would cast.

At last, the king surrendered the weapon. "Very well, dear, let's see your castling!"

Finally!

Willova faced the crowd again—wind in her scarlet waves and sun throwing sharp shadows around her skinny features—and brandished her cutlass toward the sky.

"Step forth, my Faultless,
Perfect and pure,
Make no mistakes,
Be always elegant and demure."

Her voice cracked, and I wrinkled my nose. *Demure? What good would that ever be on the battlefield? Pure?*

Black and orange sparkles whirled from the cutlass.

Oh, skunks.

A perfect, beautiful tiger cub blinked up at Willova, and for the first time Willova's face broke into an astonished smile. Her body shook—with joy and relief it seemed, rather than tension—as she knelt to pick up the cub. She held it up to the crowd, eyes darting toward where the grumble had come from earlier.

Well, skunk it all. She went for the exact same thing as me. And with a cutlass! Surely mine will be bigger at least, since it'll be coming from a scythe.

I gripped my scythe tighter and waited for that copycatting caster to get the skunk off stage.

"Very well done, Willova! My congratulations to you, of course." King Jorros bowed as Willova left the stage, her beautiful tiger cub in her arms.

I squeezed my scythe's handle harder, my lips flat.

"Next, we have Reenalyn Demensey. Please ascend the stairs, Miss Reenalyn!"

The tall blonde girl from before emerged, blushing but grinning, and walked across the stage with her unornamented spear in hand. She towered over the king by at least half a span. *Skunks, how tall was she?*

"My...uh...welcome, Reenalyn! Let's have a look at your spear."

She surrendered the weapon, and he ran his fingers over it. Several more seconds elapsed than when he'd examined the first two weapons.

"Reenalyn presents an extremely long spear—about eight spans, would you say?"

"Yes." Reenalyn nodded, still smiling brightly. "Eight spans, seven specks."

"Indeed." The king's concerned eyes flicked up to Reenalyn's face and back to the inexcusably plain weapon. "And the spear tip seems to be made of gray metal. An interesting choice. And the shaft itself is a dark wood...with no embellishments?"

So...a completely plain weapon? How could she possibly hope to cast her castling of choice if she didn't mold the weapon with the right artistic embellishments to suggest what form it should take?

Selverine stared down her nose at the girl. "I'd *hate* to be her. Frightfully tall. And with a plain, unembellished *spear* as her castling weapon? How unimaginative."

A twitter of agreement rolled through the girls around me.

I wanted to shush them—get them to quiet down before the tall girl heard and got her feelings hurt. She couldn't help being tall, and more importantly, it would be a huge advantage for her in every fight. But I didn't feel like being glowered at again. I was finally in Selverine's inner circle. And I'd already messed up once today.

Selverine hefted her trident and eyed the sharp tips with a smile. "Three points are better than one, *obviously*. She must be dull in the head. She's probably the first in her musician family to try to become a castor. All her time spent playing music for others to listen to and working odd jobs to make tattered ends meet. Not much time for useful things like learning how to fight or forging an *actual* castling weapon."

That brought Trello and Loryce back to mind. I shared my meager allowance with them whenever I could. If a castling was the manifestation of the other half of your soul, and you couldn't bring it out, then what had you done to forfeit such an important part of yourself? Only the most horrible crimes could come at the cost of a part of your soul, so failing to cast must mean you have terrible secrets.

And no one wanted to be in the company of someone so questionable. Much less give them a job.

If it was the same for this Reenalyn girl—well, I wished her the best of luck.

The king paused, squinting up at Reenalyn. "Is there anything I'm missing about this...eh...fine spear?" His voice strained.

"No, sir." Reenalyn smiled, hands clasped behind her back. "You got it all."

I cocked my head. Was she making fun of the ceremony? Or was Selverine right about her? That being a lesser-class citizen, she'd spent so much time working that she hadn't had time to improve her weapon?

King Jorros cleared his throat. "Okay then, Miss Reenalyn, please proceed." He gestured for her to step in front of him. She did, then held her spear in one hand and...covered her eyes with the other?

This girl was weird.

"Join me, my Cupid,
Brave and true,
Surefooted and witty,
I already love you!"

You already...what? You don't just say stuff like that in a castling call! She wasted a whole line saying she already loves her castling?

The crowd mumbled as a lime-green shimmer poured from Reenalyn's spear. She squealed and dropped to the ground to retrieve it before I could make out what it was.

Leaping back up, she held both arms out, palms up. A skinny green lizard rested on her open hands.

She was *excited* about that tiny thing? *That's the kind of ridiculous excuse for a castling you get when you don't embellish your weapon or spend enough time preparing.* I'd be so much more successful than this loon, despite Willova's castling.

King Jorros congratulated Reenalyn and hurriedly dismissed her, then shouted, "Kaido Felzane!"

I perked up. *Kaido.*

My tiger must turn out better than Willova's, or Kaido will surely never notice me.

I glared at the exit door Willova had disappeared through. She'd really skunked everything up for me.

"Kaido has fashioned a whip! And what do we have here...a fanged serpent carving! And these red markings on the black handle—or is it forest-green? These markings are reminiscent of an anaconda! We've not had a snake castling in all the years I can remember. Kaido, my boy, that's daring. What if the animal you cast isn't a snake? How will you ever be a true pair of fighters if it forever knows it disappointed you?"

Kaido smiled that stomach-melting, face-heating, slightly uneven smile. "I'm feeling pretty confident that nothing will be disappointing about my castling."

The crowd laughed with him, likely as taken with his confidence as I was.

The king slapped his shoulder and gestured him forward. "Well then, let's see it!"

Kaido held the whip loosely, as if readying to toss the coils while still holding on to the smooth carved handle, then flicked his wrist and snapped it at the sky.

"Strike out, my Striker,
Ferocious and strong,
May your bite be venom,
And your tail miles long!"

An olive-green mist much darker than Reenalyn's spiraled from the whip into the air and writhed as it took on the form of a snake. Kaido lifted the three- or four-foot-long hatchling serpent from the ground and held it up to the crowd, a cocky grin on his face.

"Well done, Mister Kaido! May I congratulate you on your confidence and daring. It seems to have paid off."

King Jorros beamed at him and gestured him much more kindly to the exit than he had Reenalyn.

"And next, let's welcome Princess Selverine Marrandil to the stage!"

CHAPTER 4

SELVERINE

"Selverine Merrandil, my dear granddaughter." The king gestured for me to approach the stage as I reduced my scoff to a slight eye roll. I wasn't *his* granddaughter, and he'd made it clear that being his queen's granddaughter didn't qualify me for any special treatment.

My fingers twitched, and I wrapped my other hand around them to hide the nervous tic. I would cast an avian, just like my grandmother, and everything would be fine. I would do so much better than Reenalyn, that freakishly giant mass of a girl, and her tiny squiggle of a castling.

If only he would've managed to have his own heir. I wanted to be a skunking princess even less than he wanted me to be one. But by Wager Day, I'd be the strongest member of the greatest cohort—so impressive I'd have more votes than half the other castors put together.

At least if I was going to be known for something, it would be for something I did myself.

I climbed the stairs and nodded to my grandmother. She returned the nod with an encouraging, grandmotherly smile, eyes twinkling, while her sea eagle castling stared down at me with one beady eye. He was such an impressive castling. I had to have one just like him.

A slow puff of air filled my cheeks as I handed my ornately decorated trident to the king.

"A trident with...is this etching fur or...or feathers?" he asked.

My face warmed with embarrassment that he couldn't tell, but I kept silent. He had no right to ask, and I had every right not to answer.

Feathers weren't as easy to etch as the tiger stripes on Willova Calentine's cutlass or Mella's scythe. A scythe, of all things. But Willova—there was an impressive weapon and castling pair. She and her tiger would be worth having in my cohort.

Handing the weapon back, he said, "Well now, let's meet your castling, dear!"

I held the trident high in one hand and closed my eyes. *Please manifest as an avian. Please.*

"Burst forth, my Horizon,
To rend and break,
Like the mighty talons
Of my namesake!"

I held in a self-conscious wince. Had I gone too far with the namesake part? Narellen's sea eagle was named Selvenair, and I was pretty sure I was basically named after him. I winced, worried it was too far of a stretch.

Bits of mulch dust and earth trickled toward the stage.

My eyes widened. Would I really get an avian? Judging by the colors of the dust...maybe an eagle or a falcon?

Oh please, oh please, manifest as an avian. Any avian! Even a small one. That's all I've ever wanted. And my grandmother would be so proud!

But the dust morphed into a brown body with furry ears and a short fluffy tail.

My heart plummeted.

A pile of *fur* sat at my feet.

No. No!

My eyes filled with tears before I could make out what exactly it was. A distinctly non-avian *thing* of some kind. Great skunks, why had I ever thought I could manage it? But what had I done wrong? I'd done *everything* my grandmother had told me she'd done for Selvenair!

Shaking slightly, I bent to retrieve the animal from the floor and wobbled back to my feet to display it for the crowd as required.

It was the wrong castling.

It wasn't what I wanted. I'd rather have no castling at all than whatever *this* was.

"A beautiful baby wolverine! Congratulations, Selverine!"

Wolverine. Selverine. Oh no, no, no. That's not what I meant by namesake! How was the trident not enough of a hint for a sea eagle?

The king waited a few moments, then reached out a guiding hand toward my numb elbow and directed me to the room behind the stage. I met my grandmother's eyes as I left, and she gave me a concerned-but-hopeful smile and nodded as if I'd done all right.

Her undeserved support made me feel even more miserable.

I trudged through the door without acknowledging her smile, too shaken and humiliated. I was immediately buffeted with the smiles and greetings of the other new castors. Nodding vaguely at their congratulations, I took my place by one of the small windows to watch what happened next. Not that I cared. I'd blown my one chance. You only ever get one castling, and mine had come out wrong.

"Next up, Acres Parrianther!" came the king's voice through the window.

Acres Parrianther, some guy I'd never seen before, strolled his tall, lean body up the steps, his dark locs bouncing a little in their messy bun. Mumbles rippled through the crowd as everyone probably had the same thought as me: Why would you ever choose a weapon as small as that throwing star? The smaller the weapon, the smaller the castling. Of course, any weapon too large for the castor's body to handle could have worse results. But this guy had lean muscles. He wasn't skin and bones, just not bulky like that Berroman guy.

So why something so small when he was clearly fit enough to handle something bigger?

Definitely not someone I'd want in my cohort. No way he or his castling could be any good with a castling weapon so small. Not that I had much room to talk now...*ugh!*

The king welcomed him and held up the throwing star for the crowd to see and raise an eyebrow at.

The metal shifted in his hand, and a second throwing star peeked out from behind the first. "What's this, Acres? *Two* throwing stars? You can't mean to cast *two* castlings?" Behind his amused expression, concern flickered in the king's eyes.

"No, of course not." Acres smiled, his surprisingly resonant voice echoing in the coliseum. "I have a theory that if all the pieces are crafted from exactly the same piece of metal, and with plenty of special care, I should be able to cast my castling from either of these two. Even if one were lost."

The king's mouth practically dropped open as his eyebrows rose. My own brows came together to frown at his lack of tact. Yes, it sounded crazy, though what else you'd expect from someone with a quill tucked behind his ear and pockets bulging full of who knew what, I didn't know.

Would he ever let the guy cast already? Not that casting would prove his theory about whether he could cast from either star, of course. He'd have to try with one, then let the animal fall asleep and disappear, then try with the other. No time for that on stage. But I still had to know what would come from something so shamefully small.

It better be something less than mine.

The ball of shaggy fur wiggled in my arms, but I couldn't bring myself to look at it yet. Instead, I focused on the ceremony.

The king returned the throwing stars to Acres but jumped back a little when Acres received them. "Oh!" He examined a bead of crimson on his thumb. "Well, you've certainly sharpened the edges well, Acres. Let's see your castling!"

Acres held both stars in one hand and thrust them at the sky. He gazed at them and said,

"Spring forth, my Starstinger,
Lithe and quick,
Run, jump, climb,
But never be hit!

A sand-colored swarm of dust rained down from his weapons. Some coal specks seemed to be peppered in as well. And then an ochre-yellow kitten with thick ink spots and black ears much too big for its little face stared up at Acres. A gentle smile crossed his face as he stooped to pick it up. Legs too long for its little body hung under Acres's grip as he displayed the kitten to the crowd.

Incredulous about the usefulness of that pair in battle, I avoided clapping due to the furry thing still in my arms.

How could I have failed so epically?

I looked down at it for the first time without tears in my eyes. Its brown wolverine face had a gray marking around the edges, almost in a heart shape, with a point like a widow's peak on its forehead. Little smokey ears peeked up from the top of the gray heart. Pitch-black eyes stared at me, and I felt a tug toward the little thing from deep in my core.

The bond between castor and castling shivered over me, and it was done. My heart wanted to feel right, but it didn't. This wasn't how it was supposed to start. But I'd looked in this creature's eyes, and we were bonded now. My heart ached with disappointment. I wasn't supposed to let my castling see my disappointment, but how could I hide something I felt so deeply?

I returned my gaze to the window and tucked the furry thing closer to my chest, hoping it would fall asleep soon, letting its essence drift into my trident, so I could get a break from it.

"Trinka Seranova! Please come to the stage!" the king shouted.

The shortest girl I've ever seen stepped out of the shadows by the staircase and approached the steps to the stage. And skunk it all if she didn't have a head shaved as bald as a grape and arm muscles bulging almost as much as Kaido Felzane's.

I did a double take. Her dusky neck was nearly as thick as her head, her arms as big around as my calves, and her legs seemed to be solid bulk under her loose breeches. Hardly appropriate attire. And *mismatching* boots? I grimaced. One tall with ties and one short with buttons. And where was her weapon?

"Welcome, Trinka!" The king's eyes lingered on her shaved head, and he glanced over her, his smile fading. "Um, did you bring your castling weapon?"

She scowled at him and the silent crowd. When the king seemed at a loss for words, she held something small out to him and dropped it into his open palms. What was it with tiny castling weapons this year?

"Spiked brass knuckles, I see! What inspired such an unusual weapon?" He waited expectantly for her to answer. When no answer came, he cleared his throat and said, "All right, then, Miss Trinka, please proceed."

Trinka turned from the king and raised her spiked brass knuckles as high as her short arm could reach.

"Roar with me, my Mauler,
Ferocious and huge,
Destroy any enemy,
Who dares look at you!"

The king blanched as cinnamon and pepper flecks swirled like dark snow drifts from the spiked knuckles and morphed into a chocolate-brown bear cub.

Trinka lifted the cub without expression and carried it off stage. Didn't even hold it up for the crowd. Was it not what she wanted? A bear seemed a good fit for the casting call she used. Why did she seem so dispassionate? A ripple of embarrassment struck my stomach. Had I forgotten to display my creature in my disappointment? I couldn't remember. Hopefully I hadn't embarrassed myself and Grandmother with such an oversight.

Trinka came through the door and received the same grins and smiles from other new castors busy playing with their castlings. But she walked right past all of us to stand by the exit, holding her cub close to her chest as if someone might try to snatch it. With her muscular build and her castling's potential, she might be a good cohort member, despite the small castling weapon. But who was she?

Probably not better-class if I'd never seen her before. Definitely from somewhere like Wrynford, judging by her wardrobe choices.

My wolverine, so inappropriately named *Horizon*, squirmed in my arms. If only she would go to sleep already so I could cry as soon as I was away from these people. I groaned at the small crowd still milling around on the lower stage. And we'd have to wait to be assigned to cohorts once they were through...*ugh*.

Feeling the smooth glass of one of my humming-avian earrings between my fingers, I wondered if I should take them out now. I hadn't cast an avian. But I couldn't bear to let them go. Not yet. Even if all hope for my castling was gone, they were too much a part of myself to lose.

Chapter 5

MELLA

I switched my scythe from one hand to the other, nervousness twisting my stomach. The small crowd of fellow first castors thinned as the shadows from the coliseum walls lengthened. Only a handful of us remained. My turn had to be soon.

Wiping my sweating palm over my thigh, I felt something in my pocket and reached in to see what it was.

That string from the trash pile! Will I be able to tell my castling about why I'd snagged it, or will that have to be a secret, even from them?

King Jorros beamed down at us again. "And now for Dane Velowin—Velowinzinger?" He cleared his throat, squinting at the name on the parchment. "Dane, please come forward."

What kind of last name is that?

A boy with strikingly white-blond hair pale as the king's snowy polar bear took the stairs to the upper stage, screwing up his face like he was trying to hide a wince. His hand shook slightly as he presented a large nail-looking thing to the king.

"A fine—weapon—this is, indeed. Very sharp point." He returned it to Dane with a wincing smile.

What was that thing?

Dane turned toward the crowd, brandishing the whatever-it-was.

"Charge forth, my Sprinter,
Wild and free,
Be nimble and agile,

And full of speed!"

A flurry of sand, snow, and coal spiraled before melting together into a mottled wild-dog puppy, its sandy coat patched with black and white markings marbling together over its haunches and oversized ears big enough to rival Acres's kitten.

Except...it wasn't really what I'd call a *puppy*. It stood steadily on all fours and seemed to be the right size for its paws, unlike a puppy who usually had large paws. And its head was in proportion to its body as if it were an adult.

But then the dog whined and rolled on its back, begging for a belly rub. Maybe it was just a funny-looking puppy. Maybe this Dane guy had skunked up something about his weapon. If only I could hear it speak—surely it would use baby talk just like any other new castling.

"Well done, Dane, uh, *Dane*. A beautiful castling!" King Jorros gestured him off-stage, and Dane stooped to pick up his dog.

But the dog looked awfully lanky for a new castling, and awkward as his castor held him like a puppy. My eyes narrowed as they exited. Had I seen that guy somewhere before? Something about him and his castling seemed familiar. But of course that couldn't be—his castling had only just come into existence today.

"Mella Yarinelle, please come to the stage and present your weapon!" King Jorros called.

I took a deep breath and gripped my scythe in both hands, angling it so that the bottom wouldn't scrape the stone steps. *I will get a tiger, and it will be better than Willova's. Obviously. My weapon is bigger, and my casting call is better. Nothing about being demure in battle, whatever the skunk that means.*

"Welcome, Miss Mella! Let's see your weapon."

I passed it to him, and he ran his fingers over the etchings on the blade.

"A similar pattern to that of Miss Willova, I see! How intriguing. I wonder if you will be going for the same castling?"

I kept my annoyance at his Willova comment off my face and reached to retrieve my weapon.

"Good luck to you, Mella Yarinelle! Let's meet your castling!" He returned the scythe and stepped back.

One more deep breath and I raised my weapon to the sky.

"Stride forth, my Magnificence,
Massive yet lithe,
May your ferocity be feared,
And your strength always shine!"

I looked down, holding my breath for onyx and autumn dust.

And waited.

But no shimmering flecks swirled from my scythe.

My jaw dropped, and I searched the ground in case I'd missed it and my tiger cub was somehow there, already cast and simply waiting for me.

But there was nothing.

I shook out the scythe, wondering if it were possible for a castling weapon to get...maybe...*blocked* somehow?

The crowd mumbled, their surprise and confusion rising.

"Miss, uh, Mella..." King Jorros practically stuttered, clearly as shocked as I was.

What was happening? Sweat dripped into my eyes as I stared in horror at the scythe I'd spent years preparing to wield and months smithing and etching. The scythe that was now not only refusing to cast my tiger, but refusing to cast anything at all.

Heart racing, I shoved the weapon toward the sky again and shouted my castling call louder and as clearly as I could. Maybe I'd been too soft or jittery.

But still, nothing happened.

"Miss Mella, I'm afraid something's gone terribly wrong. But it seems you need to leave the stage now for the next castor to take their turn. I'm sorry, dear." The king gestured me toward the exit, maintaining a safe distance like something must be wrong with me.

I flinched away from him and stumbled toward the back room, staring at my faulty castling weapon. On the other side of the door, the new castors stood showing off their castlings to each other.

Reenalyn, that obnoxiously smiley tall girl, cheered when I came through the door. "Congratulations! What did you get?"

She beamed at me, as if waiting for me to pull my castling from behind my back.

The shocked numbness faded abruptly as they all turned to stare. Kaido's beautiful dark eyes met mine, his anaconda castling wrapped over his shoulders and tasting the air with its tongue. Selverine regarded me with shocked disgust, her wide brown eyes looking down on me like I was muck under her shoes. Willova stood opposite Selverine, supporting her tiger cub in her arms. She stared at it with pride, the tiniest edges of a smile turning up the corners of her lips. She was the only one not looking at me. She was too absorbed in staring at her castling.

The castling that should've been mine.

I couldn't take it. I burst past Reenalyn and shoved through a door at the far end of the room.

Tears blurred my sight as I stumbled from the coliseum and into the street. Thank good fortune it was deserted for the ceremony. I got my bearings and ran for it—away from the friends I no longer deserved and the cohort members I would never train with—to my secret hiding place where I could be alone and grieve and decide what to do next.

Where I could do the one thing that comforted me that no better classer would ever consider actually doing.

I clung to my worthless scythe as I sprinted out of town, the wind of my run chilling the tears on my cheeks. Once my surroundings faded from old houses to trees, I slowed, keeping an eye out for the tree with the harp-shaped knot. Finally locating it, I brushed tears from my face and counted out twenty paces off the trail.

To the fallen log where I kept my secret.

I knelt and dug the waterproof sack from within the rotten log. Collapsing into a heap of misery and embarrassment, I dropped the scythe and pulled the sack into my lap. My head in my hands, I wondered what I could possibly have done wrong. I'd studied and planned for *six years*, just as I was supposed to. I'd chosen my weapon carefully after training with a variety of different kinds. I'd forged several serrated claw-shaped blades before finally settling on the best one, and I'd then spent about a hundred years etching stripes into it.

Where did I go wrong?

I freed my mismatched mandolin—crafted of broken pieces of borrowed things—from the sack and comfort washed over me as I clung to its familiar shape and weight.

The mandolin had been Momma's favorite. I wished Father was still like he was then, when he was the younger, kinder man who'd fallen so desperately in love with Momma that he'd married her despite her lesser-class status.

Perhaps he regretted it now. I only regretted not having more time with the woman who'd named me after one of the most beautiful things in the world to her: *Melody*.

I'd spent just as long crafting and hiding this instrument of music as I had my instrument of war. If I were a castor and got caught playing an instrument, it was grounds for arrest and thrashing and for the instrument to be destroyed. Something about *preserving professions* that didn't make any sense.

But, unfortunately, I wasn't a castor. And it was the only way I could still feel close to Momma. I needed her now more than ever. When I played, I could almost see her face again. And the sweet sounds of our hired musicians always fascinated me and made me wish I was one of them. Someone free to make carefree, beautiful music rather than strive for ever-evasive social status.

I dragged one thumb over the strings, wincing through my tears at the off sound of the chord being one string short. Pulling the fraying bowstring from my pocket, I remembered the wonder and elation coursing through my veins just a little while earlier at the thought of finally meeting my castling, when I'd found this bit of bowstring by the side of the road.

How much things had changed in such a short time.

What must Father and Mother think? How would I ever face them?

The mandolin made another wrong tune as my hand went limp on the strings and joined the other in covering my face.

I would have to go home eventually. Face their disappointment. And I'd have no explanation for why it had happened. I hadn't even felt that nervous—mostly just a little afraid my tiger would be less magnificent than Willova's. A trifling concern in light of what actually happened.

Willova, the perfect better classer dressed in extravagant riches, and walking in Selverine's crowd.

Ugh. Selverine. Frenna. Yulroe. My hard-won friendships resulting from a ridiculous amount of effort and social climbing. All for nothing. Surely they wouldn't associate with me now. Now that I was a freak. A failure. Unable to cast. I was even lower than a musician now, without ever having been allowed to play music freely.

What would my Father say to his only daughter who'd let him down so spectacularly? Which one of those dilapidated houses now loomed in our future?

Scrubbing the tears from my eyes, I picked up the fraying cord and went about freeing one string and adding it to the mandolin's arm. I pinched and curled one end of the string and threaded it under the pin at the instrument's base, and then the makeshift tuner peg on the arm. I twisted a few times, striking the new string with my thumb over and over.

Not having received an education in music, I wasn't really sure which sound was the right one. I'd pilfered my meager skills through discreet observations over the years. I decided on one that sounded like it might be right and left the tuner peg in place.

My hand brushed the arm's base where I'd carved the instrument's name: *Whisper.* Because I had to keep quiet about it.

Strumming the full set of strings, I winced again, moving my fingers to twist another tuning peg. A couple more attempts and it sounded close to right.

My fingers skittered over the strings, thrumming and picking, not really knowing what I was doing. I'd never had a lesson, of course. I found a tune that sounded kind of nice and repeated it. Soon I was humming to it, words of self-pity slogging through my mind.

"My life is over now,
To other better classers I must bow,
Father will be so angry,
How bad will my punishment be?
If only Momma was still here
She would be a listening ear

My heart misses her so much
Her music and her comforting touch."

I'd never missed Momma so much. She would've known what to do. She wouldn't have thought I was a failure, even in a situation this bad. And she would've loved that I'd made myself a mandolin and tried to play it, even though I wasn't any good. The scythe would have touched her, too, since I'd chosen it because of her father.

Swiping tears from my face, I tried to focus on something else—anything to distract me from the embarrassment and pain.

"Whisper, my only friend
A secret till the journey's end
Stealthy, quiet, never found
To my music alone be bound."

My fingers slipped, and the string squealed as a white spark shot from the mandolin's arm.

I froze, the fingers of one hand still pressed over certain strings, my other thumb in midair.

Then another spark, and another. Suddenly a swirl of cotton, soot, and chocolate twisted and wove together, coiling on the ground before me.

Just like a castling.

I stared, mouth agape, as what appeared to be an actual skunking castling took form before me. Whatever this was, it was huge! The swirling mass already reached above my head from where I sat.

The pile of dust and sparks shivered and then solidified.

A pair of bright animal eyes scowled at me from the last castling I ever expected to see.

Chapter 6

ACRES

Rolling the leaves around with my tongue, I guessed from the lack of flavor that they probably weren't working anymore. Maybe that was why I'd read the last paragraph three times without comprehension. Or maybe it was due to the big day.

Grinning, I relished my casting success once more.

After the ceremony, when Starstinger had first fallen asleep, I tried casting her from the other throwing star. And it worked. So not only had I cast an awesome castling, but I'd also managed to cast her from two individual weapons, and now she would be safer than anyone else's.

I'd given her an actual extra life.

I pushed away from my desk and looked out the window. Dapplemint plants stretched from pots on the windowsill toward the dusky sky. I took one step from my desk and carefully plucked two more multihued leaves. Spitting the ball of useless leaf matter out the window, I pressed the fresh ones into my mouth and chewed. Spicy sweetness assailed my senses, but the flavors calmed down after a few minutes.

It was their function I was after, not their taste.

I sat and returned to the book: *Fossil Fever: Facts from the Foremost Experts*. An actual fossil—a small one about the length of my little finger—weighed down my notes against the gentle breeze wafting through the window.

It was disappointing that there were so few fossils around here. The nearest place they could be found was Morrenfayre, an adjacent country to Terrenthyrs, but with the casting year's responsibilities, I wouldn't be going there any time soon. Reading was the next best thing, but focusing on the words could be challenging. They seemed to wriggle away from me and strive against my comprehension. The dapplemint leaves helped me retain what I read.

Taking a swig of water, I wished the leaves didn't dry out so quickly. They'd start shriveling almost as soon as they parted ways with the stem.

Come to think of it, that side effect could probably be useful. But no, not something I'd be experimenting with.

My family would've scoffed at me and called me a hypocrite for using and contemplating floramancy after swearing it off so adamantly.

But they'd never find me here.

Starstinger's tail flicked over the edge of my desk, her round, glimmering eyes on me.

I slipped a scrap of parchment between two pages and set the book aside. "Hey, Starstinger. I thought you were ready to rest?" *How long have I been reading without noticing she was still awake? Poor thing. I'll have to take care not to be so neglectful again.*

She pushed up to sit on her haunches, her huge black ears leaning slightly to either side like they might be too heavy for her little kitten face. "Not sleepy."

"Would you like me to read aloud to you about fossils?"

She cocked her head. "What are fossils?"

Only a few hours old and she's already surpassed human baby talk and speaks in complete sentences. If only I could learn new things that fast!

I grinned. "Just the most interesting things in the world! Fossils are the remains or impressions of a prehistoric creature preserved in a petrified form or cast in rock."

She blinked at me. "What does *that* mean?"

I chuckled and reached for her, lifting her into my lap. "It means it's what's left of special animals that don't exist anymore. The only way we can learn about what they looked like and how they lived is by finding and studying the fossils they left behind."

She curled up on my legs, tucking in her lanky paws and wrapping her slender amber-and-ebony-banded tail around herself. Her bright eyes tilted upward. "Okay! I want to hear about them."

She flashed her adorable kitten smile, and I would've read to her about social etiquette or the latest women's fashions if she'd asked. It was a nice bonus that she might be interested in fossils like I was.

I opened the book and began where I'd left off. "'The Kosmoceratops is named not for any resemblance to the stars, but for the series of ornate frills, horns, and other features the likes of which have never been discovered before in any other creature, living or extinct. Fossils suggest the creatures could reach up to fifteen spans in length, and that they inhabited the plains and woodlands of...'"

A sandy cloud *poofed* under my chin, and she was gone. I sighed and grinned sheepishly. *Fossil Fever* had put Starstinger right to sleep. Well, it was only her first day. They might interest her later. Hopefully.

"Good night, Starstinger. Rest well," I whispered to empty air.

Her dual throwing stars lay on my desk atop a stack of books. What must it feel like for Starstinger to go back into them to rest? I'd have to ask her. I grinned at the pointed metal stars, proud that my guess had been right and I'd managed to cast her from either one.

She'd never be in a situation to need the extra life—I would protect her better than that—but it was there just in case.

A twinge of fear that I'd forget her shot through my gut. I chewed the dapplemint leaves again—still there. Memory still intact. It hadn't yet helped me remember what I'd forgotten before coming here, but at least now I knew I'd never forget again.

My eye fell on the fossil again. I'd so much rather read about fossils than train to fight where there wasn't even a war.

That was the irritating thing about this whole process. To legally cast a castling, you had to do it in public during a Castling Ceremony, where you then were required to register and start training your castling for battle.

But we weren't actually at war. Not with Morrenfayre or any other country. No threats loomed. We were just required to waste eight months of our lives on unnecessary effort. Unnecessary for everyone except the winning cohort, all of whom would receive honorary positions as Grand Castor guards with guaranteed wages for life. As well as prize money.

But to guard what? Terrenthyrs? From whom?

Every year a new cohort of guards was added and the oldest one retired. But by the time they retired, they'd already been lazy and out of shape for years, enjoying their easy lifestyle provided by the king and queen and wagering nobles.

Hardly the type of people I'd aspire to become, or who I'd want defending my homeland in war.

So why all these traditions that served no purpose?

CHAPTER 7

MELLA

"Um, hello...?" I set the mandolin down slowly, my eyes locked on the gigantic avian-of-prey standing before me, so tall I had to look up to its eyes from where I sat on the ground. "I, uh, guess you probably can't talk yet—"

The giant avian looked down at itself for an instant and then popped open its umber beak and— "Ahh!"

The most blood-curdling scream I'd ever heard erupted from it as it flapped around so wildly that I lurched backward and slammed against the log to avoid its flailing wings. My heart raced, terrified of what this thing was and unsure whether to try to calm it or run for my life.

"What the bloody skunking muck am I?" it screeched at me, ruffling its feathers and nearly tripping over its huge yellow eagle feet. Long black talons bigger than Trinka's bear cub's claws dug into the ground, flinging dirt clods as it stumbled, unable to balance. A ring of salt-and-pepper feathers stood on end, crowning its smokey-gray head.

How does a brand-new castling already know how to speak, much less cuss so admirably? And how the skunk did I cast it from my mandolin?

I cleared my throat, a little terrified of drawing attention to myself. "Excuse me..."

Its crazed dark eyes jolted to mine, and it seemed to notice me for the first time. It straightened to its imperious height, laid its stormy wings over its back, and stepped in place a few times, as if to find the right footing. The crown of erect feathers made it look even more insane.

"Who the muck are you?" it asked in a much more controlled voice. It sounded feminine.

"I'm Mella. Who are you?" *You're supposed to be a tiger named Magnificence, and you were supposed to come out of the scythe! Not the skunking mandolin!*

"I'm Se...Ssss, Whisper?" She ended on a high note as if she were as confused as I was about this.

Skunk it all! Is this because I named my mandolin?

"Uh, I named my mandolin Whisper, and it seems I just cast you from it—though I didn't know that was possible. So I suppose that could be your name...but why aren't you a *baby*, um, avian? How are you able to talk?"

"I...you..." She blustered and gestured at me with a shaking wing, frowning at the mandolin, then catching sight of her avian feet and scowling even more fiercely.

"I, um...I think you might be my castling?" I winced, scared she'd be even more put out. "When I was at the ceremony earlier, my weapon"—I gestured to the scythe, and she followed my gaze—"well, it didn't cast anything. I came here to be alone and to figure out what to do with the rest of my life, and I think I accidentally cast you from my mandolin."

Dark eyes still focused on me, she swallowed and fluttered her wings as if situating them more comfortably.

"Okay. Okay, then. Hmm-hmm." She lifted a foot, bending her face toward it as if to scratch herself like a dog, and poked herself in the eye. "Ow!" Crown feathers bobbing, she sent the most penetrating glower toward her curved talons yet, then snarled at me, "So I came from that"—she pointed with the edge of a wing—"that guitarish thingy there?"

"It looks like it."

"And no one else is here?"

Oh muck. Is she going to kill me where no one will hear? My eyes narrowed. "Why?"

Her frown deepened. "Because something is clearly very *wrong*, and I need to speak to *an adult* about it."

I slumped. She didn't want to be my castling. What had I done? It wasn't like I'd *tried* to cast from a musical instrument! "Technically, I just cast my castling, which makes me an adult now."

She shot me a flat look. "Hilarious. When was the last time a weapon was shattered?"

My heart plummeted. She'd rather die by having her instrument smashed like that of the worst criminal than be my castling? What was so horrible about me? "Not for decades. No one alive has seen a shattering. That's too horrible a punishment to inflict on anyone."

She paced back and forth, muttering what sounded like, "Skunk that bloody piece of dung," and "Muck it all."

"What's so horrible about being my castling? You don't even know me. Couldn't you give me a chance?" I crossed my arms and scrubbed a lingering tear away. I thought nothing was worse than having no castling, but a castling who'd rather *die* than be your forever fighting partner and closest confidant...that hurt even more.

She paused her frantic marching, glancing up from her feet that she apparently still had some kind of problem with, and eyed me. "I'm sorry to be ruining your day, Mella. This is a bit of a shock. I'm attempting to get my bearings." She turned her glower back to her talons and paced some more.

"So you're an adult castling."

She kept staring down. "It does appear to be so, yes."

"And you're an avian."

"Un*fortunately*." She said that word with such venom I wondered why she hadn't manifested as a snake.

"I don't understand." It was rude to discuss your planned castling with your castling who turned out different, but Whisper was being so rude to me, I wasn't about to feel bad. I wanted to understand what was going on. "I wanted a tiger, I made a scythe with a tiger in mind, and I crafted an excellent casting call *specifically* for a tiger. And I somehow got an avian out of a mandolin."

Whisper ignored me, glowering at everything in sight.

"If I accidentally cast an avian when I didn't want one, why was it impossible for Selverine to get what she really wanted? I've never seen anyone with an avian castling before, besides Queen Narellen."

Whisper's head shot up, and she hobbled toward me awkwardly on her two avian legs. "Did you say *Narellen*?" Her head feathers stood on end.

I recoiled from her sudden imposing presence. "Yeah, I did."

"Narellen Marrandil and her sea eagle, Selvenair?"

I wrinkled my nose. "Yeah. Why do you already know that?"

"Tell me everything you know about her."

"Okay. If you give me a little space." I scooted a span away from her.

She took a few steps back, stepped in place a couple of times, and ruffled her wings. "You have your space. Explain." She stared down her beak at me, stern as a better classer glaring at someone like Reenalyn.

I frowned. *So pushy.* "Queen Narellen—"

"The skunking queen? That *snake!*" She growled in the back of her throat and then stopped abruptly with a look of surprise.

Scoffing, I crossed my arms. "She's not a snake! She's super nice. Just a nice, old, wise lady. She's my friend's grandmother."

Well, her granddaughter used to be my friend.

Whisper kicked back dust with one foot at a time, a murderous look in her eyes. She mumbled something about "nice" and "skunk dung."

"Okay, calm down. What else do you want to know?"

She spread her wings wide. "*Everything! Like I said. Please.*"

"I don't know what else to tell you. You know about her castling. She's been the queen since before I was born. Though she had a family before Jorros, which is how she has Selverine."

"Jorros Kellenmar? And his giant marshmallow of a castling?"

I raised an eyebrow. "Yeah. Again, how do you know all that when you've literally just been born?"

"How old are they now?"

I pushed myself to my feet and threw my hands into the air. "I have no skunking idea, Whisper. Like I said, she's Selverine's grandmother, so pretty old, I guess." I scoffed. "I'm done with this interrogation. If you don't want me, fine. I'm going home." I inspected the mandolin for injuries from dropping it, and finding it in as good a shape as ever, I wrapped it in the sack and tucked it beneath the log.

Whisper was silent, so I faced her, worried what she might be planning. Even standing a span or so taller than her, I found her just as intimidating. Her head reached past my waist. Her huge feet stretched wider than mine were long, and those talons were big enough to pierce my ankle and still poke through the other side.

I gawked at her nodding head and sinking eyelids. "Whisper...are you falling asleep right now?"

"You...have to..." Her words faded as her eyes closed and her erratic crown feathers relaxed against her neck. She took a deep breath, and then *poof*. She disappeared in a swirl of smoke and fog.

Whisper's essence was now snoozing...*in my mucking mandolin!*

She'd just dozed off in front of my eyes—in the middle of a conversation. Just like any baby castling would do when it got tired. But she was so clearly *not* a baby.

With her tense attitude finally absent, I had to think this through. I pushed to my feet and paced by the log. Assuming I could cast her again—which I should be able to—what stopped me from passing her off as my actual castling? Which she really *was*, wasn't she?

But why did she seem so much older than she was supposed to be? How could I register her? If I went immediately, they'd be suspicious I'd cast her illegally and possibly used her to commit crimes before getting registered. But they'd think the same thing if I waited until enough time had passed for her to reasonably have reached adult size if she had been cast as a hatchling today.

Frowning, I rubbed the evening chill out of my arms. She didn't want to be my castling. And I had to admit, I hadn't felt the bond form like a castor was supposed to when they first cast. Unless I missed it somehow.

But if I could figure out something she wanted in exchange for her pretending to be a normal castling and happy about it at least for long enough to get me back in Selverine's circle and keep me there...maybe we could come to an agreement.

It was too bad I'd already given her the information she'd asked for. What else would she want that I could use to bargain?

My stomach rumbled, reminding me I'd skipped breakfast. I needed
to eat, and I needed to face Father and Mother. But I'd have to wait for
Whisper to be rested enough to cast again. It would be more believable
if I had a castling the first time they saw me after failing to cast publicly.
I needed them to believe me if I was going to convince everyone else.

Normally castlings needed a few hours of sleep before being cast again,
but Whisper had only been up for a few minutes before going to sleep.
Maybe another half an hour of rest would be enough for her to stay
awake long enough to meet them.

***

"We're going to need to work on your casting call, Mella," Whisper
informed me as the cotton, smoke, and chocolate bits swirled into her
giant avian form.

That wasn't the opening I'd been expecting. "You can't change a
casting call after it's been used—"

"No, no, no!" She huffed, clicking her beak like something tasted
funny. "The strength behind it. Your passion. Your warrior's *oomph*. You
need to put more backbone behind casting me or I'm going to fall asleep
five minutes into every conversation and that will get old quickly. So you
need to get better at playing that wonky violin."

"Mandolin." I crossed my arms, embarrassed by the criticism.

"So our first step is to get you some musical education. You need to *feel*
those notes as you play them and put your heart into your voice. Okay?"

I stared at her. How did she know of so many people but not any of
the laws? "Yeah, I'd love to do that, except I'm a better-class citizen." At
least, for a little longer. Until they officially made me lesser class for failing
to cast—which wasn't the case anymore, but still didn't help under the
circumstances.

She eyed me up and down. "And?"

I threw my hands up. "And *obviously* that will make music lessons
difficult, since it's *illegal* for me to play music or own instruments that
I intend to play myself." *To think I'd just been wondering whether this*

special secret part of myself was something I'd get to enjoy sharing with my castling.

Her crown feathers tremored upward as her frown sank deeper. "Is that so? Then what the bloody muck possessed you to cast me from an *illegal instrument?* How will we ever get anything done?" She kicked up dust with her talons and resumed her pacing.

"I told you, it was—"

"An accident." She gestured angrily with a wing. "I know. You've got to work on having so many accidents."

I glowered back. "Who the skunk do you think you are to speak to me like this?"

She slowed to a halt and faced me. "I'm your *castling*, of course. And if you can't get *official* lessons, we'll just have to get you some unofficial training."

"What does that mean?"

She glared at me and threw her wings up. "Don't you know anyone who plays an instrument? How did you learn?"

I crossed my arms. "Well, of course I know *of* musicians. But they're not people I talk to. I've already got my social reputation to rebuild after botching my Castling Ceremony. I can't be seen chatting with musicians. Especially not asking them to teach me the skills that make them beneath me!"

She leaned in, squinting as if I was missing something obvious. "How the skunking muck do *accomplished musicians* fall socially beneath *you*, a spoiled child? The ability to play an instrument well takes years of disciplined practice and is an admirable feat! Musicians should be the better class, if there are classes at all."

"I'm not a spoiled child, Whisper, and musicians make a living playing music for the better class, just like anyone else with a job instead of a fortune. That's just how it is."

"What is she up to...?" Shaking her head, she eyed me again. "We'll come back to that. To answer your last question: just don't be seen."

I let out an exasperated sigh and glanced around. There *were* a lot of woods surrounding Wrynford, which wasn't terribly far from our manor in Glenmyre. Lots of space to learn things in secret. Not that I wanted to be seen heading in that direction—even poorer than the section of Polfryth City I'd walked through this morning to reach the coliseum.

But this might be worth the risk.

"Okay, fine. Assuming I'm able to find someone to teach me how to play, I'm going to need to pay them, and probably extra for secrecy. I really don't like someone having that kind of knowledge over me, though..."

Whisper raised a feathery eyebrow. "What other choice do we have?"

CHAPTER 8

DANE

These trees must be the Emberlyn Forest, right?

They were on the outskirts of the town called Wrynford, and they were huge. Limbs thicker than that Beldon guy's torso.

When King Jorros had assigned me to the Wrynford cohort after the ceremony, I didn't realize what a hike it would be to get there from Polfryth City. I'd only ever heard of Emberlyn wood before, so I could be wrong about these exact trees. But either way, the forest on the far side of Wrynford suited me fine for a new place to live.

Being up high was good. It was easier to avoid being noticed and to keep an eye out.

Sprinter decided to call it a night after we arrived. I waited for him to fall asleep and shimmer back into my weapon in a swirl of coal, salt, and sawdust, then hoisted myself into a tree. I balanced on my toes and tested the sturdiness of the bough.

Good.

I swung over several branches, impressed by how sturdy they were. I was used to ropes, not trees, and I thought tree branches had to be thicker than this to hold weight, but maybe not.

Drawing my castling weapon from its leather sheath, I brandished it at an imaginary enemy and practiced keeping my footing. I leaped up and down and spiraled around the tree as I landed on different branches, keeping my eye on my weapon rather than my boots.

"Impressive, Snowflake. Let's go."

I jumped out of my skin and barely caught myself before falling to my death. Peering several dozen spans down, I could just make out a human shape in the dim moonlight. Dropping to another bough for a closer look, I spotted the bald girl from the Castling Ceremony. The one whose castling was a bear cub.

"Hello? Didn't they assign you to the Wrynford cohort, too?" she called, her dark muscular arms crossed like she'd been waiting a long time.

"Oh, yeah." I slid off a few more branches and landed on the ground. Her eyebrows shot up.

I eyed her spiked brass knuckles, glinting in the moonlight that made it through the leaves. A set sparkled from the backs of both hands. Had she cast from two weapons, too? Like the boy with the serval?

Clearing my throat, I held out one hand. "Hi. I'm Dane. You're Trinka, right?"

Without so much as a glance at my hand, she nodded. "Trinka Seranova."

I crossed my arms, feeling more awkward by the minute. "Nice to meet you."

"Yeah, you too, Snowflake." She shifted to a fighting stance and squared up like she was ready to throw a punch.

I took a step back, wrenching my weapon from its sheath and frowning at her for bringing up my white-blond hair and albino-like complexion. It seemed we were about to spar. "What's with the nickname?"

"I'm trying to conserve energy for sparring. Your last name takes more effort than I feel like giving."

Well, I couldn't fault her for that. It was a long last name, but I was prouder of it than anything in the world, except for Sprinter. "Sorry about that. But why not just call me Dane, you know, like other people?"

"Because I'm not other people. Let's *go.*"

Well, obviously, but...

"I said *let's go.* You know, spar. No one else has shown yet, so I've been training my castling. But she's sleeping now, so let's do something productive." She gestured to the tree branches. "I saw you practicing up there. Weirdest thing I've ever seen. You look more like a spider monkey than a man, the way you flit around and climb everything. But we need experience with different fighting styles. So."

She wanted to fight in the trees?

Pulling strips of leather from her pocket, she wound them around the spikes and slid the knuckles back over her hands. "All right, so give me your best strike with that thing."

Without taking my eyes off her, I brandished my castling weapon and mirrored her stance. Wide at one end, my weapon tapered over two spans to a sharp point that looked much more impressive without the leather safety layer. It shone dully from years of use and its weight and shape felt comforting in my palm.

"What is that thing?" Trinka asked.

"My castling weapon."

She rolled her eyes and threw a punch, continuing the movement to one side and throwing me off-balance.

I stumbled and she leaped and twisted, landing a kick to the side of my head. I hit the dirt hard, the air poofing from my lungs.

She leaned over me, apparently trying to get a better look at my weapon.

"It looks like a te—*ooph*." The air whooshed from her lungs as I slammed the weapon against her chest even as my face was still planted in the ground.

She skidded back, spinning to redirect the momentum back toward me. Her foot was on its way to my face again, but I blocked it with the blunt edge.

She lowered into a crouch and regarded me as I regained my balance.

Several punches later she'd only landed one on my calf as I vanished up into the trees to catch my breath.

She gripped a low branch, hauled herself up, and landed in a crouch on top of it. She swayed a little but reached for a higher branch.

The inside of her brass knuckles scraped the bark as her petite hands gripped the limb. The weapons had to be making it harder for her to climb, but she swung herself up anyway.

Her arms flexed impressively as she landed and steadied herself. She'd climbed farther and faster than I'd expected, but I still worried about sparring with her so high up. "Do you know how to fall the right way? So that you don't hurt yourself when you land?"

Her head whipped around. "Sure. Why don't you stop flitting around and face me, Snowflake."

"Because I don't want you to get hurt falling from so high up."

She fixed me with a fierce scowl. "I doubt you've ever met someone who's fallen more than me. I always get back up. Now quit trying to be a gentleman and fight me already."

"I didn't mean to offend—" Before I could finish, she launched over to my branch and threw a spiked fist at me. *Monkey's teeth! Fine then, if that's what you want.*

I barely ducked in time. She swung the other fist and caught my shoulder with a couple spikes. The leather she used must be really thin. Snarling, I swung my weapon and deflected her next blow.

She stepped out of the way and missed the next branch with a curse. Flailing, she caught herself one branch lower and pulled herself up. I swung down to her. "Nice catch."

She bared her teeth and swung again. I dodged blow after blow. She got me with a kick to the gut, and I scrambled up another few spans to catch my breath.

This girl was brutal.

"Hiding?" she called from below.

"Letting us both catch our breath."

"That's the stupidest thing I've ever heard."

I glowered at her. "Why?"

She crossed her arms and regarded me like I was an idiot. "You think an enemy is going to let you catch your breath whenever you get tired?"

I paused, searching for a good comeback. None came. "Well, I guess you have a point."

With lightning speed, she launched several spans up and punched the tree trunk at a downward angle, anchoring her spikes in the wood. With unbelievable strength, she swung her lower body over her head, punched away from the tree, arched over me feetfirst, and landed on the other side of my branch.

"That was impress—"

Spiked knuckles assaulted me from every angle as I fumbled to defend myself. She landed several more scratches, and when I couldn't make any headway, I dropped a level. "Hey, okay, I get your point."

But she was already there, one knee raised, about to throw another kick at my face.

I dodged that one but caught the next in my shoulder. I scrambled to meet her blows. But her onslaught was too much. One branch just out of reach caught my eye. I took a deep breath and shoved away from her, hooked my boot over our branch at the last minute, and swung to the other side. I caught another bough and swung around to stand on it.

And she was right behind me again. *Monkey's teeth!*

Grabbing the branch above me, I pulled myself up a span or so, waited for her to land on the branch I'd just left, then swung both feet at her. My boots slammed into her side and knocked her off the branch.

She tumbled to the ground and landed on her back with a loud *thunk*.

"That's exactly what I was trying to avoid!" I shouted at her, dropping to the ground. "Are you okay?"

"That's some fighting style," she said, sitting up. "Where'd you learn to sneak around like a light-footed tree creature?"

"Here and there."

She raised an eyebrow. The look on her face made it clear she knew I was avoiding detailed answers on purpose.

"And the tent peg?"

I started, fighting the urge to hide it behind my back.

"That *is* what it is, isn't it?"

I held one skinny arm down to her, doubting she'd let me help her up. To my surprise, she took my hand. And almost pulled me down. I barely kept upright with her unexpected weight.

"I might be barely four spans tall, but I've got muscle on me. And the tent peg?"

"It might be." I eyed her wrist. She had a tattoo—some letters that looked like they'd been partially burned away. "What happened to your tattoo?"

She snatched her arm back, her face going blank. "It's a reminder."

"Of what?"

She took a step back. "Okay, fine. You keep your secrets, and I'll keep mine. Solid spar, *Velowinzinger*. You'll do well on Wager Day. They won't be expecting you."

I nodded and offered a friendly smile. "Thanks, *Seranova*."

She spun and marched away.

Would all the people in my cohort be this challenging?

Once she was gone, I sheathed my castling weapon and climbed back up in search of a good branch to sleep on. *What a day.* I laid back on the thick limb and looked up at the starry sky, one arm folded behind my head. The other brushed the leather sheath, and I wished Sprinter had seen the spar. I'd tell him about it in the morning.

Sighing, I focused on the stars. They looked different here. Like they were arranged in new patterns. My family had warned me that would happen when I left a few months ago, but I hadn't believed them. How could you really travel so far that you didn't even see the same stars?

I missed Sprinter and hoped he'd sleep peacefully after such a crazy day. Faking a first casting and finally discovering Mella Yarinelle's name in the same hour, then sparring with this Trinka Seranova—*wow*. Calling it a crazy day was really an understatement.

CHAPTER 9

ACRES

"Acres, can I try some of those?" Starstinger's tail flicked back and forth in a warm sunbeam as she regarded me from the desk, her black-tipped ears still far too big for her face.

Smiling, I plucked another leaf from one of the pots by the window, rubbing my tired eyes with the other hand. "Sure. It doesn't taste very good, though."

She bit it from my fingers and chewed, making an adorably disgusted face.

"Just spit it out when you're done with it."

"*Ptheh.*" She dropped the leaves on the desk and pawed at them. "Those don't taste good at all. What makes them worth it?"

I pulled my chair up to the desk and scratched behind her ears, something I'd quickly learned she liked. "I chew the leaves because they help me focus when I'm reading and retain the information rather than just forgetting it. But there's more."

"Really? What's that?" She gazed up at me, fascinated, her huge black ears alert.

"I forgot some things a long time ago I need to remember. I get closer to remembering bits when I chew the leaves. Pieces of the memories float around in the background while I read. I hope I'm chipping away at a barrier, and one day, I'll finally get the whole memory back."

Her ears twitched excitedly. "Can I help?"

I grinned and scratched behind her ears again. "You're helping by just being here. You chase all the loneliness away so I can enjoy reading more."

Her smile turned wry. "And I'm gonna make you train. I think if I wasn't here, you wouldn't train at all, would you?"

My grin faded at her surprisingly accurate speculation. "What makes you think that?"

"You cast me hours ago just as the sun was coming up and haven't left that chair." She glanced at the tidy bed. "Did you even go to sleep last night?"

I pursed my lips. Castlings really did gain intelligence too fast.

The stern look she gave me was so cute I almost burst out laughing. "Okay, okay. I see your point."

She giggled her little kitten giggle. Placing a tiny yellow paw on my thumb, she grinned up at me and said, "I'm glad to be your castling, Acres. You're cool."

Actually, I was the farthest thing from cool. But she was welcome to think that all she wanted. "I'm glad you're my castling too, Starstinger. You're really cool yourself. And you're right. Without your influence, I wouldn't train at all. Besides working at the library, I'd stay in my room and read all day."

She hopped off the desk into my lap. "I guess you're lucky to have me, then. But you know, you could go find other people to train with, too. I'll need to spar with other castlings eventually if I'm going to build up my strength and skill."

"I prefer your company to anyone else's. But you're not trapped here. You're welcome to explore and find other castlings to spar with."

She pouted. "But that's no fun all by myself! You need to come with me."

"The difficulty of that is I'm not sure where to go."

She cocked her head. "Weren't you assigned a cohort? I thought you were...I mean even if you weren't, you could just listen for sparring. I can hear it from here." One ear twitched back toward the window. "I can lead you—"

"It's not that, Starstinger. I *was* assigned a cohort, but the problem is, I'm not sure it's where I belong. I don't know whether I would fit in with better classers or lesser classers now."

Her face crinkled. "Why does *that* matter?"

"Because my family had a lot of money, so the lesser classers won't want me around. But I chose to leave it and them behind to live in this one-room apartment and get a menial job, so the better classers won't want me either. I honestly don't know which one I was assigned to, anyway. Since I didn't plan to participate in all that, I didn't pay attention."

"Acres!" She rolled her eyes.

I shrugged. "Sorry."

She cocked her head. "Acres, why did you leave your family?"

I frowned, the empty space where the missing memory should've been yawning wider than ever. "Part of the reason was because I was good at floramancy, and they wanted to use that. I didn't want to be used, so that presented a problem."

"And what's the other part?"

I sighed. "I'm a little fuzzy on the details. I think whatever I forgot has to do with my leaving. But I'll have to remember it to know for sure."

She scrunched up her face, then turned her wide eyes back to me and beamed. "Well, I want you around, Acres. You're my castor, and if anyone tries being mean to you, I'll scratch their eyes out. And then we can train with whoever we want."

She walked a circle a few times, then settled into a little coil of ochre fur and ink spots, her delicate paws curled under her fuzzy chest. Any moment she would fall asleep and disappear, which would give me a little more reading time before I'd need to take her out to train.

"Thank you," I whispered, not trusting my voice. I stroked the soft fur on her back, so immensely grateful that she was my family now.

CHAPTER 10

MELLA

W hisper wasn't interested in the long walk back to Glenmyre, so
I sneaked into our backyard hauling both the worthless scythe
and the illegal mandolin concealed in the bag to cast her once I reached
our manor.

I hid among overgrown garden plants in the backyard, my hands shaking as I barely swept my fingers over the strings and whispered my casting
call. I struggled to be firm and passionate like Whisper had directed while
also being quiet enough to escape notice.

It took a couple of tries, but then snowflakes and coal dust mingled
with soot as Whisper swirled into being. *My castling.*

Sort of.

I wrapped the mandolin again and stuffed it under some
once-groomed shrubs in our backyard. "Come on, Whisper. And remember, try not to say anything, or at least to sound a little younger than
you look, okay?"

Whisper yawned. "Okay. But we've got to work on your castling call
immediately after this. I'm already exhausted."

I frowned. She could survive for a few minutes. It's not like *she* was the
one in for a lecture.

Feeling like the overly formal and respectful approach would be
most useful in this situation, I dragged Whisper to the front door and
knocked. Hopefully Mother would answer. She was far nicer than Father
in a pinch, despite not being my birth mother.

Whisper yawned, covering her beak with a courteous wing.

"You're going to be able to stay awake for a few more minutes, right?" She nodded. Was that just the sunlight, or was she flickering already? Someone unfastened the door, and I turned to greet my fate.

"Mella!" My stepmother breezed through the doorway and wrapped her warm arms around me, her pretty brown dingo castling loping at her side. "We were so worried! Are you okay?" Pushing me to arms' length, she regarded my face.

I nodded to the dingo. "Hi, Blossom." She'd always been kind to me and didn't deserve to be ignored. "Mother, you'll never guess who—" I turned, gesturing, to introduce Whisper, but she was gone. My hand fell back to my sides as my stomach plummeted. *Muck it all, Whisper!*

"Who what, Mella?" she asked, her eyebrows pulling together as she searched the empty space behind me.

"*Mella Yarinelle!*" Father's voice rumbled.

Mother and I shared a wince. I was *so* in for it.

And Whisper skunking ditched me.

He appeared in the doorway a moment later, leaning one elbow against the doorframe, his baboon castling, Ego, glowering from the shadows with his arms crossed. "Mella, get inside and explain yourself at once."

They turned away, expecting me to follow, and I released a silent poof of air through my lips. *Oh, skunks.*

We followed Father and Ego into the dining room. Father glared at me, his eyes flicking to indicate a chair. Ironically, one of the chairs whose fallen comrade once donated a plank that became my mandolin's arm.

He certainly didn't know about that, though.

I pulled the chair out and sat, wishing Whisper hadn't just gotten out of enduring this with me. *Some castling.* How would I ever explain myself now? I'd left my scythe under the shrubs too—not that it would've done a bit of good.

Mother stood behind me, resting her hands on my shoulders. Almost like a real mother. Blossom sat on her haunches in the doorway, her shoulders drooping, while Ego sat on a chair near Father, his hair standing on end.

Father glared down at me. "I'm so disappointed in you, Mella. You've disgraced our family more drastically than I could've imagined. It's already challenging enough to maintain our name among better society without you botching your *Castling Ceremony*, of all things!"

He punctuated his frustration by rubbing his forehead. "Your mother and I have done everything we can to give you a good life. It seemed like you understood, like you were making good social decisions—making your own effort to climb the ladder." He leaned on the chair in front of him, glaring at the outdated carpeting. "This isn't working, Mella."

I turned my shamed face up to meet his dark eyes. I'd have to tell them. Make them believe me. Casting at all would be an improvement over what he seemed to think of me now. "But, Father—"

He held out a hand, then glanced to Mother. I followed his gaze, and she avoided my eyes. Which was...different.

Father cleared his throat. "Mella, your mother is pregnant."

A tiny spark of joy rose in my chest. I'd always longed for a brother or sister, but over time everything else had crowded that desire out of my head.

Reaching over my shoulder, I laid a hand on my stepmother's. "Congratulations, Mother!"

I offered her a smile. If we could just get his rage out of the way so I could show them how things were better than they seemed, then I could let this exciting news sink in and celebrate.

"You're an adult now, Mella, so there would've been some changes here anyway. But things are going to be, well, more significantly different now."

"Of course. I'd love to help Mother set up a nursery! And I'll help more with things around here so she can rest as much as she needs to." I smiled at her again. Would I be getting a little brother, or a little sister? *If I told Whisper, would she care that I was excited?*

Father nodded slowly, his eyes on the faded wallpaper now. "Those are things you can help with if you wish, certainly. But you may find yourself too busy to be of much help."

I turned back to him. Of course I would be busy training, but there was no way I'd be too busy for Mother and my new sibling. And he didn't know about the training yet.

"Mella, I'm sure you'd agree you want your brother or sister to have the best chance at a suitable life, as we've tried to give to you."

I nodded, my eyebrows drawing together. "Of course..."

He sighed. "And we can't provide such a life for both of you."

Frowning, I glanced at Mother again. Were those tear trails shimmering on her face?

"Of course not, Father. But by the time a baby is grown and needing to do any social climbing, I'll be on my own."

He cleared his throat. "Because our fortunes have been so tenuous, your mother and I have agreed that the best course of action is to start saving money now for your new little brother or sister's social future."

I nodded. "That seems reasonable." What was the issue here?

"The only expense we can cut in order to save is...you."

My eyebrows now climbed my forehead. "Wait, what?"

He flashed an impatient hand, shushing me.

All sorts of shoutable insults and pleas came to my mind, but I hesitated. Surely he couldn't mean he was...kicking me out. Right?

"Your allowance will be diverted to the family's future interests. As your bedroom is the best besides your mother's and mine, you'll need to vacate it for one of the smaller ones. It's going to become the nursery, and our youngest will occupy that room until he or she reaches adulthood. You may stay in the house and take your meals here, but you'll need to get a job in town to pay for your clothing and other necessities."

My jaw dropped. Was this real? I was being kicked out of my room...to be replaced by a *new* son or daughter? I was expected to get a *job*? In *town*? Just like some lesser classer? All because he had a new opportunity—a better child to invest in instead of me. A chance to do better than he did last time. My heart twisted.

Father continued. "You may remove any bedroom furniture that will fit into your new room. The larger pieces will remain if the baby is a girl, or be sold and replaced with more masculine furnishings if he's a boy. All of your clothes and trinkets are yours as well. Please move them today. We wish to convert the room to a nursery as soon as possible."

Slowly, I stood and faced Mother. I could see Father coming up with something like this, though I wouldn't have thought he was cold enough to enforce it. But Mother? I was only an adopted daughter to her, but she'd always been kind to me. She'd sneaked me tasty treats to cheer me up whenever Father made me cry.

"Are you really going along with this?"

Fresh tears spilled down her cheeks. She reached for my hand, grasping it with both of hers as Blossom tiptoed closer, a concerned whine in her throat. "I don't love you any less, Mella—neither of us do. You're very precious to both of us, and we treasure you. But we have another child to love now, too, and whose future we must consider."

"So you're giving up on me because you have a better option?" I wrenched my hand from hers, whirling on my father. "You've always wanted this, haven't you? I've never quite measured up to your vision of an ideal heir, have I?" *Did this mean...?* I gasped. "Do you plan to disinherit me as well?"

He straightened, crossing his arms once more. "That remains to be seen, Mella. As your mother and I are in excellent health, we expect to live quite long enough to make that decision in the future. It's nothing you need to worry about now."

"Oh, well, it's such a relief to know you haven't decided *yet* that your new child should take *my inheritance* as well as everything else!"

A sob escaped Mother's lips. I ignored her, reeling from shock.

"Please go pack up your room, Mella, and move your things into—"

"No." I raised a hand in his face now, Ego appearing at his side with a hiss. "No, I won't."

His face reddened. "I said—"

"Oh, I heard you, all right. But I have a better idea. How about I make things easier for you and disappear? You were probably hoping for that when I ran off after the ceremony, weren't you? Your life would be so much easier if you didn't have your disappointment of a daughter darkening your halls."

"Mella," Mother whispered. But if she was going to defend me, she would've done it by now. She was okay enough with this that she was going along with it. She had a *real* son or daughter on the way. That was all that mattered to her.

"I'll see myself out." I marched past their castlings for the front door, fuming and near tears. They were replacing me. And I'd have nothing left. I should've tried harder to secure a wealthy match...I was an adult now, even if I didn't want to consider marriage yet. If only I could've captured Kaido's attention!

"You come back here right now, Mella Yarinelle!" Father yelled.

With a sinking stomach, I tore open the door and ran outside. Spinning back, I leaned inside for one final word. "Oh, and by the way, I *do* have a castling. And she's unlike anything you've ever seen. Too bad you told me your whole plan before meeting her. You might've been proud to have me as a daughter."

I slammed the door and shouted at it, "Too *skunking* bad!"

Chapter 11

SELVERINE

Selvenair, Grandmother's sea eagle castling, greeted me with an echoing vocalization between a screech and a growl. It made me jump.

I don't like you either, you nuisance.

As I shoved past him into Grandmother's sitting room, he shuffled on the edge of the ugly ancient drum—a relic from some other country Grandmother liked for some reason.

Selvenair flexed his long taloned toes and fixed me with a glare. "Selverine is here," he announced.

I rubbed my nose, frowning at the avian who always made my nose itch.

"Selverine." Across the room, Grandmother entered through a door I wasn't allowed to use, the many folds of her dress draping to the hardwood floor. I caught a glimpse of the warm sunlight and green plants in her private greenhouse as she shut the door and greeted me with a smile and a quick hug. "Prompt as usual. Well done, my dear."

My spirits lifted at her praise. Maybe another supervised casting session wouldn't be *so* bad. Maybe I should be grateful she'd been willing to spend this extra time with me since the Castling Ceremony.

Selvenair soared across the room and landed on the plush chaise lounge at Grandmother's side. "I do hope you've fixed your attitude toward your castling." He ruffled his wings, one beady eye centered on me.

"My relationship with my castling is none of your business, Selvenair." It irked me so much having to address the castling I wished I would've been able to cast, and that he disapproved of my wishing my castling were like him. But I thought I'd done a pretty good job of not showing my downheartedness to the wolverine.

He stared down his beak at me. "It is my business as it affects my castor and her granddaughter's castling. I do not wish to see a fellow castling humiliated, nor do I wish to see my castor exhausted from dealing with you and your...*issues*." He blinked at me, his yellow beak too big for his small, dark head.

"I'm sure she'll have everything under control this time, Selvenair," Grandmother said softly, petting his obnoxious head.

I swallowed my grimace and scratched my nose, then raised my trident to cast Horizon on the tasseled beige rug.

"Burst forth, my Horizon,
To rend and break,
Like the mighty talons
Of my namesake."

I'd barely mumbled the end of it as dust and mud swirled from my weapon and materialized into my disappointment of a castling.

So embarrassing.

"Hello, Horizon." Grandmother smiled at the wolverine cub.

Horizon immediately disappeared behind the thick Emberlyn wood leg of Grandmother's desk. Peering out a moment later, she looked undignifiedly cute with her youngling features. Her teeny black nose twitched, candlelight flickering in her dark eyes.

I avoided the frown I knew Selvenair sent my way. I didn't need his input to recognize how right he was.

Horizon was afraid of me. My own castling, who should've felt safer with me than with anyone else in Terrenthyrs and should be ready to bravely fight with me, no matter the circumstances.

But she was fearful. Self-conscious from realizing how disappointed I was that she'd chosen not to manifest as an avian.

I knelt on the rug a few feet from the desk, holding my hand toward her. "Horizon, will you come out and train with me, please? We need to grow in strength together."

She looked me up and down, emerged just enough for the pale heart shape around her face to catch the light, and then flinched back into the shadows.

Impatience flared. "Come on, Horizon. We don't have time for this. We need to train." I reached toward her again, and she growled and skittered even further under the desk. Embarrassment warmed my face. "This is no way to behave toward your castor, Horizon. Especially not in front of the queen and her castling."

She remained where she was.

"Oh, skunk this." I reached under the desk and grabbed the little wolverine's body around the middle.

She yowled and latched on to my finger with her tiny teeth.

I shrieked and shook my hand, throwing her onto the couch. "What the skunk, Horizon! You beast!"

Blood welled up from a half-dozen tiny puncture wounds between my finger and thumb. I grabbed a dark pillow from the couch and held it under my injured hand to keep the blood off the light-wood floors.

"See what I have to deal with?" I half-shrieked at Selvenair and grandmother, pointing at the puny little fanged floof as she backed into the shadows. "If she would've just manifested as a skunking avian, I wouldn't have to deal with this!"

My grandmother regarded me with concern. "Selverine, you can't keep treating your castling so badly. You've got to be patient with her. I'm sorry that causes you grief. But be that as it may, you have cast. You only get one castling. There are no do-overs, so you ought to accept things and make the best of it. You have a fine wolverine here." She patted the desk kindly. "And the way you have treated her today, and however you have treated her in the past to cause such discomfort, is shameful."

The fury dimmed, overshadowed by shame. I hung my head. Nothing was more debasing than being chastised by my grandmother, especially when Selvenair agreed with her. Why couldn't it have been something impressive like Willova's tiger if it couldn't be an avian?

"Maybe some additional one-on-one training with members of your cohort would be a good influence on you—a chance to see what other castor-and-castling relationships look like. It would be a disgrace to reveal the state of your castling as it is presently, however. So you'll need to come up with a convincing excuse to train publicly without her."

I closed my eyes and wished once again that I would've failed at casting just like Mella, so I might have another chance rather than being stuck with this one.

Having no castling at all would be better than having mine.

CHAPTER 12

DANE

W arm sunlight dappled the forest floor as Sprinter and I trampled leaves and twigs on our way from the Polfryth City market back to our cohort's headquarters—campfire, really—in Wrynford's Emberlyn Forest. Two other people I recognized from the Castling Ceremony yesterday had shown up earlier this morning. With Trinka Seranova and I, that made four.

If that was all of us, though, we were going to be a small cohort. Hadn't all the other cohorts been eight or so strong?

Hefting the basket piled high with food from the list Reenalyn sent with me, I marveled at how far Sprinter and I had come since escaping to Terrenthyrs a few months ago. I'd even bought some of these ingredients with my *own* money—an incredible feeling.

The only feeling better than that was finally discovering Mella Yarinelle's name.

Now that I was past the shock and elation of seeing her again, it was time to come up with something to say—the right words to thank her.

But I didn't need to decide on them just yet. I had plenty of time to think of something. Sorrow for her failure to cast rolled through me. Something had gone terribly wrong—but it couldn't have been anything that was her fault. She was the kindest person I'd ever met. A much better person than I was, because I had to admit—in a selfish sort of way—her failure to cast might put us on equal footing. Maybe it would mean she'd care to know my name someday.

To think of me as more than just a random person she barely remembered.

Though it might actually be better if she *didn't* remember.

"You're thinking about Mella again, aren't you?" Sprinter grinned his toothy, canine grin, his licorice-black nose pointed up at me.

Avoiding his eyes, I rolled mine and playfully bumped his shoulder with my thigh. He'd be down for any plan I came up with where she was concerned. He understood better than anyone how much we owed her. "Maybe. But I was also thinking about our new training companions. What do you think of...of..."

I slowed to a stop as I caught movement between the trees. Sprinter froze, his nose pointed toward the motion.

A swirl of dark-brown hair breezed around a girl sitting on a log a few spans away, her head in her hands, her face obscured.

Is that...Mella Yarinelle? No way. Of course not. Not in Wrynford. But she's obviously upset. I should ask if she's okay.

She wiped her eyes as another gust of wind wafted her hair from her face.

It was *her*.

But I wasn't ready...not prepared yet. A hollow, jumpy feeling overtook my chest. I needed to get off the path immediately. Go the long way around to my cohort.

I pivoted toward the thickest group of trees off the path, crushing a dry stick under my boot. *Skunking monkey's teeth.*

She leaped up, a scythe suddenly in her hands. Beautiful sapphire eyes glared at me from Mella Yarinelle's face, the girl who'd saved my life without even knowing it.

My brain unhelpfully transformed into mush.

"Uh, sorry—to bother you. We'll just be on our feet."

What? Inwardly I cringed. Had I really just said that? *"on our feet?"* I meant to say we'd be on our way out of here! This was not how this was supposed to go at all.

Her glower relaxed into a tired expression. And without her anger, the sparkles stood out on her cheeks and in her thick lashes. Something in my chest ached at the sight.

I set the basket down and took a small step forward. "Are...you okay?"

She swiped a hand over her face and sniffed, glaring in another direction. "I'm fine." Her eyes fell on Sprinter and narrowed. "Hey, I remember you."

My heart nearly stopped beating. *Monkey's teeth, she remembers me!*

"From the ceremony. Your castling—why is he an adult?"

No, she didn't remember me. She was only talking about the ceremony. Was I more relieved or disappointed? I could just tell her now. I winced at the thought. Better to wait till she at least had a good impression of me before admitting to something so embarrassing.

Sprinter whined and stepped back, glancing up at me. My throat stuck. Coughing to clear it, I considered hightailing it deeper into the woods without saying anything else.

She held up one hand. "No, sorry. I didn't mean it like an accusation. It's been a—well, a rough couple of days." She glanced nervously behind her, then back to me. "Look, we have more in common than you might think. Could you please just tell me how he's an adult, then I'll explain myself to you. Okay?"

I blinked. I didn't want to deny this girl anything in my power to give her, but I couldn't endanger my castling, either. I glanced at Sprinter. His look of trepidation morphed into one of confidence as he met my eyes and gave one sharp nod.

"Are you sure?" I asked him.

"Yes," he replied.

She nodded at Sprinter. "Thank you. So, how did your castling emerge as a full-grown dog rather than a puppy the first time you cast?"

"I—wait, the *first* time? I didn't cast an adult the first time."

She frowned at Sprinter. "But he's right there. I saw you cast him yesterday."

"Yes, Sprinter is my castling, but he's only an adult because I cast him for the first time over a year ago."

Her lips parted as her slender eyebrows rose. She glanced around and lowered her voice. "Don't you know what the punishment is for casting without being registered?"

"Yeah. Imprisonment for the castor and shattering for the castling. So I'm really glad to have gotten him registered yesterday. We're finally safe."

"They didn't question his size?"

I glanced at Sprinter. "I mean the record keeper did look at him a little sideways, but there was a lot going on with all of us in that little room, so she didn't ask questions."

She crossed her arms and drummed her fingers on her elbows. "So as far as you know, castlings are always baby animals the first time they're cast. Never adults."

"Right." Wasn't that obvious? Why would she ask something like that? Unless... "Wait." I took another step forward, mulling over her exact words. "Are you saying you know a castling that manifested as an adult the first time it was cast?"

She gripped her scythe in both hands until her knuckles turned white.

"Monkey's teeth, Mella. Is it *yours*?"

She hesitated, not meeting my eyes. "Maybe."

I ran a hand over my head, taking that in. I'd never heard of such a thing. "Wow. How did you do that?"

Her eyes hardened. "I wish I knew."

Maybe she didn't know *that*, but she definitely knew *something* she wasn't sharing. Curiosity burned in every part of me, but I would respect her secret. I had plenty of my own I couldn't share, and blatant hypocrisy wasn't a good way to thank someone for saving your life.

"But I guess I got lucky that I wasn't able to cast during the ceremony. They would've suspected me of casting illegally. I mean, baby avians are so funny-looking—no one would ever believe that thing was a baby. But how am I going to get registered now?" She dropped her face into her hands.

She cast an avian? Wasn't that a rare thing, even in this country? "There's got to be a way for you to get registered, even though it's late."

Her stomach rumbled, and she sniffed the air. "What's in that basket?"

I reached behind me for the handle and swung it around. "It's my cohort's food."

"Oh, skunks." She dropped back to the stump, one hand running through her glossy dark hair. "I left before being assigned a cohort. When

I couldn't cast, I completely forgot about all the other stuff. You can't be assigned to a cohort without being registered."

I had an immediate and possibly terrible solution to that. Should I suggest it? Nervous jitters bounced all through me. I would. If I didn't, I'd regret it. What was the worst that could happen? It's not like I could embarrass myself much more than I already had.

"You could join us, if you want. After all, cohorts are supposed to be seven to eight castors, and ours only has four. We could really use an extra member."

Please say yes, please say yes, please say yes!

I hoped my attempt at nonchalance was working. I couldn't really feel my face with all the nerves.

She seemed to be considering it.

Hold the victory fist pump.

"Are you sure it's okay to invite me without asking the others? What about your mentor?"

"We've been a cohort for barely a day. And the mentor for this district doesn't appear to give a rat's tail about the Wrynford cohort. Whoever it is wasn't with the others at the ceremony and hasn't shown up here either. And I'm sure you'd fit in great and everything." Wincing, I hoped that sounded as welcoming as it had in my head. But would she want to join a group of lesser classers?

"What? A mentor can't just bail like that."

I shrugged. "One of our cohort members said his older brother was in the Wrynford cohort a few years ago and the mentor never showed up then, either."

Nodding, she made a face.

"Right. And since no Wrynford cohort has ever come close to winning before, the royals just don't care."

"Yeah...which means you can join us without having to ask anyone. Plus, having a cohort would help you when you do get your castling registered. At least you'd be with a group working toward the same goal as everyone else, right? Not off on your own being suspicious?"

She seemed to deliberate.

"Why don't you try it? Just for a day or two. Then if it's not the cohort for you, you can leave. No harm done."

Finally, she met my eyes. "Okay. Thank you. I'll give it a try."

I struggled to control my grin and the victory fist pump that wanted to burst out. "No need to thank me." *I owe you more than you know. And I really, really hope you decide to stay.*

***

I raised a leafy branch and gestured Mella into the clearing.

Sweat glistened on the shaved head of the short-but-muscular Trinka Seranova from where she stood. She gripped a boulder in each dusky hand and pushed her arms toward the sky over and over. Weightlifting seemed to be her favorite training so far.

Weightlifting *alone.*

Mauler, Trinka's bear cub castling, sat by Trinka's mismatched boots with her fuzzy legs curved in front of her like a human toddler. She held a small stone in each hand and tried pumping her arms toward the sky like her castor. Her cubby arms trembled a little, but she kept pushing, grabbing a blackberry with her bear lips from a nearby bush when Trinka wasn't looking.

Beldon and his gorilla—named *Brawler* despite being shy and softspoken—held on to a thick branch doing pullups.

Reenalyn poked at the fire. Her eyes met mine, and she pushed to her feet with an annoyed smile. "It's about time, Dane."

She stepped over one of the fallen logs near the firepit. "Everyone's starving. What took so long?" Swinging her blonde hair over one shoulder, she reached for the basket and then paused, catching sight of Mella. "Oh, hi! Mella, right?" She beamed. "What are you doing all the way out here?"

Mella stuttered, "I, um..."

"She managed to cast after the ceremony yesterday, after the cohorts had already formed. I thought she could join ours—since we're short."

My stomach twisted, afraid of resistance to this plan. If anyone did, I'd have something to say about it.

Reenalyn's eyes twinkled as she clapped her hands. "Oh, that's a fantastic idea, Dane! Brilliant." She stepped around me and embraced Mella in a tight, long hug.

Would Mella ever hug me like that?

Probably not. Especially if she ever remembered how we first met. And my arms were about as impressive and muscular as a tightrope.

I'd still be her friend, though, if I could.

"Mella, come with me and I'll introduce you to the others." Reenalyn, still beaming, dragged Mella nearly off her feet toward Beldon.

I followed, anxious to defend her right to join us.

As Beldon dropped out of the tree a few spans away, Brawler squealed in delight and tumbled after him. He scooped her up and waved at Mella and Reenalyn.

Reenalyn gestured extravagantly to Mella. "This is Mella. She's joining our cohort! Isn't that exciting?"

"Only if that's okay—" Mella said.

"Hey, of course it is." Beldon held out one arm with Brawler hanging from it and giggling. "It's ridiculously unfair they gave some of the better classers eight to a cohort when we have half that." He smiled at Mella and reached out his other hand. "I'm Beldon, and this is Brawler. Who's a girl, by the way, despite the name. Gosh, it's day two and I'm already tired of explaining that." He shook her slender hand in his enormous one, smiling. "Great to meet you, Mella."

She smiled back, and jealousy bubbled up in my chest. *This is getting out of hand. Get over yourself.*

Should I have shaken her hand when I found her in the woods? Was that some kind of custom in this country?

Reenalyn pivoted to face Trinka.

"Wait," Beldon said. "I don't think it's a good idea to interrupt Trinka when she's counting reps. How about you introduce her at dinner?"

Reenalyn eyed the boulders Trinka was currently armed with. "Oh, good point. Yes, I'll do that. Mella, this is my castling, Cupid." Reenalyn scooped her thick, golden hair up in one hand and pulled it off her back.

A tiny green lizard peeked around her neck, frantically looking for the hair he'd just been hiding in.

I wasn't sure how effective that one would be in battle. Hopefully he'd grow. In size and confidence.

Reenalyn let her hair fall back into place. "He doesn't speak above a whisper yet, but we're working on it. We're both looking forward to serious training with you guys!" She beamed at everyone.

Beldon's stomach rumbled loud enough for everyone to hear, and he eyed the basket still in my hands. "Is that dinner?"

Reenalyn snatched it from me. "It will be soon!"

We followed Reenalyn to the fire, and she started doling out the basket's contents. Trinka appeared with Mauler and asked for a job. Reenalyn issued orders like someone used to doing so, and when she positioned Mella next to me in the food preparation assembly line, she winked right at me as if she knew exactly how much faster Mella made my heart beat.

CHAPTER 13

MELLA

Right now, I should be seated at a richly carved mahogany dining table in Glenmyre or Polfryth City, crowded with other better-class citizens dressed in fine gowns and suits. Perhaps discussing the various strengths of our cohort or the weaknesses of others while sipping spiced cider and eating peppered lamb and soft cheeses off a golden plate presented by a servant.

With a skunking *fork*.

Instead, I sat outside on a rotten log on the outskirts of *Wrynford*, of all places, watching the pheasant and broccoli *I'd helped prepare* roast on a bonfire, no eating utensils of any kind in sight. And no talk of strategy had made an appearance yet.

Apparently, my new cohort was still getting to know each other. Probably the first cohort ever where not a single member knew another before the ceremony. No one grew up together, no one's parents were old acquaintances or potential business partners. I was beginning to suspect a couple of them weren't even from the country of Terrenthyrs. *Weird*.

"So then, Naymon told the rest of them to go skunk themselves, and no one ever found out it had been me all along." Beldon chuckled, finishing a wild story from his childhood. "It turns out there are some advantages to having so many older brothers. You're never short on free entertainment."

Reenalyn laughed and clapped her hands. "Wow. He sounds like the best big brother to grow up with, Beldon. What business is your family in?"

His face seemed to fall for a moment, but he was back to his cheery self a moment later. "Silversmithing. But the business will obviously go to one of the older ones, and I don't enjoy being in a hot cave with fire all day anyway. Being a castor means plenty of time outside, lots of fresh air. My parents and brothers all supported my decision, which was nice."

The tip of Cupid's little emerald nose parted Reenalyn's hair, and Reenalyn reached up to scratch his head. "I'm from a family of cello crafters," she said. "But my heart belongs to the violin. And that's all there is to me."

Well if her heart belonged to the violin, how did she feel about having to give it up forever to become a castor?

Reenalyn beamed at Trinka as if inviting her to go next. Trinka, who Reenalyn had introduced me to while I separated broccoli florets with my bare fingers, continued to stare into the fire. She seemed like she wasn't going to answer, so I went ahead.

"I'm Mella, and Whisper is my castling's name." They were probably wondering why she wasn't here, and what sort of animal she was. I'd just have to spring that on them tomorrow. "She's resting now after...training earlier today."

How would this group of misfits feel if they knew I'd cast from an instrument? I didn't want to make the gap any wider between us. Not yet. I needed to get better at casting Whisper so I could pull off this plan and get back into Selverine's inner circle by Wager Day. I was *not* going to lose years of hard work and my entire future.

This was a time for training myself and Whisper as hard as I could, and then getting back into society where I could prove myself enough to get into a better cohort. Then win the competition and maybe even win Kaido's handsome heart and equally handsome fortune if I could manage it, to secure my standing in society and a future of ease and luxury.

If I could get Kaido's attention, I'd have a chance at that even if I failed the competition. And better yet, maybe I'd end up successful at both. Two fortunes won on my own to wave in Father's scowling face.

Until then, though, I would need to find a job. I grimaced at the idea. Just what Father wanted.

Reenalyn nodded to me, an invitation to share more.

I hesitated. "Nothing interesting to share about my family. Dane?" I turned to him, hoping he'd take over before Reenalyn could ask me anything else.

A smile further brightened his firelit face. "My dad and mom sacrificed a lot to help me get here—they're some of the most selfless people I know. And...I can't wait to see them again once the castling year is over."

"Wait, you're not from Terrenthyrs?" Beldon asked.

"They'll just be traveling a lot. They don't have a permanent residence with their jobs." He cleared his throat and glanced around the fire a little too desperately. "How about you, Trinka?"

I narrowed my eyes at him, then turned for Trinka's answer.

Trinka pointed to her castling, the ridges of her biceps deepening in the shadows of the flames. "That's Mauler. Don't mess with her. You already know my name. Don't mess with me. I'm not here to make friends. I'm just here to fulfill the cohort requirement. I don't want the job. Just the prize money."

Reenalyn's eyebrow shot up, but she masked it by hopping up to check the food. "All right, I think it's done now." She twisted the pole to swing the grate off the fire. Heat rose in smokey tendrils from the pheasant and vegetables. "Dig in!"

Beldon, Reenalyn, Trinka, and Dane each grabbed a piece of pheasant from the grate. With their bare hands.

Skunks.

Not wanting to appear too obviously out of place, I plucked off the last piece and blew on my fingers. After a moment I bit into the roasted pheasant and chewed, surprised the wild, smokey flavor actually didn't taste too bad.

Instead of maintaining conversation, everyone ate quickly, then picked off vegetable bits from the grate.

"Mm, that was delicious." Beldon sighed, sitting on the ground and leaning against a fallen log. He laced his fingers behind his head and contemplated the stars.

"My little sister's favorite," Reenalyn said, pulling something out from behind her log. "Another tradition in my family is to play music together after dinner. Do you mind if I play a little? It feels weird not to."

I stared in amazement that someone I'd just eaten with was not only a cook but also a *musician*. But she had to give up music to become a castor! She couldn't play ever again.

"Aren't you supposed to give up music if you become a castor?" Dane asked.

Reenalyn grinned sheepishly. "You're supposed to, yeah, at least not for money. But I know plenty of people who haven't given it up. I mean, the lashes would hurt, sure. And they would destroy my instrument, too, which would be the worst. But I'd rather risk it and enjoy this violin as much as I can than bury it in a closet to collect dust for the rest of eternity. If they destroy it, I'll just save for another one. It's a risk I'm willing to take to keep that part of myself. Besides, no one who cares would come to Wrynford, much less the woods behind it. But if it makes you all uncomfortable, of course I won't—"

"Nah, go ahead and play. Some music would be nice. Let's hear it." Beldon grinned.

Scandalized, I watched with rapt attention as Reenalyn's violin bow caressed the strings and sent emotion zinging through me. A melody more beautiful than the finest better-classer silks and more wistful than windchimes poured out like a smooth stream over Reenalyn's shoulder. With her eyes closed, her arms wove through the air as her bow danced over the instrument fast, then slow, then fast again, her long torso swaying with the beat.

Each note touched something fragile and unfamiliar inside of me.

Emotions roiled in my chest. Sadness, loneliness, pain, but then hope. Every few seconds, notes of hope and promises of goodness soared from Reenalyn through the breezy leaves. A tear rolled down my cheek. Was it sorrow or joy? Her music made both coil through me at the same time.

When her eyes opened and she lifted the violin from her shoulder, everyone else's mouths hung open. Except Trinka's. But her dark eyes were wide, her narrow brows lifted in surprise.

"Reenalyn, that was beautiful," Dane said.

The rest of us nodded, wide eyed.

"Wow." Beldon ran a hand through his dark hair. "You're good. Why in the world aren't you a head musician in one of the noblest houses? You could make a decent living with that kind of skill."

And you could teach me how to play so I can cast Whisper with more energy. If I could just tolerate these circumstances for a few months, I could hone my fighting skills and train Whisper as much as possible. And then most importantly, I could learn to play well enough to cast her with enough energy to stay awake for an entire day. If I could do that, there was a good chance I could get away with passing her off as a normal castling.

That future looked much sunnier than what I'd brooded over the past couple of days. That was it. I'd ask Reenalyn to teach me to play the mandolin proficiently. Tonight.

The fire cast shadows around Reenalyn's cheerful smile as she placed the instrument back in its case. "Thank you. I love playing music so much—it's my favorite part of myself. But I like playing for the enjoyment of the people I love. And for myself when I feel like it. It wouldn't be the same, playing behind a curtain for rich men who don't even listen. And making a living with it would take a lot of the magic out of it for me. I like it as it is now—something I do in my free time. Sort of like something I get away with. That, and I just really wanted a castling."

"Wow," Beldon repeated. "Respect."

Embarrassment colored Reenalyn's cheeks. "So we'll start training tomorrow morning, then? Does everyone have a place to sleep tonight? My family lives in central Wrynford, about half an hour's walk from here. Our house is crowded but anyone's welcome." She smiled at each of us.

"I'm good. My brother's place is nearby, too, so I'll stay with him." Beldon turned to Trinka and opened his mouth.

"I don't need a place," she spat.

He pressed his lips together and focused on the flames.

"Dane? Mella?" Reenalyn glanced between us.

"Sprinter and I enjoy sleeping under the stars."

Their eyes turned to me. I couldn't be seen spending time with these people in Wrynford. Out in the woods with no witnesses was one thing, but staying in one of their houses? "I, um, already have plans."

"All right, then." Reenalyn stood and stretched. "I'll see you all tomorrow morning." She hefted her violin case and headed for the trees.

"Hey, Reenalyn?" I darted after her, struggling to keep up with my much shorter legs.

She turned, smiling. "Changed your mind?"

"No, thanks for the offer though. It's just...do you know how to play mandolin, by chance?"

Reenalyn grinned. "Yes! I love mandolins."

"Great! Um, do you think you could teach me how to play?"

"Of course. I'd love to!"

"Thanks. The only thing is...since, well, it's just that with my um, background, I'm not supposed to play, even more so than you. I wouldn't want you to get in trouble..."

She rolled her eyes. "Don't worry about it. Like I said, no one cares about what we do all the way out here. We'll be fine. And besides, no one should be forbidden from playing music. It's simply too wonderful."

"Yeah..." if only Trello and Loryce had known it wasn't such a big deal here, on the outskirts of Terrenthyrs's poorest town. Maybe they could've been happy here, with the freedom to play music at least for themselves sometimes.

But still, if they loved it so much, why risk losing it by trying to cast?

"Reenalyn, what would you have done if you had failed to cast? You couldn't have gone back to music as a profession, even if you could have snuck playing in the woods sometimes."

She shrugged. "I also clean houses sometimes—I probably would have looked for more opportunities for that. Or I could have worked in my parents' shop."

"But you must have had aspirations to be a sought-after musician, if you worked so hard to perfect your violin skills. Right?"

"Well they're not *perfect*...but yes, I did once. And then I decided I'd rather have a castling." Her carefree smile made her look genuinely happy, like a child without a care in the world.

"Okay, well, thank you, Reenalyn. I'm going to search for a job tomorrow, so I'll be able to pay you soon."

She brushed away my words. "Remember the part about how I don't like to do music for money? Don't worry about it."

More money to save for clothes and food, then. I could hardly complain about that. Especially with only three months to save for a gown for the ball. And to have it fitted. I didn't even know how much that would cost.

Petting Cupid's spiky head with the tip of one finger, she continued. "Figuring out a training routine will probably take two or three days. How about we get started after that?"

"Uh, yeah. Sounds great." It was a little later than I'd like, but for free lessons from someone so skilled, the wait was worth it.

"Perfect. See you tomorrow." She gave me another hug as if we'd known each other for years rather than hours and disappeared into the trees.

CHAPTER 14

ACRES

"So what exactly is a library?" Starstinger asked in her kitten voice.

I glanced at her from where she sat on my shoulder as I walked down the cobbled street to work, my satchel and waterskin tapping my leg with each step. "A library is a giant house of books. A castle of books. Every wall is lined in books, and there are a bunch of shelves, too, with books on both sides."

Her eyes rounded. "There are that many books in the world?"

I chuckled. "There are a lot more than that!"

"Wow. It makes sense you would work there, then. If there are so many books."

"That's right. And it's wonderfully quiet. Much better than—" I had to let the sentence trail off as I struggled to remember what I'd been about to say. Had I worked at a loud place before? Of course I had. But...what job had it been?

A shadow burst from an alley and blocked my path. I caught Starstinger before she could roll off my shoulder, my other hand going to my throwing-star pouch. "Let me pass."

The dark-haired man, his crossed arms as big around as my thighs, scowled down at me. "I need to get into the library. I know you work there. Get me in."

"I'm sorry, sir, but no one gets in without a pass. A guard stands out front, and he'll check to see if you have one."

"I don't, but you're going to find a way to get me in anyway," he growled, a snow leopard castling hissing at his side.

"I'm telling you, man, I can't get you in. My pass will only work for me and my castling. No guests."

He took a step closer and loomed over me, shadows creasing his thick biceps. "Then you can find me all the books on hybrids in that mucking library and bring them here."

I slid Starstinger from my shoulder and held her next to me instead, to keep the man out of her face at least. "Bring books out to you? No, sorry, I can't. If you lose or damage them, I'll be out of a job and lose my library access. And I'd have to pay for them."

"Then we've got a problem, haven't we?" he ground out, his heavy brows slanting lower.

The snow leopard, its gray-and-black markings resembling the mixed colors in the man's unkempt hair, growled at me. No, not at me. At my Starstinger. Fear and anger roiled in the pit of my stomach.

How dare she?

Starstinger squirmed from my grasp, dropped to the ground, and hissed up at the snow leopard. Exposing her dainty canines, she pasted her too-big ears against the back of her skull.

I shifted to shield her a little better from the castling who was twice her size and glared at the man.

He considered me, his menacing scowl fading slightly. "Look, kid, I'm telling you, I need that information. It could be important."

"How so?"

He dropped his voice and glanced at the mouth of the alley. "I've seen them—hybrids. I've seen a lot of them. But they're not just animals. They're hybrid castlings."

I raised an eyebrow. "Hybrid castlings? How's that possible?"

He scowled at me again. "Why do you think I need the books, you idiot?"

I frowned deeper. "Where are all these hybrids, then?"

"I've seen them on the road to Morrenfayre. Closer to Morrenfayre than here. And...they're strong."

"All the way in Morrenfayre? Then what does it matter if a few unusual castlings are all the way out there?"

"Twice the animal, twice the power."

The snow leopard growled at Starstinger again.

"Stop doing that!" I shouted at her. She didn't even look at me. "Please ask your castling to give mine some space, sir."

"No, I don't think I will." He somehow moved even closer, daring me to back down. "If the threat of hybrid castlings doesn't matter to you, maybe a direct threat to your own castling will give you the motivation you need to get me those books."

The snow leopard's paw darted out and swiped Starstinger across the face, throwing her head into my shin hard enough to bruise. Starstinger scrambled to keep her footing and yowled like a wildcat as she launched her slender body at the other castling.

I stumbled after her into the swirl of feline screams and blood splatters, ignoring the sparks of pain as I struggled to pull her free. "Call off your castling, man!" I bellowed, shoving my bare hands between the cats.

With no help from the man, I finally got a hold of Starstinger and aimed a solid kick at the leopard. Before I could straighten, the man yanked me back and aimed a punch at my face. I barely ducked out of the way as Starstinger dug her claws into his fist. With a curse he released me.

Dodging a pounce from the leopard—whose claws raked down my calf—I ran for the main road with Starstinger in my arms, desperate to be in sight of the library guard in case the man and the leopard came at us again. As much as I hated to admit it, they were far more than Starstinger and I could handle.

But they didn't pursue us onto the main road.

At last, I rounded the corner and spotted the guard a few hundred spans away. He stood at the top of the stone stairway to the library entrance, his wolf castling at his side.

I kept my pace. "Starstinger, are you okay?"

She sighed. "She was a good fighter."

I blinked and slowed to a jog. "What? Aren't you supposed to cuss me out for interfering?"

"We're lucky to be alive, Acres. You were right to interfere—her skills far outmatched mine. But if the man had been quicker, you and I wouldn't have stood a chance."

Stubbornness and guilt warred in my gut. As my scratches burned and my ankle ached, I wondered if maybe training wasn't as much of a waste of time as I'd originally determined. Obviously, it could be useful even if there wasn't a whiff of war in the air. Why hadn't I given more weight to the practical benefits of combat training?

Because I'd sworn not to get mixed up with people like that in Terren-thyrs—that's why I left home in the first place—at least a part of the reason. And here I am again.

"I'm sorry I didn't do a good job of protecting you, Starstinger."

"It's okay, Acres."

I was out of breath before reaching the top of the stone steps. I'd have to think through this later.

"Identification?" Jaion asked.

I cocked an eyebrow at the guard who let me in almost every morning.

He grinned and opened the door. "What the skunk happened to you, Parrianther? Looking a little grubby to be trusted with books today."

"I'll clean us up before touching anything," I snapped, carrying Starstinger past him. "But listen, this guy in the alley just accosted us demanding I get books out of the library for him."

Jaion frowned. "Seriously? Where?"

I pointed to the alley. "You should go chase him off before he injures someone else or worse, convinces someone to sneak books out for him. His castling's a snow leopard."

Nodding, Jaion sent his wolf castling for a guard to cover his post and I darted inside, finally breathing a sigh of relief. We were safe in here.

I slid into the first quiet corner I could find and set Starstinger in a reading chair. The drying blood in her mussed fur hurt my chest. I realized anew how petite she was. Delicate, almost. I should've done a better job protecting her.

"Do I look that bad?" she whispered.

"Worse," I teased, digging in my satchel for the cloth I'd wrapped some fresh dapplemint leaves in earlier. Shaking the dried, brown leaves loose into the bag, I pulled the empty cloth out and dabbed some water onto it from my waterskin. I started by gently wiping at the blood on Starstinger's foreleg.

She pulled her arm away, and I looked up with concern. Was she angry with me?

"Better clean up my face, Acres. I can clean the rest of me." And she dipped her head to lick at her foreleg.

Fair enough. I focused on the scratches across her face, deep enough to still be oozing blood in a few places. How could I have let this happen?

Once Starstinger looked almost new, I cleaned myself up as best I could, and we headed to the returns section and the overflowing restock cart.

"Acres?" Starstinger whispered, brushing softly against my uninjured leg.

"Yes?" I pushed the squeaky cart slowly to keep the noise to a minimum for library guests.

"What are hybrids?"

The cart jerked to a stop. In the panic of the moment and our injuries afterward, I'd completely forgotten that part. "Ah, I believe a hybrid is a mix of two different species. Which is interesting because most of the time, different species can't breed. The offspring usually doesn't have the right genetic material to survive. But sometimes, if two species are very similar, they may be able to produce offspring that will live to adulthood. Like a zebra and a donkey."

"Oh. Could a serval make a hybrid with, maybe, a tiger?"

"Maybe. I don't know for sure. But Starstinger, you know castlings can't breed, right? It's inarticulate animals that can produce offspring."

"Oh." She sprang up onto the cart and deftly slammed her paw against a book, stopping it from sliding off. "Have you ever seen a hybrid?"

I pushed the cart forward again. "No, I haven't, actually."

She pushed the book back on top of its stack, then sat on her haunches facing me, her ink-spotted ochre tail swishing behind her. "I think that man and his castling really had. And that he thought it was scary."

I paused in front of the *History of Terrenthyrs* section and swiped up a book to check its title. "What makes you think that?"

"Didn't you see the fear in their eyes? But they weren't afraid of us."

Putting the book in its place on that shelf, I thought back to the snow leopard's scowl, the sneer on her castor's face. "You might be onto something, Starstinger. I mean, what do people fear most?"

She cocked her head, her ears erect as I pushed the cart to the next section.

I scooped up a small stack and walked down the row. "What they don't understand. People feel more comfortable once they have knowledge about something."

Her kitten voice rose above a whisper. "So they can fear it less?"

"Possibly," I whispered, sliding another book into place and inspecting the next title. "The question is what makes them think the supposed hybrids were castlings rather than wild animals." I thought for a moment. "You know, I really can't imagine how someone could do that. Is it possible to cast a hybrid?"

We locked eyes and said at the same time, "We should find those books."

***

There wasn't much on hybrids. Nothing in the *Myths and Legends* section, and only two mentions in the *Creatures* section. With both of those books hidden from sight in my satchel in case we ran across the man and the snow leopard again, and *An Analysis of Fossilized Texture: Scales, Fur, or Feathers?* under my arm, I strolled home with Starstinger at my side. I couldn't wait to start reading.

Walking through the wealthy half of Polfryth City was my least favorite part of the trek. I could've lived without the sight of the enormous manors and the way the owners stared down their noses at me if they bothered to notice me at all. It was too unsettling—how much they reminded me of what I'd left behind.

Shouts and clanging weapons rose from the next manicured lawn, and I hurried over to see what was going on.

Several people stood with their castlings at their sides. They must've been new castors—I recognized many from the Castling Ceremony. A beautiful cheetah castling was among them, at least three times Starstinger's size. Fear for her safety rose in my stomach again. *At least she has two weapons to be cast from. But still.*

A woman who must've been the cohort's mentor instructed one group as her hyena castling sat by her side. Abruptly, the castors crowded around the woman as their castlings followed the hyena across the yard.

I had sort of been assigned to a cohort after registering Starstinger, but not having cared about training at the time, I hadn't paid much attention. Was it a better-classer cohort or lesser-classer? How would I ever fit in either way?

Even so, maybe Starstinger and I would be better off among those learning how to defend themselves, even if they didn't accept us as comrades.

"You know, Acres, we could get through those books a lot faster with two sets of eyes."

I glanced down at her. "You want me to teach you to read?"

That was something I could help her with right away. It could definitely be an advantage, right? Most castlings didn't learn to read as far as I knew.

"Why not?"

I grinned. "That's an excellent idea."

Excited to get started, I picked up the pace through the city, hurrying past the row of shops and vegetable stands.

The mouthwatering fragrance emanating from my favorite tavern, The Braided Loaf, called to me, but we had work waiting on us. I passed it with a wistful stomach rumble but reminded myself we had almost two-thirds of a loaf and plenty of cheese at home.

As well as one type of training I was actually good at.

Adjusting the strap of the heavy satchel, I hefted the other book under my arm and smiled down at Starstinger. We had some reading to do.

CHAPTER 15

MELLA

Wind danced through the Emberlyn trees as Whisper and I strolled from my mandolin's old hiding spot—my new sleeping quarters—toward the Castors of Wrynford's camp.

"Could you try to act less conspicuous?" I frowned at Whisper as she struggled to walk and kept throwing her enormous wings out for balance.

"You try walking with these worthless avian legs." She yawned.

"Whisper, seriously, it's been ten minutes! Just keep your eyes open for a reasonable amount of time today, *please*. And starting tomorrow, I'll be getting mandolin lessons so I can cast you with more energy."

She glared, her crown feathers standing on end. "You try having all your energy rely on an incompetent child. *Then* you can talk."

I glared ahead. *Ouch.* "You try having a grouchy bitch for a castling," I mumbled.

Reenalyn's golden hair shone through the trees ahead.

"Look, just, please *try* not to act like you're older than us, instead of a new castling, okay? Only Dane knows you're an adult. Better to keep it that way."

She ambled on without acknowledging me, her wingtips getting messier with each flailing step.

We entered the clearing behind Dane and Reenalyn. Beldon sat on the other side of the empty firepit. He waved, then caught sight of Whisper.

His eyes widened. "Whoa! Mella! What a castling! You were holding out on us!"

Dane and Reenalyn whirled. Reenalyn beamed at us, and Dane's jaw dropped.

"Good morning, everyone. This is Whisper." I gestured to her as we reached the logs. She straightened into a standing position and held still. "Whisper, that's Reenalyn and her castling, Cupid." His little green face barely peeked through her hair. "That's Dane and Sprinter, and Beldon. Where's Brawler? And Trinka and Mauler?"

Sprinter's dark muzzle and ears leaned to the side to peer around Dane. Huge blotches of black and white patched his sandy coat in a strange and beautiful pattern.

"Trinka disappeared when Mauler fell asleep. Haven't seen her in a while," Beldon said. "Brawler's taking a nap, too."

"Before training?" I asked.

"We started at daybreak," Dane offered. "When you didn't show, I was afraid you might've changed your mind about us."

Humiliation warmed my face. Yet another change I'd have to deal with: getting up *early*. Yuck. Despite the discomfort of sleeping on the forest floor, I'd still overslept. I used to rise even later than this. "Sorry, I'll try to be on time tomorrow."

Reenalyn smiled and beckoned to me. "Come sit. We're just taking a little break. We've been discussing our strengths and weaknesses."

I swung my legs over the same log I'd sat on last night. The thick bark scratched even through my leather pants. Whisper tried to grip the bark in her talons and pull herself up but fell backward in a flurry of feathers and curses.

Baby castlings don't cuss like that, you idiot. Who's incompetent now?

All eyes were on me, and I guessed from their expressions they were probably wondering why I wasn't helping her.

Because she'd probably scratch my eyes out if I got my hands too close.

But I needed to keep up the farce.

"Whisper, do you, uh, need a hand?"

She was on her feet now, glaring at the log. "I suppose so."

Awkwardly, I picked her up around the middle and nearly fell back over the log from her weight. How could something that heavy ever get airborne?

Straining my muscles, I managed to regain my balance and set her next to me. A puff of air shot through her beak. Crown feathers erect, she ruffled her wings and shuffled her feet. Avoiding my eyes.

"Hi, Whisper." Reenalyn smiled, Cupid's emerald head peeking out her sleeve as she waved.

Crown feathers quivering, Whisper nodded in Reenalyn's direction.

Beldon glanced away, straining his neck like he was looking for someone, then focused on us again. "Whisper, you're humongous. How tall are you?"

She glowered at him. "Seeing that I've only existed for two days, I haven't yet had the chance to measure my stature."

I resisted the urge to hide my face in my hands. If there had been any chance we could convince them she was an immature castling, it vanished with the word *stature*.

Seeming to miss her annoyance, Beldon plowed on. "I was just wondering if you're taller than Trinka. I'd bet a whole silver that you are."

Trinka, who walked into the clearing at that moment, rolled her eyes. "We're not going to stand back-to-back for you to measure us, Berroman, so keep your money in your pocket."

Smart girl. Whisper would probably snap both your heads off if you tried.

A ray of sunlight glinted off Whisper's beak as she began to nod off.

I elbowed her. "Stay awake!" I hissed.

She started and shuffled her feet and feathers again, glaring at the circle of people.

Hopefully no one noticed.

"Well, strength-wise, I think we can all agree Trinka's the fiercest," Beldon said, grinning at her.

She scowled at him and pushed off from the tree she'd just leaned against. "Excuse me?"

He blanched. "Um, I was just trying to give you a compliment. Watching you train this morning—you're clearly good."

"Considering we've known each other all of *a day and a half*, how about we state *our own* strengths and weaknesses today and comment on others once we've actually spent time studying them." She didn't say it like a question. It was a command. "For example. My height is my greatest weakness. My greatest strength might be that people underestimate me because of it." She sat on the log and glared at Beldon.

Whisper dozed again, and I smashed her toes. She flinched and scowled.

"Ah, right," Beldon said. "My greatest strength is probably my size, I guess. And my weakness could be...aim. I'm terrible at throwing or kicking things. Not ideal when you're also the biggest target." He grinned wryly, the same look he'd had while talking about his brothers last night.

I'd always longed for a sibling. Was Mother's pregnancy going okay? I hadn't even asked how far along she was. How much had my old room been transformed into a nursery by now? Had Father thrown out my things already?

Whisper adjusted her footing, her talons scraping against the bark.

"I guess I have two main weaknesses." Dane looked at the dead fire, seemingly avoiding everyone's eyes. "I get bad sunburn because I'm so pale I practically glow in the dark, and I've obviously got the body of a twelve-year-old."

Beldon cackled, and Dane grinned sheepishly.

He was slimmer than Beldon—but so was every guy I knew. Even Kaido. But he didn't look twelve to me. Just leaner.

"And what about your strength?" Reenalyn asked him.

Dane said, "I can climb pretty well."

Trinka snorted. "That's an understatement. Even so though, what are you going to do with that when we're in the coliseum and out of these woods?"

"I guess I have a few months to figure that out." Dane didn't seem concerned.

Reenalyn looked bothered by their bickering. "I'll go next. My weakness is trouble focusing. If there's a lot going on, it's hard for me to keep my mind on one task."

"You *are* aware lots of people will be fighting all around you in a war, right?" Trinka asked.

"Of course." Reenalyn looked surprised. "That kind of busyness won't distract me. It's...other types of crowds."

One of Trinka's dark eyebrows rose. "What's that mean?"

"It's just a thing with me." Reenalyn shrugged and smiled at Trinka.

Beldon beamed a cheerful smile at me. "Mella, tell us yours."

"Well, um...I guess a strength is determination. A weakness is not having enough money."

Trinka snorted again. Reenalyn asked, "What about a mental or physical weakness that could affect your fighting, Mella?"

"Oh, um, knowing when to strike, maybe? I've been reprimanded for waiting for the opponent to attack first." A poof of dust and smoke swirled next to me.

Skunks, Whisper!

Sure enough, her spot on the log was bare. "Oh, I guess she was tired from...training with me, this morning, before we got here. That's why we were late."

Reenalyn smiled. "Oh, okay. Well, I need to work with Cupid on his speech while he's still awake. How about you four divvy up sparring pairs while Brawler and Mauler rest and I work with Cupid?" Reenalyn disentangled Cupid from her hair and set him in her lap.

"I'll take the new girl. What do you say, Mella?" Beldon grinned.

"Uh, sure." I eyed his brawny build, not at all enthusiastic about starting with the biggest opponent, but I'd have to face him eventually. The better I did with this cohort, the more I'd be able to impress the king and queen and convince the nobles to bet on me on Wager Day. And then get transferred to Selverine's cohort. And there was Kaido to win over as well, just in case.

"I'll take Velowinzinger and Sprinter," Trinka said, the sun glinting off the sheen of sweat on her smooth head and crossed arms.

Dane gulped and punched Sprinter's shoulder. Smiling, he said, "Really, my first name is fine—you don't have to bother with my last name. And of course we don't need to both take you on at once."

She frowned at him. "Think I can't take it?"

"Well, um, I wasn't saying that."

"Great. Then both of you give me your best shot."

"No weapons, then?" Dane asked.

"Whatever suits your fancy."

Dane and Sprinter glanced at each other as they pushed to their feet.

Trinka stepped away from the firepit and into the clearing free of logs, beckoning to them, her hands free of weapons. I couldn't remember what her castling weapon was.

"Any day now, boys."

Sprinter dashed at her with a snarl, Dane right on his heels. Trinka knocked Sprinter aside with one arm and caught Dane with a feint to the side, followed by a solid punch to the face. They reeled away from her, circled, and dove again.

After evading them, her brass knuckles appeared on her fingers, one set on each hand, with a leather strap over the sharp points.

"Okay. Let's make this more interesting." She nodded at Dane's weapons belt.

I cocked my head. Spiked knuckles on each hand? Hadn't she only had the one set at the ceremony?

Dane drew his strange nail-like weapon and swung at Trinka. She deflected with an iron fist and spun the movement into a jumping kick that caught Dane's shoulder, knocking him to his knees.

"Wow." Beldon sighed. "I said she was amazing, didn't I?"

"Yeah." I chuckled weakly, wincing as she threw a snarling Sprinter into a tree. "I don't look forward to taking her on."

"I do." He turned to me. "But hey, we're supposed to be sparring ourselves right now." He smiled and drew his mace from his belt. Its leather casing made it look less intimidating.

I took a step back, reaching for my scythe. "So how does that thing help with your aiming issues, then?"

He grinned, rotating his wrist so the spiked ball flew in a blurry circle on its chain. "It's a close-range weapon, for one thing. Plus, it's big, and it's got a lot of piercing points." He watched it spinning, his huge hand flexing. "And it's fun."

"All right. Let's go."

Smirking, he cocked an eyebrow. "How about you come at me first. I promise I'll take it easy on you."

"Okay, condescending asshole." I lunged, raising my leather-covered scythe high overhead to jab the handle into his fist. He'd be expecting the blade.

"Ow!"

The mace plunked to the ground, and I rolled it away as I shoved the scythe under his chin. "Dead. Oh, and thanks for taking it easy on me, Beldon. I don't know what I would've done otherwise." I couldn't help but grin at him.

His eyes bugged. "Skunks. Okay. Respect. Let's go for real then."

"Good." I lifted the scythe from under his chin and backed into a crouch.

Beldon retrieved his mace and regarded me with a calculating smile. "So the better classer fights dirty. I'm impressed." He braced the mace at his side.

I rolled my eyes. "Impress *me*, then."

He lunged. "You're on!"

***

"You're not bad at all, Mella." Kneeling in the sand, Beldon scooped a handful of spring water to his lips, the afternoon shadows of Emberlyn trees stretching over his sweat-soaked tunic.

"Thanks." I dragged my arm over my mouth and sat on the cool ground.

He sat next to me, facing the spring. "So the badass scythe—What made you choose it?"

"My mother's family were wheat farmers. I remember visiting when I was young and seeing all the people harvesting with scythes. And in the evening, some of them would spar with them. My grandfather was very good. That was the first thing I thought of when my instructors asked what weapon and fighting style I wanted."

"Really?"

"Yep. Why the mace for you?"

He chuckled. "Looks-wise, because it's badass. And practicality-wise, because, like I said, I'm better at close range."

I nodded. "It is impressive-looking. I bet forging all those spikes was a process."

He rolled his eyes. "You have no idea." Throwing himself back, he folded his arms behind his head. "Hey, so do you know a better-class girl named Yulroe?"

I turned to him, but he kept his eyes on the rippling surface. "Yeah, Yulroe Dinburr?" Why would he ask about her?

"Do you...know how she's doing?"

"Um, fine, as far as I know. She cast a...what was it?"

"A cheetah." He rasped a broken laugh and scrubbed a hand over his eyes.

Odd reaction. "Oh, right. As far as I know, she's fine. Why? Is she a friend of yours?"

"Yeah, something like that." He sighed. "*Was,* anyway. We were sort of together." He laughed again. "But she dumped me after the ceremony."

Ah. "I'm sorry. How long were you together?" I'd known she had a secret boyfriend, but a lesser classer? That was interesting.

He finally turned toward me. "You're less shocked that a better classer and a lesser classer were together than I would've expected."

I shrugged, not in the mood to discuss my parents' love story, which seemed much less magical now than it had when Momma had been alive.

Beldon stared at the ground. "Almost a year. But I guess casting an herbivore was the last straw."

I turned to him, gaping. "That's ridiculous! When Brawler's full grown, she'll be able to heft a cheetah in one hand and chuck it from one side of Terrenthyrs to the other. That's such a lousy reason. I never liked Yulroe."

With a jolt of surprise, I realized that was actually true.

He smiled genuinely for the first time since mentioning Yulroe's name. "Thanks, Mella. You're pretty cool, for a better classer."

"You're pretty cool too, for a lesser classer." And I realized that was true, too.

Maybe sparring with these people—and getting to know them a little—wouldn't be so terrible after all.

Chapter 16

DANE

"**S**eriously now, what *is* that thing?" Mella asked when I brandished my castling weapon against her scythe. With Whisper passed out again and Sprinter helping Reenalyn coax a little courage from the shy Cupid, I had Mella all to myself.

Which, as it happened, I didn't mind one bit.

The sun shone through the dense foliage and glimmered on her fair skin. I took a steadying breath of the sweet summer breeze and tried to focus on her eyes. Which were as deep and cobalt as the sea and didn't help me calm down in the least.

"It's my castling weapon. It's almost like a roundish short sword." Maybe I could explain it to her one day. Maybe then she'd want to know my whole story. I shook myself. Today was not the day to go into all that. Especially not the fact that I'd become a thief despite her generosity.

She shrugged, her dark ponytail swinging and short bits of hair playing around her face in the breeze. "Okay. Let's see if you use it like a sword."

She crouched, and her blank, appraising expression rooted me to the spot. She was flying at me before I'd even taken up a fighting stance.

Monkey's teeth!

I parried her blow just barely and slid to the side. She was there again, the leathered scythe swinging toward my legs. I leaped over it and glanced at the branches above me out of habit. I was definitely the better fighter in the trees, but I didn't want to weird her out or give myself too much of an advantage.

She swung once more, and I ducked. She blew past me, and I could've kicked her squarely in the back. But something held me back. With a roar, she continued that momentum into another swing, feinting low and then striking my thigh hard when I tried to jump over her blade. I landed on my butt.

So much for impressing her with my battle skills.

Smirking, she held out a hand.

I stared at it. Her *hand*. She was inviting me to *touch* her hand.

She quirked an eyebrow. "You want a hand or no?"

And I was taking too long being an idiot. Again. I snapped out of it and wrapped my fingers around hers, trying in vain to ignore the hot sparks flying through me from where her skin touched mine.

Then it was over, and she was crouching again, ready to spring.

I had to push past this. If I was going to have a chance at making a good impression, if our cohort was going to have any chance of winning, I had to pull myself together.

I sprang at her first this time, but she deflected me easily. I tried again, and she tripped me onto my face in the dirt. Monkey's teeth, but she was a brutal opponent. Maybe I didn't need to try to take it easy on her. After all, she'd held her own against Beldon earlier, and he wasn't stumbling all over himself in love with her.

Her hand flashed out again, and I took it.

She darted to my side, and I met her blow, but the leathered edge of the blade still left a raw burn line over my shoulder.

"Monkey's *teeth*!" Maybe the trees weren't so bad an idea.

She lunged again, and I grabbed the branch above me and swung out of the way, throwing myself over it to land in a crouch where the limb met the trunk.

Mella regarded me from the ground. "You going to stay up there all day?"

"Why don't you join me?"

Her eyebrows rose, and she straightened from her crouch and held her scythe like a walking stick. A relaxed pose.

"Up there? Won't we fall?"

"*I* won't."

"Well, *I* might."

I shrugged, pretending nonchalance. "If you do, I *might* catch you." Of course I *would* catch her.

She eyed me. "Fine. How do I get up there?"

"I'll give you a hand." I altered my footing to better distribute my weight, leaned down, and reached toward her. She took my hand, sending all sorts of shivers zinging through me. Did she have any idea what she was doing to me? I hoisted her up to my branch, and she immediately stretched her arms out for balance, her scythe clasped in one hand.

"Whoa. Okay, so have you actually ever swung a weapon in the trees before?"

I grinned. "Sometimes. Want to give it a try?"

She took hold of a nearby limb. "Sure."

Smiling at her, and at ease in my element, I laughed at myself for thinking this would give me too much of an advantage. I clearly *needed* an advantage with how proficient she was on the ground.

I would take care with her safety, though. I'd seen people fall to their deaths, and that would not happen to Mella Yarinelle. I jabbed my castling weapon toward her, and she stepped back, blocking me with the scythe. She missed, and I halted my jab in time to avoid hurting her.

"Skunks, how do you balance?" she spat, grabbing another branch to steady herself.

I looked at my boots, placed just right on the branch to distribute my weight, leaving both arms free. "It's in the footing, mostly. If you keep your feet in the right place, balancing is easier. Like this." I pointed to my boots, and then glanced at hers. "You also don't have enough space over there. Here."

I pulled myself one branch higher and gestured for her to take my place where the branch met the trunk. It was thicker there.

She shimmied to the spot I indicated and glanced at me again.

I pointed to one of her boots. "Move that foot a little to the right. And shift those toes outward more. Just a bit less than that. There. Does that feel more comfortable?"

"Maybe. I'm not sure yet."

"Do you want to get down?"

"No, I want to give this a try. I've never seen people fight up high before. It could be a useful skill."

"It is." I dropped back to her branch and stood where she'd stood before.

She narrowed her eyes, and then her scythe came flying out of nowhere at my face. I ducked and missed it, then struck her shoulder with my weapon, accidentally knocking the scythe from her grasp.

"Oh—sorry!" I dropped to the ground, retrieved it, and lifted myself back to our branch, holding it out to her. "Sorry, I didn't mean for that to happen."

She took it from me, her eyes searching mine. "How did you do that?" Her eyes glowed bright in the shadow of the tree's branches, distracting me again.

"I, uh, just got out of the tree and back in." *Poetically stated.*

"But you did it so fast, and with one hand! Were you raised by a pack of wild monkeys or something?"

I laughed. "No. I got used to heights at my last job. I, uh, tended ropes. Got good at balancing, I guess. And actually, I hate monkeys."

"Wow. That's a fascinating skill. Can you teach me?"

Her radiant smile took my breath away. And she wanted to know more about my domain. *Mella Yarinelle, nothing would delight me more.*

"Sure, no problem." I grinned, and she grinned back. It lit up her face so much that I could barely stand it.

She stepped back against the tree trunk. An image of me wrapping my arms around her and pressing her against that tree trunk, her lips pressed to mine, drifted through my mind, making my balance stutter. Would she ever want me that way? My stomach clenched with the knowledge of how inept I was at this. I didn't know the first thing about getting a girl's attention.

"So your last job..."

I blinked. "Yeah, and speaking of jobs, my current job is at a bakery not far from here. Have you heard of The Braided Loaf?" Of course she had. She'd seen me there. She just didn't remember.

"Yeah. I know it."

"Well, I heard the funniest story there the other day..." I launched into a pointless rendition of something I'd overheard to distract her. I wanted to tell her everything about me. But she didn't need that information now.

When I finished, she laughed, and the sound of it undid me all over again. She had the most beautiful, musical laugh.

"Speaking of sandwiches, I'm famished. Want a sandwich?" A spark of pride lit inside me at the thought of the coins I'd earned myself jingling in my pocket. I could actually afford to treat her to a meal. With my own money. How things had changed since the first time we saw each other.

"Oh, actually, yeah. Food sounds good. But, um, how do I get down from here?"

"Do you want my help?"

"Yes, please. I don't feel like falling to my death today."

I chuckled. "Sure, want me to take your scythe first?" I held out a hand, and she gave it to me without hesitating. A good sign. Castors don't throw their castling weapons into just anyone's hands.

Dropping lightly to the ground, I laid the scythe next to my weapon and leaped back into the branches. "Um, would you rather I carry you to the ground, or catch you?"

"I'm not sure I can make myself jump, honestly," she admitted.

"Okay." Did my voice just crack?

She watched me, and I knew I was taking too long. It shouldn't take so much time to prepare for this. "Oh, right."

She stepped forward and threw an arm around my shoulders. Somehow, in the midst of all the swirling sparks, I managed to put an arm around her back and one under her knees. With Mella Yarinelle in my arms—my actual arms—I dropped to the ground.

And thank good fortune I didn't land on my butt this time.

My arms had forgotten how to work. I should put her down, but she had her arms around my neck, and her beautiful bright eyes were smiling at me. I couldn't bear for that moment to end.

"Thanks." She unwrapped her arms and hopped to the ground. I have no idea what my arms did, but they seemed to let her go without too much difficulty. "So what's the fastest way to The Braided Loaf from here?"

"Uh, this way." I gestured toward the path I usually took and thrilled again as she fell into step beside me. More time with Mella, and I hadn't completely humiliated myself yet. At least, not that she'd noticed.

"I wonder how Sprinter and Reenalyn are coming along?" she mused.

"Sprinter is...annoyingly wise for his age. I bet he'll be able to get Cupid out from behind Reenalyn's hair and into sparring shape in no time."

"Hmm. It's too bad that my joining you made your numbers uneven."

A miniscule price to pay to get to see you every day. "It's not so bad. We can take turns sparring. And fighting two or more to one isn't a bad idea. Something to be prepared for. Maybe something our mentor would recommend...if he bothered to show up."

Hmm. Maybe there is actually something I could do about the numbers.

She frowned. "I can't believe the mentor completely ignores the Wrynford cohort every year. What a skunk. I don't know how we'll ever outperform the other cohorts with fewer people *and* no mentor to tell us what we need to improve."

Reaching behind her head, she pulled the tie out of her hair and let it fall around her shoulders, knocking the breath out of me once again. A moment later she'd scooped it up into a smooth ponytail, most of the loose wispies contained.

I blinked myself back to the moment. "Um, yeah. The odds are stacked against us. But I'm not giving up just because some mentor doesn't think I'm worth his attention. It'll be hard work, but we could show them."

She turned her electric eyes and earth-shattering smile full on me. "I like the sound of that."

CHAPTER 17

SELVERINE

"**D**ead," I pronounced with my trident at Willova's throat as she lay where I'd knocked her. I blew a strand of brown hair out of my face and stepped back, sweeping the leathered trident off her neck.

Nodding to concede the match, she shoved to her feet, her red hair swinging. She brushed herself off, and her sweaty hand left marks on her fine suede dress—hardly the kind of thing I'd wear for sparring. Catching sight of her casting cutlass, she bent to retrieve it and stumbled before getting a hold of it.

Sometimes she was all grace and poise. Sometimes she moved like a stiff old lady.

The hardwood floor of the second ballroom, which we now used for sparring, had to hurt. The grassy ground outside was probably a little better. But Willova had looked over her shoulder so much the first time we sparred, she was no challenge at all to take down.

She seemed to find training indoors less distracting. Being incapable of defending herself outside would certainly be trouble for her, but at least sparring indoors with her gave me the chance to hone my skills against someone who paid attention.

Finally retrieving her cutlass, she inspected it for damage.

Willova was an okay fighter. And her tiger castling was sure to be one of the best with a little training. But even so, Willova herself was so awkward and self-conscious that it wasn't worth staying angry with her.

I eyed the frustrated angle of her eyebrows as she inspected the weapon, clearly annoyed at herself for dropping it.

"It's that extra arc of metal around the handle," I informed her, eyeing her cutlass's pommel, where a thin strip of metal wrapped over her hand for better stability. *Probably because she's always so sweaty.*

Her shoulders slumped as she examined the pommel. "I see what you mean." Her voice was too soft. "I didn't want it too tight, but as loose as it is, it's easy for your trident to wrench it off my hand."

Which I'd done multiple times.

A drop of blood plunked to the floor, and her eyes flicked to a thin cut on her hand.

"How'd that get there?" I asked, taking a look at my leather-tipped trident points. "Oh skunks! One of my leather tips ripped. Good thing it was just a light scratch. I'll have to get that fixed. Sorry, Willova."

She stared at the cut for a bit too long. What was her problem? It wasn't like she was going to get an infection from such a small wound. I'd get the leather tip fixed. And anyway, those were only required for three and a half more weeks. She'd need to get better at avoiding worse injuries.

"Can you alter a castling weapon after casting?" she almost whispered. "I mean, if you notice an imperfection?"

Stretching and flexing my hands, I raised one eyebrow. "No, you can't. But it's not that big of a deal, Willova. Just practice angling your hand differently to prevent me from getting a trident point in the gap." I gripped my fingers and stretched them back, loosening the cramped muscles from holding the trident for so long.

"I've already been trying that all day. Is your hand okay?" she asked.

I crossed my arms. "Just a cramp. But Willova, I first noticed the gap two days ago and tried to exploit it multiple times. Today was the first time I succeeded. If it takes you some time to learn to deflect a strike, that's okay. You don't have to be perfect the first time you face me. We spar so we're better prepared for real battles when they come."

"That's an interesting way of looking at it," she mumbled.

"What do you mean?"

"Not expecting yourself to be perfect. How will you ever get perfect if you don't expect perfection of yourself?"

I scowled. "Skunk off, Willova. I'm aware of my imperfections. I don't need you pointing them out to me. I've got plenty of other people for that."

"I wasn't...I'm sorry. I didn't make myself clear. I meant how could *I* ever make *myself* perfect if I don't expect perfection of myself all the time?"

I threw my arms out. "Look, I don't know, Willova. Just give yourself time to learn like everyone else. You have way too high expectations for yourself."

She stared at me like I'd just spoken another language. "I don't think there's any such thing."

"Okay, fine. Whatever, Willova. Let's take a break. It's time to eat lunch anyway."

"Shouldn't we work a little more first?" she asked.

I spun, frowning at this difficult person. "I thought you were too busy staring at your hand."

She clasped her hands in front of her like a child being reprimanded. "I'm sorry, Selverine. I'll work harder to maintain an appearance of pleasing aesthetics and symmetry worthy of the family Calentine."

I made a face at her. "What the muck are you talking about?"

"I, um—" She held one wrist and looked at the floor like she was embarrassed. As her hand squeezed her wrist, her long sleeve pulled up a little, revealing an indistinct line of black ink.

"What's that?" I pointed, stunned that Willova Calentine might have a tattoo.

Her eyes went wide, and she yanked her sleeve down. "Oh, nothing. Sorry. Maybe you're right. It does seem like a good time to get some lunch, doesn't it?"

A blush nearly as deep as her red hair colored her otherwise bone-white face, and I narrowed my eyes. What was up with this weirdo?

Chapter 18

MELLA

After eating a delicious sandwich from the Loaf, I left Dane to work his shift and headed back to the Emberlyn forest on my own. I finally reached my mandolin's hiding place and pulled it out from under the moss-covered log, considering how grouchy Whisper would be about having fallen asleep so easily this morning.

I strummed my mandolin and sang my casting call, and she appeared in a swirl of snow, coal, and sawdust. And surprise, surprise, her crown feathers were already sticking straight toward the sky.

I crossed my arms. "I know you nodded off earlier than was ideal in front of our new cohort today, but may I remind you I've arranged to have lessons with Reenalyn in the morning. So there's no reason to be mad at me."

"You almost dropped me in front of the others this morning. Hardly an impressive first impression," she spat.

I let my arms fall as the smile melted from my face. "You're upset about *that*? Why didn't you just fly up onto the log? Why is everything *my* fault?"

"Last I checked, you've had a few thousand times as many days in your body as I've had in this one. In theory, that would make you able to handle yourself with more skill than me. You are clearly too weak at casting, and we need to work on strength training as well. And I never said everything was your fault. We don't have time for your dramatics."

Heat suffused my face. "Excuse me for trying to *help*. Last time I do that! Maybe you should learn to fly like an *actual avian*."

Her crown feathers shivered as her glower deepened. "That is precisely my intention, Mella."

I crossed my arms again, furious. "Fine. What's your brilliant plan?"

She glanced around, ruffling her wings and shuffling her feet. "Do you see that rock over there?"

She pointed with one wing, her sleek feathers fanning out. Her wings were quite a bit longer fully extended than I'd realized. That one alone looked as long as I was tall. Which wasn't much more than five spans, but her full wingspan added up to a significant amount.

I followed her line of sight to a hefty rock dappled in what sunlight could reach it through the thick Emberlyn trees. "Yes, why?"

"Do you think you can pick it up?"

"No."

"Great. Go try."

I crossed my arms. "No."

She brought her feathers to her forehead in a pose of frustration. "Do you want to walk in front of the royals in six months with me waddling behind you like an intoxicated duckling?"

"Nope. That's why *you're* going to learn to fly."

Glowering, she took a slow breath. "Even so, we need a backup plan in case that doesn't work. And do you really want me to fly in and land on the floor, or to land on your shoulder? Think how much taller and more imposing we would be as a pair with me on your shoulder. I look dumpy on the ground in this body."

We stared each other down.

"Whisper, nothing about you is dumpy."

"The way I walk right now is *intensely* dumpy. You *do* want to impress your friends, don't you?"

Skunks. She got me.

I marched over to the stone and dug my fingers under it. Dirt shoved under my fingernails as I tried to get a good hold on it. I heaved it up and tossed it to the side so I wouldn't squash anything living under it.

"There. Happy? Now show me you trying to fly."

For the briefest of seconds, uncertainty flashed across her face, erasing the hard determination. "Okay, then."

She spread her magnificent wings—coal and snow in bands all the way down each feather—and took off at a furious waddle. Her talons gouged deep wounds in the ground. Wind shivered through her feathers.

Flapping madly, she achieved about a speck of air before hitting the ground and stumbling to keep her footing.

She turned to face me. "There. Your turn. Pick it up again and carry it to me while lifting it over your head."

I looked at her, then the rock, then back at her with eyebrows raised.

She glared unblinkingly. Eagles were capable of the most impressive glares.

I stooped to pick up the stupid stone, then heaved it and held it against my body. It slipped with my first step. I gripped tighter and kept on toward my glowering castling.

I reached her and dropped it at her feet. "Happy? Now my back hurts. That accomplished nothing."

"The more you do it, the more your body will adjust and the less sore you'll be. It'll take some time."

"We'll see. Your turn."

She hopped onto the rock and stretched out her magnificent wings, then sprang into the air. Her wings came down and up, down and up, down, and up... The wind sang through her feathers.

And then she faceplanted.

I was tempted to cackle at her, but managed to hold it in as I walked toward her. "Whisper, are you okay?" I bit my lip.

Struggling to her feet, she swayed and fell backward. She took a deep breath and exhaled slowly with her eyes closed. "I *hate* this mucking *skunk* of a body."

Pausing, I watched her lay there for several beats. Hopelessness emanated from her.

I reached over, ripped a leaf from the branch next to me, and closed the distance. I knelt in front of her talons and held out my forearm. "Can you pull yourself up by my wrist?"

She contemplated my wrist, then gently grabbed hold of it without touching the points of her talons to my skin, digging the claws of her other foot into the ground. She pulled herself up awkwardly, flapping her wings, then releasing my wrist and hopping around to get her balance.

"Whisper, you keep talking about 'this body.'" I eyed her, and she looked away. "What body did you have before?"

Slowly, she met my eyes. "One without wings."

"How did I cast a soul who already had a body into a different body?"

"I have no idea."

"But how—"

"Mella, we must convince the royals I am a normal castling. They cannot discover my true nature."

"Why?"

"I need you to trust me. It's the only way I can survive. Which means it's also the only way you can get back to where you want to be."

Her crown feathers clung to her neck now as her eyes pleaded with mine. What could be so important? Who or what had she been before?

Could I trust her?

I couldn't be sure. But I needed a castling, and she was my only option. "Okay."

She seemed to wilt with relief. "Thank you. Please know that even though I am not truly your castling, I appreciate your trust, and I will not abuse it."

"Okay, if you explain that one to me."

"I had a different castor before you, Mella. He's dead now."

My eyes widened. "But how could I have casted you if you already had a castor?"

Her crown feathers draped limply around her head, her eyes sad. "I don't know."

Squinting at her, I had another question. "Do you think Queen Narellen had something to do with this? Is that why you hate her? And King Jorros and their castlings?"

"I will avenge his death on them." Her voice was steel, her eyes as sharp as daggers.

Concern shivered through me.

"Okay, but can you wait until after my castling year? If my castling destroys the king and queen, it won't look good on me. Any chance I have to get back into society will be ruined."

She turned her flinty gaze on me, regarding me for a long moment. "And you'd really rather be accepted by heartless murderers into their world of tea parties and fancy dresses than see justice served?"

I cleared my throat. "Well, when you put it like that...honestly, I don't know. I find it hard to believe they're as bad as you say."

"You are blinded by foolish desires for acceptance no matter who it comes from."

I scowled. "And you're the most annoying castling I've ever met." *Especially if you do something ridiculous like murder the skunking royal family—that would destroy whatever flimsy ribbons of status I may still be able to reclaim.*

She took a deep breath, her vicious eyes closing. "I will do my best to wait until it is *convenient* for you to get my revenge. All right?"

Technically that time would never come. She'd have to keep being my castling permanently if I won, because taking out the king and queen would never be a good look. Plus, this was all ridiculous. Narellen was Selverine's grandmother, for skunk's sake. But if this was the best I could get, I'd take it for now.

I nodded and held up the leaf. "Okay. Thank you."

"What's that for?" She darted a glance at it.

"The dirt on your beak."

She made a face, then closed her eyes and leaned toward my hand, allowing me to clean her beak.

"There. All better."

"Thank you, Mella. Now please don't hate me, but you really should pick up that rock and carry it around as long as you can. If I'm going to restrain myself until the end of your casting year, it will be gratifying to see the looks on their faces when you show up out of nowhere and beat their most prized cohort. So I will try taking off again. We will master these things together, like a true castor and castling. Hand to claw?"

She held up one clinched foot, and I raised my eyebrows.

"What's that mean?"

"It means we're a team no matter what happens. It's something castors and castlings say to each other—at least, it used to be. You say it and then you bump fists, like this." She held up one foot again.

"All right then. I like it." I bumped her toe knuckles. "Hand to claw."

***

"Which one is she again?" Whisper asked as we strode through the woods far too early for the music lesson.

"Reenalyn's the one with the long blonde hair."

"And the puny green lizard?"

"Hey, be nice. He'll grow." I glanced at her. She really did waddle. Why was she having so much trouble walking?

A glimmer of gold flashed through the brush. Probably Reenalyn's hair. We emerged into the clearing with our log benches and firepit a few moments later.

"Mella! Good morning!" Reenalyn sang with an enthusiastic wave. She was clearly one of those people who were unaccountably cheerful at unacceptably early hours.

I waved back and tried to smile. Suddenly, I worried I may never learn how to play well enough. Never half as good as Momma.

But then Reenalyn was right in front of me, taking hold of my free hand and cheerfully dragging me over to a log. "I'm so excited to get started. Are you excited?"

She hugged me again like we were old friends.

"Um, yeah. A little nervous, too."

"There's nothing to be nervous about! This is going to be fun." She turned to Whisper and leaned as if she were going to hug her too. But Whisper gave her a horrified look, and she stepped back.

"Oh, not a hugger. Sure thing." Instead she tapped Whisper's head like she would a human child and said, "Okay, well, let's get started."

She finally sat next to me eyeing my makeshift mandolin. "How much experience do you have?"

I smiled wryly. "Basically none. I've just messed around some. I don't actually know anything."

"We'll fix that quick! No worries. May I?"

I nodded and she took the mandolin gently, showing me how to hold it properly and a better way to wrap my fingers around the neck without twisting my wrist so much.

"Now, try this." She skimmed her fingers over the strings, showing me a chord a few times.

"Like this?" I tried to imitate her.

"Really close! Move your pointer finger just a bit—there. Now try again."

This went on for over an hour. Whisper got bored and fell asleep, but Reenalyn never made me feel like an idiot for not getting it on the first try, and she was even more excited than I was whenever I did something right. But my fingers, which were a little sensitive at first, were aching now.

"Wow. What should I do about my fingertips getting ready to fall off?" I shook out my hands.

Reenalyn laughed. "Yeah, you'll have to push through that till callouses form, unfortunately. It took a while for me to get these, but they'll come." She turned her hand over to show me the ends of her fingers.

I made a face. "You don't mind having those?"

"No, of course not. I love them. They help me play better. Why?"

"Well, they're, um, not *pretty*." I didn't mean to be rude, but I didn't love the idea of my fingers looking like that. Callouses were a sign of lesser classer's work.

Reenalyn laughed again, thankfully not offended by my lack of tact. "No one can see them when I'm playing."

"Yeah, I guess."

"Trust me, it'll get so much easier to play once they come in. They'll be worth it."

If they would help me cast Whisper more effectively, then she'd be right. "That case you have for your violin—how much was it?"

"Oh, I don't know how much in silvers. I played my violin at the carpenter's sister's inn every evening for a year to earn it."

I had to have heard her wrong. "How long?"

"I don't remember exactly, but it was a little over a year."

"Wow. A whole year. I'll need to find out how much that is in silvers, then. And it'll have to look like it's something else. Hey, weren't you training to be a castor at the same time? Why'd you spend so much on something nice if you knew you'd have to hide it for the rest of your life?"

She shrugged. "I needed something to keep my violin safe, and I wanted it to be pretty for me. Not for anyone else."

What was the point then, if it wasn't to impress anyone? "Anyway, I'll need a job too. Like Dane. To pay for a case and my share of food and a gown for the Grand Castors' Ball."

Reenalyn looked askance at me. "So Mella, you're not interested in Dane in the slightest, are you?"

"Huh?" I faced her. "What? No. I mean, he's nice, but I've got my eye on someone else."

She handed my mandolin back. "Oh, that's right. The boy with the anaconda. Kaido, right? Too bad the guys around here can't catch a break."

I stared at her. "How...how'd you know that? And what do you mean, 'the guys around here can't catch a break'?"

"Well, I knew about Kaido from the ceremony. As for Dane, he's out of luck because he's been starry-eyed at you all along, but your heart's already claimed. And Beldon's out of luck because he's had his heart broken recently. He wonders if he could like Trinka, but she's *so* not interested. Trinka doesn't like anyone, though. So it's not someone else with her like it is for you."

I blinked, surprised at the turn the conversation had taken. "Wow. I didn't realize you were so close to Trinka. She doesn't seem like the type to open up."

"Oh, you're right. She's not. I could just tell."

I squinted at her. "You could *just tell* all of those things about Trinka? And Dane and Beldon?"

"Of course. I mean, you've been here two whole days now. Can't you tell any of it?"

"Two whole...?" I trailed off, wondering what I was missing. "No one can *tell* that much about a person just by observing! Especially not for a couple of days."

She frowned. "Okay, maybe so," she halfheartedly conceded. "But then how do I know you like Kaido, but you're frustrated he hasn't noticed you, and you're worried he's noticing Selverine or Frenna, but you don't want to give up because even though you're frustrated, you still think he's attractive and would benefit you in some way? And I figured all that out just from the ceremony. And it wasn't like I was only watching the two of you all day. There was a lot going on. Crowds make it hard for me to focus. Remember? That's my weakness."

My jaw dropped. How in the world could she know all that?

She looked worried now. "What's wrong?"

"How can you possibly tell so much from a *look*?"

She sighed dramatically. "I just can. I don't know why. I used to think everyone else could too, but more and more it seems like most people are blind to this kind of stuff."

Eyeing her, I crossed my arms. "Okay, then. Does Frenna like Kaido?" She was wealthy enough not to need his fortune—not that that would prevent her from going after it anyway.

"Oh, yes. Very much."

"Bloody skunking muck!" I kicked up a spray of dirt and grass and tiny pastel petals, throwing my scythe to the ground. How would I ever get him to notice me if he had so many other options?

Reenalyn stared at me, and I realized I'd just thrown my castling weapon, what she thought was my real castling weapon, right in front of my castling. I retrieved it and sat back down.

"Well"—she cleared her throat as if nervous I'd throw another tantrum—"for what it's worth, she feels helpless about him, too."

"Why?"

She shrugged. "No idea. I can see the feelings, but not often the reasons behind them. At least, not as quickly. I have to know a person longer to understand on that level."

"Okay." I crossed my arms. "Then who does Kaido like?"

Reenalyn started counting on her fingers. "Frenna, and Yulroe, and—"

"Skunking mucking skunk butt!"

Reenalyn frowned. "*And* you, and Selverine, and the girl who got a panther, probably some others, too. But you can't expect me to remember them all. He likes a lot of girls. Doesn't really seem like a guy worth your time."

I ignored her presumption and grinned. "So he *has* noticed me, then!"

She looked concerned. "Well, yes, but—"

I smirked. "Ha! I'll beat Frenna yet."

Reenalyn gave me a funny look.

"Wait," I said, "you don't like him too, do you?"

"Pfft, no! Of course not. He's...not someone I could respect. Besides, I'm not one of the girls he's into."

"I don't understand how you can know that, but why do you think that is?"

She shrugged, her long blonde hair cascading over her shoulders. "I think he wants someone shorter than he is, and I'm not." She paused, curling a finger through her hair. "Sometimes I wish I was shorter. I really like wearing my hair up, you know? In some kind of elaborate, decorative updo." She chuckled and dropped her gaze to the ground. "But I'm too tall for that kind of stuff."

"Well, back to Kaido, can you tell, like, the order of who he likes most?"

She rolled her eyes, but also smiled a little. "Kind of."

I straddled the log and perched my chin on my fists. "And...?"

Chapter 19

ACRES

*T*he acrid scent of charred wood singed my senses as I whirled around, struggling to find something that made sense. My family, their arms crossed as they glowered down at me for refusing to be used. The weight of their stares was too much.

The burning building I'd once lived in. The few things I'd run back inside to save.

A mysterious man in fine clothes wearing a single leather gauntlet. I couldn't see his face—I couldn't see any of him, really. But some impression of him. There was the missing memory.

I lurched up from the sweaty sheets, my heart racing. But it was already gone.

Skunks! I'd almost had it.

I dropped back to the pillow and concentrated on slowing my breathing. If I could fall asleep, maybe I'd get it back. I'd been so close!

Ages later, I was still wide awake. I gave up the useless effort and swung my legs over the edge. Time to cast Starstinger and go for a walk.

***

The fragrance of smoked ham and warm bread made my stomach growl as I approached The Braided Loaf with Starstinger at my heels. She'd made incredible progress reading over the last few days. She was already so fast we'd both read the sections on hybrids and found no mentions of hybrid castlings.

So I'd started going back and forth between reading and fretting over what to do about training. Last night, I'd been so absorbed in *An Analysis of Fossilized Texture: Scales, Fur, or Feathers?* that I'd completely missed the stars coming out and the sun rising a few hours later. The daffodil yellow of the afternoon sun had already deepened to the burnt rose of early evening when I'd woken from the nightmare.

Ugh, I'd been so close.

I opened the door, and the aroma of fresh-baked bread wafted by, making my stomach growl. Only a handful of other people were dining at this time of day. Someone's ring-tailed lemur castling hopped onto a vacant table and nabbed a crumb. A hyena sat next to a group of men, the table next to it having been pushed out of the way to make room.

No snow leopards. Whew.

A pale boy with white-blond hair met me at the counter. "Welcome to The Braided Loaf. What'll you have?"

"The wild mushroom, bacon, and burroot sandwich on a full braid of bread, please."

"Sure thing." He held out his hand. "Four pennies." His bright blue eyes met mine, and he did a double take.

Ignoring the weird look, I handed over the coins, headed for an empty corner, and took a seat with my back to the wall, just in case. Starstinger sat beside me, curling her black-and-yellow tail around her paws.

Is there anything I can do besides joining a cohort to make her safer? Is it even possible to join a cohort at this point?

The same guy brought my sandwich to me on a smooth wooden plate.

"Thanks." I breathed in a whiff of salty burroot. My mouth watered as I eyed the wild mushroom, burroot, and bacon sandwich with some of the Loaf's special sauce dripping from it.

"Enjoy." He walked away. But before I could take the first bite, his dark boots appeared at my side again. "Hey, didn't you cast at the ceremony a few days ago?"

I lowered the sandwich back to the plate, annoyed that he felt the need to interrupt my overdue breakfast-dinner. "Yes."

"Acres, right?"

I raised a brow. He remembered me? I didn't remember him. "Yes."

He held out one pale hand. "Hey. Good to see you again."

I shook his hand, then pointedly returned both my hands to the act of lifting the sandwich to my face. Eyeing the crispy crust and creamy sauce, I opened my mouth.

"I'm Dane, from the Wrynford cohort. And I've been looking everywhere for you."

The Wrynford cohort. Skunks. I lowered the as-yet unbitten sandwich. "The Wrynford cohort?"

"Yeah. The one you were assigned to after the ceremony but apparently don't give a monkey's tooth about."

Skunks. My stomach squirmed, relief and discomfort clashing. "What about it?"

He crossed his arms, frowning. "Why haven't you shown up to train?"

"I—I didn't think you all wanted me. You already have four people. I would've made the number uneven and sparring more challenging." *And I didn't want to waste my time preparing for a battle that isn't happening or a frivolous job I don't want.*

"Oh." He dropped his arms. "Who've you been training with?"

"Me, myself, and I. And Starstinger." I gestured to her, and she purred up at Dane from under her too-big ears, flashing one of her winning kitten smiles.

He smiled back before returning a serious gaze to me.

"Well, we have five people in our cohort now, and a sixth person would even things up. And make us closer to the eight members the others have. Why don't you join us? You can't win the tournament by yourself, anyway. You have to have a cohort."

"I don't care about the competition." My frustration with the whole process burst from me. It was true, but here was an opportunity to train myself and Starstinger to better defend ourselves. Why was I throwing it away?

He crossed his arms again. "Even if you don't care about the rest of your team, don't you care about what's best for your castling? For her to be able to hold her own in a fight?"

I blinked, annoyed at his insinuation that I was too selfish to care about Starstinger. "Of course I do. That's why I work with her every day."

"Oh? And working with *you* will prepare her to take on a bear? Or a wild dog? Or the literal *hundreds* of other castlings—most of whom are bigger than she is?"

This mucking guy. He had me. Wasn't this what I wanted anyway? For Starstinger? I glanced at her and raised an eyebrow.

She tilted her head, looking ridiculously cute. "Well, I *have* been telling you how nice it would be for both of us to get more extensive training." She beamed at me, the tip of her tail flicking over her paws.

Here was my solution, then. Even though this Dane guy would walk away thinking he'd convinced me rather than he'd provided me with a solution I'd already been grudgingly looking for. "Fine. When and where?"

Dane nodded, his arms still crossed. "We start training an hour before sunup. In the Emberlyn Forest on the outskirts of Wrynford. It's kind of hard to explain exactly where. How about you meet me by the river an hour and a half before sunup, and I'll show you the way?"

I glowered at him, drawing out the silence. "Sure." I shoved a much-anticipated bite in my mouth and chewed slowly, savoring the delicious flavors and hoping the annoying guy would be gone by the time I took the next bite.

Chapter 20

MELLA

Just days ago, I walked this same road with Selverine, Frenna, Yulroe, and the others toward the coliseum. A somebody with a scythe and a dream. Now I was a nobody with an eagle and a secret. And almost no coin left for my share of the cohort's food. And more importantly, nowhere near enough coin to purchase a dress for the Grand Castors' Ball. I needed a gown striking enough to earn Kaido's attention in the midst of my many competitors and begin to bring my plan together.

I braced my scythe handle over my shoulder and strode toward Polfryth City in search of a job.

"Excuse me."

The hoarse voice startled me, and I jumped back. "Oh, Mrs. Brenslow. Hello!" I smiled at the old woman, her wrinkled face wrapped in tattered shawls. She wore the usual patched dress and mismatched shoes. "I'm so sorry I haven't been back to Brekken Fennyl Road in a while. I was preparing for the ceremony and...I've been training since."

Were beggars allowed into the ceremony? Would she know I hadn't cast, or would she assume I had? I wouldn't lie to her. But my coins were sparser now than when I used to think I had it rough at home. I reached in my pocket and felt six coins. I could spare one for her. How long had it been since she'd eaten?

Mrs. Brenslow waved away my apology. "How was the ceremony, dear?" She grinned, showing off wide gaps from missing teeth whose absence had lost her the flautist position she'd once had in a wealthy noble's estate.

If she knew my circumstances had changed, she wouldn't take my coins. "It was great. I'm afraid I'm in a hurry, but here, take this. Okay?" I placed the coin in her bony hand.

She held it against her bosom. "Miss Mella, dear, you are so kind. Thank you."

Half turning to go with a smile, I thought of Jeffers, another unfortunate musician whose hands had grown too arthritic to play the harp. And Miralie, who'd been disowned by her wealthy family when she'd been caught making more than illegal music with the pianist in their house orchestra. I'd missed her little son's first birthday last week. And Trello and Loryce, who'd failed to cast in their ceremonies.

"Wait, Mrs. Brenslow."

I stepped back to her with the remaining five coins in my fist. But *I* needed them, too. And not just for a nice dress—I had to pay for my own food now. What if I couldn't find a job? How would I impress Kaido, or afford to eat? I could put the coins back in my pocket and just wish her a good day.

I took one of her hands and dropped all five coins into her palm. "Could you also give one each to Jeffers, Trello, and Loryce, and two to Miralie for her and her son?"

Her wrinkly face glowed as she closed her hand around the last few coins I had to my name. "Thank you, Miss Mella. You are a blessing, dear."

If only Mother and Father agreed with you. I smiled. "You are too kind, Mrs. Brenslow. I hope you have a lovely day."

"The same to you, Miss Mella."

We waved to each other, and I watched her go, wondering how Miralie's little boy was doing and fearing I'd never earn enough to pay for my share of food and keep my place in my new cohort. And my only chance at a future.

But I couldn't have turned a blind eye. They needed it more.

So. Back to the job hunt. I'd learned enough blacksmithing to forge and etch the scythe. I didn't particularly care for it—with the heat and the soot all climbing down my lungs—but I gave it a shot.

No deal.

I visited carpenters, bakers, weavers, barbers, and seamstresses, but not even the more feminine jobs had openings. Disgruntled, I hopped onto a barrel to consider my circumstances. I squinted through the dimming sunlight at all the places that had turned me down, feeling sorry for myself as my stomach growled. My fingers found the braided leather on my scythe's handle. *Leather.*

The one place I hadn't tried yet.

Sliding off the barrel, I hurried to the leatherwork shop. My last hope.

***

"I'll see you tomorrow." The leatherworker's calloused hand shook mine, and he smiled tiredly beneath his mustache. "The extra help around here will be useful."

His badger castling waddled up to him and held out a piece of leather for his inspection.

Relieved and nervous, I tripped on my way out the door. A strangely shaped piece of leather had caught my boot.

"Just kick that out of the way," the shopkeeper said. "Must've fallen off the scrap pile. My last assistant kept forgetting to take it out. You can start with that tomorrow afternoon."

I nodded and shoed the awkward leather triangle toward the pile of scraps, then strode out the door.

Leather scraps? That might just solve the other part of my problem—an inconspicuous case for when I had to take the mandolin with me. I'd just need a needle and thread.

I saw plenty in the seamstress shop. I wonder if I could—

I bumped into someone and staggered back. "Sorry—"

"Mella, hey. Haven't seen you in a while." Kaido mucking Felzane stood in front of me in all his tanned glory, grinning like the heart-meltingly gorgeous guy he was. He leaned against the wall, looking me over with a smirk.

My heart galloped, and my hands suddenly felt clumsy. I fumbled with my scythe and nearly dropped it. "Kaido, hi."

Stabbing the handle into the ground and holding it still, I put on my best smile and stared into his eyes.

Like me. Like me. I'm way better for you than Frenna or any other girl. How long will it take you to see that?

His anaconda hung around his shoulders, its head resting under Kaido's ear and its tail wrapped around his waist.

"Where's your...oh." He pushed off the wall, his smile vanishing. "I forgot. You didn't cast anything, right? Skunks."

Plummeting into my toes, my heart suddenly felt much less exhilarated. But I *had* cast something, just later. And too old. And the wrong species. *Ugh.*

But I *had* cast. I was just as good as any other girl.

He wouldn't tell on me for being unregistered, right? I shouldn't just assume...the consequences if I were wrong...but I couldn't let him forget about me.

I widened my smile and looked around conspiratorially. "Actually, Kaido, I *did* cast that day."

He raised his eyebrows, flexing his crossed arms. Eyeing my scythe, he nodded at it and said, "Show me what you've got."

Trying to keep my jitteriness from showing, I stepped a little closer, never looking away from his eyes. "You have to wait like everyone else. The king and queen don't know yet. I'm waiting for the right time to register her, and I can't let them find out about her before I do or it will look bad, you know? I'll register her soon, and it will be so worth the wait. My animal is...very special." She was certainly...*unique*, at least.

He grinned at me. "What if I'm not good at keeping secrets?"

I blanched. Skunks, I'd done the wrong thing. They couldn't find out about her before I registered her myself. And neither Whisper nor I were strong enough for her to stay awake a decent amount of time. I had to keep her a secret until she could reasonably be full grown, because no one could find out she was cast from an illegal instrument. Besides the lashings I would get, what would they do to Whisper?

He took another step closer, his eyes locked on mine. "Hey, calm down. The price of my secrecy isn't steep."

I frowned. Price? He was going to *charge* me? And I'd just given away my last coins!

His lips crashed against mine in a sudden molten rush. My heart zoomed from my toes to somewhere too high to describe. I dropped the scythe and wrapped my arms around his shoulders.

Was this victory?

Victory was *so* nice.

He let go, grinning.

I couldn't speak. I just stared at him, already completely fallen for him. "Kaido…"

He laid a finger over my lips. "Shh. I'll see you around. Your secret's safe with me." He stepped back, never taking his rich brown eyes off mine, then turned into a side street and disappeared.

Holy skunking muck. Did that just happen? Maybe this will be easier than I thought.

CHAPTER 21

DANE

"Hey, Dane!" Reenalyn waved enthusiastically as Sprinter and I approached the fire circle after training in another part of the woods. I sat on one of the logs, catching my breath after a serious workout. Sprinter lay at my feet, still panting.

"Hey, Reenalyn." I smiled back at her, wishing it was Mella who was so excited to see me. But Reenalyn was always excited to see everyone. It was nice.

Beldon approached with Brawler and Mauler wrestling in his wake. Trinka leaned against a tree with her arms crossed several spans back.

No Mella.

I scratched between Sprinter's ears. "How do you feel after sparring?"

He huffed out a sigh. "Exhausted. Sleepy." He tended to keep his answers short and quiet around others, since the more he talked, the more he was clearly not the young puppy he should be.

"Same," I said. "I'm starving, too. I hope we'll eat soon."

"Mella!" Reenalyn waved her over to us as she and Whisper entered the clearing.

I tried not to stare at Mella's glossy hair rippling in the breeze, or her confident stride, or her hand wrapped around her scythe...

"Stop ogling before you get drool strings. Ladies don't care for drool strings, let me tell you," Sprinter mumbled under his breath.

I lightly swatted his shoulder. "Shut up."

He chuckled, his canine lips poofing out each time.

I turned my focus on Whisper instead. An imposingly huge avian of prey, she was really something. But the awkward way she waddled and leaned forward clashed with Mella's graceful step. How was it possible for something so big to fly? I'd never seen a wild avian more than half her size.

Mella hugged Reenalyn, Cupid scuttling to perch on Reenalyn's head. Then Mella hugged Beldon.

Ugh. Something twisted in my chest. Would she have hugged me, too, if I would've been over there?

Mella nodded at Trinka, who nodded back, then she waved to Sprinter and me with a smile.

She had such a nice smile. Definitely the prettiest one I'd ever seen.

"This is the part where you wave back," Sprinter hissed out the side of his mouth.

Oh, monkey's teeth, yes. I waved vigorously, smiling at her. She looked away, her smile fading. *Too much.* I winced and sat on my hands. *What an idiot.*

Sprinter eyed me, grinning. His tail thumped against the log.

"Knock that off," I hissed, glowering at him.

His tail wagged a bit faster as he chuckled again.

I rolled my eyes, but they wandered to Mella again, as always. She was walking toward me—toward *me!*—the huge eagle waddling behind her.

"Hey, Dane." She sat on the log next to me, just half an arm's reach away.

"Uh, hey, Mella. And Whisper. Good to see you both." I realized I was still sitting on my hands and quickly picked up a piece of bark to fiddle with while searching my entirely blank mind for anything to say.

An awkward silence bloomed. Then I remembered Acres Parrianther.

"Oh! I forgot to tell you, there was another guy assigned to our cohort who, um, had some trouble finding us."

Part of me wanted to tell her how many hours I'd searched for that guy just because she mentioned she'd rather have even numbers for training, but would that sound childish? Like I wanted a pat on the back? I didn't want to come off that way.

"But I ran into him today, and I'm meeting him tomorrow morning to bring him here. We'll have six, then."

Her grin widened. "That's fantastic! Lucky that you ran into him."

"Yeah. Lucky." I chuckled, sharing a look with Sprinter.

"Then we can all spar at once and no one will have to sit out." She stared ahead, maybe watching Reenalyn and Beldon roasting something over the fire.

She had a light dusting of freckles on her face, so subtle you wouldn't know about them unless you'd been lucky enough to sit close to her.

Suddenly she was facing me, apparently waiting for a reply. What had she said? "Oh, uh...okay?"

Skunks. Was that the right answer? I had zero idea.

Her eyebrows drew together as she regarded me. Must've been the wrong answer.

I glanced away, my face heating. "Um..."

"Which will be nice," she said.

"Yeah." What was I agreeing with? Heat rushed into my face as I tried to imagine what we were supposed to be talking about.

Another awkward silence fell. I searched for anything suitable to say. I was too full of feelings—which were not suitable for discussion—to grasp at any appropriate topics.

"So...do you mind?" she asked.

"Mind what?"

She gave me an exasperated look that would've worried me if it wasn't so adorable. "That I got a job at the leatherwork shop across the street from The Braided Loaf. Like I was just telling you."

"Oh! No, why would I mind? Congratulations! That's great." It was more than great. Possibilities of walking with her to and from work and maybe eating lunch together swirled tantalizingly in my future. Would she finally remember me? Did I want her to? "But wait, you're better-class, aren't you? Why do you need a job?"

She rolled her eyes, but hurt lingered in her expression as she stared straight ahead. "It's a long story."

She breathed deeply, and I couldn't help noticing the way her body moved as she exhaled.

Would asking be showing I cared, or seem nosey? "Do you want to tell me about it?"

"I just...I'm living in Wrynford now, so I need to act like it. My parents...well they didn't even give me a chance to explain about Whisper. They just let me know that failing to cast at the ceremony was an unwelcome addition to a rather long list of my shortcomings." She ground her teeth.

"If there's anything I can do—"

"Just wait till they see Whisper and me on Wager Day. And if Kaido..." She trailed off, looking askance at me.

"What about Kaido?" Who was he?

"I just have bigger plans than leatherwork for the rest of my life, I guess." She licked her lips.

Why did she do that? Why was it so distracting?

"Dane, I—"

"Grab a stick and get your butts over here! It's roasting time!" Beldon called out to us.

"We should tell them about the guy you found," Mella said, sliding off the log. Whisper shook herself as if from a trance and followed her.

I could've strangled Beldon, even if my arms were a fraction the size of his. If he could've waited a few more seconds, Mella would've finished her sentence, and I wouldn't be perishing with curiosity. Instead, I watched her stroll across the leaf-littered ground to Reenalyn, Whisper waddling by her side.

Beldon looked over his shoulder and grinned as Trinka walked up to the fire. He smiled at her an awful lot. Maybe he was into her, not Mella. Hopefully.

"I think her castling has a thing for me." Sprinter sighed.

I blinked, sure I'd misunderstood. "What?"

"Didn't you notice how the eagle never took her eyes off me the whole time they were over here?"

"Uh, no. I guess I was slightly distracted by the beautiful girl of my own species. Why would Whisper be staring at *you*?"

Sprinter frowned, his ears swinging back against his head. "Don't sound so shocked."

I rolled my eyes. "Sprinter, you're a gorgeous wild canine with eyes that shine like the blistering sun. I wasn't surprised someone was admiring you. Just that it was an eagle instead of another canine. Besides, Whisper seems a little old for you, doesn't she? And pretty grouchy, too."

"All right, *Dad*." Sprinter huffed.

I chucked and scratched between his ears again. "If you don't want to get teased, then don't start the teasing."

He pointedly looked away from me, his black nose to the sky. "And before you try telling Mella what her eyes shine like, consider comparing them to something pleasant rather than *blistering*. Unless you want to dig yourself out of an even deeper hole."

"Hey!" I stopped scratching.

He ignored me, sniffing the air. Standing, he stretched and yawned. "I'm going to check that food out." He trotted off to the others, leaving me behind.

I rolled my eyes. *Castlings.* What had Mella been about to say?

"Dane, I'm hopelessly in love with you and will you please come over here and kiss me right now?"

Probably not.

"Dane, I think I like you. Want to hang out more often?"

Maybe.

"Dane, I noticed you seem to drool after me wherever I go. I just wanted to let you know it makes me uncomfortable, so please stop doing that."

Ugh. Probably.

***

After eating a dinner of campfire potatoes and peppers with bacon, we sat under the stars and watched the flames.

"Trinka?" Mella asked. "Are you related to the Seranovas from Glenmyre?"

Trinka laced her fingers behind her head and closed her eyes. "No."

Before Mella could say anything else, Reenalyn dragged her to her feet and got her to agree to one more spar before calling it a night. Mella and

Whisper versus Reenalyn and Cupid. Cupid had barely fought anyone yet—he was so small and shy. Whisper seemed like an odd choice,
but the more experience the better, I guessed.

"Seranova..." Beldon mumbled from where he sat.

Trinka's eyes opened, and her frown deepened at Beldon's voice.

"Does that mean something about the stars? A constellation or
something?" he asked her.

"No idea."

Whisper leaped and snapped at Reenalyn's shoulder. Again, something seemed off about the way her legs extended. But Mella swept in
to block Reenalyn's downward spear thrust, also blocking my view.

I'd rather watch Mella than Whisper, anyway.

Beldon continued as Trinka focused on Mella and Reenalyn. "My
last name, Berroman, means *keeper of the fish barrels* or something,
which is funny because most of my family doesn't even like fish. And
none of us have ever been fishing, or on a boat."

Finally, Trinka took her eyes off the spar and faced him. "Why tell
me this?"

Mella and Reenalyn jogged back a few steps, heaving for breath as
they analyzed each other.

"Because it's interesting. Have you ever been fishing?" Beldon
asked.

Trinka's eyes unfocused, and she was silent for several moments.

Beldon waved a hand in front of her face. "Trinka?"

Her eyes flashed. "No. I haven't been fishing."

She narrowed her eyes on the spar as if she were focusing hard and
trying her best to ignore him.

"Okay. So you're definitely not an undercover adult, or someone
from a secret fight training academy. And you're not from the Glenmyre Seranovas or from a fishing family. Emberlyn wood producers?"

She rolled her eyes. "You're still curious where I'm from?"

He grinned sheepishly.

"Well, stop." She huffed, facing the sparring pairs again.

"Why won't you tell me?"

She sent a scowl at him. "Why do you need to know?"

"It's the sort of thing friends find out about each other. Don't you want to know where *I'm* from?"

"No, I don't. And didn't I say from the beginning that I'm not here to make friends?"

"Oh. Okay, then. Fine." He crossed his arms and leaned back, finally focusing on the fight.

Poor Beldon. He's having about as much luck as me.

Trinka watched him, apparently confused, then turned away.

"See how Demensey does that thing every time she kicks?" Trinka nodded at Reenalyn. "And always lands on her right leg?"

I followed her gaze as Beldon said, "Oh. Yeah, I see what you're talking about."

"Yeah." Trinka gestured to Mella and Reenalyn. "That's useful information. Why anyone has their last name is not useful information."

"O...kay..." Beldon raised an eyebrow.

Her eyes narrowed. "Not that I should help you, since you clearly already have all the advantage you need."

He grinned. "All the advantage I need?"

She gestured to him. "You're at least a full head taller than everyone but Demensey. I'm not going to explain how height and strength are an advantage in a fight."

Beldon looked down at himself, shrugged, and turned his attention back to Mella and Reenalyn.

Trinka took several deep, slow breaths like she was trying to calm herself.

Interesting.

Yeah, even if Beldon might be into Trinka, she definitely didn't like him. That was too bad.

Chapter 22

ACRES

S quinting through the dimness, I wished I was at home reading instead of out in the middle of nowhere trying to find Dane and my new cohort. Did sparring have to take place outside?

Twigs crunched somewhere up ahead.

"Is that you, Dane?" I called.

"Hey! You found the place. Great! Follow me and I'll introduce you to everyone."

Usually the pale blue-grey light of morning before sunrise meant I'd read straight through the night again. But today it meant I was up so early it should be unlawful.

Yawning for the hundredth time, I entered a clearing behind Dane.

I could just make out a girl with dark hair sitting on one of the fallen logs they'd dragged into a circle around the firepit. Was that Mella from my blacksmithing class? She looked about as lively as I felt.

She glanced up at me and squinted, then smiled. "Hey, Acres. You're our missing cohort member?"

I waved awkwardly. "Looks like it."

"Good morning!" a tall, blonde girl appeared out of nowhere with the energy of a blinding bolt of sunshine. "Who are you? Would you like some breakfast? What kind of castling do you have?"

"Uh..." I could barely register one question let alone multiple.

"Acres, this is Reenalyn. Reenalyn, Acres." Gesturing back and forth between us, Dane squinted at my half-dead eyes and chuckled. "Since he's asleep on his feet, I'll tell you he's the missing guy who was assigned to the Wrynford cohort with us. He's joining now and his castling is a serval named Starstinger."

Slapping my shoulder, he said, "There. Now all you need to tell her is whether you want breakfast. Which I can tell you, you do."

"Right. Sure."

Reenalyn threw some things over the fire. Soon they sizzled, making my stomach growl.

"Something smells good!" A huge guy said, strolling through the trees with a gorilla at his side.

"Acres, meet Beldon. Beldon, Acres. This is our missing cohort member."

"Right on. Even number again, woohoo!" he pumped his fist, then took a seat on the log closest to the fire, sniffing the air appreciatively.

"Trinka's the other one, if you're wondering about the even number thing." Beldon added. "She's sort of evasive most of the time. But you'll meet her eventually. She's probably less than five spans tall, but three times as scary."

Blinking slowly, I nodded. "Short girl—scary. Got it."

"Yeah," his voice rose as he winced, "but I wouldn't recommend commenting on her height in her presence. If you value your life."

"Right. Thanks."

"Breakfast is served!" the overly cheerful girl announced. "Dig in!"

***

They really weren't too bad, all in all. But after a few hours of sparring and answering questions, I'd had enough time around people for one day.

Now for some quiet target practice. Without company.

I scraped a target shape over the bark of a good-sized tree and practiced throwing my stars at the center.

"Acres, didn't we just join a cohort?" Starstinger wove between my ankles, brushing her tail against my legs.

"Yes. And I know where you're going with this—you wonder why we aren't sparring right now. Well, we just met them, they already have a routine, and it will take some time to integrate ourselves. So for now, while they do their thing, we can practice out here."

"Except that's *so boring*, Acres." She threw herself on her side and sighed dramatically.

Sliding the throwing star still in my hand into its leather pouch, I turned to Starstinger. "Look, I joined the cohort like you wanted."

"And I appreciate that, Acres, but we're not doing anything different."

"It's been less than a day!"

"And that's almost another whole day we haven't spent getting in better shape to defend ourselves!"

I paused, guilt weighing in my gut again for letting us get attacked and intimidated by that man in the alley. But I *had* tried. I was here now, wasn't I? That should count for something.

A twig snapped behind us, and Starstinger was on her feet in front of me before I could pull the star back out.

"Just me." A girl with skin even darker than mine approached, her bear cub castling at her side. "One of the Wrynford cohort members. You're the dual-weapons guy. Throwing stars?"

Holding the star at my side, I raised my other hand in greeting. "Yeah, that's right."

"Trinka Seranova, and this is Mauler. Sorry we missed introductions."

"Acres Parrianther." I nodded to her castling and gestured to mine. "This is Starstinger. I was just getting in some target practice."

She crossed her short, muscular arms, eyeing the throwing star in my hand. "So why'd you do that? The two castling weapons, I mean."

"Safety. This way—in theory—if one is ever shattered, there would be the other."

"Like an extra life?"

I nodded. "Precisely."

She ruffled the hair between her castling's perked ears. "Wish I would've thought of that." She squinted at me. "What are you eating?"

I hadn't realized I'd been rolling the leaves around in my mouth. They were about out of flavor, which meant they weren't working to boost my memory, either. "Dapplemint leaves. I struggle with focus sometimes, and they help with memory retention. I'm trying to see whether they'll improve muscle memory as well. But I'm not actually eating them. Just chewing. It releases the oils."

The bear cub castling, Mauler, wrinkled her nose. "Ew."

I shrugged, wondering if I could spit the leaves out in front of them, or if that would seem rude.

Trinka eyed me. "Does it really help? With general memory retention, I mean?"

I nodded. "Yes."

She eyed me. "Floramancy, huh?"

Skunks. Sure, it was technically floramancy. But I was *not* a floramancer. "I'm not into potions and all that, if that's what you're asking. I'm just making use of one floramantic property that has a positive effect on my memory."

"But what would you do if you didn't have any on hand for a battle? Wouldn't it be dangerous to get too used to it and then not be able to perform well?"

That was an interesting question. "It's not addictive, if that's what you mean. It helps with *storing* memories. Your mind can bring them back on its own, as long as they're stored effectively."

"Huh. Seems like it would be more useful to have something to take memories *away*. I wish there were some leaves for that."

"No, you don't." How could she think that? "Having someone take your memories away is the same as someone else deciding who you are and what you care about without you even knowing what they're changing. It's...unacceptable."

Her gaze drifted to the side. "You haven't seen my memories."

I scoffed, the annoying edges of memories still out of my grasp tickling my mind. A flash of my older sister's teary face. My mother's pleading hands. They wanted—what? "You've never had yours taken away against your will."

She glowered at me. "Does getting knocked out and not remembering what happened count? Having to piece together the story by which body parts are injured—the aftermath of choices taken away from you. Seems at least as bad to me. And forgetting it all would be better than reliving it."

I eyed her, a teeny part of my brain feeling compassion for whatever she wanted to forget, but most of me annoyed that she thought being forced to forget was better than being forced to remember. I'd rather remember everything—all the good and all the bad—than constantly wonder what I'm missing.

Her suspicious gaze widened. "Are you trying not to mention that there *is* a way to have some memories...removed?"

I glared at her. "There used to be. But I wouldn't recommend it. There's no way to guarantee which memories you'll lose. You might forget a key part of who you are."

"There's an awful lot I wouldn't mind getting rid of."

I spun a throwing star and turned back toward my target on the tree. I was done with this conversation. "Can't help you."

"All right. See you around, Parrianther."

Chapter 23
SELVERINE

Tossing my sweaty amber bangs out of my face, I danced away from Willova, barely avoiding her cutlass as it arced toward my knees. My boots clicked against the hardwood floor until I'd put several spans between us. Catching my breath, I stared her down.

Willova Calentine had the pain tolerance—or at least self-controlled stoicism—of a battle-worn boot.

She held still, crouched, and brandishing her cutlass, her hand twisted over and through the cutlass grip a bit differently so more of her hand filled the space.

I'll take it easy on her and avoid the handle wrenching for today. I wonder if I could twist it out of her grip more easily with her hand at that angle?

I saw my chance and lunged. But she spun and blocked my advance.

"Nice block."

"Nice lunge." Sparring was the only time her voice came out at a normal volume, one I didn't have to strain to hear.

I ducked in again while the words were still leaving her mouth.

Her cutlass was almost too slow but still managed to beat me. And—*whoa!* She threw me back and caught my shoulder with the point—thank good fortune it was still leather-tipped.

She stopped just at my throat. "Dead."

I stepped back and pivoted to catch her by surprise, but she saw me coming and blocked me again, hooking my ankle with hers and knocking me to the ground.

"Dead," she repeated.

Okay. Forget taking it easy on you. I snarled and leaped to my feet. That gap between her hand and pommel guard was all mine. *Right. Now.*

I feinted a blow to her shoulder and then shot for the gap, but with one of the outer points rather than the middle. *Bet you don't see this coming!*

She tried to block me, but the change meant an angle she wasn't expecting. But the trident still bounced off her pommel guard and tore her fighting tunic, despite the leather tip.

I rose from my crouch, eyeing the tear. "Sorry, Willova, I didn't mean to…"

Where the tear should've revealed a sliver of pale skin, dark onyx peeked out instead.

I pointed. "What's that?"

Her eyes widened, and her hand flew to cover the spot. "Oh, it's nothing."

Panic shook in her voice. *Panic?*

"Is that *another* tattoo?"

"No!" she snapped, then closed her eyes, taking deep breaths. "It's nothing. I don't have *any* tattoos. Listen, do you have thread and a needle somewhere around here? I can't go home with it torn like this."

The fear in her eyes when she finally looked up sparked my curiosity. I raised an eyebrow. "Sure. If you tell me what it is."

"It's truly nothing, Selverine. It's the tear I'm worried about. Please, can you let me mend it?"

She so rarely made eye contact, but the frantic way her emerald eyes searched mine worried me a little. Would she be punished for her torn clothing? What could parents expect of a new castor who spent all her time sparring? A few ruined garments would hardly be the worst outcome.

"Okay. Sure." Maybe she'd gotten a tattoo her parents didn't know about and would be displeased with. But then why hide it from *me*?

Turning toward the door, I gestured for Willova to follow me. "Come on."

***

"Thank you," Willova said from the foot of my bed, snipping the tail off the thread.

Why she didn't just hand it to a servant at home, I couldn't guess. Why she even knew how to sew something herself—how many times had she mended her own clothes before? "No worries." I leaned out my bedroom window, watching a flock of avians soar overhead. What an amazing thing it would be to fly.

Willova's elbows joined mine on the beige stone windowsill. She took the same crossed-arms-head-down pose as me. "Are...are you worrying about who to take to the ball?"

I blinked. "What? No. That's the *last* thing on my mind right now."

It made my nose itch, thinking about that. I scratched it absently, feeling a jolt of pain as my fingernail caught skin I'd already rubbed raw. I hadn't realized I'd been scratching it so much.

Waiting for her to ask the obvious questions about what was on my mind, I pressed my fingers against the irritated skin on my nose. I wanted someone to want to understand. *How can I possibly have time to worry about the ball when I'm too busy training to be good enough without a decent castling?*

Of course I felt guilty for being disappointed in my castling, but I also felt eternally frustrated that I couldn't get a redo. It was *so* unfair.

I'd done everything I could. I'd given it a hint in my casting call that it was supposed to be like my namesake, Selvenair, the avian I was named after. I'd even chosen a trident, shaped so much like a taloned avian foot, and etched feathers into it. And still my weapon's soul decided it should come out looking like a *skunking* wolverine.

What the muck.

"Well, when you do start thinking about it, you could consider my brother, Drazdan. He's a...um...pretty good dancer. I guess."

I turned fully toward her. "Did you just roll your eyes at your own suggestion?"

"What? No." She turned away.

I glanced up at the sky again, empty of avians now. "Why are you trying to set me up with Drazdan? I thought you didn't like him."

"I...he's okay. Great, actually. And he likes you."

"And that should matter to me why?"

She let out a strained chuckle. "I don't know. I just think you should ask him to the dance. That way you wouldn't have to think about it anymore. Since it's not much of a priority for you."

I peeked at her without turning my head. The girl had an unusual obsession with getting me and her brother together. This was at least the third time she'd mentioned it. Why? If she thought setting me up with him would somehow thank me for the thread or any other small favors I'd done over the past couple of weeks, she shouldn't have grimaced every time she said his name. I got a bad vibe from just the idea of him. Nothing I could put my finger on, just a feeling.

But as a sort of royal heir, I'd be even more expected to bring a guest. *Bleh.*

Come to think of it, I couldn't remember what the boy looked like. "What's he look like? Is he attractive?"

Her face remained expressionless. "Yeah, he's attractive. His hair is darker than mine—more of a mahogany-brown color. And not a single freckle."

"Gosh, why don't *you* just date him? If you're so into his look."

She chuckled. "Really, he *is* nice-looking. I wish I looked more like him. The hair and complexion, anyway."

I glared her up and down. "Willova, you've got perfect skin. What are you talking about?"

"I wear a paste over my face to hide the freckles. Drazdan was born with perfect, clear skin. No imperfections."

"You wear makeup?" I asked, incredulous.

Makeup was for old rich men and women who wanted to look younger. And freakishly expensive. Willova didn't need it. I wondered what she'd look like without it, and if I would start needing some for my nose.

"Yes. The freckles are...pretty numerous. Distracting. Unattractive. And asymmetrical."

I slouched off the windowsill and dropped onto my bed. "Again with the symmetry muck. What's your deal?"

When she didn't answer, I leaned up to get a better look at her. Her arms were still crossed, her shoulders hunched like she was ashamed of something. And a stark black design peeked out from where the resewn fabric bunched out of the way.

Well, that's not symmetrical.

I flopped back down and laid an arm partially over my eyes. "Okay, fine. I'll invite Drazdan Sir Handsomeskin to the stupid ball."

Her shoulders lifted—so that was the victory she was after? But why? Had he asked her to ask me?

Then she slouched again, as if she weren't actually pleased. "Okay. Great. Would you like me to deliver the invitation?"

I threw the other arm over my face. "No. I'll invite him myself. Tomorrow maybe."

"Okay. Thank you."

"But first, I think you need another go at that rip. It's still showing a bit of the secret non-tattoo you don't want anyone to see."

She went as straight as that huge blonde girl's spear.

"If you're trying to hide it, it's not working. Though if it makes you feel better, I can't tell what it is."

"Thank you for warning me. And for the thread. I would appreciate the chance to hide this better."

"Sure thing." I faced my closet and frowned, considering what to wear. "It's really too bad the ballroom isn't big enough for castlings to attend as well."

Willova leaned against the windowsill. "You want to take your castling to the ball?"

I laughed harshly. "No. But I overheard Mella Yarinelle the other day—that girl who failed to cast. She told Kaido she'd somehow managed to cast afterward. I want to see what she's got. If she's actually got anything."

"Wow. Well, you could always find where her cohort is training and do a little spying."

"I've tried. The Wrynford cohort would have to be hiding out somewhere in the Emberlyn Forest. But I haven't been able to track them down."

"I could help."

I shifted to a sitting position, raising an eyebrow.

"I've been in the Emberlyn Forest a few times. I know a few clearings where people sometimes camp out." She shrugged.

"That would be great, but when do you have time for it? You're always in such a hurry to get home."

She crossed her arms, regarding the wood floor. "Drazdan sees fit to keep a close hold over my time. But if we went during a training session I've already got his permission for, it could work."

A conspiratorial smile spread across my face. "How about tomorrow?"

Chapter 24

MELLA

S unlight dappled the forest floor where Whisper and I prepared to train. Flexing my bicep, I pushed against the little muscle with one finger to make it look bigger.

If only.

"I'm pleased with my flight progress, Mella." Whisper sighed. "I just wish I were able to get farther off the ground."

"Even with gigantic wings? All those lighter-than-air feathers for catching the wind? You've got those, haven't you?"

She sighed heavily, hanging her head. "That's not all I've got, and that's the problem. I'm too heavy, Mella."

"You're right about that." I ran my fingers through my hair, eyeing the makeshift shoulder pad I'd constructed from leather scraps and leftover thread. "Whisper, you've got to stop being so vague with me. Don't you trust me enough by now to tell me what's really going on? What do you mean that wings aren't all you've got?"

She eyed me, then wilted, her crown feathers lowering against her neck. "Try not to lose your mind, okay?"

I raised my eyebrows. Was I actually going to get a straight answer?

Glaring at me, she planted her feet and straightened. And straightened even higher. Suddenly she was over a span taller.

I took a step back. "What...?"

She stuck out one incredibly long leg and I saw it. Her taloned foot and avian ankle were the same yellowish color. But the brown-and-white feathers only went so far up her leg before being replaced by sandy fur. And her upper leg was shaped wrong.

"As you can see, something is clearly wrong with this body. These...these legs look kind of like my old coyote legs from the first time I was a castling. They're misshapen, but they've been growing slowly ever since you cast me. That's why it's gotten harder and harder to walk, and harder to fly, because of the added weight."

"So you're...a mix of two animals? Like a hybrid?"

She nodded. "It appears so. And it's exceedingly important Narellen doesn't discover this. I don't think she would recognize me, but if she did...you and I both would be in grave danger."

"But why? What's her problem with you? I can't imagine Narellen being dangerous. She's a nice old lady."

Whisper regarded me, her bright eyes flashing. Then she sank to the ground and sighed. "Do you remember how you told me no one alive has seen a shattering?"

I nodded.

"That's not entirely true."

I raised an eyebrow. "Really? But what does that have to do with your legs?"

"I'm the one who was shattered."

My mouth dropped open. That couldn't be true! "What?"

"And the reason I hate Narellen is because she ordered my death and my castor's imprisonment."

"She ordered you shattered? But why?"

"Someone framed my castor for an attempted assassination of the last king, who was Jorros's father. They sentenced my castor to death for the false offense. And I—his castling weapon—was shattered right in front of his eyes."

"King Jorros framed your castor for murder?"

She glowered at the ground. "That's right. But my castor wouldn't have done such a thing. He gave no indication of such intentions. But I was separated from him immediately after and then shattered. We never got to discuss it. I don't even know whether he was put to death or died from his injuries in prison."

How awful to part from your castor under such circumstances and be shattered immediately. Without even a goodbye? "Whisper, I'm so sorry."

Her face hardened as her crown feathers shot back up. "I don't think we have the whole story. Something's missing. Something Jorros didn't want everyone to know. Jorros and his castling, Glacier, and Narellen and Selvenair deserve to die for what they did."

Alarm shot up my eyebrows. "Well, let's not kill them all yet. Let's get through the Grand Castors' Tournament first. How about that?"

If my castling went rogue and murdered the royals—besides the obvious problems with that plan—my miniscule chance at a good future would burn to smithereens.

I understood the importance of hiding the extra legs though. "So the leg thing—that's why you never fly over anyone's head. It's because you've been hiding the fact that you're a hybrid."

She nodded. "Yes."

"How did I go from failing to cast, to casting a rare avian, to casting a hybrid? I didn't even know a hybrid could be a castling. I've only heard of travelers coming across strange animals in the wilderness who seemed to be made from multiple animals. But this?"

Her wings rose and fell in an avian shrug. "You sang a casting call over an instrument instead of a weapon. That's all I know."

I picked up the makeshift shoulder pad. We'd have to use it, then. To protect Whisper's identity. "It's time for a crash course in using this thing."

She nodded, carefully scratching her beak with one giant talon.

I pulled off my tunic and slid the small pad over my shoulder. With the band in place, I reached for the strap behind my back.

I turned to Whisper. "What do you think?"

She stared forlornly into the distance, maybe caught up in memories.

It seemed to me the method used to put a loved one to death wasn't something most people wanted to know. But she was right—it had only been a short time for her. Maybe knowing would help her process. Maybe I could find out for her. All castor and castling deaths were recorded with their registration parchments. And the registry was kept in the Glenmyre library.

"What was your castor's name?"

She waddled behind me and nosed the strap into my hand with her beak. "I don't speak his name. It's too painful. For me, it's as if I lost him two weeks ago."

"Of course. Thank you for confiding in me, Whisper."

She nodded, and her eyes grew hard again as she glared at the leather pad. "I'm sorry you have to go to so much trouble because of my wretched feet. If I could've come back as I had been the first time, it would be so much easier."

I slid the strap through the buckle, still considering how to find out exactly what had happened. She'd manifested as a coyote in the past, and her late castor was male. That should be enough to start. If I could just access the registries...

"Your feet and talons are impressive, actually. I wouldn't call them wretched. Eagle feet are much better for grabbing things and climbing."

She grunted and eyed my shoulder. "That looks bulky. Is it comfortable?"

"Comfortable enough."

She frowned at it. "Will your tunic really fit over it?"

I slid it back on without too much difficulty. "How's this look?"

"You look like a hunchback."

I shot her a glare.

"But...once I'm standing on it, I don't think anyone will notice. What if you use your scythe like a walking stick with that arm?"

I frowned at the scythe. What a worthless thing I'd spent all those countless hours perfecting. Reduced to a castlingless walking stick.

"Yeah, that's a good idea." I leaned my shoulder toward her. "Come on up. Let's try this out."

***

A breeze played through the leaves at eye level, instead of far above. Metal chinked as Dane blocked my scythe with his strange giant-nail weapon. I stepped back, sliding my foot over the branch to keep my footing like he'd taught me.

"Nice job," he said, leaping over a couple of higher branches. He fell back to hang from his knees ten spans above me, grinning. "Think you can catch me?"

I laughed. "Not unless you let me."

His upside-down eyes gleamed. "I'll let you then."

Rolling my eyes, I hefted my scythe and reached for the next branch. I wondered if I could do the same thing he was. I glanced at the fork in the branch I was standing on and slid the scythe handle through it.

Climbing to his branch, I awkwardly hooked my knees over it like he had. Falling backward, I squeaked before my knees caught me. Dane's hands flashed out to steady me as my tunic flopped over my face.

"Skunks." I shoved it back into place and tucked the edges into my waistband. "Oops." I laughed, but he didn't say anything. I faced him, and his face was beet-red. "You're not seriously blushing because of my tunic, are you?"

"No!" His voice cracked. I raised an eyebrow, but he wouldn't look at me. "Your mandolin—it's made of pieces of different things. Can you tell me about them?"

He blushed like he was embarrassed. About my tunic? He couldn't have seen more than a little midriff. Hardly anything to be embarrassed about.

"Sure." The branch swayed, and a thrill of fear shot through my stomach as I flailed for balance. Realizing I was fine, I let out a giggle.

"What?" He finally looked at me.

"I was just thinking how funny it is that we're having a conversation upside down. It's kind of fun."

He smiled back at me. His smile was actually really nice.

I let my arms hang over my head and closed my eyes, picturing each carefully pilfered piece of my homemade mandolin. "The arm is from a cherrywood dining room chair that broke. I was swinging my practice scythe in the house—which I was definitely *not* allowed to do—and crashed into the chair. It was one of the good ones, too. I knew Father would be furious, so I cleaned it up, threw out the pieces, and spread the other chairs out a bit, hoping its absence would go unnoticed."

I shooed a fly away from my face. "We haven't had guests in the dining room for as long as I can remember, so as far as I know, that's our little secret." I winced. "I've still got the scar though."

"Scar?"

"Yeah. A couple of the broken pieces scraped me up pretty bad when I fell. Couldn't sit down right for weeks."

"Ouch."

Opening my eyes, I faced him. "Skunks, Dane. You should probably sit upright for a bit. All the blood's rushing to your head."

His eyes shot open, and his face got even redder. Avoiding my eyes, he swung himself up with uncanny grace and straddled the branch where it met the tree, leaning back against the trunk.

My knees ached, so sitting upright seemed a good idea for me, too. I struggled to pull myself up, absently wondering what kind of abs a person would need to swing right up like Dane had.

"Want a hand?" He was there, right next to me, hand outstretched. I took hold of it, and he pulled me up so I was sitting, my legs dangling.

His fingers lingered around mine, and then the warmth was gone. He sat next to me, his hands braced on either side of him. Though rather pale, his hands were...nice. I'd never noticed anyone's hands before—other than Selverine's, whose long dainty fingers and golden skin I envied. No guy's, though. It was kind of a weird thing to notice. I'd have to pay closer attention to what Kaido's hands looked like now.

Dane's light-blue eyes met mine from behind shaggy white-blond bangs. "What about the strings? Where'd those come from?"

"I poached the strings and tuning pins off a broken guitar I found in the street. It looked like someone had gotten bashed over the head with it." I winced. I'd forgotten that part. "But it was just lying there in pieces, so I sneaked out after dark and swiped what I could."

He looked at me. "Aren't mandolins supposed to have pairs of strings?"

"Yeah, that's right. How'd you know? I thought you didn't play any instruments."

He shook his head. "I don't. I don't know anything about music, really. I just overheard some musicians talking about what a pain it had been to restring a mandolin because of the double strings at the Loaf the other day."

"You overhear a lot of things there, don't you?"

He laughed. "Yeah. Some ridiculous stuff, too."

I grinned. "Like what?"

He shrugged. "New castors talking trash about people in other co-horts. Parents talking about the muck their kids get up to. Younger kids arguing about who will cast the best castling one day. Random muck from the Emberlyn wood transporters about what they encounter on the road to Morrenfayre."

"Random muck on the road to Morrenfayre? What kind of muck?"

He rolled his eyes. "There's this one guy who's the worst. He's friends with some of the mill workers, and they all eat at the Loaf when he's in town. He always orders his sandwich without bread—just the in-sides—and makes up all kinds of stuff about the wild animals in the woods. Animals that look like combinations of multiple animals, stuff like that. No one ever believes him. I think he's just trying to impress them. His castling is a gorgeous snow leopard, though, so I have no idea why he'd feel the need to compensate with crazy stories."

"Multiple animals combined? Like a hybrid?" I tried not to let my jaw drop. "What does he say about them?"

"Yeah, that's what he called them. Claims to just see them. They conveniently run off whenever he gets close. He never brings up battle wounds, so he hasn't tried to take any of them on. If he's even seen anything at all."

Maybe this guy was just a bored drunkard looking for some attention, but what if there was some truth to what he claimed? "What kind of combinations has he seen?"

Dane's eyes fell on mine. "You believe him?"

I tried to laugh it off. "No, of course not." I waved the idea away with one hand. "I was just curious."

"Well, usually large species. Chimps and lions and rhinos. That kind of stuff."

I nodded, pretending to be more interested in watching the leaves sway in the breeze. His eyes bored into my head. How could I find out more about hybrids without risking Whisper? I'd have to think about that later.

For now, maybe some misdirection. "Anyway, back to the mandolin. It's not exactly a true mandolin, because it should have pairs of strings. But I only ever had the chance to pilfer the one guitar's worth of strings. Plus the body is shaped differently. As for where I got the body..." I rolled my eyes at that memory.

"What?" A half smile quirked Dane's mouth.

"It's a wooden shipping container for sample thread spools. Father's in textiles, and he'll send a container of small samples to potential clients from time to time. He kept a few on hand in his office. They were such a perfect shape for what I wanted, and I was pretty sure he wouldn't miss one of the *shipping* containers, of all things. One day, I sneaked one from his desk, but I found a parchment with some disturbing numbers on it. That was when I first understood why the parties had stopped and the new dresses were so much fewer and simpler than before."

Brushing hair from my eyes, I continued. "When he caught me snooping, he shouted me out of the room and slammed the doors. Fortunately for me, I still had the wooden container in my hand. He hadn't even noticed in his rage. So I fastened the lid and butchered sound holes into the sides with a kitchen knife."

"So you really did make it by yourself?"

I shrugged "Yep. Only way for me to get one."

"What made you want one?"

"A mandolin? It was my Momma's favorite instrument. She used to play and sing to me when I was little." I blinked. I'd just confessed that Momma was a musician. Skunks! "But, um, please don't tell anyone. I'd rather that not be common knowledge."

He nodded. "Sure. Is that what made you want to play an instrument? Even illegally?"

"Yes. The hired musicians father occasionally employed fascinated me—especially the string players. They could make such melancholy tunes, but somehow it made the sadness easier to bear. Not that I had much to be sad about, other than missing my momma. I was a spoiled kid, even in spite of the declining fortune. I had no idea how easy my life was back then."

He shifted to face me. "What were you sad about? Besides losing your mom."

I glanced at the dappled light pouring through the leaves. "Not getting my way, a lot of times. But what really occupied most of my pouting and wistfulness was—ironically—wishing for a sibling. I was lonely and wanted someone to play with, especially after losing Momma. Funny how *that* worked out."

"What's funny about it?"

I sighed. Shouldn't have let that one out either. Why was I slipping up so much around this guy? "My stepmother's pregnant."

His eyebrows rose. "Really? Well, congratulations." He peered at me. "But...you aren't excited? Why? Because of the stepmother?"

I shook my head, staring at the forest floor far below. "Not because of her. She's all right. And I want to be happy for her. I want to know who my little brother or sister will become. But—and I know it isn't the baby's fault—Father decided to replace me. Since I've turned out to be a disappointment. They didn't just turn me out because of the Castling Ceremony. It's because they have a new child who might be able to secure their futures, unlike me. And they wanted to stop spending money on me so they can save it for him or her." I nearly fell off the branch and stopped angrily swinging my legs.

His hand slid a speck toward mine, but he didn't touch me. "Mella, I'm so sorry. That's an awful way for parents to treat their kid."

"And so embarrassing." I leaned on my hand next to his and scrubbed my face with the other. "Please don't tell anyone."

His hand slid another speck toward mine. I wondered what it would feel like if he took my hand—not to help me up, just to hold it. I imagined it would be nice.

But I couldn't give him the wrong idea. I was all in for Kaido. Dane was a great guy, but Kaido was my ticket back into society. And *so* gorgeous.

And then Dane's hand covered mine, his fingertips brushing over my skin and leaving little pricks of something pleasant behind.

It did feel nice, but also wrong. I snatched my hand away.

I wanted Kaido, not Dane, and I would be hurt and furious if Kaido was out holding other girls' hands. I wasn't that kind of person.

"I'm sorry, Mella..." Dane's face was stricken, his eyes not meeting mine. "I just meant to let you know I want to help if there's anything I can do. I can't imagine how hard all that has been to deal with."

I slid down to the next branch, embarrassed that I'd hurt and embarrassed him and chastising myself for leaving my hand where he could easily take it. "It's fine, Dane."

"Wait, where are you going?"

"I'm about to be late for work. I need to, um, do some leathercraft stuff."

I slipped ungracefully and barely caught myself. It took a moment of fast breathing to catch my breath enough to consider the long jump down.

"Can I help you?" Dane asked from right in front of me. How he moved so silently, I'd never understand. And I found I *did* want his help. I liked how it felt when he picked me up and jumped to the ground with me in his arms.

But that wasn't right. I shouldn't be enjoying that with him when I wanted Kaido. "No, thank you. I can get it."

"Okay." His voice sounded sad.

Had I somehow led him on? I hadn't meant to. Skunks. I also had no idea how to get down. And even if I wasn't trying to impress Dane, I didn't want him watching me fall flat on my face. I sank to a crouch on the lowest branch, wrapped my arms around it, and tried to lower my legs. My feet slipped out from under me, and I wound up dangling and swinging my legs. My toes were still a couple of spans off the ground.

No way would I stick that landing.

Dane was suddenly behind me, on the ground. "Mella?"

I dropped, desperately hoping my feet would find the ground before my butt did.

Dane's hands caught my waist, keeping me upright. My feet hit the ground, and I swayed against Dane's chest, catching a whiff of smokey pine. My breath whooshed past my lips as if I *had* gotten my breath knocked out of me.

I jumped away from him.

"Sorry, Mella, I just didn't want you to get hurt."

"No worries." I brushed my hands off on my pants, needing to run my fingers over the etchings on my scythe handle to get the feel of Dane's hands out of my mind, and for something to do while I avoided his eyes. Heart sinking, I glanced up into the tree, where my scythe still hung.

Dane followed my gaze. "I'll grab it."

He launched into the leafy branches, and I tried to ignore how much I missed the warmth of his hands. Where in the world did that come from? I'd been too open. I shouldn't have talked about such personal things. But it had also been nice. I wished Kaido would ask me about those kinds of things.

How long until I could see him again?

Chapter 25

DANE

Shadows lengthened over the forest floor as I stared at the tree line, still hoping Mella would return to our cohort eventually.

At last she entered the training ground alone with her scythe in hand, and I almost stood to greet her. But embarrassment from this morning held me back. It was easier to watch from back here than to risk looking like an idiot again.

"If you're thinking how it would be better to hide than go talk to Mella, I'm highly disappointed in you," Sprinter drawled.

I frowned down at my castling's dark eyes. "Ouch. Why would you assume that?"

Sprinter eyed me, his huge black ears twitching. "Because you've been practically drooling over her since she walked through the trees."

"Shut up."

"Right on the mark."

"Skunk you."

He huffed through his lips. "Rude. And I don't think you'd actually want that, would you? I'm pretty sure my getting sprayed would make your weapon smell like essence of skunk butt even after I've fallen asleep."

I wrinkled my nose. "Gross. How did we go from Mella to essence of skunk butt?"

"Good point. Let's go back to Mella. Like, literally, walk up to her."

I rolled my eyes. "Guess I walked into that one."

"Not quite. Your feet would have to be in motion for actual walking to take place."

I threw my hands in the air and let them slap against my knees. "I give up."

Sprinter's laughter puffed his lips out so ridiculously I couldn't help a reluctant grin as I stared at my stupid skinny hands in the fading light of evening.

"Here are your options, Dane. Either go talk to her, or I'll get her and bring her over."

"No and no. She doesn't want to talk to me. Why isn't there a *minding my own business* option?"

His voice went low and soft. "Because you need humans in your life. I know how much you miss those we left behind, and I don't want you to lose the chance to train with Mella over one little embarrassing moment. Are your feelings for her so weak you'd rather give up after one mishap?"

I scoffed. "Of course not. But I'm not going to force my presence on her if she doesn't want me around."

"She likes your company, Dane. Just give her some time, and she might come around. Even if she doesn't, isn't the chance worth the attempt?"

I scowled at nothing, my chest aching more than I wanted to admit.

"I know you have more than just a crush on her, Dane."

"Do not."

He huffed another laugh. "Spoken like a man, indeed."

I threw a stick at him.

He chuckled and turned toward Mella. "What if she gets used to training with Beldon and makes it a habit? He's a good-looking guy. She might forget all about you."

Skunk Sprinter and skunk Beldon and his muscular build.

But he was right. I didn't want that to happen. And of course the chance she could ever return my feelings was worth any risk. As long as I didn't do anything stupid like this morning, maybe it would be okay.

He started to make his way toward Mella.

"Wait! Okay, fine, you obnoxious mutt. I'll go talk to her. I don't need you to do it for me."

He grinned slyly and waggled his eyebrows. I'd always admired how he could do that, as a *dog*. I hadn't been able to figure it out.

"Just behave yourself, *please*," I said.

"Rest assured, I will behave exactly as I see fit."

My eyes rolled again. "Oh, great. I'm so comforted."

Mella's forest-green sleeveless tunic over her leather leggings made her dark hair stand out even more attractively against her ivory skin. And she was talking to Beldon. Who was at least a full span taller than me. And ripped.

I was overthinking things. She wasn't interested in me as more than a friend. At least not yet. But that didn't mean she *hated* me, right? Talking to her again couldn't be so bad. I could ask her why she chose a scythe as her castling weapon. That was surely a safe topic.

My chest felt light and heavy at the same time. Mella's ocean-blue eyes met mine, and the words I'd had in mind got jumbled.

"So if it's weight training you want to work on, that's the best way to start," Beldon finished with a flourish, Mella's eyes flicked quickly back to his.

"I can help you if you want," he said. "Show you how to do it without straining your back and shoulders."

He shoved up his sleeve to show off his bicep. Which was also about a span bigger around than mine. *Monkey's teeth.*

"That's how I got these. So believe me, it works. You'll have stronger arms and increased upper body strength in no time."

"Yeah, I'd appreciate the help—especially arm and shoulder strength. That's where I'm weakest." Mella nodded, more interested than was necessary in his mucking biceps.

"Definitely good to focus on for swinging a scythe. But you'll need a strong back and torso, too. Good arms and shoulders require back and core strength for support."

She fixed her hands on her hips and smiled at Beldon. "Teach me your ways, then. I'm in."

Oh, please.

"Great! Follow me and I'll show you this limb I use for pullups."

Mella followed him without another look at me. Suddenly my chest felt hollow.

Skunking Beldon. Muck him.

Sprinter whined, and I dropped my gaze to his. "I tried, okay?"

He hung his head, the disappointment in his gaze stinging me. "Didn't look like you talked to her at all to me."

"Whatever. We don't have time for this anyway. Let's run." I jumped into a sprint right there, suddenly overtaken by a restless energy I needed to use up.

A moment later and Sprinter was at my side. And *finally* off my case.

CHAPTER 26

ACRES

I was deeply engrossed in a description of kosmoceritops dinosaurs in *Fossil Fever* when there was scraping on my windowsill. I looked up to see a pair of arms pulling themselves through the open window. My chair squealed against the wood floor as I shoved it back and dropped my sandwich on the desk, hoping no sauce had defiled the pages.

"Who's there?"

Trinka's bald head and dark face appeared, bathed in candlelight, as she hauled herself the rest of the way in. "I know you've got something against removing memories, but if you've got any floramancy stuff that might do it"—she slid past the dapplemint leaves in their little pots on the sill—"I really need some. Hi, Parrianther." She dropped to the floor, surprising me again by her short stature.

"Hi." I frowned. "I really don't think—"

Trinka sat on my bed. Starstinger regarded her, her tail flicking. Where was Trinka's castling tonight?

Eyeing me, Trinka took a deep breath and said, "Yesterday, I had a nightmare involving some terrible memories, and I...I stabbed my castling by accident." She winced, covering her face with her small hands before shaking it off and pulling her usual emotionless expression back into place.

Skunks.

"Fortunately, it was with my second set of spikes and not my castling weapon. Thank good fortune I didn't know how to make two castling weapons, because if it had been my casting spikes...I could've..." Her voice quivered, and she pursed her lips, struggling to keep the emotion inside.

Holy skunks. She'd almost ended her castling in the worst way. Even with enough injuries to a castling's animal form to scar their weapon, they could eventually heal. But if a weapon were shattered, or a castling's animal form injured with its own weapon, there was no coming back.

Her voice trailed off, and her eyes flicked away. She took a heaving breath, her lips quivering as she wrapped her arms around herself.

And I couldn't blame her.

With a sniff, she straightened and uncurled her arms. "I need a memory-erasing plant or something, Acres. Better to lose a part of myself than to lose my castling because of memories I didn't want anyway."

I glanced at Starstinger. Her eyes were on me, ears pricking. Trinka had a point.

I eyed the trunk crammed under my desk.

Revulsion and nervousness and unpleasant feelings welled up. But if it could save her castling...

Helping one person with a little floramancy wouldn't make me become the thing I hated. It was just one.

Nodding gravely at Trinka, I reached over and plucked a dapplemint leaf from the windowsill.

"Take this first. It helps with focus. Chew this and think hard about the memories you want to lose. Don't think about anything you want to keep. You'll be at risk of losing those memories, too, if you think of them now."

"Floramancy is the art of potion making. Where's the potion?"

"It's more like the art of combining the right ingredients, under the right circumstances. A potion doesn't have to be liquid. Breathing in a powder could be just as potent or worse than swallowing a liquid."

With a shrug, she took the leaf and popped it into her mouth, making a face at the strong taste.

I rose from my desk chair, lifted it over my desk, and set it by the window. The trunk screeched over the wood floor. When it was finally out, I laid my hand on the lid and took a deep breath.

The hinges creaked as I raised the lid and leaned it against the dresser, stale vanilla rising from aged oak slats. The old set of clothes I'd been wearing the last time I saw my family were shoved in a crumpled sack in one corner. Some of my grandmother's things took up the rest of the space. A dusty music box I knew from several failed attempts didn't open sat atop a stack of ledger books. I should've burned those. But most of them were written in her hand, and it didn't seem right to let everything of hers be lost.

A single old quilt lined the bottom. Rolled-up parchments too faded to make out rested in front of the ledgers, topped with the last note she wrote me before she died.

Funny how heavy the sight of certain objects could make your body suddenly feel.

Clearing my throat, I plucked up the sack from the corner, revealing more books. Floramantic books. Those wouldn't have been hers. The sight of them angered me. I threw the chest lid down and plopped the sack on top.

After so long trying to forget this was in there, it felt odd to bring it out now. But if it could save Mauler's life, it was worth it.

With a deep breath, I opened the sack.

Bits of long-dried plant fibers clung to those clothes. I retrieved a scrap of parchment from my desk, slid its edge against the fabric, and gently lifted one tiny, blue-green fiber.

The translucence had faded to opacity in its time drying out in the chest. Would that increase or decrease the effects? My floramantic knowledge was rusty.

As I'd intended it to be.

"Trinka, are you absolutely sure?"

"Yes, Parrianther, do it already. What's the holdup? We're trying to save my castling here."

"I realize that." With a sigh, I slumped. How could I explain this to her when I barely remembered it all myself? "Look, just promise me you'll never ask me again after tonight, okay?"

If I'd just gotten rid of this stuff instead of hanging on to it in case I got the chance to pay back whoever stole my memories with a taste of their own floramancy, I wouldn't be in this situation.

"Why is this such a big deal to you?" she asked.

"I don't know. That's the problem. But I do know accomplished floramancers are dangerous. Hang around them too much and eventually you'll disagree about something and end up on their bad side. And they don't just steal your stuff or knock you around a little. They can erase your identity without you even knowing." I lifted the edge of the sack and peered inside.

Trinka stared at me. "What are you doing?"

"This plant doesn't grow around here. I'm lifting it from a tunic I had on when I was exposed to a great deal of it."

She leaned around me, peering at the fiber on the parchment. "Will there be enough?"

I chuckled, laying the parchment on the desk and retrieving another scrap. "This stuff is a little more potent than dapplemint. You won't even need this whole piece right here." I sliced the tiny fiber in half with the other piece of parchment and swept the bigger half back over the sweater. Cinching the sack closed, I dropped it in the chest and let the lid slam.

"This should do it." I handed her the parchment bearing the little blue-green dot of deecho fern. "Just slide it into your mouth. I wouldn't pick it up since it's easy to lose."

She accepted the parchment and eyed the dot, then dumped it into her mouth.

"Now think only of the memories you want to lose. Since you won't remember what you lost, you can tell me something about them so I can ask you once it's over and confirm whether they're gone. Otherwise you'll never actually know whether anything was removed."

She eyed me. "So that's why you're against removing memories. I'm sorry that happened to you, Parrianther. But I'm not sharing these memories. Ask me if I remember the Proprietor. If I look as confused as you do, we'll know it worked."

I nodded, watching her face for signs.

A crease appeared between her eyebrows. Gradually, her face hardened into a grimace.

Her arms curved around her middle, and she bent forward, eyes squeezed shut. A tiny cry escaped her lips as she leaned further off the bed. She was about to tumble off.

"Trinka, careful—" I stooped to break her fall.

When my hands touched her skin, the room faded into a dark place with pulsing lights and bad smells. Crowded with people. Jostling. *Pain. So much pain and humiliation and fury. Concentrated between—*

I shoved myself back, Trinka collapsing to the floor and retching. Wastebasket forgotten, she sputtered and heaved all over the wooden boards.

"Trinka!"

That shouldn't have happened! Had there been some other effect due to the long time the deecho fern had spent drying? Was there something in the sweater fibers that had reacted with it?

Trinka pushed herself to her knees and then to her feet. "I'm sorry about that, Parrianther. Do you have anything I can clean that up with?" She scrubbed her tunic over her mouth, looking like she might retch again.

Picking up the drying cloth I'd used after bathing yesterday, I got on the floor myself. "No. You sit down. You need to rest."

"I'm not going to let you clean up my puke." Her voice was weak and hoarse.

What had I done?

"It's my room. Sit." Ignoring her glower, I cleaned the floor and dropped the cloth in the wastebasket. The foul smell lingered, though, so I took the basket to the window and dumped it, leaving the basket to air out on the open sill behind the dapplemint plants.

I turned to Trinka, who still stood next to my bed. "What was that place?"

Her eyes flashed, her face twisting into a glower. "What place?"

"How did you show me that memory? Where was it?"

She was fiery with indignation. "I didn't *show you* anything, Parrianther! What the skunk did you see?"

"A dark room. Weird lights. It smelled awful. And it hurt..." I glanced down and quickly returned my eyes to hers. "I'm sorry, I didn't mean to—I mean, I've never seen someone else's memory. I don't know how that happened. But...I understand...why you wanted to forget."

She was at my throat, her spiked knuckles pricking pain below my chin as she slammed me against the desk and held me there. She was incredibly strong, especially for being so petite and weakened by the bad deecho fern. A sheen of sweat glistened over her bald head.

Starstinger darted around her and leaped onto my shoulder, baring her teeth in Trinka's face. A brilliant shrieking growl ripped from her throat.

Trinka held on, leaning the knuckles even harder against my skin. "Parrianther, if you *dare* speak of this to anyone, it will be the last thing you ever do."

Another ripping snarl erupted from Starstinger, and Trinka dropped me, backing up.

"There was a flash of running from a fire. Which I've never done. Did I see one of your memories, too?"

I stared wide-eyed. "What color was the smoke?"

"Green."

"Muck. Yeah, that happened to me."

"Then why did I see it? And why the skunk are my memories still there, Parrianther? Did I say to ask me about anything besides the Proprietor?"

"No. That was all."

She punched my bed and cursed. "All of them...they're still trapped in my head! What went wrong?"

"I don't know! I've never seen that happen before. Ever. The only risk I knew of was losing the wrong memories."

Rigid as a statue, she glared at me, her clenched fists trembling. "Nothing you *remember*, anyway."

My jaw clenched as the old, familiar terror trickled down my spine. Had it happened to me before? Countless times, even? I'd never know. If I wasn't careful, I'd find myself curled up in bed, sweating for days, too suspicious of what was real and what was only suggested to function. I ran a thumb over the scar on my nose—the side effect of someone else choosing who I was.

It was best not to dwell on that. I might as well enjoy my life now.

I laid a hand over Starstinger's back, focusing on her warmth and soft fur. Her prickly defense of me wasn't something I could've dreamed, was it? I would choose to believe that *she* was real, at least. I needed some kind of anchor. She leaned against me, letting me know she was there while keeping her fangs out for Trinka's benefit.

With an apparently great effort, Trinka made herself sit on the bed and drop her gaze from mine. She took two deep breaths, then unfisted her fingers.

"Well, if I'm cursed with them forever, at least now I know I can survive reliving them all in horrible clarity. That...that was worse than what I usually see."

"It made you remember them more sharply?"

She nodded without meeting my eyes.

"I'm so sorry, Trinka." Guilt made me feel small and too noticeable all at once. But I had no idea anything like that could happen.

Starstinger growled, the rumbling vibration ringing through my hand.

"Well, let me know when you figure out what happened. These memories have to go."

She leaped out the window, narrowly avoiding the wastebasket, and disappeared.

Starstinger slinked off me to watch Trinka's retreat.

I glared at the trunk again. I didn't want that life. Floramancy was not for me. I'd sacrificed everything to get away from it.

But I owed Trinka for what I'd accidentally made her live through. And for seeing...how was such an intrusion possible? Not only did I owe her, I now understood why she wanted to forget. And there was still danger to her castling if memories continued terrorizing her.

A potion was involved somehow. But what ingredients? There may have been traces of dapplemint still on my tongue. And the deecho fern had been freshly plucked when they'd used it on me. Was the dried-out-ness what made it stand out stronger? Or was that what allowed me to relive the memory with her when I touched her?

The tedium of addressing the innumerable variables hung over me like a dead weight.

I removed the unwanted floramancy books from the trunk and shoved it back under the desk. With a sigh, I returned my chair to its place and set the books to the side. The dropped sandwich still sat on some parchments.

Wild mushroom, bacon, burroot, and The Braided Loaf's special sauce, all on a braid of barley bread. Would they tell me the ingredients of the sauce and the bread dough if I asked? Maybe Dane could get it for me. But I couldn't tell him why without betraying Trinka.

With a sigh, I picked up *Fossil Fever*, found my place, and marked it with a scrap of parchment. Between training and trying to figure out what happened with Trinka's memories, it would be a long while before I'd read more about fossils.

Chapter 27

MELLA

I couldn't forge a registration record for Whisper until I knew what a registration record looked like, and for that, I'd need to get into the library. And I no longer had access to Father's pass. But I knew someone who had one I might be able to borrow.

But how to get into the library and find the registration records without drawing attention to the fact that Whisper wasn't actually registered?

Maybe asking about hybrids was the way to do it. Acres wouldn't assume I was asking because I had one, right? Just casual interest. Dane mentioned patrons at the Loaf talking about them. That was normal enough, wasn't it?

I pushed away from the tree trunk I'd been stalling against and crossed the breezy clearing toward Acres. If anyone knew about books, it had to be the guy who worked at the library.

He leaned against one of the logs around the charred firepit, a book propped open against one bent leg and his long locs piled on top of his head.

"What are you reading?" I asked.

"A book about plants." He sighed. "Probably sounds boring to you."

I shrugged, sliding down to lean against the same log. "I can't say plants are one of my favorite subjects, necessarily. But...I am curious about hybrids. Do you know anything about those?"

His brows rose as he snapped the book shut. "Yes, I've heard of them. What do you want to know?"

Something in his expression threw me off. He usually looked like he'd rather be reading than talking and couldn't wait to get back to his books. But he seemed intensely focused now.

"Just...heard some people talking about a sighting outside of Terrenthyrs. I was wondering if there was any truth in it. Just out of curiosity. Do you think...would the library maybe have some books on them?"

He tapped his book against his leg. "Yes, they do. But I've read them, and there's nothing useful in them. Nothing more than a mention."

Of course he'd already read them. "I'd still like to read them, out of curiosity."

"Sure." He cracked the book open, running a dusky finger over the page. "Go ahead and check them out. Let me know if you find anything I missed."

"Well, I'd like to, but unfortunately...I don't have access."

His eyes narrowed. "Oh. So you want me to get them for you."

"No, I'm not asking you to do the work for me. I was just wondering if you could sneak me in to look for myself?"

I had to be there, too, to get a look at that castling registry.

He eyed me. "When do you want to go?"

"Maybe...now?" I winced, not wanting to annoy him.

Rolling his eyes, he pushed to his feet and stretched. Through a yawn, he said, "You're lucky I take every chance I can to escape sparring and leaf through books instead." He turned a wry smile on me. "Come on. Let's go."

***

Leaning against the cool stone wall of the alley by the library, I folded my arms and waited while Acres went in the front with his pass. If only Dane were here. He'd probably have some funny story or something interesting to make the time pass.

Or Kaido...he'd help the time go by in a more *interesting* way. I grinned, thinking about when he'd kissed me.

The shriek of rusty hinges had me leaping off the wall and into a crouch.

Acres's spectacled face appeared through a hidden doorway. "Come on!"

He beckoned to me, one loc falling loose from the knot on his head to sway in his face. Shoving back my annoyance, I followed him in.

I blinked rapidly as my eyes adjusted to the dim library. Tall shelves came into focus, stretching up to cavernous ceilings. A boy slid a ladder on wheels further down a shelf, scurried up it, and ran his finger over spines far above our heads.

"So hybrids. Should be in the *Creatures* section if they were reshelved properly. Follow me."

Acres led me from the high-ceilinged room and down a stone hallway lined with a disturbing number of unmarked wooden doors. What if the castling records room was unlabeled? Sweat broke out on my forehead as I hurried to keep pace with him.

After another hallway and two flights of stairs, we reached another room with a ceiling not quite as high. The arched doorway had a plaque reading: *All Things Animalia.*

Acres darted through the doorway, and I wondered whether a castling record room might also fall in that category. Following him, I scanned between the shelves.

Acres was frowning at a sign for Antidotes on the first shelf. "Antidotes should be in the Herbs and Floramancy Wing." He squinted at smaller writing underneath it. "Oh, this is only antidotes that can be made from animal venom. Different type of antidote. That makes more sense."

I cleared my throat. "So hybrids should be down this way, right?" I glanced at the shelves, finding H and pausing to read it more carefully. *Hazardous Creatures of Terrenthyrs and the Surrounding Lands, Herpetology: the Pros and Cons of Reptile and Amphibian Castlings, Hyena History: A Biography of Lyndell Maysen...*

I frowned. Hybrid—H-Y-B—should've been between herpetology and hyenas.

"Acres, look at this," I hissed.

He joined me and frowned at where my finger pointed.

"No hybrids."

He crossed his arms and held his chin with thumb and forefinger. "They must not have put that one back yet since I returned them. Or someone placed them in the wrong section. Maybe the *Myths and Legends* is where someone put them."

"Where's that? Can we check?"

He shrugged. "It's worth a try. Down that hall."

"Okay."

He glanced longingly at the shelves we'd just checked. "Mella, would you mind if I spent a few more minutes in here? There's a book I need to pick up."

I brightened. My chance to look for the records room. "Sure. I'll just go see what I can find."

And while the hybrid information was potentially valuable, the registration information was much more so. If I could prove Narellen and Jorros weren't to blame for what had happened to Whisper's castor, my future social standing would be safe from her, at least. And if I found they *were* to blame...I may need to keep that information to myself, at least until after the ceremony.

I winced with guilt. But I couldn't risk losing everything over Whisper's grudge.

Acres nodded distractedly and backtracked to the second *F* shelf. I waited a few seconds and then headed for the hallway.

A closer look revealed small wooden plaques on each door describing what was in them. Disappointingly, they were mostly for storage and unlocked. The records room was sure to be locked, which was another hurdle I'd have to deal with if I ever found it. But rooms for storing spare parchment and materials for repairing book bindings were not helpful.

I tiptoed back through the *Creatures* section and into another hallway. This one was shorter and doorless. Scanning the next room for signs or plaques, I rounded the corner and slammed right into a guard.

"Oh, I'm so sorry. Excuse me." I smiled as genuinely as I could, grateful for the dim room that would hopefully hide the guilty heat in my face.

He squinted at me. "I'm sorry, can I have a look at your library pass?" My smile faded. *Skunks.* "I, uh..." I had no excuses.

So I bolted.

"Hey!" he shouted, stumbling after me.

I skidded around a shelf and paused to listen for footsteps. Instead, I heard the man reciting a short poem about strength and stealth. *Oh skunk it all.* He was summoning his castling.

A moment later the howl of a wolf sent fear shivering down my spine. Most castlings were good at sniffing out a trail, but canine castlings tended to be the best. Of course. And useful castor that I was, I had my worthless scythe but no actual castling weapon. Or, well, casting *instrument.*

So it was me versus this guard and his wolf. *Fanskunkingtastic.*

I ran through another short hallway and knocked over a cart of books before backtracking and taking a different route, hoping to throw off my scent.

It didn't work. The growling wolf was right on my tail. I flew through an open door and whirled to slam it after me, wishing for an iron bolt to throw into place. But I'd have to settle for a chair. I hooked my toes through a chair back and pulled it to me, doing my best to fix it under the door handle despite the wolf throwing his weight against it with enough force to knock me over. The chair squeaked in place but held. For now.

I took in the room. Wooden chairs and bench seats lined three long tables. Two shocked girls—with a weasel and a possum playing on the table amidst stacks of books—stared at me open-mouthed from the other side. A staircase wound around the perimeter of the large, circular room, slowly getting higher until it reached the top level. Several archways led into other areas off the staircase.

I bolted for the stairs.

Claws and teeth scraped at the door as the wolf's frustrated growls shivered the air. I stumbled and slammed my knee against the metal railing. *Skunks!*

The chair clattered away, and the snarls grew louder as the wolf and his castor erupted from the door. The feral yellow eyes locked on me immediately, and I stumbled to my feet and ran as fast as I could to the next archway, hoping there was another door I could close.

My knee aching more with each step, I tore through an archway only to find there was no door to close. And the room didn't have any hallways branching off it. It was just a little room with a sign reading *Agricultural and Property Line Records.*

So I was in the right place for records, then?

Snarls grew closer as the wolf zoomed up the stairs, the guard's boots clomping after it.

Well, the closest I'd been to the right place, anyway. I raced out of the room and back onto the stairs. The wolf was only a handful of spans behind me.

I took the stairs two at a time, launching myself forward.

The next archway was only a dozen steps away. The sign came into view: *Birth and Death Records.*

Still the wrong skunking kind! The next one was too far away to read the sign. The wolf was right on my heels, slobber dripping off its exposed teeth as snarls ripped out of its open mouth.

The guard slipped and went down. The wolf paused to look back at its castor, who might have just wiped out on the drool. A tendril of humor bubbled up in my chest. I couldn't wait to tell Dane and Sprinter about that.

Then the wolf was after me again. I was almost to the next archway. The sign was nearly close enough to read. One more step...

The wolf's claws scraped against the stairs as it launched into the air. It landed full on my back, slamming me onto the steps and knocking the breath out of my lungs.

"Just sit still, and I won't bite you," the wolf growled, panting and dropping bits of slobber on my hair and neck.

Ew! Gross!

"Racer, you okay?" the guard shouted from below us.

"This way. She's down," the wolf called back, more slobber dripping from his mouth.

"Yuck! Okay, you got me, you win. But could you please stop drooling on me?"

It sounded like he licked his lips, then resumed panting. "If you hadn't made me run so hard straight up a staircase, it wouldn't be a problem."

"Skunk you," I hissed.

His left paw rested between my shoulder blades. Maybe I could twist just right to escape...

The paw grew heavier, huge claws against my back, though they didn't pierce my skin. "Don't even think about it. If I have to chase you again, I'll still beat you, but I'll be a lot more irritable about it. You don't want to make me more irritable, kid."

A growl rumbled from his throat on the last word, and unfortunately, I had to agree with him.

"Well done, Racer!" The guard heaved for breath behind us. "How did you get in, hmm? If someone snuck you in, they're going to be in big trouble."

Skunks, Acres. I'd been too busy trying to escape to think about him.

"I don't know who you're talking about."

"I'm sure you don't." The guard scoffed as he knelt next to me.

The paw lifted from my back, only to be replaced with two rough hands on my shoulders, hauling me to my feet. My legs felt like jelly after climbing so many stairs so quickly. I'd need to work on that if I ever got out of here.

"What's your name?"

"Selverine Merrandil." I didn't know why I said it. But I wasn't going to give him mine, and maybe I could use her high position to get out of this.

He raised an eyebrow. "I do know what Princess Selverine, the Queen's own granddaughter, looks like, and it's nothing like you. Your *real* name, please?"

The wolf stepped into the next alcove to stretch out, his eyes still bright and focused on the guard and me. I looked up at the sign to see *Construction and Mapping of Cities Records.*

With a glower, I returned my eyes to the guard's face and tried to pay attention.

"I don't have one," I replied.

Frowning, he tied my wrists together and gestured for me to precede him down the stairs.

Sullenly I obeyed, furious at failing. What was I going to do now? I couldn't bear to have Father and Mother summoned here to break me out. But I had no proof of being a castor without being able to cast Whisper, so the only way the guard could handle this was to treat me like a child.

I hoped Acres wouldn't get in trouble, too.

At last we reached the bottom of the stairs. Something shiny zoomed across my line of sight, and the pile of books in front of the two girls crashed to the ground.

"Whoa! That's no way to treat these books, young ladies!" The guard held out my rope to the wolf, who took it with his teeth, as the guard strode over to scold the confused girls.

Another shiny object appeared out of nowhere and sliced through my rope. In the time it took for the wolf to realize what had happened, an arm yanked me behind another bookshelf.

Acres dragged me through a maze of shelves and darted under the staircase, the wolf's claws clacking in pursuit. Shoving a cart full of books in front of us, he whirled on me and glared darkly enough to make me feel even worse.

"Wow. This is definitely the last time I ever sneak *you* into the library. What the muck, Mella?" Acres's eyes were exasperated as he threw his hands out, grasping a book in one of them.

"I'm sorry, Acres, but I can't leave yet," I whispered.

We both hushed as the wolf ran past us, my scent trail from earlier confusing him.

Crossing his arms, Acres eyed me. "Fine. But I'm leaving, so good luck getting out of trouble again. You're welcome for the rescue, by the way."

"Right—thank you, Acres. I really appreciate it. Really, a lot."

"Mm-hmm. If that's true, then leave now with me before you cause any more trouble and get my library pass revoked. And me fired. Which would *really* piss me off."

I winced. I didn't want to ruin that for him. And I knew about that back door he'd let me through now. Maybe I could sneak in another time so he wouldn't be associated with me if I got caught. "Okay. Fine. Can I have a quick peek—"

He swiped an angry arm through the air in front of him. "No." A couple other locs had come loose and swung in his face. "We're leaving. Now. Or at least, as soon as Jaion and his castling leave the room."

He peered between the messy stacks of books. Several moments passed with nothing but the sound of our breathing.

Finally, he slid the cart over the tiniest fraction of a speck, then a little more. The coast was clear. "I'm going to go find the throwing star I cut you loose with and check the hall for guards. Would you grab my other throwing star? It should be stuck in one of those books that fell."

Nodding, I crossed to the now restacked books and leafed through for the throwing star, which I now understood was the shiny thing that had knocked down the books and caused the distraction.

Finding it, I headed toward the hallway Acres had taken.

"Acres Parrianther! What were you thinking, chucking your stars at me!" someone shouted further down.

Oh no.

Acres said something in a calm voice I couldn't quite make out.

I backed up a couple of steps, and a door I hadn't noticed in my haste wore a faded plaque: *Castor and Castling Records.*

Well, it's about time.

I turned the handle. But it was locked. Shocker.

"If you think you're ever coming back in here again, you're dead wrong!" the guard shouted.

Oh, no, no, no!

Wrenching the knob did nothing. It was solidly locked. *Skunking skunk muck! I can't have lost Acres his library pass for nothing! I have to get in there!*

Acres spoke again, pleading with the guard now.

Wincing, I traced a finger over the space between the door and the wall, but there wasn't enough room for me to wedge anything in there to trip the lock. There was a huge space between the floor and the bottom of the door, but a muck-ton of good that would do me.

The star, though... It could, in fact, fit through that crack under the door.

But that was a terrible idea. The king's speech echoed in my mind. *"A castling call is sacred. No doubt you'll all know each other's calls like the back of your hand before long, but except in an extreme emergency, it is never acceptable to take someone else's weapon and attempt to cast their castling."*

I barely knew Acres. I'd already gotten him in so much trouble today. But Whisper was in danger. This did qualify as an emergency, and he'd already lost his pass. I might as well do it.

Dropping to my knees, I gently slid the throwing star under the door and kept one finger on it, hoping I could remember all of Acres's castling call.

A scuffle sounded down the hall. Was the guard throwing Acres out?

Moments later, a shimmer of black and ochre shone under the crack, and then a soft little paw poked at my finger.

"Hello? Acres?" the little-girl voice said.

"Hey, Starstinger, this is Mella from Acres's cohort. We're in the library and I need your help. If you could please unlock this door..."

The door swung inward, and I stepped toward it. But then claws launched at my face and dug into my shoulders.

"Ouch!"

She displayed an impressively menacing glare for such a small, cute castling with oversized ears. She removed one paw from my shoulder to take the throwing star out of her mouth and let out a petite but serious snarl.

"If you're the reason Acres is getting thrown out of his favorite place, I'm not doing a single thing to help you!" she spat. "I'm going to find him, and I'd better never hear you bothering him again. Got it?" The sharp daggers in her scowl shouldn't have been possible in a face as cute as hers.

I nodded, holding back my wince at her dragging her claws slowly through my skin.

She replaced the throwing star in her mouth and leaped off me, prancing down the hall.

How would I ever make this up to him?

Guilt weighed heavy in my chest, but I'd have to worry about that later. Whisper's life depended on forging her registration parchments, and mine depended on finding out what had really happened to her castor.

I closed the door behind me. Finding a stack of blank castling registration forms, I went about filling one out for Whisper. I spent a lot of time rifling through parchments, looking for this years' castors and castlings, then stuffed Whisper's registration form toward the bottom and breathed a sigh of relief.

I'd done the most important thing.

I stepped back and frowned at all those stacks of parchment. Now to find all the castors who'd cast a coyote in the last—what?—like, sixty years.

CHAPTER 28

DANE

S quinting at the sky, I stepped into the shade of the Emberlyn trees to cool off. The breeze was nice, but Terrenthyrs summer was proving to be a lot warmer than Terrenthyrs spring. It was amazing the difference a couple of months could make, especially when I spent the majority of them sweating in spars.

Sprinter trotted from my side to join the other castlings where Beldon held one arm out, signifying an imaginary starting line.

"And...go!" Beldon shouted, slicing through the air with his thick arm. Tails whipped and claws gouged the forest floor as Mauler, Sprinter, Starstinger, and Whisper raced over the leaf litter under Brawler and Cupid, who leaped and skittered through branches. The gorilla and iguana practically flew through the trees, kicking bark flecks to the ground.

It was Mella's idea to race them against each other. They were just as competitive as their castors, so they gave it their all and pushed themselves to the limit. Mella ran next to Whisper, cheering her on. Acres let her pass him as he jogged next to the castlings on long legs.

I'd been trying to help by bringing him to our cohort, but it seemed like he and Mella were no longer speaking. I wonder what happened?

The rest of us ran after them, and I grinned as Sprinter took the lead on the ground. Whisper struggled more than the others, but her wings came open, and she caught some air every few seconds. Hopefully these exercises were strengthening her wings.

At last the finish line rope with leather scraps came into view. Sprinter had fallen a bit behind Mauler, but he put on a burst of speed and kicked dust in their faces as he flew into the rope and skidded to a halt. Brawler caught a thick branch with both hands and swung all the way around it twice to slow her pace, Cupid right behind her, wrapping his long green tail over branches to slow his momentum.

"Great job, Sprinter!" I scratched behind his ears and patted his back as he smiled, his tongue lolling to one side. Lowering my voice to a whisper, I said, "Remember how I suggested you not win every single one of these, or it might start looking like you're not as young and inexperienced as you're supposed to be? Well, your competitive side's showing, and you really should lose the next three at least."

He nodded but kept up the grinning and lolling.

Mauler high-fived Brawler. "I was totally in front of you the whole time," she teased.

"In your dreams," Brawler said in her deep raspy voice and smirked.

"Cupid!" Reenalyn's arms stretched toward the tree for her castling, but he didn't leap into them like usual. Today, he waited till she held up one hand, then he crawled over it onto her shoulder, calmly wrapping his tail around her upper arm and holding his head out from her hair. More dignified than I'd ever seen him.

I smiled. It had taken a few weeks, but he was finally gaining confidence.

Mella held one fist toward Whisper, who clinched one set of razor-sharp talons and bumped knuckles with her. "That was incredible, Whisper. You caught so much wind! Maybe a little more healthy competition is just what you need."

Whisper nodded, eagle eyes bright. "My legs held up better than I expected. Maybe there's hope for this body yet."

Mella blushed and looked askance around our group. I flicked my eyes away, but not before she caught me.

I winced, that ache ripping through my chest again. If only she would be happy to catch me looking at her. If only I'd ever catch her staring at me the same way. But it had been exactly sixty-three days since I'd learned her name, and she hadn't shown any more interest in me.

Sprinter whined and set one paw on my boot. I glanced down to find his wide, dark eyes on me, his ears drooping.

"I'm all right. Just...you know."

He nosed my wrist, and I scratched his head again, but his lips remained closed.

"Beldon." Brawler raced up to him on her feet and knuckles. "Mauler and I want to go swimming now. Haven't we trained enough for today?" Her deep voice was the last octave of feminine before reaching masculine.

"I could use a swim, too. Who wants a river party?" Beldon raised both hands and eyed the rest of us.

With a cheer, the twelve of us headed for the river. Brawler and Mauler disappeared in front while Whisper brought up the rear, walking alongside Mella as Sprinter strolled by me. Ahead of us, Starstinger draped herself around Acres's shoulders, her pretty obsidian eyes turned up to chat with Cupid, whose entire upper body emerged proudly over Reenalyn's shoulder, unobscured by her hair.

Trinka and Beldon led the way, Beldon counting off something about various professions on his fingers while Trinka rolled her eyes.

"You're making excellent progress, Whisper. Well done," Sprinter said, slowing to match her pace.

I smiled in agreement at Mella. She smiled back. Was it just me, or was there hesitation behind her eyes? I hoped I hadn't made her uncomfortable. She was just so interesting and unbearably beautiful. It was hard to keep my eyes off her, even as I tried to give her plenty of space.

She trained her eyes on our companions' backs. "You know, I've been meaning to tell you two a funny story."

I raised an eyebrow, excited that she'd thought of us. "Oh?"

"A little while ago, I was at the library. Well, I wasn't supposed to be there. And a guard with a wolf castling chased me down. I thought they had me, but then the guard bit it because he slipped on the wolf's drool."

Sprinter's jaw dropped. "*Drool* made you think of us?" He eyed me with barely contained chortles.

"No! It was just funny. It distracted the wolf long enough for me to almost get away. They still caught me in the end, but the man wiped out on his own castling's drool! How do you even do that?"

"Wow. That is crazy." I glared at Sprinter. "Why were you not sup-posed to be in the library?"

She lowered her voice. "Registering Whisper. At least, making sure a registration record exists for her." She grinned. "I got away with that."

"Nice!" How had she managed that?

"Yeah," a frown darkened her features. "But Acres snuck me in, and they revoked his library pass."

"Oh, so that's why he's been extra sullen."

She nodded, pushing a branch aside and staring ahead.

The sparkling river shimmered through the trees, and we emerged into the clearing. Mauler and Brawler were already splashing around, shrieking and laughing. Boots kicked aside, Beldon tugged off his tunic, threw it on the ground, and sprinted into the water in just his trousers with a bellow and a tidal wave. Reenalyn raced right behind him, Cupid gripping her shoulder for dear life, his newfound dignity replaced with a comical look of terror as they rushed for the water.

Acres pulled off his boots, rolled up his pant legs, and waded out shin-deep while Starstinger remained draped over his shoulders, her eyes closed and face turned toward the sun.

Trinka walked a little ways around the river and sat in a beam of sunlight, stretching her legs in front of her, a rare neutral expression brightening her face as Mauler dunked Beldon with her huge bear paws.

Sprinter trotted ahead of me and dipped his head to lap at the water, while Whisper stepped just deep enough for the water to cover her taloned feet, her tail raised to keep her feathers dry.

Suddenly I was even more conscious of Mella's presence next to me. Should I dive in with just my trousers like Beldon? Or be more like Acres?

"Um, are you going to—uh…" My question died in my throat as I faced Mella Yarinelle wearing nothing but thin creamy underthings.

"Huh?" She glanced back at me as she stepped toward the water.

"I was…just asking…clearly you are…going swimming, I mean."

She grinned. "Yeah, the water looks incredible. Come on." She ges-tured to me and then strode into the river, the murkiness Beldon, Brawler, and Mauler had stirred up obscuring her body speck by speck as she waded farther in.

"Mm-hmm." Sprinter raised an eyebrow, his lolling smile returning. "Drool strings, remember?"

I glowered at him. "I am *not* drooling." I wiped a hand over my mouth just in case, though.

"You did pick up on the part where she told you to come in after her, right? Or were you too...shall we say...*distracted*?" He waggled his stupid eyebrows again.

"Yes of course I heard," I snapped. "I just can't decide whether to leave my tunic on or not. I won't look as incredible to her without my shirt as she does to me. I'll just leave it on."

My legs were still locked in place.

Sprinter frowned. "Then what are you waiting for?"

"I just don't know what to do once I get in the water."

"How about you start by stepping in. I'm right behind you. All you have to do is get close enough for one of those crazies to splash you in the face. Then you can splash back and then you're in on the game. That's all it takes."

Mella shrieked as Beldon's splash drenched her hair, sending rivulets of water pouring over her bare shoulders.

Sprinter slapped a paw against my shin. "No drooling, remember?"

I rolled my eyes and took a step toward the river, where the girl I was already too shy to speak to properly was swimming in nothing but underwear.

Chapter 29

SELVERINE

Wiping sweat off my forehead, I frowned at the never-ending tree shadows all around us. "How did you become so familiar with the Emberlyn Forest, Willova? It all looks the same to me."

We'd barely been looking for an hour and had already eliminated three clearings. Between those and a few failed expeditions before today, there couldn't be that much forest left. Surely we'd find Mella's cohort soon.

Willova brushed a leafy branch out of the way, creeping forward with more of a hunch than normal. Maybe she was sore from sparring yesterday. "I spent some time in Wrynford as a child."

"Why'd you—"

"Ouch." Willova paused, her dress caught on the log she'd just stepped over, revealing an ink-black mark on her calf.

Wasn't that where I'd scratched her with my trident yesterday? There hadn't been a tattoo then. Weird.

"You know, if you want to hide those secret tattoos, maybe you should wear some leggings under your dresses."

She unsnagged the fabric, obsessively smoothing it out and checking for holes.

"What was that one? Some kind of symbol?"

"No. It's nothing important." She hurried ahead.

I dashed after her, ducking under a few low-hanging limbs. "If it's nothing, then why'd you get it tattooed? And why are you so touchy about it?"

"It's *not* a tattoo—not permanent. And it's not a symbol of anything. It's just a scribble."

"It looked much fancier than a scribble—"

"Are you still planning to invite Drazdan to the Grand Castors' Ball?"

I frowned and crossed my arms. "Way to throw in a subtle subject change."

She glanced away, like she wanted to hide her expression or something.

"Yeah, I'm still planning to ask him to the ball, I guess. I'm just weirded out by the fact you keep bringing it up and looking like you ate a lemon every time, so I haven't gotten around to it yet."

She stared into the distance, and it pissed me off.

"Come on, Willova—"

"Shh!" Her hand flashed out to cut me off. "Voices. Over there."

Crouching behind her, I followed her pointing finger and tried to hear past the breeze rustling the leaves. Was it finally them?

The voices were still too low to make out, and I couldn't see anyone. So I crept toward the sound, passing Willova and keeping close to the ground.

"Remember, loosen your elbows a bit," a male voice said. "You'll get a better workout if you don't push your elbows all the way in every time you push up, and it's better for your joints."

"And you do how many of these at a time?"

That was Mella's voice. I could just see her pushing up from the ground to sit on a log, sweat marks down the back of her tunic. Where was her mysterious castling? I'd finally find out what it was today!

I crept closer, peering through the scrub. Mella sat facing my direction on a fallen log. The guy sat in front of her with his back to me, a huge gorilla leaning against his back, its knees bent like it was doing a wall sit.

He laughed. "A lot. But how about you do three reps of ten throughout the day for now? That's more than you started with and not enough to hurt yourself. A sustainable way to build shoulder and back strength."

Something moved behind Mella. Was it her castling? I stared at what must be the top of its head, impatient for it to show itself.

"Thank you for this training, Beldon." A voice I hadn't heard yet. And it wasn't the gorilla. Was it coming from behind Mella? "It will be very useful."

The guy smiled and waved off the comment. "No problem! Glad to help. And glad there's still something I'm better at than Mella." He chuckled and Mella slapped his arm.

"Sometimes you really do act like a bunch of children." And with the flap of a wing, the most majestic avian I'd ever seen stepped out from behind Mella and leaped onto the log.

My mouth went dry as my pulse raced. What was *this*?

"Well, Mella? More pushups? You might as well practice now that you know how to do them right." The eagle eyed Mella before turning to the boy.

Mella's castling was an avian.

A skunking gorgeous eagle, of all things.

How'd she done it? Oh, she'd be hearing from me about this. If she knew how to cast an avian and didn't share it with me...she'd *known* what I wanted. She'd teased me about it. She'd known how to do it, and she hadn't told me.

So she'd only been *pretending* not to be able to cast at the ceremony. She'd wanted to show off for everyone later, perhaps when an avian would look more impressive fully grown, with full plumage. Although, this castling didn't look a few months old. It was enormous with glossy feathers and piercing, bright eyes.

Had she specifically wanted to spurn me? For what? Being royal? Or what I'd said about her mother?

My fingers spasmed, and I bit back a curse as I stretched them as far as they would go to make it stop.

A hand touched my shoulder, and I whipped around. Willova's eyes were wide as she looked between me and the eagle.

"Yeah. Looks like that's Mella Yarinelle's castling. What the skunk."

"That's unbelievable," she whispered. "Um, I've got to get back home. Do you want to come with me, or watch them for a little longer?"

With a scowl, I tore my eyes from the castling that should've been mine and faced Willova. "You go ahead. I'm not leaving yet."

***

Mella and her eagle—whose name was *Whisper*, of all the ridiculous things—sat with the others around their fire, some kind of meat and vegetables roasting on a grate over the flames. Scowling, I fisted my twitching fingers. How in the skunking muck did she get a better castling than me with a name like *Whisper*?

Huh. Wasn't her scythe's name Magnificence? *Does she have a different castling weapon?*

That couldn't be it. A scythe just like the one she'd had at the ceremony leaned against her log.

Even if the weapon had been the problem, she wouldn't have had enough time to make a new one by now. Certainly not for her castling to have reached an adult-like appearance. Plus, it would've been expensive. Too expensive for a family with financial struggles.

How had her family's fortunes started falling? I couldn't remember, but as far as I knew, not a soul had visited the Yarinelle house for ages. Had they gone so far as to sell the furniture?

Glowering at Mella, I considered whether breaking into her house might be worth it. What could I find on her? Surely a little muck was hiding around there somewhere, waiting to have her name dragged through it, that traitor. After I'd welcomed her into my inner circle and pitied her for failing to cast.

What would be the most memorable revenge?

CHAPTER 30

ACRES

I headed for The Braided Loaf much earlier than usual. I'd spent the last few weeks experimenting with possible combinations for whatever had happened the night Trinka came to me for help, and so far, I hadn't learned anything except a dozen different ways to make myself sick.

Guessing wasn't cutting it. I had to get the ingredients from Dane. He'd been tight-lipped about them so far, but today...

Was that Mella knocking on a door a few blocks down?

What are you up to now, Mella?

Crossing my arms, I watched as a woman and her coyote castling answered the door. She and Mella spoke for a few moments, Mella's shoulders slumping more and more by the second. Finally, the woman closed the door and Mella turned toward me.

Her eyes widened and then narrowed. She approached with a glare. "Following me, Acres? I thought we weren't speaking."

She avoided my eyes. I hoped that meant she really was embarrassed about what she'd done. I still couldn't believe she'd had the audacity to cast Starstinger.

"I want to know what you really wanted in the library. It clearly had nothing to do with hybrids, given what Starstinger told me about the room you had her unlock."

She pursed her lips and fell into step beside me.

"Actually, I *was* curious about hybrids. That wasn't a lie. But I did have some other information to look up that was a higher priority."

"Which was...?"

She stared ahead.

"Come on, Mella. You owe me big time for everything you did. Can't you let me in on the secret? What does it have to do with that lady?"

"Look, Acres, it's not my secret to tell."

"Okay, fine. I know you broke into the castor and castlings records room because Starstinger saw it. And Starstinger's also seen you speaking to a handful of other castors—all with coyote castlings—over the past few weeks, which leads me to believe you're looking for a coyote castor, but I haven't found the reason yet. Am I correct?"

She continued to stare straight ahead, her hands fisted at her sides.

"I'll take that as a yes."

"Why does it matter to you?" she hissed without looking at me.

"I'd like to know why I sacrificed my skunking *job* for you, not to mention my library pass. It's annoying not to have access to books anymore." *The good ones, anyway.*

"Look, I'm no better off than you right now. I've checked every single one of these names. There's only one left, and I won't get any help out of him."

"Why not?"

"Because Bennet Rohiece died decades ago. So I'm back to knowing nothing."

"How disappointing."

She rolled her eyes. "I'll see you around, Acres." She turned down a side street and disappeared around the corner.

Good riddance.

***

"Acres! Welcome back." Dane greeted me with a wave from the counter at the back of The Braided Loaf.

I tried to smile back, even though he was talking too much again. I'd need to come across nicer if I was going to convince him to help me this time.

"Uh, the usual sandwich today?"

"Yes. And we're going to have a chat while you make it."

His brows rose as he calculated the cost. "Okay, sure. But you know I can't help you with that. Four pennies."

I paid and leaned over the counter, prepared with a new angle. "Thanks to you and your little guilt trip about me joining your cohort, I have now lost my job and am in a difficult situation I can't even begin to explain. The only thing you can do to remotely improve this is to give me the recipe for the Loaf's secret sauce."

It was only indirectly his fault. But nothing else had worked so far, and I didn't want to reveal Trinka's troubles without her permission. And since she'd said talking about what I'd seen would be the last thing I'd ever do, I wasn't going to ask for it.

He frowned, glancing at a man carrying two sandwiches, and a pile of sandwich ingredients without the bread to a table.

"This way." He nodded toward the door into the kitchen and I followed him through.

"I can't imagine how the sauce recipe could help you with losing your job." His brow furrowed as he sliced a wild mushroom and a section of burroot, then piled them onto my sandwich with bits of cheese. "Of course I'd give it to you anyway, if I could. But as I've said, I don't have access to it. I only make the sandwiches. The owner prepares the sauces and fiercely guards the recipe."

I leaned further over the counter, annoyed at how unthreatening my spectacles and skinny frame made me. "Look, Dane, I need the ingredients to help another cohort member. Without them, something might happen that could lose us the competition."

If Trinka lost it again and accidentally stabbed Mauler, that would definitely not help us, especially with already being the smallest cohort.

Throwing a few thick slices of bacon onto the sandwich, he poured a ladleful of sauce over it all and raised a pale eyebrow. "Who?"

I shook my head. "She swore me to secrecy."

"Mella?" He bumped the bowl of spices, throwing way too much over half the sandwich.

"Watch it!"

"Sorry! Is it Mella?" he brushed off some of the excess spices.

I frowned at the mess he'd made of my meal. "Maybe. I said I can't tell you, and I'm not going to break my promise. Just get that recipe and bring it to me before I finish this extra-spicy monstrosity, okay? It's really important. A castling's life depends on it."

Squinting at me, Dane laid the other slice of bread on top of the disaster and handed me the plate. "Right."

Hopefully a castling's life would be enough motivation. If not, I'd have to try Mella's method of sneaking Starstinger under the owner's door one night. And I was still too pissed at her to admit the possible merit of that idea.

"I'll see what I can do."

With a nod, I took the plate and strode back through the kitchen door. The other server passed me with a frown. Hopefully he wouldn't prevent Dane from doing what I'd asked.

Sitting at a table toward the back, I took a bite of the sandwich. Crisp crust gave way to a delicious combination of sauce and veggies.

"Another hybrid story, really?" someone complained from the table next to me.

My ears perked at the word. From the corner of my eye, I saw a woman and two men bent over sandwiches, a beaver, a ferret, and a snow leopard seated with them.

Snow leopard?

Glancing sideways at them, I looked for the dark-haired man who'd attacked Starstinger and I outside of the library.

Skunks! It's him!

I shifted to face away, straining to hear their conversation past the racing pulse in my ears. Had he learned anything about hybrids in the months since then?

"I'm telling you, it's not a story," the snow leopard man said, spearing his breadless-sandwich ingredients with a fork. "I've seen them plain as day in Morrenfayre, walking around with humans like regular castlings. Them and a load of avians."

"You're full of muck." The woman rolled her eyes and stroked the beaver's head.

"No, I'm not! There's always a few around the mills where I drop off Emberlyn shipments. I'm telling you, I know what I've seen."

A piece of parchment appeared between my face and my sandwich. "I had to copy it fast, so I did the best I could." Dane frowned as I snatched the parchment from him. "I'd better not lose my job over this."

One of the men at the other table chuckled. "Sure you do. Just like you remember the last shattering here forty years ago when you were just a little speck of a boy picking up a delivery with your father, hmm? The shattering that no one else remembers?"

"My father remembered it, too, before he died. That Mr. Bennet was always so nice to us kids. Brought us candy and taught us to stand up to bullies. I'd never forget something so wrong as that man's castling being shattered."

"But none of the rest of your family remembers it either, do they?"

"Give him a break," the woman said, standing and stepping over the bench seat. "Let him believe what he wants. We've all got jobs to get back to."

Bennet? Hadn't Mella just mentioned a Bennet?

"Hello, Acres?" Dane raised an eyebrow. "Distracted with the old wood hauler's stories, huh? And I'm supposed to believe you needed this information to save a castling?"

I shook myself. "Are you saying you might've missed an ingredient?" If he had, it could ruin everything.

"I'm saying you're lucky I got what I got and you'd better not ever ask for something like this again. Now go save that castling, and if anyone sees that list, you didn't get it from me."

Shrugging, I lifted the sandwich and took a big bite.

And I remembered.

A man in fine clothes wearing a single leather gauntlet, his face invisible to me. A neighbor my grandmother didn't like.

Not a neighbor. A stranger to me, but someone she knew. And despised.

He knew her too. He'd said something to her, something mundane I couldn't quite remember, and she recoiled and rushed me away. She'd known him, though she hadn't recognized him at first.

He'd laughed as we hurried away. And when I wouldn't stop asking about it, she'd made me forget.

My own grandmother. The only person I thought I could trust. She'd made me forget that encounter. But why?

Back to the present, I stared at the sandwich in my hands, realizing I'd never finished chewing that bite. I chewed and swallowed with my eyes on the dripping sauce.

What the skunk was in that sauce?

Chapter 31

MELLA

My fingers danced over the mandolin's strings, a beautiful melody pouring from them and singing to my heart. I was doing this *myself*! Momma would've been so proud. It would've brought tears to her eyes.

And Reenalyn had been right—daily practice for a couple of months had drained the wimpiness from my fingertips and left them with helpful little callouses. Selverine or Frenna might think they looked weird, but they were a small price to pay for the incredible feeling of making music. Not to mention how much they helped me cast Whisper more strongly. She couldn't get more than a few spans off the ground, but she could stay awake for hours now.

And I understood Trello and Loryce's perspective better now. The desire to have a castling and the desire to feel the way playing music could make you feel were both big things. Having to choose between them would be horrible.

Reenalyn picked up her violin and bow and joined in with some kind of harmony. She never failed to baffle me with how good she was at making things up on the spot. Her notes blended perfectly with mine and made me smile.

With a mischievous grin, she increased the tempo, daring me to keep up. My fingers flew. The rhythm soared. Reenalyn leaped up, her feet keeping time with her wild fingers. And then she brandished her bow toward the sky, one finger of the other hand wiggling on the last string to finish out the final, beautiful, ringing note.

I slumped, set the mandolin against my log, and stretched out my fingers. "Whew! Reenalyn, how am I supposed to build confidence if you make a point of one-upping me every time we finish a lesson?" I teased.

I'd learned over the past months that once the music got a hold of her, there was no breaking her free until she'd explored it to her heart's content.

"I don't know what you're talking about, Mella. You were absolutely amazing!"

Cupid, who'd managed to keep his perch through the entire practice session, finally dove off her shoulder and rested on one of the logs instead, his green body almost twice as long and much thicker than when we'd first met.

"Thanks." I smiled. "I obviously owe everything to my incredible teacher."

I stood and bent into a dramatic bow, flourishing one arm. I would really miss Reenalyn once I got transferred to a better cohort. I hoped I wouldn't be matched against her. Honestly, she was more fun than Selverine or the others. It was too bad she didn't have a place in high society. If we all managed to get placed into better cohorts, maybe I could take Reenalyn with me. That was an exciting thought.

But Selverine and Yulroe and Frenna already didn't like her. They wouldn't understand...it probably would complicate things.

Social muck was exhausting and disappointing.

She laughed and laid her violin lovingly in its case, followed by the bow. Her fingers caressed the instrument as she secured it in its felt lining and closed the lid with a smile, then slid the case into a nondescript sack.

I needed something to get my mind off eventually leaving Reenalyn...Kaido told me my smile lit my eyes the last time I saw him. Over the last few weeks, we'd managed a few stolen moments together. Hopefully, the second part of my plan was coming together.

"What are you grinning about now?" Reenalyn asked.

"Oh, nothing."

"You know I know you're lying, right? I can't help sensing a sudden flare of Kaido-related emotions." She raised an eyebrow.

I rolled my eyes at her teasing. "Oh, come on, Reenalyn. You must've never seen him up close. He's *gorgeous*. There's literally no one else as attractive as him."

She grimaced. "His body, maybe. But the rest of him is rather—well—skunked."

I choked on a cackle. "Reenalyn Demensey, is that the first time you've ever cussed?"

She rolled her eyes. "Well, has he asked you to the ball? It's only a couple of weeks away now."

I sighed. "No, not yet."

"Why don't you ask him, then?"

"I keep meaning to, but every time I see him, we spend a lot of time kissing, then I get too nervous to ask."

She shot me a look.

"Okay, okay. Before you start on how I shouldn't be too nervous if I'm already kissing him, let me just remind you how dreadfully many admirers he has. Admirers *you* told me about, I might add."

"Well, no matter what *I* think about him, he'd certainly be an epic fool to miss going to the ball with you." She grinned.

"Right. The disinherited ex-daughter of a meagerly wealthy family barely holding on to their fortunes by the threads of their better child's diapers. What a catch."

If I couldn't win the competition or win Kaido's heart, I'd be living in the Emberlyn Forest of Wrynford long after my cohort found careers and started families. If I could just convince Kaido I was worth marrying in a year or two, and hold his attention for that long, then my life would be back in order, and everything would be okay.

"Mella Yarinelle, you stop talking so badly about yourself or I'll have to break that mandolin over your head." A teasing smile peeked out from her mock-stern expression.

My arms tightened over my instrument, though I knew she was teasing. If castlings could be killed by their weapons being shattered, then Whisper could be ended by damage to my mandolin, too.

It was a good thing my boss at the leatherworks shop hadn't minded my taking scraps. After a few weeks of work, I'd had enough pennies for good quality thread—which I'd purchased from a tiny shop in Wrynford rather than from the seamstress who'd turned me down for a job, or any of the places that stocked Father's textiles. I'd made the shoulder pad first, to protect my skin from Whisper's talons, and then constructed something to protect my castling instrument.

I placed the mandolin in its mismatched leather case now, tying the fastenings in place.

Reenalyn said, "You're still going to help with my hair, right? I want to do this elaborate updo with braids and everything, but I don't know if I can pull it off."

I smiled. "Of course!"

It had been years since I'd had a lady's maid, thanks to father's diminished fortune, so I had a little practice with hair styling.

Reenalyn clasped her hands. "Thank you so much!"

"Reenalyn, why are you always so happy?" That wasn't the exact question I'd meant to ask, but I was curious.

She seated herself on the log next to me and cocked her head. "Am I?"

I raised an eyebrow. "Uh, yeah. Like literally all the time. I've never seen you in a bad mood. Not ever."

"Oh." She looked down at her hands. "Well, I'm not *always* happy. But I guess I like everything I spend my time doing, you know? I enjoy playing instruments and helping my family build them to fill orders and admiring them in others' homes when I clean. And now I always have Cupid with me. He's so much fun."

She beamed at the little lizard, who smiled shyly back from his dappled patch of sunlight on the log.

"I think he thinks I'm a bit more than he bargained for." She winked at me as if I should know this obvious fact, which I kind of did. "But he's getting used to me. And he's grown at least a span and a half already! I'm just as proud as I can be of him."

"Huh. Okay. Does it have anything to do with your...like...romance-sensing abilities?"

Reenalyn glanced away, wrapping her arms around herself. "It might if...if there was ever someone who noticed *me*. It seems my heightened senses come with a blinding effect on everyone around me. Or maybe it's just how too tall I am."

Her laugh came out kind of strangled. Very non-Reenalyn-ish.

Cupid skittered over the log, laid a little emerald lizard hand on Reenalyn's knee, and gazed up at her with concern.

Reenalyn smiled again, and somehow, sincerity glowed from her face despite the obvious hurt. "I think it's more like I decide to be happy—to focus on the good things—even when there are bad things around me. It's kind of like a fierce, determined joy, I guess. Sounds pretty silly though, saying it out loud."

She let out a laugh and curled Cupid's tail around her finger like most girls would twirl a ringlet of their own hair.

"You *choose* to be happy? How do you just *choose* that?"

"Hmm." She rested her chin in one hand and drummed her fingers on her cheek. "It's like this. Say the conductor of the orchestra I was in before casting yelled at me for a bad note. If I focused on the one bad note, I'd feel terrible about myself and make another mistake, and it would keep compounding. But if I focused on the hundreds of other notes I played well and remembered I'm a good musician despite an occasional mistake, I'm more likely to keep up the good work."

She stroked Cupid's back. "I'd also think of how proud my family was when I got in the orchestra, and how much that helped my parents with all my siblings. And how my little sister, Angelira, looks up to me. And the good things just keep coming until I'm more grateful for them than any mistake can compete with. And I stay happy, even if something's trying to bring me down."

I crossed my arms. "That's great for you, being a master musician and only messing up *occasionally*. What about someone like me, who messes up more than gets it right? How can I be *fiercely joyful* when everything keeps going wrong?"

"But it doesn't all keep going wrong, Mella, does it? You had trouble at the Castling Ceremony, but you still cast almost immediately after. And your castling is fierce and beautiful and so unique and eye-catching!"

But she's not really my castling and doesn't want to be.

"And you made new friends you might not have met if you'd cast that day and been assigned a different cohort."

Yes, but...losing my standing with Selverine and Yulroe and the rest after all my hard work...that was a load of skunk muck.

"And you're improving so much at the mandolin!"

Very slowly.

"And getting stronger from training!"

A little.

Her face went kind of wistful and conspiratorial at the same time. "Aaaand, you have *admirers*."

"Admirers with an 'S,' hmm?" She wasn't just referring to Kaido with that gleam in her eye. She was thinking of Dane.

Who wasn't bad looking but far too pale and always uncomfortable around me. It made *me* uncomfortable. I wanted Kaido and his dark eyes and tawny skin and that adventurous grin. It had been ages since I'd seen him. Between training and my turns for shopping and cooking for my cohort, while also keeping my job at the leatherwork shop, our moments alone were shorter and fewer than I'd like.

I crossed my arms. "Dane doesn't count."

"But it must be nice to know *someone* thinks you're attractive, right? That someone's so attracted to you, talking to you makes him adorably nervous?"

I grimaced, then remembered her confession before about feeling like people were blind to her. Which was ridiculous. She was definitely prettier than Selverine or Frenna or Yulroe, now that I thought about it. So what if she was taller and broader than them? She'd be better in a fight for sure.

"You know what I think, Reenalyn? If guys around here aren't attracted to you, it's not because you aren't pretty. You're really beautiful. The problem is they're intimidated by you. Guys don't like to admit when a girl is better at something than they are. You're taller than most of them, a better fighter than probably all of them, and definitely the best musician. They can't compete with that."

Her eyes went wide, and her mouth slacked slightly. She gazed at me, then at nothing.

"Come on, don't tell me you've never thought of that before." I lifted an eyebrow.

She turned her astonished eyes back on me. "I haven't, though. Do you really think so?"

"Definitely."

"So all the things I've gotten good at, things I thought would make up for being too tall...it's only made it worse." Her expression crumpled, and I immediately regretted my speculations.

"Reenalyn, no. That's not what I'm saying. I'm saying there's just no one good enough to deserve you around here—at least not that you've met yet. Maybe someone will come to Terrenthyrs one day and sweep you off your feet."

The corners of her mouth turned down.

"Uh, or there could be someone awesome around here you just haven't met yet. Or someone who's just too stupid to realize how awesome you are, but surely will soon."

Her lips quivered, and she tore her gaze from mine to stare at the ground.

"Oh no, Reenalyn, that was supposed to make you feel better, not worse. I'm sorry it didn't come out right."

"I'm not sure how it makes me feel. I'll have to think about it."

"Sorry I said anything. I was just trying to help, like you were trying to help me."

She patted my shoulder and smiled tentatively. "No, thank you for telling me. Sometimes I see so much other people don't that I can be blind to what's obvious to everyone else."

"Well, okay." With a sigh, I tied the last tie on the makeshift mandolin case, wishing for real fastenings like on Reenalyn's wooden case and feeling awful for opening my big mouth.

***

The breeze grew cooler as the sky faded late in the afternoon. I sat on a log and stretched my tired back after trying to balance Whisper on one shoulder all afternoon. Reenalyn returned from working with Cupid, and the others followed soon after.

Everyone brought something to share for dinner tonight. Brawler and Mauler rolled around in the grass and chased each other around tree trunks, loud laughs and shouts replacing their little-girl giggles of a couple months ago.

Beldon swung his huge legs over a log near Trinka's but grinned at me instead of her. "How'd mandolin practice go, Mella?"

"Oh, um, all right, I guess." I smiled, remembering the amazing harmony Reenalyn and I had played together—the best keeping up I'd been able to do to date.

"She did great!" Reenalyn shouted from the other side of the fire. "Don't believe anything she says!"

I chuckled, wondering if Reenalyn really felt as happy as she looked, or if our conversation still bothered her. "I'm learning. Reenalyn's a great teacher."

Beldon grinned. "Sweet. Why don't you play something for us?"

I'm not ready to play for an audience! My stomach sank right into the ground. "Oh, um, well..."

Reenalyn smiled at me encouragingly.

Oh, whatever.

I pulled the mandolin into my lap and strummed a few chords, keeping my eyes on the strings and off my audience. Though I felt several pairs of eyes burning into me.

"Do you guys remember this old children's rhyme?

Ask Wexel for the truth,
You can trust his word,
Brellna will be the first
To guard your secrets in this world.
To Karmell you can take
Your very greatest fear,
To tell how great you'll be,
Thornyn is always there."

I messed up once but did pretty good otherwise. I stood and bowed dramatically, straightening to find Beldon crossing the distance with his palm held up for a high-five. "That sounded awesome! Nice job."

I returned the smile, touched by his encouragement. "Thanks."

Behind him, Dane smiled and clapped, nodding when I caught his ice-blue eyes. Reminded of Dane's feelings toward me, according to Reenalyn, I nodded quickly and returned my attention to Beldon, who was speculating whether musicians should do finger stretches like bodybuilders stretch their arms.

"Oh, yeah. Thanks for the tip," I said vaguely, still aware of Dane and wondering what he was thinking.

A commotion from where Brawler and Mauler wrestled had Beldon and Trinka swinging over their logs to check on their castlings, and without the huge mass of Beldon to shield me from Dane's view, I felt uncomfortably open and available for conversation.

Oh, skunks. He's standing up. And walking this way. I don't want to hurt him, but I don't feel the same way...

I pretended to adjust the mandolin's tuning pegs—anything to look busy.

"That sounded great, Mella," he said, taking a seat beside me. Sprinter leaped lithely up next to him and sat on his haunches, his black ears twitching.

"Thanks." I didn't want to give him the wrong idea by being too nice. But no reason to be cold or rude. I faced him and smiled, hoping it was friendly—but not *overly* friendly.

His answering grin lit up his face. The firelight gave his pale skin an attractive glow that made it look less pasty than usual. His snowy-blond hair lacked the charm of Kaido's carefree dark waves, though his eyes were really a nice color. An icy blue much more striking than mine.

"So." Dane shifted his feet and laid his hand over his castling weapon. "What's the story with that song?"

"It's a kids' bedtime song. Haven't you heard it before? The people in it are mythical magical people with special abilities."

"Abilities?"

"Yeah, like Wexel could always tell when people were lying. And Karmell, he could keep a secret. You could tell him anything, and it was impossible for anyone to get it out of him. Brellna was more interesting. She could tell when someone had a secret, and unless they'd told Karmell first, she could tell what it was." I laughed. "That would make for a lot of interesting situations, if it were real."

"What about Thornyn?"

I grinned, thinking of Momma. Thornyn had been her favorite. "Thornyn could see the future. Mainly just the good things. She could tell you whether there was a chance of things working out well for you—help you decide which course of action would have the best results."

"Wow. That would be useful."

I nodded. *You have no idea.*

"You know, legends usually have some truth in them. Maybe they *are* real."

"Maybe. But if they were, it was long ago. That's a really old story."

Dane blinked, and I realized I'd been staring into his eyes far too long for a non-overly friendly vibe. I turned to the crackling flames and searched for a subject change. "Have you ever considered picking up an instrument?"

He shook his head. "Not really. I never had the chance to learn." He sounded like he might've liked to.

"I'm sure Reenalyn could teach you, if you wanted. She seems to know everything about every instrument."

"Maybe someday. For now, I'm too busy training and working to have time for that."

"Yeah, I get that now."

"Can I ask you something?"

Oh boy. "Um, sure."

"It's pretty personal."

I winced. *Skunks.*

"About your family."

Oh, not as bad as I thought at first. I kept my focus on the dancing flames. "Sure."

"Do you think you'll ever meet your little brother or sister?"

Well, that wasn't what I'd been expecting. I frowned, not interested in discussing anything so personal with him at the moment. I never should've told him about it before.

"Sorry, I didn't mean to stick my nose in your business. It's just that while siblings can be a lot to deal with, they can be really great, too. I can't describe how much I miss mine. And I just wanted you to know I had a lot of awesome times with them. Lots of good memories. And I wouldn't want you to miss out on your sibling's life and regret it later. I'm sorry your parents took so much joy out of it for you."

"Yeah, me too."

I wasn't sure how else to reply. I didn't hate the kid. Father's choices weren't its fault. And I *did* want to know him or her. But how would I go about that? It would be a lot easier if I were able to win Kaido and the competition both.

But for now, I needed to get the attention off my family issues. "How many brothers or sisters do you have?"

"Three."

I turned back to him, raising an eyebrow at his tone. He sounded both wistful and...guilty?

"I have a brother. And two sisters. But my...*parents*...they take care of a lot of people." His gaze finally stopped burning into me and rested on the fire instead.

Something about his siblings was painful for him. I was curious, but being too interested might give him the wrong idea. Maybe more small talk would be safer.

"Well, if you're able to learn, what instrument would you choose?"

"I don't know. I've never actually thought about it before. I've seen plenty of instruments, but I've never touched one, much less tried to play it."

"Would you like to hold mine? My mandolin, I mean?" Flushing, I shoved it at him, hoping to distract him.

"Oh, thank you." He accepted it and ran a hand over the arm and strings, lightly feeling each one.

Huh. Dane really did have attractive hands. His fingers were the per-fect proportion to his hand and wrist, and gentle with the mandolin. Veins rose slightly in a few places, which for some reason was appealing. I'd forgotten to pay attention to Kaido's hands.

I'd have to pay better attention when I saw them next. I'd meant to last time I'd noticed Dane's hands, but Kaido was always so distracting I kept forgetting.

"It's really cool that you made this. I like how it looks. It's more *you* than any other mandolin, with pieces of yourself put into it like that."

I smiled and looked away, again fearing I'd give the wrong impression.

"It's a lot like a castling weapon, actually."

I stiffened, keeping my eyes on the embers. Had he figured out my secret?

"What do you mean?"

"Just how we put our own desires, our gifts, into our castling weapon, similar to how you made this mandolin, you know?"

"Yeah, I guess you're right." He'd cared enough to pay attention to every detail I'd told him. I hadn't told Kaido the first thing about my mandolin. We should talk more next time.

"My siblings would've liked your mandolin."

So we were back on his family. Well, better than on the unnecessary details of my life. "Thanks. Next time they come to visit you, you're welcome to show it to them if you'd like."

His face clouded. "Thanks, Mella. I'm sure they'd like it, if they were able to come."

I wasn't sure what exactly that meant. "Where are you from anyway, Dane? How do you not know about Wexel and Thornyn?"

"Around."

I raised an eyebrow at his evasive answer.

"Really, I've lived a lot of places. I'm not from anywhere in particular."

I could tell there was something he wasn't saying, and a beat too late I realized I'd been searching his eyes for too long.

Again.

Standing, I packed up the mandolin, quickly tying the leather fasten-ings. "All right. I've got to talk to Reenalyn about our dresses for the ball. See you tomorrow." I waved in order to hopefully not be rude in my abrupt leaving.

"Goodnight, Mella. See you then." His voice was soft, and the sadness was mostly gone. His face was so open, so...hopeful? But hopeful about what?

Reenalyn walked by just then, sitting a few logs over.

I called out to her, thankful to have the perfect distraction. "Reenalyn! We still need to talk about our dresses—"

"Oh, right! Have you decided on your design? If you've written it down, I can drop it off with mine tomorrow."

With a sigh, I pulled the folded parchment from my pocket. My first plan had been pretty elaborate—I was barely going to be able to afford it, even with the extra shifts at the leatherwork shop.

But I wanted to make things right with Acres, and that meant purchasing a new library pass for him.

I'd made up for the lack of baubles with a deeply plunging neckline and a tighter waist. There was, after all, elegance in simplicity—if done right. I was confident my new design would impress Kaido and leave enough money for me to get Acres to stop scowling at me.

"Yes, here it is." I handed the parchment to Reenalyn with a smile. "Thanks, Reenalyn."

"Of course!" She unfolded the parchment, beaming at the sketch and the design notes. "Ooo! I love this!"

As I stepped over the log to sit next to her, I realized I was surprisingly excited about what Acres's face would look like when I shocked him with the new pass.

And what Kaido's face would look like when he saw me in that dress.

Chapter 32

ACRES

S tarstinger's eyes danced with mischief. "You're going to explode soon if they don't shut up about the Grand Castors' Ball, aren't you?"

She was right. If I had to hear one more word about dresses or dates, I might just puke. Mella and Reenalyn seemed to have lost interest in any other subjects. They'd finally walked off, but I could still hear them from the firepit.

"Basically."

She laughed and curled up in my lap, her long tail wrapping around her body and covering her front paws.

Shivering slightly in the cool evening air, I stroked her back, amazed at how soft her fur was. "We'll go as soon as we're done eating. It's been a long day."

I watched the flames licking at the food on the grate and wished it would hurry up already.

"Hey, Trinka." Beldon waved a pocketknife at Trinka as she walked into the clearing, sweaty and grouchy as ever. I avoided her eyes, frustrated and ashamed that I still hadn't found a floramantic solution for her.

"Berroman." She nodded at him and took a seat on a log a few feet away.

How did he not get the hint? I knew nothing about girls, but even I could see she was as interested now as she'd been two and a half months ago.

Which was not at all.

"Aren't you curious about what I'm doing?" he asked, his eyes on the knife in his hand.

I followed his gaze. He was scraping ribbons of dark wood from a stick. Trinka frowned at his work. "Not particularly."

"Well, that's too bad, because I'm going to tell you anyway."

She stared at the fire. "Great."

"I noticed you sometimes tap your hands on the log to keep the beat when Mella and Reenalyn play their instruments."

Her eyes snapped to his, suspicious.

Did she do that? I hadn't noticed.

"I do not."

He chuckled. "Yes, you do. So I'm making you a pair of drumsticks. We'll be able to hear you keeping the beat then, and it will make the music sound even better. The percussion is always the best part. Here." He handed her one smooth piece of wood. "This one's already finished."

"Um, Berroman..." She pinched the stick between her fingers and held it out like something gross that might bite.

The dark sheen on the wood stood out in the firelight. He'd carved them from Emberlyn wood? That was much harder to work with than any other variety. He must really be trying to impress her. Too bad he had no chance.

Trinka held the drumstick out to him. "I don't play music."

Mella and Reenalyn were still talking about dresses, so I worked harder to ignore them.

"That isn't playing music, really." He scraped another ribbon from the stick in his hand and ran his thumb over the space. "It's just keeping the beat. It's fun. Why don't you give it a try?"

"I don't think that's the best idea." She handed the stick back more insistently, and he accepted it without a fight.

"I had a feeling you'd probably say that. So I brought backup." He produced a set of panpipes and tossed them at Trinka. "These I found and spent no money or effort on whatsoever. So they don't count as a gift. Plus, they're softer than drums, if you don't want to stand out."

She caught them, looking like she'd considered letting them land on the dirt instead. "Berroman, I don't want to be a part of the little orchestra."

His hands stilled, and he looked at her. "Are you sure? Being a part of something is really nice. I don't like to see you feeling excluded."

She narrowed her eyes. "I don't feel excluded. I exclude myself on purpose."

"Maybe you'd have more fun if you didn't."

"I'm not here for fun, Berroman. I'm just here for the castling year and the prize money."

He sighed and focused on the stick again. "Okay. If that's what you want."

She frowned.

"What are those?" Dane strode behind the circle of logs and took a seat a few specks from Trinka, eyeing the instrument.

"Panpipes, Snowflake." She tossed them, and he snatched them out of the air. "Try them out. They sound like wind in the trees. A good instrument for you."

He blew into them, and they made a hoarse, reedy sound.

"No, hold it parallel to your body, not out from your lips like that," Beldon corrected him.

He played a few notes, then glanced at Sprinter's erect ears.

"It's a nice sound, isn't it?" Dane asked.

The blotchy dog nodded, staring at his castor as if waiting for more.

He shrugged and played some more. "These are really fun, Trinka. Where'd you get them?"

She tossed her head at Beldon. "Berroman."

"I just gave them to Trinka, but she doesn't want them, so they're all yours."

He glanced between Beldon and Trinka. "Oh, okay. Thanks, Beldon."

"And it looks like I have a new pair of drumsticks." Beldon sighed, then drummed on the log on either side of him. Tucking them in his belt, he crossed the circle to where one smaller log lay upright. Lifting it with no trouble at all—even though it probably weighed twice as much as me—he set it in front of where he'd been sitting. "Not a real drum, but it will do. What do you say, Dane? Want to join the girls' illegal orchestra?"

He grinned. "I'm in."

I hoped they wouldn't ask me to join. Music was not a strength of mine. Though my grandmother used to sing. She had a great voice. At least if I remembered correctly.

My head ached again. After remembering the leather gauntlet man my Grandma had removed from my memory, I couldn't help wondering how many times my memories had been tampered with. I'd known about one of them, and now two. But were there more?

CHAPTER 33

SELVERINE

S weat slid down my temples as I strained at my castling call, begging Horizon to appear.

But she refused.

And the only thing greater than my annoyance was my shame for disappointing the queen.

Grandmother sighed and sat back in her silky chaise lounge, her eyes closed and her lips pursed. "Selverine..."

Apparently her disappointment in me was too much for words. Which was great.

But I'd been saving my news for a moment just like this. Before she could find the words to scold me or fruitlessly encourage me to keep trying, I laid my trident on the other sofa and faced her.

"That girl who failed to cast at the Castling Ceremony—she actually has a castling now. And it's an *avian*."

The queen stared at me, then asked with polite interest, "That girl cast an avian?"

"Yes." I gestured to Selvenair, towering over me from his perch on the enormous ancient drum. "Even bigger than him."

"How interesting. Did you ask her how she managed that?" Grandmother sipped her tea as if this was nothing notable. And it irritated me.

"I spied on her cohort in the woods—we're not close enough friends for her to tell me details."

Grandmother set her teacup on a saucer. "And you're sure it wasn't just a tamed wild animal? It was an actual castling?"

Crossing my arms, I frowned. "Of course I'm sure. She talked. I watched her beak move. She wasn't a tame animal at all."

"How interesting," Grandmother said again. "With such a fascinating castling, maybe this girl—what was her name?"

"Mella Yarinelle."

"Maybe this Mella Yarinelle would be a good friend for you. Maybe someone who could help you learn how to cast with more efficacy."

I bristled. The last thing I wanted was to be around Mella and the castling she didn't deserve, especially when I was skunk dung at handling my own castling.

"I don't know."

Grandmother smiled. "I'm sure you could find it in your heart to befriend her. Think of what you could learn. In fact, it might be a good idea to add this Mella and her incredible castling to your own cohort. It could increase your chances of winning, I'd imagine."

I winced. I didn't want to win with Mella at my side. I wanted to beat that skunking cheater. She couldn't have acquired an avian any other way, I was sure of it.

"Maybe," I conceded to avoid a fight. But I already had plans, and I didn't want to change them. Especially not this way.

The queen lifted the teacup to her lips once more. "I'm confident you'll do the right thing."

CHAPTER 34

DANE

S printer lay on his back and rolled around in the soft forest dirt under the Emberlyn trees. The early morning sun glinted off his fur, and I yawned and closed my eyes against the bright light.

"You look ridiculous," I told him.

A dust cloud formed around him, rising to his feet flopping in midair. "You're just saying that to make yourself feel better," he said.

He was right. And he knew that I knew it. But I wasn't going to admit it out loud, and he knew that, too. "Come on already, Sprinter. We've got to go."

He stretched long and slow, then rolled to his feet and shook himself off.

I fanned the air in front of my nose to avoid breathing it in. "Essence of dust and dirty dog. Delightful."

Sprinter huffed a laugh and tossed some dirt at me with one paw.

I kicked dust back at him with a grin. "Knock it off. They're not going to let me into The Braided Loaf looking like I've been hanging out with you all day."

We strolled into town for my shift at the Loaf. The rhythmic clink of blacksmith hammers and the whoosh of bellows filled the air on our way.

After a few hours, the smell of fresh barley bread had my stomach growling, and I decided it was time for the good old lunch break. I made myself a sandwich on a full braid of barley bread with extra meat and sat at one of the tables out front.

Sprinter sat on the bench next to me, overlooking the street. He cleared his throat, drawing my eye to him mid-chew. "So don't look now, but your crush is walking this way."

Of course I looked up. And choked on my sandwich.

"I said *not* to look!" he hissed.

"That is the *least* effective way to get someone not to look!" I hissed through a mouthful of sandwich.

"At least she didn't see you do that. Should I wave her over, or do you want to choke more first?" He grinned at me, his tail wagging the slight way it did when he was giving me a hard time.

"Please don't. We've already established I've made enough of a fool of myself." I glanced up from behind my sandwich.

Her hair was down today instead of in the usual ponytail. The sun shimmered off it as it bounced with each step.

How could someone be so beautiful it hurt? Did her hair feel as silky as it looked? I imagined running my fingers through its softness, my hand finding the back of her head to pull her in for a kiss...

Suddenly a hand was at the back of her head. I did a double take. Another guy walking down the street had suddenly stopped, and he was holding her, as *he* pulled her in for a kiss!

"What the skunk!" I only meant to think the words, but they seemed to have shot out of my mouth. And suddenly I was on my feet, my hands on the table, muscles flexing to vault me over it.

"Dane!" Sprinter was in front of me on the table, showing his teeth in a threatening gesture he'd never aimed at me before. The shock of that was enough to bring me to my senses.

I blinked. "I've got to stop that!"

He put one paw against my chest, pushing me toward my seat. "Oh, really? Dane, that would be a decent idea if she *didn't* want that guy's attentions, but look at her. She's smiling. And nobody's making her wrap her arms around him."

I rubbed my eyes and focused on them again. Monkey's skunking teeth. Sprinter was mucking right.

I sighed and dropped back to my seat. Some tall, dark, and disgustingly handsome guy had his arms around her, one hand pressed against her waist as he leaned low to reach her lips with his.

"Ugh." I had to look away. The sandwich had turned to tar in my stomach and threatened to make a reappearance.

"I'm sorry, Dane." Sprinter shifted between me and them, blocking my line of sight.

"I guess I don't have any right to be upset. It's not like I ever manned up enough to tell her..."

Tell her what? That I thought she was gorgeous and kind and incredible? That I...had feelings for her? *Bleh.* What a stupid thing to say. I barely knew her, even after nearly three months in the same cohort, and she knew me even less. Of course she'd prefer this giant guy with a hot tan to a scrawny ghost-pale—

"Dane?" Sprinter's eyes held none of their usual mirth. The concern in them made me feel like even more of a child for how much this affected me.

"I'm fine," I growled.

He cocked his head, a slight smile curving up one side of his muzzle. "That sounds about right."

Exhaling, I unfisted my hands and laid them on the bench on either side of me. "Let's get out of here. We've got supplies to pick up for the Loaf. We're wasting time."

The smile gone from his face, Sprinter jumped down and resumed his place at my side, nonchalantly switching from his usual side to the side between me and the piece of skunk muck who was still—holy skunking muck—*still* kissing Mella. Didn't he have anything better to do with his worthless life?

No. No, of course there would be nothing better than to spend time kissing Mella Yarinelle. If you were the guy she wanted to kiss back.

CHAPTER 35

MELLA

I had spotted Kaido waiting for me across from the Braided Loaf.
Grinning, I smiled and waved, picking up my pace. When I had
reached him, he wrapped his arms around me and pressed my back
against the cool shaded wall of the inn.

Being in Kaido's arms felt like nothing else I'd ever experienced. With
one warm hand on the small of my back and one cradling my head, he
pressed his lips to mine.

I smiled through the kisses, melting into him. Delighted to have kept
his attention after several weeks of not seeing each other. Perhaps it was a
sign I would be successful in pulling this off. If I snagged Kaido Felzane,
the only child of a rich family of Emberlyn wood processors and whose
father was an advisor to the king, I'd be richer than Father had ever been
in all his life—than he'd ever dreamed of being. Performing well enough
to win the competition would be pure bonus. Not even necessary for
living a good, comfortable life.

Finally, I pushed back to get a breath in, giggling. "Kaido..." I looked
into his dark eyes and melted some more.

He smiled that lazy smile, his eyes heavy lidded, and leaned in again.
"You are *so* hot."

"So are you," I whispered back, then grimaced. That was probably a
lame thing to say. But what do people talk about in this situation? "So,
Kaido, how's training been going? I bet Striker has grown a lot. I know
my castling sure has."

He backed up a little but kept his hands around my waist. "Oh, you're serious?" he asked, the yearning huskiness ebbing from his voice.

"I was...? But if that's a stupid question, never mind." *What an idiot.* You don't talk about anything when you're kissing because you're *kissing*!

"It's going great. Striker and I are at the top of our group. No one can get past us. We always beat everyone."

He grinned at me as if I should be impressed. Which, I guess I would be if it were true. But beating everyone every single time? That seemed hard to believe, even for someone as fit as Kaido. It meant his team wasn't trying very hard, or he was lying. One person just didn't win every single time.

But maybe I misunderstood. He wouldn't *lie* to me. And I *had* seen him train before we all got our castlings. He *was* good. So...it *could* be accurate.

I ignored the nagging feeling that he was exaggerating. I really just wanted him to kiss me again. It made me feel like I still had worth, despite being practically disowned. I held in my grimace at the thought of Kaido ever finding out. What would he think? I hoped the long swim I'd taken in the river this morning had rinsed off the smell of the leatherwork and sweat.

"That sounds nice." I tried to sound sexy as I leaned in for another kiss. He obliged. It was warm and rich and made me dizzy.

He never asked me about how *my* training was going. But that was probably because I was such a good kisser he couldn't resist making out with me for as long as possible. Right? Especially since we lived far enough away from each other and were so busy training that we hardly ever got to hang out.

Something pestered me, but I didn't have time for it today. I was busy.

"You are so sexy, girl." The huskiness was back in his voice, forcing my eyes closed to better absorb the sound. His lips brushed mine, sending shivers all over.

"Wait." I giggled, stretching up between him and the wall. "You haven't let me say what I came here for yet."

"Oh, I know what you came for, Mella," his honeyed, husky voice whispered in my ear as he pulled me closer.

"Wait, seriously." Smiling up at him, I rested my hands against his chest and pushed him a few specks away. His rich, dark eyes drank me in and hypnotized me. "I, uh"—giggling again—"I wanted to ask if you'd like to go to the ball with me."

Of course, I'd spent days psyching myself up to believe he'd say yes, but when his smile faltered and he hesitated, I second-guessed everything.

"I mean—" I didn't know what I was going to say, but he cut me off.

"I'd love to, Mella." He grinned that grin and laid it on mine again. "Mm, good."

"Yeah. I think so, too. You know, we find ourselves right by an inn. What do you say to getting a room? To celebrate that we'll be going to the ball together." His nose brushed my neck, and tingles shot from the contact.

My heart beat faster. A room? Did he mean...

Well, it wasn't like I hadn't thought about it. And I was in a pretty romantic mood just now. And he was now my date to the ball. Kaido Felzane. Surely an easy way back into Selverine's social circle. And an excellent match to rub in my parents' faces.

"Okay, sure. Yeah." I smiled shyly, my heart bounding now.

He unwound from around me, his absence suddenly making me feel cold. I shivered a less-pleasant shiver than before.

But then his warm brown hand slid down my arm and clasped my fingers, pulling me toward the inn's side door. His other hand rested on the stair rail.

His wonky-shaped hands with their stubby fingers and palms that didn't match them.

My stomach drifted from the pleasant place it had been hovering and back down to where it belonged. Suddenly I didn't want those hands on me.

Maybe it was just nerves. It wasn't like I'd done this before. I had enough going on without starting *that*, too. After the ball would be better. Or maybe to celebrate Wager Day. Yes, that would be perfect.

And surely all hands were different—Kaido couldn't be the only person with odd-shaped hands. I just needed to notice more people's hands. Then they wouldn't be so weird to me. No, that was too weird. Why did I give a muck about anyone's hands? No one else did that!

And why was I focusing on his hands when the rest of him was so beautiful? And my ticket back into society?

"Oh, Kaido, I'm sorry," I mumbled, pulling my hand from his. "I just remembered I'm late for a training thing. We had to reschedule for today—you know. So stupid." I chuckled lamely.

The glorious light went out of his eyes as he ran one of those wrong-ish hands through his hair with a frown. "Fine. Whatever."

"I'm so sorry. But I'll see you at the ball next week." I smiled and stepped on my tiptoes to kiss him.

His lips were unresponsive.

I stepped away. "Are you okay?"

"Sure. I'll see you later." He brushed past me and into the street, leaving me alone in the shadows.

I winced. *I must've really disappointed him. I guess I should be flattered, though, that he's so attracted to me, right?*

Strangely, another pair of hands floated through my mind. A finely shaped pair of hands that were much too pale to be attractive. At least, I used to think so. I brushed away the thought.

Remembering the shivers and sparks from a moment ago, I took a deep breath and smiled to myself as I strolled onto the cobblestone road to head for the woods.

This ball was going to be amazing.

I hoped.

CHAPTER 36

ACRES

S tarstinger's dual throwing stars glimmered in the candlelight. Her tail flicked back and forth, hanging from where she curled up on my crossed feet on the desk.

I frowned at the letter in my hand. "It only says that tonight is the ball, Starstinger. It doesn't actually say I'm required to attend."

"Yes, it does, and you're very late," she purred without opening her eyes. "You taught me how to read, remember?"

"What? Where? No, it doesn't." I frowned at her, afraid she was right.

"Right under that bit about how you're to go without your castling."

I frowned at the letter again, then tossed it on the desk. "That's open to interpretation."

"Then you'll take me with you?" She rolled onto her back and stretched luxuriously, reaching toward the ceiling with her tawny paws.

"Then I'll stay right here so neither of us has to bother with it."

She licked one paw upside down, her bright eyes fixing mine with a you-know-that-won't-work look.

I sighed and pulled my legs off the desk as she dropped primly to the floor on all fours. "But I don't have a date."

"You probably aren't the only nervous kid showing up alone. Just go find someone there."

I pushed to my feet and stretched less glamorously than Starstinger, looking around the room for my ballroom attire. The stiff suit pants and jacket were somewhere under the open books and notes sprawled across my bed. I'd experimented with every ingredient and combination of ingredients in the recipe Dane snuck for me, but nothing produced the effect I needed.

I was guessing that the combination of the dapplemint and deecho fern must have caused the memories to stay rather than go. The fern's aged dryness likely had something to do with the unexpected reaction as well. But there had to be something in the sandwich ingredients that made the details stand out so clearly. I just couldn't figure out what.

But why had I seen them when I touched her? The never-ceasing question.

I did need a break—Starstinger was right about that. But dancing in a crowded room hardly fit my idea.

My eyes fell on the floramancy books I'd pulled from the trunk after Trinka's visit. I'd avoided them at first, but now there was just the bottom one left to read. Not that the others had been much help. With a sigh, I pulled it from the stack.

No matter what I find in here, no matter how helpful it could be, I will not use floramancy again once I'm done with helping Trinka.

I took a deep breath and opened the cover, and was surprised to find a sheet covered in handwriting. Recognizable handwriting—my grandmother's tidy print. The musty scent of old parchment swirled through my nose as I read the faded script.

Dear Diary,

Father says he means to marry me off to Mr. Dorrow's son. I cried when I found out, and Drae punched a hole through one of his fresh paintings when I told him. He said we should run away together, but Father heard him.

I haven't seen him since.

I blinked. Mr. Dorrow's son? Could that be her first husband? I'd heard he'd died before they'd started a family, and she'd married my grandfather after that. I flipped the book over to the back cover, and there it was.

Property of Lirna Blythlie.

Blythlie. I hadn't heard that last name in a long time. My grandmother kept a journal when she was young? And it made it here with me without my even realizing it?

Tiny forepaws tapped my shoulder. "Acres, the ball, remember? You need to go and make good connections and all that. This book will be waiting for you when you get back."

I shrugged, my eyes fixed on my grandmother's handwriting. "Actually, I should keep reading. This is much more important—"

She slid over my shoulder into my lap, her paw slamming the cover closed. "Acres. You're letting your cohort down by not showing up. *Please* go, and then you can stay up all night reading and miss a whole day of sparring tomorrow, and I won't say a thing. Just please at least make an appearance."

I did have a bit of a headache from reading so much. And the last few months had proved Starstinger could be a stubborn serval when she wanted to be. "Fine. I guess I could go for a few minutes, just to get you off my back."

She grinned. "Thank you." She eyed the mess on my bed. "Now just to dig your dress clothes out of all that..."

Chapter 37

MELLA

It was finally the night of the Grand Castors' Ball. Music poured from the mahogany double doors of the Great Hall, and excitement mingled with a little disappointment that I didn't get to walk in on Kaido's arm. But he'd said he couldn't wait to see me in the note he'd sent, so I stepped through the doors and breathed in the extravagance.

No expense had been spared in the decorations. Or in anyone's dresses, it seemed. Colorful gowns of all shades and materials shone, sparkled, and whispered over the dance floor. I stepped to the side to avoid falling into the dancers and glanced around for Kaido.

I ran my fingers over the straps of my midnight-blue silk dress with a rather revealing neckline, making sure it was still in place. Modest silver lace trimmed the edges—not my first choice, but decent all the same. And I had to do without pearls to pay for Acres's library pass.

My dark hair was piled into a loose bun sort-of-thing with a few strategic strands pulled free to frame my face. I couldn't say I'd spared no expense, but I'd spared as much as I could. I hoped Kaido would like it so I'd be that much closer to never having to worry about expenses again.

A crimson velvet gown with a plunging neckline to rival my own adorned Selverine, setting off her flawless tan skin. A thick pitch-black sash tied around her waist accentuated her figure. Her light brown hair was pulled to the side in a complicated braid with emerald stones pinned throughout. Her ever-present blown-glass green humming-avian earrings dangled from her ears.

Next to Selverine, nearly invisible in her shadow, stood Willova, the girl who'd cast a tiger, who I didn't even have the time to despise anymore. If only my biggest problem were still casting the same castling as someone else in my year.

Willova's striking scarlet hair was parted simply and left wavy, hanging past her waist. She wore a long-sleeved gown made of ornately patterned fabric. It swished around her ankles as she moved stiffly, probably because of how tightly she'd had the bodice drawn. Her face was carefully blank.

Trinka had chosen to wear her fighting leathers rather than a traditional ball gown. Her casual dark clothes stood in stark contrast to the bright formal attire worn by most.

"Mella!"

Whipping my head around, I searched for whoever had called my name.

Reenalyn waved at me in a pale pink gown with her hair in a half ponytail. I waved back, frowning slightly at her hair. She'd been so excited to wear it up in the elaborate design she'd been planning and practicing for months. Why was it mostly down like that?

I stepped toward her as she took a sip of punch nearly the same color as her dress, worrying our conversation about boys being intimidated by her height might've caused the change.

But a boisterous laugh caught my ear—one I recognized—and I looked past her to finally find Kaido. Reenalyn followed my gaze and glanced over her shoulder. She rolled her eyes at me with a grin. But she had to be wrong about him.

I grinned back as I strode toward them, then slid my eyes to Kaido in his tall, gorgeous suit talking and laughing with a group of other better classers. I brushed aside the self-consciousness that threatened to stall me and put on my best smile, then skidded to a halt as Kaido wrapped an arm around Frenna's waist, pulled her to him, and kissed her right on the lips.

My pulse drummed in my ears as I stared at them, hoping when the man faced me, it wouldn't be Kaido. Maybe I'd thought I'd seen him when I hadn't...

But I knew. In my plummeting heart, I knew.

But why?

Kaido finally came up for air, Frenna's fuchsia lipstick smeared over his disgusting lips. Swiping a suit sleeve over his mouth, he turned and caught my eye.

I must've expected him to look guilty, to apologize, because it surprised me when he held my gaze with a cruel smile and slid his hand tighter around Frenna, drawing her closer. With a smirk, he turned his back on me.

What was I supposed to do now? I felt...I don't know what I felt. But I couldn't stand this crowded room a moment more. I needed to leave. Now.

I whirled, sickened by the smooth whisper of silk against my skin—this wretched dress I'd spent every cent I could spare on for him.

What an idiot!

I'd waltzed into this mucking ball, thinking how much Kaido would love this dress. Blah, blah, blah.

And he'd been a skunking piece of muck.

After how he'd acted last time I'd seen him...I'd been so naïve. He didn't give a muck about me. He was only using me. Like so many other idiot girls had been used by handsome men.

And I'd skunking *splurged* on this dress! Midnight-blue silk with a plunging neckline my parents would never have let me get away with back home. Gripping fistfuls of unbearably expensive fabric in both hands, I marched for the exit.

I could've paid for a room in Wrynford, instead of sleeping on the forest floor.

How many coins could I have spared to help Mrs. Brenslow and Miralie and Jeffers?

And Acres's library pass—I could have bought it for him ages ago instead of putting it off just a little longer.

Tears pricked my eyes, but I willed them back. I wouldn't let him see me cry. That snake! How could he do this to me? Suddenly decide Frenna was a better choice—maybe because she wasn't such a chicken.

But had it been sudden? Coldness washed over me as I realized how easily he could've been leading both of us on this whole time.

Thank goodness I hadn't gone into that stupid inn.

But still. No Kaido, no chance at his fortune.

I fisted my hands, determined not to let this stupid thing ruin my plans. I'd just have to win the Grand Castors' Tournament. Not rely on anyone else's fortunes.

I should've decided that in the beginning. *Idiot.* Then I might not have wasted so much on this *stupid* gown. I didn't even have a wardrobe to keep the thing in now.

I, fool that I was, had been determined to make it up to Kaido after chickening out on him the other day. I was sure this was the perfect way to show how obsessed I was with him and how much I wanted to please him and his gorgeous face.

Skunk him. And skunk his ugly hands.

Suddenly Beldon's hands flashed out, and the next thing I knew, he was whisking me from my angry march onto the dance floor.

"Whoa. Um, hello." I avoided his eyes, trying to blink away tears. "I'm not really in a dancing mood right now, Beldon. I need to go."

"You know," he said with a thoughtful expression, "I bet I know exactly why Kaido cast a giant snake."

Surprised and annoyed that he'd brought Kaido up, I met his eyes and glowered.

"Well, it's obvious," Beldon said matter-of-factly. "He's compensating for...*other things* being disappointingly small."

Chuckling in spite of myself, I smiled as a sudden appreciation for Beldon overshadowed my pain. "Thanks, Beldon. You know, I bet you're right." *And I'm so relieved not to know from experience. Ugh.*

"I definitely am. Now, do you trust me?" The mischievous glint in his eye didn't inspire confidence.

I raised an eyebrow. "I did until you asked it like that. Why?"

He chuckled. "Just pretend you *do* trust me and get ready."

I widened my eyes in alarm. "Ready for what?"

And then he spun me out into the whirling mass of dancers. I lost my grip on his hand and flailed for balance, and then slammed smack into someone whose second-hand suit smelled like smokey pine.

CHAPTER 38

DANE

How long was I required to stay at this ridiculous event in order for it to *count*? I'd seen plenty of past winners. Shaken hands with a few of them. Dodged a question about which family I was from.

I wanted to get out of here, cast Sprinter, and go for a run. Maybe a bit of leaping and swinging to tire myself out. A good distraction that would thoroughly exhaust me was exactly what I needed.

The image of that oaf Kaido with his meaty hands all tangled in Mella's hair had been seared into my mind since I'd seen them in the street. I'd do anything to get it out of my head, and to forget how incredibly stunning she looked in that gown tonight.

Seeing her left me speechless. A kind and wonderful soul who could fight like a total badass and look...indescribable in that dress.

It was more spectacularness than one person should be allowed to have.

And it was indecently unfair that I had to notice it so much. It squeezed something in my chest, and I didn't like how that felt. Not when things were like this.

Skunk it all.

It didn't matter how long I was supposed to be at this stupid thing. I'd been, and now I was leaving.

With a new determination, I turned toward the door and slammed face-first into a different pair of attractive breasts.

Stumbling back and spluttering apologies like an idiot, I tilted my head up to see Reenalyn's face. "Oh, monkey's teeth, Reenalyn, I'm so sorry. I didn't...did I hurt you?"

She laughed her musical, delighted laugh and held out a hand.

That was quite possibly the last response I would've expected after coming eyeball-to-cleavage with her. "Um, shouldn't you be shouting at me for running into you?"

She laughed again and took my hand without waiting for me to accept hers. "*I* stepped in *your* way, Dane. I know you didn't run into me on purpose."

She laid my other hand on her waist and swept me onto the dance floor.

Which was incredibly uncomfortable. I'd never danced with anyone before, and I only wanted to dance with one person ever. "Um, Reenalyn...?"

"Shh! It's okay. Trust me."

Reenalyn's impressive stature made me feel further dwarfed than I already was by Mella's preference for that imbecile Kaido, and being eye level with her low neckline wasn't helping me understand what was going on. At least the steps were simple. But her hip swayed under my hand with each one, and a painful wish that she were somehow Mella stung my chest.

"Trust you about what?" I finally managed.

"I'm going to twirl you, and then you just need to grab hold of whatever you run into, okay? Gently, though."

Alarm rushed through me. "Wait, what? No! Don't do that—"

But it was too late. I was spinning out from her, my hands suddenly free and my balance gone. I flailed my arms, trying to get control of myself. And then Mella tumbled into them, crashing against my chest and bringing my flailing to an immediate halt.

She was here.

In my arms.

Her face turned up and her red-rimmed eyes met mine and...she'd been *crying?*

I would murder every speck of life right out of Kaido and flay him alive and feed his remains to wild animals and then...

Out of the corner of my eye, I glimpsed Kaido's filthy arm around some blonde girl, and I understood.

He'd dumped *Mella Yarinelle* for someone else. Unbelievable. Clearly, he was the most astoundingly dense waste of existence ever born.

Mella took a step back and wiped away a tear, and suddenly, I knew I could either swallow my fear of her rejection and take her hand and try not to trip all over myself, or lose this chance forever.

Sprinter had asked if the chance she might return my feelings someday was worth the risk of a little embarrassment. Maybe a lot of embarrassment. And more rejection.

It *absolutely* was.

The chance to help her feel better was *alone* worth the risk that she might reject me again, even in front of all these people.

Barely able to believe I was doing it, I reached for her hand and rasped, "Can I have this dance?"

It's MAY I have this dance, you skunking idiot!

One moment her hands were swiping away tears, and I knew with gut-twisting certainty she'd take another step back, then another, and she'd pretend she'd never crashed into me.

But then, by yet another miracle, she nodded and took my hand.

Her warm palm slid over mine, her fingers curling over the back of my hand, shooting sparks up my arm.

For a frozen moment I wasn't sure I could actually take her waist without freaking out.

But then somehow, I did.

Her other hand slid up my arm to rest on my shoulder, absolutely assaulting my senses and destroying my concentration.

With a gulp, I stepped to the side, and she followed my lead.

And I was dancing with Mella Yarinelle.

Wow.

"I'm sorry for running into you," I said. "Are...are you okay?"

Of course she's not okay! What kind of question was that?

"I'm fine. Just a total idiot." She stared at the air between us, her galaxy eyes unfocused.

That bastard had made *this girl* of all people feel like an idiot? He'd reached an all-new low, and that was saying something.

"That's not true." If tonight was one for miracles, please let Mella not hear every time my voice cracked with nerves.

"What? That I'm fine or that I'm a total idiot?"

"Both."

She cracked the smallest of smiles, and that place in my chest that had squeezed so painfully now glowed with warmth.

If I wasn't careful, my inward freaking out was about to bleed over into outwardly freaking out.

What else could I do to make her smile like that again?

I tried to control my voice. "Am I right?"

"Well, I guess you're right about me being not fine. But completely wrong about my idiocy status. I am one hundred percent the biggest idiot in Wrynford—in all of Terrenthyrs."

"Hmm." I squinted at the ceiling, pretending to deliberate. Her hip swayed under my hand with each step, sending unbearably pleasant tingles through my fingers and up my arm. "I guess we'll have to agree to disagree."

An ever-so-slightly bigger smile.

My chest leaped with delight, and somehow it translated to my fingers in hers twitching. My thumb brushed her knuckle by accident, and I held my breath.

Skunks! Did she notice?

Her eyes fell on our hands, and my chest emptied of all emotion, hollowing out for her to let go and back away.

But she *stayed*.

She gazed at our hands and remained in my arms.

In a rush, feeling pumped back into my chest. I could breathe again.

"Yeah, I guess so," she whispered.

"Do you want to tell me what's wrong?"

No! That's going to scare her off! Don't be pushy just because you're curious about how much of a skunk Kaido made himself.

Her rich black lashes rose delicately as she lifted her eyes to mine, still slightly red from how much that scum had hurt her. But there were no more tears. Was that because of me?

My chest squeezed with a combination of pain for her and thrilling admiration of how close she was to me right now.

If only she could understand how enthralling she was. If only she could see herself through my eyes, to understand how much I wanted to tell her. It filled me so full I could never begin to explain without everything bursting out in an avalanche of nonsense.

What if she forgave the bastard for whatever he'd done? A wordless shout against anything so horrible screamed inside me, but I restrained it.

In this moment, her tears were dry, her eyes bright, and her gaze timid but so nearly warm I almost shook with a desire for her to understand how okay it was to be herself. She didn't have to say anything else. She could just be. In my arms. As long as she liked.

Please, just one more dance.

"Actually, Dane, I'd rather talk about literally anything else, if you don't mind."

"Of course. We can talk about whatever you want."

She smiled again, and I beamed, my chest full of happiness and victory fist pumps.

"I was wondering if you and Sprinter could help Whisper and me with this technique."

She launched into a hypothesis, and I hung on her every word, my gaze sliding between her lips and her gorgeous eyes.

The next dance began, and then the one after that, but she showed no sign of noticing the transition. Maybe this could be the beginning of something between us. But that couldn't be rushed. I'd had several months to sort things and decide how I felt about her.

She didn't remember me, so she'd had barely any time at all, and she'd been deceived by Kaido. Maybe now there was some kind of chance for us. Maybe. Hopefully.

But for tonight, I would dance with her as long as she'd let me, and I'd do whatever I could to take her mind off the snake-headed skunkass, to bring that perfect smile back to her lips.

No matter how long it takes, Mella Yarinelle, please, don't let this be the last time I get to hold you.

CHAPTER 39

ACRES

This is such a waste of time.

I'd rather be at my desk pouring over tedious floramancy notes, sick from another failed experiment, even, than at a ball with far too many sweaty people dancing around and being loud and bumping into me.

My desk was quiet. And covered in interesting books and scrolls, with bits of rocks and small fossils holding them in place.

But instead, I'm here. What's the shortest I can stay?

Loud music had been assaulting me since I first strode through the doors a little while ago. I found a nice dark corner to lurk in—hopefully unnoticed—behind some empty tables far from the musician's stand.

Dresses of crimson, azure, amber, and sapphire sashayed in some pattern I couldn't comprehend. I probably should've taken those dancing lessons back home instead of reading.

Actually, my time had definitely been better spent perusing field guides and philosophies.

I took a deep breath, fantasizing about the smell of books, and instead picked up on notes of chocolate and plumb and something spicy.

Refreshments?

Servants came toward me laden with wooden platters of food and drink. They were heading for those stupid tables all along.

Catching sight of the crowd coming, too, in the wake of deli-
cious-smelling treats, I slid behind a tapestry.

Which was already occupied.

"What the muck!" the girl hissed, stepping back and then in my face
again to keep from being seen.

Leaning as far out of her way as I could without being seen from
outside, I said, "I'm so sorry. I didn't know yo—"

"Shh!" She waved a hand in my face. "Don't let him hear you!"

I held my tongue and peeked around the tapestry to see who we were
hiding from.

Far too many people crowded around the punch for me to know who
she meant.

Once the crowd started dispersing with their goblets of pink liquid,
she took a step back and jumped when she landed on my foot. "Skunks.
Are you hiding too?"

I winced, shifting my weight to the foot she hadn't impaled with her
heel. "Sort of. Who are you hiding from?"

"That skunk, Drazdan Calentine. I don't know why Willova...well,
never mind. He got his punch and he's walking to the other end of the
hall. Thank good fortune." She rolled her eyes. "Acres, isn't it? You cast
a serval. Stargazer?"

I tried to stop my eyebrows from shooting right off my head. This
girl knew who I was? Who was she? I should've paid better attention.
"Starstinger, yes."

She nodded and held out her hand. "Selverine."

Princess Selverine? Skunks.

"Nice to meet you." I shook her hand. It was slightly sweaty. Sliding
my hand over my pant leg, I wondered if some punch might help her feel
less worried about this Drazdan guy.

My many unfortunate brushes with floramancy left me suspicious of
unfamiliar refreshments. But I couldn't think of anything else to say, and
I didn't want this girl to think I was an idiot. Besides, I'd eaten some
pelinary petals to neutralize anything suspicious at lunch. They were
probably still working, right? "Punch, Selverine?"

She smiled. She had a nice smile. "Sure. Thanks."

I slipped out from behind the curtain and filled two goblets with the foamy pink liquid. It smelled sharp and fruity, but I couldn't detect anything suspicious. Some pelinary petals to counteract the overtalkativeness of some drinks would've been nice, but I didn't have any on me.

Glancing around, I slipped behind the tapestry without being seen.

CHAPTER 40

SELVERINE

"Thanks, Acres." I accepted the goblet of punch and took a sip.

He followed suit. "So what did this Drazdan guy do?"

I eyed Acres, his unexpectedly deep, attractive voice grabbing my attention. Yes, I certainly did remember that from the Castling Ceremony. And from spying on Mella in the woods. He was in her cohort. Could he be useful?

"Drazdan's just...weird."

"So am I, I hear." He lifted the punch and sipped.

With his locs bunched into a knot and his spectacles as big as his face, he had a unique look. He wasn't a bad-looking guy, though. *I'd wager he's decently attractive behind those spectacles. I hope this makeup on my nose is doing its job.*

And he acted like a normal person instead of throwing heavy-lidded leers at me and trying to convince me he was better than all the other guys in the room. Which was a nice change and a plus for someone to be stuck behind a tapestry with.

"I'm not talking about his looks. I'm talking about his...like...*vibe*. He just...creeps me out."

It wasn't as if I had to marry—and why would I pay attention to any of them if I did? I didn't give a skunk's butt about a single one, and the king had other plans for passing on the kingdom. Didn't they realize he didn't care for me? It was obvious with every cold look and pointed glance away from me.

Though, if this Acres wanted to prove me wrong about the worthlessness of the male population of Terrenthyrs, I wouldn't mind hearing more of his exquisite voice. Hopefully he wouldn't wind up being just like the rest of them.

Peering around the tapestry, I glared at Mella, looking unhappy as she danced with that guy who'd cast a gorilla. I hoped *she* was unhappy. I'd have my revenge on her yet for keeping the secret of avian castling from me.

Before the night was out, I'd convince her my cohort wanted her as long as she could perform on Wager Day. Then I'd find out how she'd done it, then let slip about her low-birth mother. If that wasn't enough to get her removed from my cohort with an unsalvageable reputation, I'd make her life miserable enough that she'd remove herself.

I glanced around the curtain to check on Drazdan, and several pairs of eyes besides his turned to mine. Shoving the curtain back over me, I tried to steady my heartbeat. *What the heck?*

"Wow," Acres said, blinking like he'd just woken up. He wiped away a splash of punch from his lips and stared at me differently than before. "You're really hot."

"What?" Disappointment clouded my changing mood, despite the resonance of his voice. Maybe I could turn his apparent infatuation into something useful against Mella, but the idea exhausted me. I was more disappointed than I should've been. He'd turned out to be just like everyone else. What a shock.

Wiping his mouth again, he offered me his soiled arm. "May I have this dance?" He grinned with all his teeth in a way that didn't seem natural.

Definitely misjudged this guy. Just your typical creep.

"That's a hard no. I'll see myself out."

I stepped out from behind the tapestry to find nearly all eyes on me. Drazdan was wading through the crowd in my direction. I spotted Kaido and darted for him. He was at least a manageable creep. Much better than Drazdan.

I threw an arm around him and dredged up a smile. "Hey, Kaido. How's it going?"

One arm came around me, his other still around Frenna in a lavender gown. To my surprise, she looked even happier to see me than he did. Not at all annoyed at my embracing her date. She just took another sip of punch and smiled at me.

"Hi, Selverine. How are you?" She beamed like I was the best thing since casting the animal you most wanted as your castling.

"Uh..."

Other people were beaming at me, too. And those who weren't were sending me nervous smiles.

"Selverine!" Drazdan had caught up to me. *Skunks.* I faced him, letting go of Kaido's overly eager arm, and felt nauseous. Drazdan gazed at me like I was his long-lost true love. Which I most definitely was *not*.

He grabbed my hand in both of his and knelt in front of me before I could escape. "Selverine, will you marry me?"

CHAPTER 41

ACRES

Wow, that girl Selverine looked amazing tonight. But apparently everyone else thought so, too. Nearly the entire room stared at her. They'd all want to beat me to her, I was sure. I tore out from behind the tapestry and strode after her, setting my goblet on a table. I had to get there first, or I'd have no chance with her.

She crossed the hall toward Kaido Felzane and threw her arm around him.

No! Don't choose him! Give me a chance, please!

I stumbled, and some guy cut in front of me. Regaining my footing, I raced him to Selverine. But he beat me to her and was down on one knee before I could knock him out of the way.

What? Why didn't I think of that?

But she looked shocked and then angry. Good—surely she was waiting for me. I took a step toward them, but she slid around him and darted for the door.

"Wait! Selverine!" I shouted, reaching toward her as I tried to follow her through the thick crowd.

The crowd moved with me, scrambling after her. I lost sight of her in the midst of so many people.

The further away she ran, the more hopeless I felt. But why did I feel hopeless? What had I been thinking anyway? I'd only ever spoken to her once.

Shaking my head, I allowed the others to push past me and tried to clear my thoughts. I didn't know her at all. What was I thinking? I didn't want to marry that girl. What had gotten into me?

That's enough socializing for one night. I'd done what Starstinger had asked—for the most part. Now I needed to get back to work.

I pushed through the sweaty dancers just outside the door, holding my breath. Several half-finished and full goblets sat in the hands of the few people who merely craned their necks to see what was going on.

Hmm...

Frowning, I turned and saw that people running after Selverine gripped empty goblets, and shimmering glass shards covered the cobblestones in places. But almost no liquid spills.

Had all the crazies drunk more punch than those who stayed at the party?

What the skunk was in that punch? And why didn't my pelinary petals neutralize it?

CHAPTER 42

SELVERINE

I stretched my cramping fingers, trying in vain to keep a graceful stride. It was more of a pissed-off run for cover.

What was Drazdan thinking, *proposing* to me? I didn't even know the guy!

I glanced over my shoulder. My following had trickled down to a small handful of obnoxious shadows. As soon as I was in the palace, I could shut them out.

What in the world had happened to make them act like this? And *Acres* even. He'd seemed decent, not like Kaido or Drazdan.

Having more disappointment over his brazen attitude than everyone else's behavior didn't make sense. But at least I was almost home. My grandmother would know what to do.

"Good *night*!" I called as I restrained my annoyance enough to shut the door calmly.

"Selverine?" Grandmother called from the stairs.

So she wasn't in bed yet. Good.

"You're home rather early from the ball. Are you well?"

"Grandmother, you'll never believe what happened."

She rang for the teakettle and dropped leaves into two cups for us as I launched into the weird way everyone was acting. "And I was graceful about refusing Drazdan, even though I'm sure everyone else thought it was just as ridiculous as I did. I'm sure you would've been proud of me."

A servant entered and set a teakettle on the tray in front of Grand-mother, then bowed and left.

"I just can't figure out why he did it. We didn't even *go* to the ball together, Grandmother. We just met there, and chatted less than five minutes before he left to stuff his face. A few minutes later and he was on one knee proposing. I can't imagine he could've taken anything I did as a sign I wanted anything to do with him, much less to *marry* him."

Grandmother handed me the steaming cup, and I took a sip of calming liquid. The refreshing scent of spiced chamomile floated up in a curl of steam, calming me. I kept the bit about hiding behind a tapestry with Acres Parrianther—from the Wrynford Cohort, of all things—to myself. For some reason, I didn't feel like sharing that.

Her kind face wrinkled in concern. "What a night you've had, dear. Yes, you certainly were right to refuse the boy. I, too, wonder what could have possessed him to make such a bold move. How strange."

"You know, all the weirdness seemed to happen after they brought out the refreshments. Maybe...I don't know. Maybe one of the snacks was off? Some expired ingredients, maybe? That still wouldn't ex-plain why *everyone* caught a sudden case of Selverine-obsession rather than an upset stomach, though."

Her eyes held mine as she took a long sip of tea. Lowering the cup, she asked, "Have you discussed this with Horizon?"

I fought the urge to slump and tried not to fist my hands. "No. I know I should, though." I reached for my trident.

"Wait." Grandmother's teacup clinked against the saucer. "Have more tea first. Then, you're right, when you're more relaxed, you should include her in your deliberations."

I pulled my hand back to my lap. More tea? Did I still seem upset? Well, I wasn't in a hurry to discuss my choices with the little floof anyway. If she even bothered to show up, which she probably wouldn't.

Grandmother stood, retrieved my half-full cup, and set it by the teapot.

"I can finish that—"

"Of course, dear. Let me just top it off for you." She poured more tea into the cup and then dropped a dainty spoonful of something else into it and stirred.

"What was that?"

"Something to help you calm down, like before. You've had such an unusual and stressful night. You should relax and get a good night's sleep." She tapped the spoon on the cup's edge and laid it on the tray. With the cup held between her hands, she returned it to me. "Here you are, dear. Did you let Mella Yarinelle know of your intentions to bring her into your cohort after Wager Day?"

"Thank you for the tea." I accepted it without meeting her eyes. "Unfortunately, I wasn't able to talk to Mella before everything got weird."

I took a sip, thinking how nice it would be to escape the strange evening in a dreamless sleep. Grandmother's tea was perfect for a dreamless sleep. When I woke after drinking it, I never remembered a thing.

"You'll get another chance to discuss it with her, I'm sure. Now drink up. Then you can cast your castling."

I took another sip, then frowned. "But I don't want to cast my castling. She isn't what I wanted."

Grandmother smiled, gesturing for me to sip again. "That's right. She's not. You're angry with her for manifesting as a wolverine rather than an avian, aren't you?"

She was absolutely right. I completely loathed that ridiculous excuse for a castling.

"And you liked having everyone pay attention to you after they drank Jorros's punch, didn't you?"

Did I? That was an odd question. The king's punch? What did the king have to do with the punch? "It was kind of weird—"

She frowned. "Take another sip, dear. And one more. There. Now, wasn't it nice that everyone paid so much attention to you tonight? Just like you deserve?"

The overwhelming rightness of what she said settled in my head. It made *so* much sense. I did deserve for everyone to want to be my friend, to do whatever I wanted. "Yes. It was a nice feeling, having them all focus on me and treat me like the royalty I am. I deserve their respect and admiration."

"You absolutely do, Selverine. Whenever people act like they did tonight, you should let them and help them understand that you do deserve their awe. You can command them as you like, and they have to do what you say, as long as you mean the commands you speak. You can do that, right, Selverine?"

"Definitely. It makes perfect sense."

Narellen nodded, her expression dimming to sadness.

"Grandmother, what's wrong?" I had to help her, the poor thing. She shouldn't be upset.

"It's just too bad your castling is such a disappointment, isn't it?"

Anger roared through me. She was absolutely right. That wretched castling.

"She's the reason things aren't right. The only thing wrong with your life, you know."

"She is. Such a disappointment."

Her eyes brightened a little, like she had a good idea. "Maybe it would be better not to have any castling than to have such a disappointing one."

"You're absolutely right. I'd rather not have any castling if I can't have an avian. Horizon is not my castling."

She nodded. "You should keep her from continuing to ruin your life. Shouldn't you?"

"I should. Immediately. I'll shatter my trident. Then she'll never humiliate me again."

"No!" Grandmother blocked my trident by sitting on the couch between it and me. "No, you can't let anyone *know* you cut her off. People who don't understand would talk. We don't need their interference, do we?"

I frowned, confused. "Wait, I didn't mean that. I wouldn't ever shatter—"

"Your tea is getting cold, Selverine. Drink up."

I drained the cup and smacked my lips. "Mm."

Grandmother smiled. "Now. This is what you should do about your troublesome castling."

She laid out a plan, and it made so much sense. She was so good at strategizing. I would do precisely what she suggested.

"You must forget this conversation until it's time, all right? It isn't quite time yet." She reached for my teacup, filling it up once more.

I accepted the warm drink from her. "Yes. You're absolutely right."

CHAPTER 43

ACRES

"It wasn't so bad, was it?" Starstinger greeted me from the foot of the bed when I walked through my door.

"Well, I think I offended the princess, so that wasn't ideal."

Her kitten smile fell as her ears stood straighter. "You did what?"

"And that's not all," I told her, sliding out of my shoes and flopping into the desk chair. I told her what a weird night it had been. "So you see, I would've been way better off sitting here reading like I wanted to anyway. And now there might be someone floramancing party drinks, with something pelinary petals aren't enough to neutralize, to top it off. Should I be worried about that? I feel like I should probably be worried about that."

Starstinger stretched her lanky body all the way out, her sharp claws winking out from between her toes. "Well, at least you spoke to some other human beings." With a yawn, she curled into a ball and wrapped her twitching tail around her feet.

Plucking a dapplemint leaf from the windowsill, I frowned down at her. "That's all you've got to say? What about the floramancy?"

She shrugged. "Didn't you eat pelinary petals at lunch?"

"Yes."

"Then you learned something valuable tonight—either there's something they can't work against, or their effect lasts for a shorter amount of time than the hours between when you ate lunch and when you drank the punch."

"You make a good point."

"Of course I do." She grinned.

"All right, well, I've been to the ball now." I stuffed the leaf in my mouth and retrieved the journal. "Can I please read?"

Propping my feet on the desk, I blew dust off the cover, flipped back to page two, and ran a finger over my grandmother's neat handwriting. What would I learn about her in these pages?

Starstinger stuck her tongue out at me. "And you can skip training tomorrow, and I won't say a thing, as promised. Good night, Acres."

She closed her big eyes and rested her head on her paws. She'd grown into her ears a bit, but they were still a speck or two too big for her head. Which was adorable.

"Good night, Starstinger."

I read about my grandmother's forced betrothal to her first husband, who was a horrible man indeed. About her best friend's baby being born. I could've lived with fewer of those details. And about her performances playing the harp.

I read another page and paused, confused by the change in tone. Her writing suddenly sounded like it came from a different person. Were there missing pages? I checked, but it didn't seem like it. All of the sudden she was gushing about the new queen and how wonderful she was. Several pages later, she alluded to someone named Bennet having his weapon shattered.

A shattering?

But she glossed right over it and went on about the queen. And not another mention of playing the harp. Had she stopped playing it? Did someone steal it?

I flipped the page and found several empty. She'd just stopped writing. Why? Had someone else written the last few entries? If not, what had caused the change in her?

I wracked my tired brain, but then my candle flickered and went out. I realized by the ache in my shoulders that I'd been reading for hours. Starstinger was nowhere to be found—must've passed out a while ago.

With the candle out, the faint blue haze of morning was visible around the curtains' edges. I yawned, deciding I could probably make more sense of this after a little nap. I slid under the corner of covers not covered in books and notes and drifted to sleep.

***

"Mella!" I waved her over from the campfire the next morning, stuffing the last bite of a sandwich in my mouth.

Something was really weird about all this, and she was the only person who might be able to connect it. And apparently it bothered me enough to meet the others for training even after Starstinger had promised to give me the day off.

Mella eyed me suspiciously but walked over. "So we're on speaking terms again?"

"Listen, you said the coyote castor who died in prison was named Bennet, right?"

"Yeah." Her eyebrows drew together.

"I overheard someone talking the other day about a shattering forty years ago."

She crossed her arms, failing to keep a straight face.

"And it happened to someone named Bennet. And I found my grand-mother's journal, and she mentioned the same thing—a nice castor named Bennet having his weapon shattered. But what bothers me is the whole tone of her journal changed right after it happened. She started writing a ton of muck about what a wonderful person the new queen was, and she stopped caring so much about—other stuff that had both-ered her before. And she stopped playing the harp. I hadn't even known she'd played an instrument. But she gushed about it in the diary until that day."

Mella's jaw dropped along with her crossed arms. "What if the laws about playing music started the same time as the shattering?"

"Yeah, looks like it. But why? It's never made sense that musicians, who have to work so hard for their skills, are punished with lower status for it."

She frowned, staring into the distance.

I eyed her. "What are you thinking?

"I'm not sure. I need to think about it some more."

"Come on, Mella. You owe me an explanation after everything that happened in the library."

"I know. I'm still really sorry about casting Starstinger and about you losing your library pass. But I just don't know what all this means. I need to talk to Whisper."

She turned on her heels, and my arm flashed out to stop her. The moment I touched her, a swerving sensation came over me, just like the night Trinka came for the deecho root.

And all at once, I *knew*.

Mella's castling was different.

Whisper came from the mandolin rather than the scythe, and she'd manifested as a coyote to someone else before. Possibly Bennet?

And something about Mella's fear of being found out.

"Let go of me!" she hissed, tearing her arm from my grasp.

I stumbled and landed heavily on the ground, my head dizzy. Had the same thing that happened with Trinka just happened with Mella?

But how had I done it?

"Acres?" Mella leaned toward me but didn't touch me. "Are you okay?"

I sat up and rubbed my temples. "Muck."

"What just happened? It felt like you just...sucked energy out of me or something."

Oh no. I hadn't taken her memories, had I? "Did your castling used to be a coyote?"

Her confusion hardened into a scowl. "What the skunk—how'd you know that?"

So she still knew everything I did—no memories lost from those I'd just seen. But explaining it would be too difficult. I needed to record exactly what happened so I'd at least know what might've influenced it. But it was unlikely Mella had any deecho root on her.

"Have you eaten at the Loaf recently?"

"What? No, not in a few days. Why?"

So what floramancy made this happen?

"Did you see anything weird just now? Thoughts that weren't your own?"

"Acres, you're not making any sense. Why would I have seen someone else's thoughts? Yours?"

I pushed myself up and shakily stepped back. "I've got to go. I'll see you later." I stumbled into the woods toward my apartment.

"Acres! Wait! Acres?"

"I'll explain later!" I called over my shoulder.

I had to figure this out immediately. Was I closer to finding the potion to help Trinka, or just that much more lost and confused?

CHAPTER 44

DANE

S weat darkened the underarms and back of Mella's forest-green sleeveless tunic as she propped her scythe against an Emberlyn tree and leaned against its base. "Good spar, Dane."

"You, too." She was so fast, it was ridiculous. But I'd won this match, and I was proud of that.

I couldn't believe my luck at getting to spar with her so much more often since Reenalyn and Beldon had set me up to dance with her. Something changed that night, and there wasn't the same awkwardness between us.

She hadn't fallen madly in love with me, which would've been nice, but we were more like good friends now, which was better than before. I'd even gotten close to telling her how I knew her from before. One of these days, I'd actually do it. I wasn't sure I was ready for her to know yet.

Mella's eyes went to Sprinter, who was loping up to us. He nosed my side, silently requesting ear scratches. I patted his head and scratched behind his ears.

Mella asked, "Do you think they'll notice Sprinter is basically unchanged since the ceremony?"

I sighed, sliding down the tree trunk a few specks from her, enormously aware of her presence. "I've been worrying about that every minute since before casting. But there was nothing I could do to disguise him as a puppy, since when a castling is cast, they just are as they are. They can't take a disguise or anything with them. He did do a pretty good job acting like one, but he clearly had adult proportions."

She nodded. "Yeah. I guess it helps that I was able to hide Whisper for the first six months, so her age won't be as noticeable now. But being an avian, she won't go unnoticed. Hopefully most of them will just be impressed." She made a face. "She's better at flying, but I worry we could be disqualified or something for being an enigma."

"Has that ever happened before?" I hadn't heard of it.

"Not that I know of. But no one besides the queen has cast an avian, either."

"She wasn't punished though, was she?"

Mella frowned. "I don't think so. I don't actually know. We learned the histories of our royals, but I don't remember that part of her story."

"It might not be bad. And your parents will see you and realize what a huge mistake they've made and want you back."

"Yeah."

I stared at her, eyes wide. "You wouldn't go back to them after they treated you like that, though, right?"

She shrugged. "I guess not. It's just a nice thought, you know? It would be nice to get my normal life back. But I intend to get it in a different way. Them taking me back would be a shortcut, but they won't. Father needs to keep his social standing, and even though I wasn't enough to do that before, he could get that through me if I win."

Her father's treatment of her angered me to no end. "Mella, none of that is your fault. Something is seriously wrong with him. Don't you think family should always be more important than *social standing*?"

"But what if your family is bringing you down?"

"Then I guess you find a way to lift them back up."

She raised an eyebrow. "You left your family to come here."

Ouch. "I did, but not because I wanted to get away from them. And I'm planning to go back for them after the Grand Castors' Tournament."

Was that a shadow of regret behind her eyes? Why? Would she miss me?

"Okay. But what if our cohort does win and you get a chance to be someone important if you stay? Someone who'd get their high lifestyle paid for and didn't have to work a regular job and who would be well-known and invited to all the parties and—"

"I'd still go back for my family, Mella. No amount of social status can make a bunch of fake friends worth giving up people who truly care about me, people who've made sacrifices for me. Haven't you ever had friends or family like that? Surely you wouldn't give them up for hundreds of people who only pretend to be your friend because of what they can get out of it."

She glared at me. "My social aspirations aren't up for criticism here, Dane."

Shoving to her feet, she was about to walk away.

But she wasn't really so shallow. I knew better. She was the most giving person in the world. She'd just never felt true friendship long enough—she didn't know how important it was. If only I could get past my deeper-than-friendship feelings for her enough to show her that kind of fierce friendship.

"Mella, wait, please." I stood too.

"What?" With her hands on her hips, she glared daggers at me.

"I'm sorry for offending you. I didn't mean to. It's just that I wish you could experience the kind of real friendship I've been lucky enough to have. People who love you and would do anything for you, no matter who or what you are. And not for what they can get out of you. It's the best feeling, and I wish you could feel it too."

"That's great, Dane. Thanks so much." She whirled again, and I jogged after her.

"Think of Reenalyn. Isn't she your closest friend? She's helped you with the mandolin. And you two are always talking."

"Yes, we're friends. And I'll always be friends with her and everyone else in my cohort. But that doesn't mean I want to live in Wrynford my whole life."

If that was what she wanted, fine. I couldn't change her mind. But if that meant I only had a few more weeks to spend with her, I wouldn't waste a single second.

I pumped my arms to keep pace with her, Sprinter loping at my side. "Have dinner with me at the Loaf sometime. Celebrating accomplishments is something else friends do, you know, and we've both come a long way in the last few months."

She slowed to a stop. "Dane, I don't think that's the best idea."

My chest ached that she still didn't return my feelings. But this wasn't about me. This was about her never having known what it was like to have real friends. She needed to know so if she did go back to her old life full of fakers, she could remember how fulfilling life could really be and maybe get another chance at it.

"As friends, Mella. Let me celebrate our castlings' progress with you."

Still facing away, she drummed her fingers on her arm. I could picture the exact face she was making, even though I couldn't see it. Not wanting to hurt my feelings, but not wanting to encourage me and hurt me more later.

One thing might convince her. But could I risk it? I took a deep breath and realized I'd want her to know something deeper about me before we went our separate ways. Yes, it was worth the risk.

"I'll explain about the tent peg."

Her head lifted, and she turned slowly, regarding me with those heart-wrenching ocean eyes. I tried not to let emotion shudder through me. Would I really be able to convince her it was just as friends? I could handle it, but could I really tamp down my feelings? I had to try. She couldn't go back to her old life without knowing riches and social standing weren't everything.

"As friends?"

"Yeah. The Braided Loaf?"

"All right. I look forward to hearing about how that tent peg became your castling weapon."

I nodded. "I'll tell you the whole story."

Chapter 45

MELLA

I jogged away from Dane, throwing my frustration into every step. Ever since that dance—which had felt like it was over much too quickly for having lasted until the lights were dimmed and everyone else had left—he wouldn't stop going on about *friends*.

I completely deserved it after rejecting him for Kaido over and over. Of course it would look mucky of me to switch my affections from Kaido to Dane the moment Kaido dumped me. Like I couldn't handle being single. But it seemed enough time had passed that Dane didn't feel as he had before.

"Mella!"

I slowed and found Reenalyn jogging toward me, Cupid bouncing on her shoulders. I tried to smile. "Hi, Reenalyn."

She stopped in front of me and took a deep breath, looking more subdued than her usual sunny self. "I've barely seen you since the ball. How are you doing?"

The genuine concern in her voice was the only thing that stopped me from snapping at her. It wasn't her fault my heart was so late to the game. "I've been busy with tasks for the leatherwork shop, but I'm fine. I don't really want to talk about it."

Selverine wouldn't have looked as concerned as Reenalyn, wouldn't have tried to help me in the first place. And I was really going to leave this group of good people who cared about me for a cohort of people who didn't?

"Should Beldon and I have stayed out of it? We just wanted to help—"

Closing my eyes, I took a step back and breathed slowly as guilt and frustration churned in my chest. "Reenalyn, it's fine. I appreciate you trying to help, but I just don't want to talk about it, okay?"

She pinched her lips, her eyes moist. She felt so bad for me she was about to cry.

Kaido had smirked at me. Yulroe would've laughed. But not Reenalyn. Or Dane.

"Look, Reenalyn, I really need some time alone to think. Okay? Don't worry about me. I just need some time."

She nodded and turned to leave without a word.

I started jogging again. How had I gotten into this mess? I'd never intended to stick with these people, but they'd treated me like I belonged. And they'd been nicer than everyone else I knew.

But what about Dane?

My feelings for Dane had come on much more slowly than my attraction to Kaido, but it was... Different. He never tried to get anything out of me—which was clearly all Kaido had been interested in. And Dane talked with me about everything—sparring, castlings, even the harder things like our families. And he asked me questions about myself like he genuinely wanted to learn.

Why had this attraction never been more apparent than when he reminded me that we were just friends?

It was what I deserved. For him to have moved on. What I had stupidly wished, at one point. But skunks did it hurt more each time I saw him since we danced.

Going to dinner with him *as friends* was sure to *not* help that. But I was curious about the tent peg, so at least it would answer that question. And I simply liked being around him. I even missed him. Though it had been uncomfortable how much he'd seen through me.

I slowed to walk the rest of the short distance to my mandolin's hiding place. If only I could erase the ghost of his hand on my waist—though it had been a few days since the dance, the weight of it was so fresh—or the way my hand looked so *right* in his. Or how he always talked to me about everything like Kaido never had.

I couldn't remove all the surprising impressions I'd gotten from being so close for so long, either. How much taller he was than I'd thought. How much broader his shoulders were. How he didn't just have nice hands, but nice arms, too. All that climbing in trees. And he had this one smile I only ever saw when he looked at me. That smile seemed to mean something special.

At least, it might have before I'd mucked everything up.

Ugh! Why hadn't I seen through Kaido's muck earlier on? Then maybe things could've been different with Dane. My heart squeezed. I should've listened to Reenalyn.

I sat on the log and reached under it for the case. Pulling it out, I undid the ties and released the mandolin. I stared at it, trying to pull my focus from the memory of being in Dane's arms to the task at hand. Wager Day was almost upon us, and we needed to practice.

With a sigh, I strummed my casting call.

Chapter 46

SELVERINE

S lumped in a chair in Grandmother's sitting room, I rubbed my aching forehead with both hands.

Wager Day was finally here, and my castling weapon was broken. Physically, the trident was fine. But something deeper was wrong. Horizon was uncastable. Unreachable. I'd recited my casting call three times in the last few minutes, but nothing worked.

My pulse hammered in my ears. Why wasn't it working? My castling wasn't anything that spectacular, but still. I couldn't walk onstage with *no castling*!

An unfamiliar twinge of concern for Horizon's well-being pricked in my chest. Was something the matter with her?

Straightening, I lifted the trident and gripped it as hard as I could. I pulled myself up from the chair and stood, placing my other hand on the trident as well. I tried once more, pouring all the energy and passion I could dredge up into the call.

Nothing.

I fisted my shaking fingers. It was too late. The ceremony was about to begin—the citizens ready to choose who to bet on. I'd just have to go without her.

***

The little room off the upper stage we'd each disappeared into six months ago with our castlings was a different sight now. The various castlings had grown considerably, and together the castors and castlings filled the space to nearly bursting.

Most of them congregated with awed whispers—probably gawking at Mella's skunking eagle. I ignored them, taking advantage of the breathing room by the window overlooking the stage.

I eyed the many castlings. Horizon had barely grown since I'd first cast her, but the rest looked nearly adult-sized.

Adding that to my many frustrations, I peered out the window. The king and queen reclined in their arena thrones, their backs to me and their castlings at their sides. At their feet sat two huge stone basins. I frowned. Usually there was only one. Why the extra basin?

A burst of surprised coos came from the huddled castors. I frowned, wishing Mella's admirers would shut up already.

The king addressed the crowd and drew out a few cheers, then called out for Beldon Berroman to approach the stage. The huge boy pushed through the new castors and castlings with his humongous gorilla—really, castlings that big shouldn't be allowed.

Then the king called Willova, and I knew despite the sweat stains darkening the underarms of her overly fine, long-sleeved dress, she'd do fine if she'd quit overthinking every little thing. Faultless sauntered at her side, her striped back now reaching Willova's waist.

Then that giant of a girl named Reenalyn Demensey—what a last name. She beamed at everyone as she struggled to pull the lizard from her hair and strode from the room. At least the little green thing was considerably larger now. I rolled my eyes as Kaido Felzane entered the stage with Striker wound around his shoulders, and then braced myself for my own name.

"Selverine Merrandil!"

I pushed through the door, my trident in hand and no castling at my side. *Just call the next name already and get everyone's attention off me!*

I'd never win against a castor and castling by myself. Not that Horizon would've been much help, small and fluffy as she was. She could've at least *shown up*, though. My hands balled into fists as I wondered again what in the world was wrong with her.

The sun glared as I stepped next to Kaido, avoiding the queen's eyes. She wouldn't be pleased to see I'd not cast at all. And she'd be even more displeased to find I'd actually lost the ability altogether. I didn't even know that could happen.

I hoped my makeup covered my nose well.

If I couldn't figure out anything by my turn to fight, would my cohort get rid of me? Surely not. I was the queen's granddaughter. Technically a princess. Not that it would feel good to only be tolerated because of that. Skunk that castling! Why was she doing this to me?

I kept a calm mask over my growing terror as Acres Parrianther and his serval, Starstinger, crossed the stage. Then the short and bald Trinka Seranova and her black bear—surprisingly close to Trinka's height already, even on all fours—joined us, followed by the ghostly Dane with that unpronounceable last name and blotchy canine.

They each took their places on stage, and it was time for Mella Yarinelle.

The king called her name, and a wave of gasps rippled through the crowd when she strode through the door. I rolled my eyes.

Mella crossed the stage with a smile, her scythe held like a foreboding ebony staff at her side and the wretchedly spectacular eagle mounted on her shoulder.

A hush spread through the crowd as this incredible creature took everyone's breath away.

It was even more enormous and impressive this close, already larger than Selvenair, and unlike any wild avian I'd ever seen. It was gorgeous. Painfully beautiful and fierce to behold.

It was everything *I* should've had.

A roar of cheers and applause broke out as the crowd rose to their feet, a couple even standing on their seats.

My stomach twisted with jealousy and frustration. Why couldn't I have a redo? Why'd there have to be only one chance to cast a castling for life? *Ugh!* But I'd rather have some kind of castling than no castling at all! Wouldn't I?

I caught my grandmother's eye and quickly straightened, schooling my features to hopefully shield my pitiful jealousy.

What the actual skunk, Mella.

Mella and her eagle bowed slightly and took their spot a few castors down from me.

I leaned out to look past them.

The king gawked as much as the peasants. My grandmother alone had enough self-control to appear unaffected by this revelation.

Finally, the king sputtered out the names of the remaining castors and castlings. With eyebrows raised at Mella, he gestured for silence. "What a surprise we've had from one of our castors today!" Everyone applauded again. Obnoxiously. "And I'm delighted to say, my queen and I have our own surprise for our competitors."

I glanced away from the eagle to narrow my eyes at him. A new surprise?

He pulled four more strips of parchment from his pocket and made a show of balling them up and dropping them into the other basin. "In the past, sparring pairs have been obliged to fight with their weapons and castlings in every match, no exceptions. However, in order to further challenge our competitors and get the best impression of their success so far, we will have a different drawing for each pair to determine whether they will fight with only weapons, only castlings, both castlings and weapons, or nothing but their own hands and feet. What say you?"

He raised his hands to the crowd, and they erupted in cheers. Again.

What? Wasn't the point of this whole thing to see how well we'd all trained our castlings? Sure, the wagerers would get an idea of our dedication to training, but Wager Day has always been about the castor-castling relationship. Why change now? Surely Grandmother hadn't orchestrated this because of my failure?

But I wouldn't argue. A tiny surge of hope floated up in me at the idea that I had a fifty-fifty chance of not even being expected to show off my castling after all. Maybe this horrible development wouldn't ruin the whole competition for me. That would give me time to fix it before the Grand Castors' Tournament. Or maybe...did this mean it would be possible to recast? To get a second chance? If my castling had disappeared, but not died, could I get a new one? I had to get Mella's secrets out of her immediately.

My spirits rose at the thought. Maybe some good could come of this after all.

The king gestured dramatically to the stone basin and made a huge show of pulling out a name. "And our first castor today is..."

The king's voice faded behind my annoyance. Two castors parted from the line, followed by their castlings, and faced off in the ring. Who they were didn't matter.

All that mattered was that I was going to get back at Mella for this.

Someone elbowed Kaido, who's shoulder bumped mine as a result. "So when are you going to go crawling back to the Yarinelle girl, huh, Kaido? Unless you're really over her. In which case...hello, Mella."

"Back off, man. We both know she's still into me. Don't bother trying anything. Eagle Girl's all mine."

I rolled my eyes. They were welcome to her, and may they be as obnoxious toward her as they'd been to me. I glanced around for that Drazdan Calentine, hoping *he'd* get a load of Mella and redirect his attentions her way.

I considered the plans I'd come up with for revenge, mulling them over. Maybe I could make use of every single one of them. The only reason I hadn't managed to pull one off yet was because Grandmother had been forcing me into so many useless training sessions that I'd had no extra time.

Good thing all that work would be helpful today.

The line had thinned further without my noticing. Hopefully my own match would end as quickly as these seemed to.

"And Crous takes the victory! Well done, Frenna and Crous!" The king dipped his hand into the first basin and pulled out two more strips of parchment. "Yulroe Dinburr and Willova Calentine!"

Yulroe and Willova? That would be an interesting match, especially if they got to spar with their castlings. A tiger versus a cheetah. An obvious weight advantage for the tiger, but speed and dexterity for the cheetah.

I'd pay attention to that fight.

Willova had improved since we'd started sparring. She was a pretty good fighter once she got into it. She just had no confidence in her abilities, so once she messed up at all, she couldn't move past it. I couldn't imagine what her problem was. Always so humble and nitpicky about herself. Hopefully she wouldn't let it get in her way today.

Selecting one of the strips from the second basin, the king examined it. "Castlings *and* weapons! Willova and Yulroe, please enter the ring with your castlings and weapons. Please keep in mind if the castling of the winning castor is defeated by the loser's castling, the match is a draw and both participants will await an additional turn."

Willova crossed to the stairs with Faultless, her tiger castling, her right hand clutching her cutlass. She gripped it hard enough to whiten her knuckles. Probably not a good sign.

Yulroe strode right behind Willova, her shoulders back and her dark dreads tamed into a side ponytail. Her cheetah castling, Bolt, pranced next to her. Confidence practically dripped off Yulroe and Bolt both, while Willova seemed freshly squeezed out.

Willova trotted backward a few steps, moving to the other side of the ring while keeping an eye on Yulroe and Bolt. The two pairs squared up.

They were far enough away I couldn't hear them from up here—probably nobody in the stands could hear them either. I wondered what they were saying.

Then Yulroe made the first move, flying at Willova's shoulder while Bolt and Faultless leaped up and met midair, their back legs swinging as they dropped to the dirt floor, yowling and swiping.

Yulroe gained a span, and then another, as she used the advantage of her height over Willova's average stature. Willova's face remained expressionless as she blocked and parried, never gaining a strike of her own but never showing emotion about it either. Stoic as they come.

Finally she got creative and dropped her cutlass to punch Yulroe in the face, then with the toe of her boot tossed the cutlass back into her hand. That was an impressive move.

She gained a little ground then, pushing Yulroe back. Her red hair swung with each strike, and the beads in Yulroe's long locs bounced against each other, throwing sparks of sunlight.

And then a line of deeper red flashed open on Yulroe's exposed shoulder, and she let out a frustrated scream and glowered at Willova.

Willova's face was still blank, but her arms and shoulders were halfway raised as if she was shocked she'd won.

See? I told you, you could do it.

I realized I was proud of her, which seemed funny. But then the king was scooping out the next set of names, and my ears perked up.

"And our next pair will be...Mella Yarinelle..."

Skunks. Choose me. I'll fight her right now. My fingers twitched around my trident, ready for some good swings and blows.

"And Selverine Merrandil! Let's welcome our next sparring pair! And"—he made a dramatic dip toward the second basin and plucked a piece of parchment from within—"castling weapons will be allowed, but no castlings!"

No. Way. I couldn't believe my luck. I could've cheered along with the crowd.

Applause and shouts filled the arena. They were probably all cheering for Mella and her avian. But I'd show them. I was expected to tell her about the queen's wish for her to join my cohort, but I didn't have to let her win.

"Castors, please enter the ring and fight to first blood!"

I scowled and marched down the stairs into the dusty arena.

Mella hesitated, the avian still perched on her shoulder. If only those glorious talons would clench around her collarbone just a *little* too hard.

Mella crouched and held her arm up to an empty seat. The castling stepped down her arm to the chair. Rising, Mella followed me to the arena, taking the opposite side.

She grinned at me, and if any part of me had been unsure when said revenge was going to happen, that indecisiveness left me immediately.

I crouched and moved to the middle of the ring, brandishing my trident. Mella copied the move, her scythe raised.

Curiosity burned in me more than my duty to deliver the queen's message. "How'd you do it, Mella?" I hissed low enough for only her to hear.

"Do what?"

I jerked my chin toward the gargantuan avian perched on one of the seats, standing as tall as the man sitting next to her. "That."

She shrugged, swinging her scythe around once in a circle. "I said my casting call, and she appeared. That's all."

My eyes narrowed. She was *so* hiding more. Okay, then. I'd managed to dig up a few things about her family since I'd first discovered her castling. Maybe I could put that to use. "I imagine times are difficult for your family, Mella. Considering how much your fortunes have declined."

Was that too vague? Hopefully it would keep her guessing how much I knew.

Her focused stare broke into a grimace, pain darting across her face before she could stop it.

I struck at her shoulder.

She blocked me at the last moment and shoved me back, bringing down a strike of her own at my ribs. I dodged and jogged a few paces back, bouncing on my toes. Ready for her next move.

"So it's true then? Fortunes *are* quite low? You know, Mella, Frenna and I were just talking about visiting to see how you've been faring lately. Would you like us to come to your home? To have a look around inside?"

She controlled her features better this time, then spun and launched herself at me, her scythe making a sloppy arc toward my left as her anger outmatched her focus.

I grinned. This would be easier than I thought.

"It would be a shame if the decline of your family fortunes—and the mysterious condition of your home—were to become common knowledge."

Her eyes sparked as she scowled, heaving deep breaths.

"And the musician status of your dead mother...it would really be something if that were to get out."

She gritted her teeth and lunged at me.

I dodged and slammed my trident flat against her back, nearly knocking her to her knees.

"That could be avoided...if certain facts about avian castlings were to pass between us." I waited three beats to let that sink in, then darted forward again, launching at her neck.

She tripped out of the way, blocking me clumsily. So I *had* gotten to her. Good.

"So what'll it be, Mella? Are you going to let me in on your avian secrets, or should I let everyone else in on your family's?"

Worry and indecision flashed on her face, then she scowled. She came at me with even more rage and force than any of the last strikes. I blocked each one, awaiting her secrets. I'd won, and these were her last few moments of keeping them to herself. But they were within my grasp at last, and skunk it all if I wasn't going to try casting again. There had to be a way to get a better castling.

She paused, all her strength in her scythe pressed against my trident.

"Well then, Mella? I'm listening."

"I said my casting call, and Whisper appeared." She heaved a breath. "That's all."

Glowering, I tossed her off me, snagging her ankle with my foot and kicking her feet out from under her.

"All right." I hooked her scythe blade with my trident, ripping it out of her grip.

She scrambled to her feet and launched at me, but I blocked her with her own blade at her throat.

"What's that say right there, Mella?" I flicked my eyes to the name inscribed on her blade, and she followed my glance.

Her eyes hardened slightly.

"Interesting that your castling's name doesn't match the name you inscribed on your castling weapon. Has anyone even seen you cast before?"

She scowled, taking hold of the scythe handle and jamming the other end into my toes.

I winced and pulled back, brandishing my trident. "What's your *real* castling weapon, Mella? Tell me how you did it!"

I struck toward her shoulder to draw first blood, but she rolled away at the last instant.

She was suddenly on her feet, her scythe flying toward me. I threw up my trident to block, but the teeniest edge of the huge curved blade caught my sleeve.

Skunks! Skunks! Skunks!

But I didn't feel it break the skin.

My heart pounded in my ears.

"You only get to choose silence on one side: either me or you."

I spun and threw my trident at her thigh, slicing through both leather and flesh.

Mella's chest heaved as she regarded me for several loaded seconds. "That was unnecessary, you know."

I scowled at her. "What?"

She eyed my shoulder where the scythe had just barely brushed. It was bleeding. I stared at it, my stomach sinking into a puddle that was quickly swallowing up my pride. *Skunks!*

"You win today, but what about when I spill your secrets to—"

"Go ahead, Selverine. If you think the only way to beat me is to do something underhanded, then be my guest. I still beat you today, and I'll still beat you in the Grand Castors' Tournament."

I barely held in the urge to punch her stupid face. "Tell me how you did it," I hissed one last time, knowing it was hopeless.

She just stared at me.

"Fine. You be quiet. I'm about to get loud." I spun and stormed out of the ring.

Oh, it was on. And I was *so* not going to have her in my cohort.

CHAPTER 47

MELLA

I gritted my teeth against the pain in my thigh, mostly just pissed I'd let Selverine unnecessarily slice me. Skunks. And all her muck about my family—if I ever did manage to be a part of the winning cohort, which was less and less likely, that could be a big problem. Winning could get me into the right circles, but muck about my family could damage my reputation and get me tossed right back out. What good was being among the best if you were still the worst in the room?

And worst of all, no one had ever seen me cast. And if she pointed that out...even the Wrynford Cohort would surely have questions.

Ugh! Skunking Selverine!

King Jorros's flourishing movement as he reached for the first basin caught my eye. Teeth clenched, I sat next to Whisper and tugged my ruined fighting leathers around the wound to slow the bleeding.

I glanced up in time to see the king draw two pieces of parchment from the first basin and one from the second. "And our next sparring partners are...Kaido Felzane and Reenalyn Demensey! With both castlings *and* weapons! Let me remind you, Kaido and Reenalyn, that if the castling of the winning castor is defeated by the loser's castling, the match is a draw and both participants will ascend the stage to await an additional turn."

Reenalyn leaned on her spear, smiling at Kaido.

I squinted at her. Yeah, she was beaming at him. Like she was into him or something. That...seemed off.

Kaido smirked at the other better classers as he strode down the stairs in front of Reenalyn.

Swaggering into the ring with Striker around his shoulders, he smirked and coiled his whip in both hands. Reenalyn was still smiling sweetly at him, and it was weirding me out. She...surely she wouldn't have made up all that stuff about him being trashy because *she* wanted him, would she? I mean...I didn't think so. But why look at him all starry-eyed? She'd never looked at him twice as far as I knew.

He feinted to one side, then struck out with the whip toward her ankle. She dodged it quickly, but pretended to trip a little, as if he'd managed to hook her.

His smile darkened, and he glanced up at the crowd as if to encourage applause.

It would've been so easy to take him down while he was distracted. But she didn't.

Why didn't she strike while he was gloating?

His eyes returned to her, and she looked nervous now. Why would she be nervous? She was just as skilled as Kaido if not more.

He struck again, his whip wrapping around her wrist before she could stop it.

Oh no.

He yanked her toward him, leaving his legs wide open for a good ol' kick to the groin.

Which Reenalyn didn't take advantage of. *What the muck, Reenalyn? Take that skunk down!*

He flicked his wrist and the whip uncoiled, then struck out for her again. She caught the edge under her foot and slammed it down before it could wrap around her legs, then let it go so he couldn't rip it out from under her.

Well, at least that made sense. Nice one.

Scowling, he stepped cautiously forward.

She tossed her spear around so the blunt side faced him, which made no sense! *Reenalyn, you know how to hold a spear!* Did someone floramance her before this started?

Behind the fighters, Cupid danced nimbly around Striker, maybe trying to tire the large snake out.

And then suddenly, brandishing the spear, Reenalyn leaped at Kaido, aiming for his chest with the blunt end.

He dodged and swiped at her chest with one hand.

What the...? Did he really just go for her breast in the middle of a public fight? What a piece of skunking muck!

They paused a few spans apart, both breathing heavily, their eyes racing over each other to decide their next moves.

He flicked his wrist toward her face.

She grinned her first real grin of the match—finally a smile that didn't look like she was simpering after him like I had when I was an idiot.

Shielding her face with the spear handle, she let the whip curl around it several times at lightning speed, then wrenched it back. Had she done that on purpose?

With an outraged shout, Kaido lost his grip on the whip. It was out of his hand and across the arena.

Striker hissed at Cupid, who snickered.

Kaido sprinted toward her, and she crouched, eyeing his torso.

He aimed for her hip with one fist.

She dodged but didn't see the other fist. It struck her breast, throwing her back. She cried out and stumbled. Kaido laughed and aimed a kick at her side, knocking her from her awkward crouch to flat on the ground.

Cupid hissed.

"I'm fine! Stay on Striker!" she spat back.

Kaido loomed over her, his legs spread as he bounced from foot to foot.

"Ready for more, tramp?"

She considered him, but then Striker was in front of Kaido, also looming over Reenalyn, and Cupid hopped onto Reenalyn's side, hissing at the anaconda.

Striker regarded him with about as much respect as Kaido had for me.

Cupid tensed, then lurched to the side and leaped off Reenalyn, clamping his little jaws over Striker's nose.

The snake flung his head back.

Right into Kaido's crotch.

I shot to my feet, ignoring the pain in my thigh. Had that actually happened?

Kaido froze, then dropped in a fetal position, eyes squeezed shut in agony.

Reenalyn pushed herself up and retrieved her spear. She hefted the sharp end toward Kaido's face and lightly nicked a line from his nose, over his lips, toward his chin.

She scowled down at him and said, "First blood's all mine, Kaido Felzane. Now take a look at that crowd." She gestured to the spectators. "Most girls you chase are here today and will think of this moment when they see that scar over your lips."

It was a bright-red line now. Not dripping, but a clear sign of first blood, making Reenalyn the winner.

"I'm sure you'll find other girls, someday, and make up some story about how it's a battle wound. But at least as far as Terrenthyrs is concerned, no one will want to kiss the guy who got knocked in the balls by his own castling right after hitting his female opponent in the chest. Seriously desperate fighting tactics that *still* lost you the match. Have a nice life, Kaido. And don't mess with my friends."

Reenalyn held out an arm for Cupid to climb, then stood. With a smirk at Kaido, she walked out of the ring with her head held high.

Holy skunks! She'd been pretending to be into him and an incompetent opponent to get him off his guard! All the openings she could've taken advantage of, but she waited it out and let him make a fool of himself in front of everyone. And marked him for the skunk he was.

And warned him against messing with her friend again.

She'd done it all for her friend. Me.

Warmth filled my heart. Was this what Dane meant when he went on and on about real friends?

Chapter 48

SELVERINE

I threw my worthless trident onto a chair and flopped into a chaise lounge across from it. Willova followed me in more gracefully, sitting in another chair with her cutlass at her side and Faultless at her feet.

"Selverine, it will be okay. You still have a chance to beat Mella at the Grand Castors' Tournament."

I shifted away from her, ashamed. That wasn't all I was upset about. She had to know by now I'd lost my castling, or at least something was wrong. Even though I'd lost, I had to have some wagers on me by now simply for being royal, even though that was a silly reason. How could I appear before all those people at the Grand Castors' Tournament with no castling?

The queen's entrance may have spared me from a drawn-out silence with Willova, but it only brought more stress. I'd also failed to ask Mella to move to my cohort. I couldn't stand the thought of seeing her every day and being reminded again and again of her stupid castling.

"How did it go with getting Mella into your cohort, Selverine?" Grandmother asked as she gently lifted my trident, set it against the wall, and sat in its place.

I took a deep breath, dreading her disappointment so much that I couldn't find the words to tell her I'd failed. Not even failed, really, just never even tried. I just couldn't.

"Judging by what I saw in the ring and the fact that you're avoiding my eyes, I assume it didn't go well."

I dragged my gaze to hers. "I'm sorry, Grandmother."

"It is disappointing that I was relying on you, and you failed to deliver."

I flinched, ashamed.

"Fortunately, I sent a runner with a message to Mella as she was leaving with her cohort. She replied that she would be happy to meet me for tea tomorrow to discuss her impressive performance today."

My cheek twitched. Mella, invited here? Tomorrow? To discuss her *impressive* performance? "Grandmother, you can't really mean to—"

"Don't presume to tell me what I can and can't do, Selverine. I am the queen. You would do well to remember that." She rose from her seat and swept from the room.

I'd forgotten Willova was even here, but she shifted in her seat, and I flushed.

"I'm...I'm sorry you had to see that."

"It didn't seem that bad to me."

I faced her. "You didn't think that was humiliating?"

"She just talked. Didn't even raise her voice."

I dropped my gaze to the floor. "She doesn't have to."

"It could be a lot worse, you know," she whispered so lightly I could barely hear.

Glancing up at her, I frowned. "I don't see how that's possible."

Now she was the one to look away. "It's just...not as bad as it could be."

"Willova—"

"You really should clean your shoulder wound, you know."

Ugh, I did *not* want to think about that stupid thing right now. Scowling at it, I said, "It better not scar."

I didn't want to remember this mucking skunk of a day every time I looked in a mirror.

"I...I could show you how to keep it from scarring. If you want."

"How?"

"Do you have any Emberlyn wood here?"

I looked around the room. "Sure. Most of this furniture is made of it. Why?"

"Any that you can burn?"

"Burn the most valuable type of wood there is? Willova, you don't *burn* Emberlyn wood like common firewood."

She sighed and nodded at my damaged shoulder. "Do you want that to scar?"

I rolled my eyes and shoved to my feet. "Fine. Let's go to my room then. I don't want to give the queen anything else to be upset with me about."

We left the room and walked down the hall, then up the stairs to a landing and my bedroom. Closing the door behind us, I surveyed the furniture for something that wouldn't be missed. The hairbrush on my vanity stood out.

"Here." I crossed the room and held it up for Willova's inspection. "How about this?"

She took it and examined it, running a fingertip along the wood grain. "Yes, this is Emberlyn wood."

"Great. Now what?"

"Where are the matches?"

"Matches?"

"To start a fire."

"It's not cool enough for a fire."

"We need one."

"Fine. Probably on the hearth. I'll call a servant—"

"Why?"

"To *start* the *fire*, obviously."

"We don't need a servant. I just need the match."

"*You* know how to start a fire?"

Willova nodded.

"We both have servants for starting fires. Why do you know how to start a fire?"

She shrugged. "I'm Drazdan's only servant. So I start the fires at home."

Willova placed the hairbrush on the hearth and picked up a match.

"What? Your own brother treats you like a servant?"

"It's what I deserve. One day, if I can learn to be perfect, I won't have to be anymore." She struck the match and lit some kindling in the grate, then blew on the orange embers.

"That's what all your muck about being symmetrical and worthy of the family Calentine is all about? Not having to be a servant in your own home anymore?"

Her brows furrowed, dark red lines against her pale skin. "Yes, I guess so."

Was this why she was so stiff sometimes? Sore from servant labor? Did the tattoos have anything to do with this? Knowing Drazdan, my suspicions rose.

"Willova, what happens when you don't do one of your tasks perfectly?"

"I'm punished for my imperfections. Drazdan hopes that one day he'll be able to punish all the imperfections out of me." She grasped the horsehair end of the brush and stuck the handle into the coals.

"Oh no, Willova, please tell me you don't let him, like, beat you or anything?"

"I don't let him do anything."

"Oh. Good."

She moved from a crouch to sit on the floor, her hands clasped in her lap and her eyes on the flames. "What?"

Sitting next to her, I peered at the reflection of the flames dancing in her green eyes. Something still bothered me. Was she safe in that house with Drazdan?

She pulled the brush out once with the tongs, squinted at the blackened handle, then stuck it back in.

What felt like ages later, she finally pulled the hairbrush out and smiled at it. "It's ready."

"Ready for what? Are you going to make an ointment with it or something?"

Picking up the brush end in her hand, she laid the tongs on the hearth and scooted closer to me.

"It sort of already is, I guess. Hold still."

She pressed one hand lightly to my collarbone, then touched the charred handle to my scratch.

I expected it to burn and nearly pushed her away, but to my surprise, it felt soothing. She lightly traced the torn skin, leaving behind several black lines, as if the charcoal was ink.

Like a tattoo.

"Willova, is this what I keep seeing on you? You do this to heal your sparring injuries?"

"That's not exactly why, but it's a nice side effect." She was still touching the strange charcoal to my skin. What was left to do? Was there a secondary cut I'd missed?

"What's the real reason, then?" I asked as I tried to see what she was doing.

"Come look." She stood and pulled me with her, guiding me to the vanity mirror. I turned slightly to get a better look at my shoulder and *wow*!

Where there had been an ugly, irritated, reddish slice, now an ink-black work of art decorated my skin. Something between a flower and a star swirled over my wound with little squiggles and flourishes covering the injury.

"Willova, how did you learn to do this? Why haven't you ever told me you're an artist?"

She shrugged, smiling a little. "It's just private, I guess."

"Why, though?"

"It's hard to explain. But I'm glad you like it." She pulled a face cloth from the vanity and wrapped it around the charred handle. "Be careful with this. It washes off, but it will stain fabric if it touches it before setting. Give it a few minutes."

"Yeah, okay, but what aren't you telling me?"

She sighed. "It's just a way to make my injuries my own, I guess. Rather than letting them belong to someone else."

"Okay." I mulled it over. "I still don't get it."

"And I need to be getting home. I'll see you tomorrow, Selverine."

She let herself out of my room and closed the door behind her.

Making her injuries her own...surely she only meant sparring injuries, right?

CHAPTER 49

MELLA

"You agreed to tea with that piece of muck? On her territory?" Whisper paced next to the river, crown feathers quivering as she gestured wildly with her enormous wings. "What if it's a trap, Mella? What then?"

She was losing her cool again. As usual.

I examined my reflection in the river, considering whether I should wear my hair up or down.

"It's not like I can *decline* an invitation from the queen. And it's just *tea*, Whisper. With Queen Narellen, who's a nice old grandmother. How bad could that be?"

I tried to focus on the wind whispering through the leaves rather than on Whisper's non-whispery tone. Or my trepidation at seeing Selverine again after the horrible threats she'd made during the spar. Maybe I could smooth things over with the queen's help and still have a chance.

"Are you planning to *drink* the tea?" Her talons scraped gouges in the soft earth as she narrowed her piercing eagle eyes at me.

"Uh, yeah. That *is* what you do with tea."

"Mella! You can't accept any food or drink the enemy gives you! What if it's laced with something? She could slip in floramancy to knock you out or injure you. Or worse, make you *talkative*. You could reveal where you cast me from. Or who I am! It is of the utmost importance that doesn't happen. Do you have any idea how dangerous that could be?"

"Since you've only reminded me about a hundred times, no. I don't think I do. Maybe you should elaborate."

She covered her face dramatically with one wing and sighed. "At least ask Acres if there's any floramantic precautions you can take before we go. Something to neutralize anything that might make you overly talkative, maybe?"

I crossed my arms. "Sure. I'll do that." I needed to talk to him anyway. "And I'll let you know how it goes."

Her eyes widened as her beak dropped. Something looked funny about her beak—like it opened wider than it should or something. But she snapped it closed before I could get a good look.

"You think I'm going to let you go waltzing off alone to have tea with Narellen Merrandil?"

No way was I letting Whisper anywhere near Narellen. Not when my future was partially dependent on Narellen liking me. "I think you don't get a say. You'll pass out sometime between now and then, and I won't cast you before I go."

She scowled. "Why would you do that?"

"Because I'm honestly concerned you might try to murder Narellen if you get close enough. Which would not only be unnecessary but would also eternally bar me from any decent social standing in Terrenthyrs."

She glowered at me.

It was really amazing how piercingly a harpy eagle could glower. It was like her eyes were shaped specifically for delivering the most scowly glowers in history.

"I promise not to murder Narellen at her tea party. Please, Mella, take me with you. I may not be a true castling, but I care for you and your safety and want to be there to ensure it."

Her eyes slightly less glowery now, I considered whether I could trust her.

I gave her a once-over. "I don't think it's a good idea. I'm sorry."

The scowl was back—a truly spectacular sight. "Fine."

I raised an eyebrow. She was surrendering that easily? "Fine?"

"Yes. Fine, I'll just have to stay awake until then."

"Ugh! Whisper, please. Just let me do this."

She resumed pacing. "No."

"Whatever. You won't be able to stay awake that long anyway."

"I guess we'll see."

***

I waited till the last possible moment to head to the palace, hoping Whisper would fall asleep. But that stubborn eagle stayed awake, just like she said she would. So I marched toward the castle with Whisper on my shoulder. I considered being late or not showing up, but that would also damage my reputation. And how likely was I to ever get another chance to request that the queen stop Selverine from doing whatever she could to damage my reputation?

Worse than worrying about Whisper's behavior was the roiling in my stomach over what the queen wanted to discuss. The message had said she wanted to speak about my performance on Wager Day and my cohort options, which hopefully meant I was about to get the opportunity I'd been longing for from the beginning. The chance to be a part of a cohort where my abilities and determination would matter. Where I'd actually have the chance to win.

But Dane's words haunted me. All that stuff about real friends. Because as much as I didn't want to admit it, it rang true.

I couldn't give up my life, though. My future. Proving I didn't need Father's money.

But I'd miss them all so much. And Reenalyn's actions on Wager Day...

A servant answered the door and showed us to a sitting room. An odd wooden thing—a drum, maybe?—took up the whole view until we were through the door. The rest of the room was filled with plush sofas and chaises.

Queen Narellen sat on a rich chaise lounge with her sea eagle perched on the cushion next to her. Selverine frowned at me with her arms crossed from the opposite sofa, her castling nowhere in sight. *Skunks.* How could I make that request of the queen with Selverine right there?

Come to think of it, I hadn't seen her castling since the ceremony a few months ago. She must be nearly full grown by now.

If I joined her cohort today, how would I get back in her good graces with the castling she'd always wanted perched on my shoulder? Not that I wanted to be friends with her as I had in the past, not after all her threats. Dane was right about her being fake. But I still needed connections among the better classers. That was still my priority.

At least, I think it is. Isn't it?

I couldn't be questioning my top priority!

"Hello, Mella." Queen Narellen greeted me with a soft smile. Her wavy gray hair was pulled back from her face and hung comfortably behind her.

"Hi, Queen Narellen. Thank you for inviting Whisper and me to tea." I smiled and nodded a bow.

Whisper's talons dug into the leather shoulder pad painfully. The sharp tips hadn't poked through yet, but bruises were forming.

I turned to Selverine, whose only greeting was a blink, not bothering to shift her bored expression to something more welcoming. I squinted at her nose. It looked like one side was reddish. Maybe it was the lighting.

"Please take a seat, dear."

I sat in the chair she indicated and leaned to let Whisper sit on the arm. Belatedly, I realized I should've brought a piece of leather to protect the chair from Whisper's talons, but it was too late.

She'd better not mess it up on purpose because of her stupid vendetta against the queen.

I sent her a look, but she was too busy taking in the sea eagle, who glared regally down at us.

Queen Narellen poured steaming tea from a pale floral pot and handed the cup to me. "Here you are."

The wrinkles around her eyes and mouth gave her smile an even more grandmotherly appearance, further supporting my annoyance with Whisper.

She was just a nice old lady.

I smiled back. "Thank you."

"Of course, dear. Now"—she leaned back and rested her hands in her lap—"tell me about your beautiful castling. Miss Whisper, you are the only avian castling I've ever met besides my own."

She gestured to the sea eagle, Selvenair, who nodded his white-feathered head at Whisper and went back to staring.

"Well, I'm not sure what went wrong the first time I tried to cast her," I lied, not interested in getting in trouble for owning a contraband mandolin, "but I tried again later that day and somehow it worked. Have you ever heard of that happening before?"

I raised my cup to my lips, glad to have swallowed some pelinary petals from Acres before coming in. It would neutralize any floramancy in the tea. *Thank you, Acres. Even though I'm sure I don't need it in the least.*

"No, actually. I've heard of people failing to cast, but never casting after failing. It's a most admirable accomplishment." She beamed at me, taking her own sip.

Selverine scoffed from the corner, scratching her nose. Not sure how to address that in a helpful way, I kept my eyes on the queen. "Thank you." I eyed the sea eagle again. "How did you cast your sea eagle, if I may ask?"

Taking another sip, she gestured to an ornately carved table on which rested a crossbow. "With that weapon there."

Whisper bristled at my side. Did she recognize the weapon?

That wasn't *dust* on the crossbow, was it? *Must be fading from age. A castling weapon used every day wouldn't be dusty.*

Narellen reached over and petted Selvenair's head. He closed his eyes, then regarded us again. "You hail from a better-class family, correct? The Yarinelles of Yarinelle's Textiles?"

I paused in taking a sip. She'd gone digging up who I was? Of course she and Selverine had been discussing me. How much did they know? I swallowed and nodded. "Yes."

"And do they keep a steady set of musicians in your home? Such that they leave their musical instruments in your house?"

She tilted her teacup, her eyes on the contents.

That was an oddly specific question. My heart stuttered, and I hoped I was controlling my face. "No, we don't keep a steady set. My father prefers to try different ones from time to time. And he finds music distracting from his work, so we rarely entertain in our home."

"Hmm." Her eyes nearly disappeared as she beamed at me over her cup. "Are you enjoying your tea, dear?"

"Yes, thank you. It's very good." I took another sip to prove my point.

"Mm. Did you do anything unusual or special to cast your avian?"

I swallowed the tea, miraculously not choking on it. "Um, no. I just cast her. I wasn't even trying for an avian."

My calm slipped. Lying could get so complicated.

"See, Selverine? I told you nothing had changed." Narellen sipped again. "She didn't hide anything from you to best you. Why don't you stop being so suspicious and be friends with her again?"

I turned to my once friend. Dane's words floated through my mind. Had she ever really been my friend?

"No, really, Selverine. It was completely an accident." That much was true. If I'd known beforehand, I absolutely would've told her so I could get higher on her list of friends. "I know how much you wanted an avian and we were friends. I wanted you to succeed. If I'd known anything to help you, I would've shared it."

But what does that have to do with whether we keep regular musicians? Why would she suspect music has anything to do with Whisper? I kept my hands flat on my lap so the new calluses wouldn't be visible.

"As for the matter of regular musicians," the queen added, "I recently had to let mine go and was curious whether you had any recommendations, dear?"

Oh! That's all? I laughed so hard inside that for a moment, I feared I may have let it out. But no, I'd maintained control. "I'm honored you value my family's insight on musicians, Queen Narellen," I said, impossibly relieved. "Since I've been away from home while training with my cohort, I'm not sure who my father has hired most recently."

She looked at me expectantly.

"But I could give you the names of those I remember, if you'd like."

The queen set her cup on its saucer and smiled warmly. "That would be perfect, dear. Thank you. Now, more importantly, I'm sure you're ready to discuss more than your family's musicians."

I tried not to gulp. Did she suspect I had a contraband instrument? Had she seen the callouses?

"Of course I wouldn't ask you to come all this way just for that. I have a proposal for you."

I fought an urge to glance at Whisper but kept my eyes on Narellen. "A proposal?"

"I can only imagine your discomfort the past several months—living with lesser classers in Wrynford. It seems like the castor of such an incredible castling deserves to have a better chance at Grand Castor status."

My pulse raced as my eyes widened. Was she offering me a transfer to Selverine's cohort? Everything I'd hoped for and worked so hard to achieve!

"How would you feel about switching cohorts? To Selverine's, perhaps?"

Her words washed over me, and a thrill swirled in my stomach. Victory was within my grasp!

Then why did I feel such strong reservations about her proposal?

An image of Whisper and me standing with the winning cohort—*our* winning cohort—floated through my mind. Kaido beaten. My parents proven wrong. All other cohorts beneath me.

My stomach sank. Another image swiftly followed. My Wrynford friends, beneath me. Not sharing in the victory but looking on from somewhere far away. Perhaps regretting all the things they'd taught me and the fun times we'd had together.

But I'd have Selverine and her friends again. I'd be back in high society, just like I wanted.

I flicked a glance at Selverine, who was scratching her nose again, and her icy glare sent my eyes away immediately.

Dane's annoying words about true friends echoed in my head. Selverine didn't fit the description. Neither did Frenna. Or Yulroe. Or anyone else I knew from Glenmyre.

But Reenalyn did. And Beldon. Acres. Even Trinka.

And Dane.

I nodded to Queen Narellen, casting my eyes to my teacup as I made a decision that would dictate the rest of my life. "You're certainly right. I would have a better chance as a member of Selverine's cohort." I took a slow sip and swallowed. Complete confidence in my choice settled over me, and I met the queen's gaze. "But I can't accept."

Her eyebrows rose high on her wrinkled forehead. "No? May I inquire why not?"

Dane's words came to me again, and I couldn't help but smile. "I've made some real friends in Wrynford, even though it's not a place I ever would've chosen for myself. I appreciate your generosity, but I'd like to stay with them."

***

Whisper stepped from my shoulder onto a low branch, and I lowered myself to the ground. Legs crossed, I dropped my head into my hands. "I cannot believe I just did that."

Whisper's feathers rustled, then went silent. "I'm proud of you, Mella."

Startled, I turned my gaze to her. "What?"

"You made the right choice. I am so proud of you, and I'm going to redouble my efforts these next few weeks to help you and the others win despite everything against you."

"Wha—I—thank you." I leaned back, my palms sliding over cool dirt. "But you know I didn't make that decision because of your vendetta against the queen, right?" I quirked an eyebrow at her.

Just because I'd chosen my real friends didn't mean I was going along with her conspiracies.

She nodded. "Of course. I'm so pleased you chose your true friends over shallow, societal relationships. Your life is going to be much happier."

"Well, that's good to know." I grinned and lay all the way down, covering my eyes and holding out a fist. "Hand to claw?"

She leaped down from the branch to stand by me and bumped her talons against my knuckles. "Hand to claw."

"And you know what else?" I asked.

"What's that?"

"The castors of Wrynford *are* going to win."

***

I walked toward the campfire in search of another sparring opponent, feeling weirdly energetic after making my choice. Beldon, Reenalyn, and Dane sat around the dead firepit. Reenalyn's elbows rested on her knees, her chin in her hands, as she contemplated the ashes. Dane slouched, one hand resting on Sprinter's head. Beldon rolled the handle of his mace between his fingers, staring at the ground.

"What's gotten into all of you?" I asked. We only had a couple of months left until the Grand Castors' Tournament.

Acres's knotted loc bun stuck out over another log as he leaned on the other side of it, and the sound of spikes biting into wood over and over came from nearby.

Beldon halfway glanced at me, his clever fingers not missing a beat. "What else should we do? None of us guys got wagers. Trinka got one and doesn't care. Reenalyn technically got one too, but only one despite beating her opponent. They're chalking it up to a mistake, though, and practically disqualifying her."

"What?" I turned to Reenalyn. "They're disqualifying you?"

She swung around on her log to face me instead of the firepit and nodded sadly. "Yes. Apparently it wasn't a true victory because his own castling took him out, even though it was Cupid's doing. Apparently it was indecent of me to take first blood from his face. Though it wasn't indecent for him to grope me in front of everyone."

I scoffed and met Cupid's shy eyes from behind Reenalyn's hair. "Firstly, Cupid, that was an epic move. I will always admire you for it."

Beaming at him, I remembered the look on Kaido's face when Cupid's attack on Striker sent the snake's head launching back into Kaido's crotch at top speed. Cupid's green snout emerged from Reenalyn's golden waves, and I took it as a sign that he appreciated my words.

"And Reenalyn, I have a question for you. I saw a lot of openings you didn't take during your fight with Kaido. I know you had to have seen some of them, so were you trying not to win too easily? To make it more believable than beating him right away?"

A small smile lit up her face. "Actually, I didn't take those openings because I didn't need them. I wanted to take first blood the way I did for a reason, and if I'd taken those other chances, I would've cut him on his arm or thigh, which wouldn't have been as satisfying."

I raised an eyebrow. "Why first blood on his face? To remind him of your victory every time he looks in a mirror?"

She shook her head. "No. To remind any girl in Terrenthyrs who saw the fight that he's not as fantastic as he thinks. And to hopefully make at least some of them think twice before kissing him." She grinned a little wider. "And all that was punishment for how he treated you, of course. I told him so at the end."

Crossing my arms with a smile, I said, "Yeah, I heard you. Brilliant!"

She grinned so big her eyes disappeared. "It was pretty brilliant, wasn't it?"

My heart felt bigger and warmer than ever before, and I was again so proud and relieved I'd chosen to stay with my cohort. "Yes, it was. Thank you, Reenalyn. It was an awesome fight. I'm sorry it cost you wagers, though. But with Kaido's father as one of the king's advisors, I bet they would've come up with a reason to disqualify anyone who beat him."

She nodded. "Maybe."

Dane finally spoke up, and my heart jumped at his voice. Had I been avoiding his eyes? This was ridiculous. I had to get a hold of this.

"So what are you going to do, Mella?"

"I don't know what you mean..."

"I mean you don't have a chance of getting back into society with this cohort, and you won your match. So which cohort are you transferring to?"

Guilt flooded me at the assumption I'd be leaving. But of course he would think that—I'd made it clear I wanted to get back into high society all along. But not anymore. "I'm not transferring. I'm sticking it out with you guys. And we are going to win."

The sound of spikes violently attacking wood stopped, and the others and their castlings all turned to me.

"I'm serious. We didn't have a great Wager Day as a cohort, no, but we still have time to get stronger before the Grand Castors' Tournament."

Beldon let go of his mace handle and placed his hands on either side of him. "But even if we somehow did win, we won't have the income from the wagers. Just the one-time prize money."

"Yeah, and you wouldn't get the life you've been working so hard for," Dane added.

I nodded. "But you'd get the prize money to take back to your parents, Dane. And Beldon, you'd be able to start your own business. And Reenalyn, you could buy some nice things for your siblings. Acres could buy more books. Trinka could do whatever she wanted."

Reenalyn watched me closely. "But what about you, Mella?"

Honestly, I wasn't sure. All I knew was I was happier around these people than anyone from high society. Even though some of them would go home to their families, I would still have Beldon and Acres, and Reenalyn most importantly. Maybe I could buy myself a little shack near her family's house and keep working at the leather shop during the day and playing music with Reenalyn in the evenings. That wouldn't be so bad.

"I'm the one who's going to whip the rest of us into shape."

CHAPTER 50

SELVERINE

F renna's arrow pinged against one of my trident's teeth.

Whew. Barely missed that one.

With a battle cry, I aimed the points at her and dove.

Something slammed against my side, and my trident and I hit the ground, leaving Frenna unscathed. Her lynx castling landed lightly next to me and bounded back to Frenna's side.

"Selverine," Yulroe approached with her longsword drawn and her cheetah castling by her side, "I'll never understand why you don't just train with your castling."

Shoving to my feet, I brushed myself off. "As I've told you, Yulroe, I *do* train with my castling." Hopefully the lie wasn't as plain on my face as it felt. "The queen keeps us so busy training with her that my poor castling needs to rest by the time you all are up and ready to spar."

Stooping, Frenna retrieved the arrow, inspecting the tip. "I mean, the more time she trains the two of you personally, the more valuable you both are to our cohort, and the more likely we are to win the tournament. So it doesn't bother me."

"Yes," Yulroe sheathed her longsword, "but how will our castlings ever learn to fight as a team if Horizon's never here to train with them?"

"Quit worrying, Yulroe!" I snapped. Taking a breath, I added more calmly, "I promise, it will be fine." It would be. I'd make her come out and train. Somehow.

"Hey Yulroe," Crous called from a few dozen spans away, running a hand through his blond hair, "heard from your lesser-class boyfriend lately?"

Tucking a thin braid behind her ear, Yulroe rolled her eyes. "Ex-boyfriend, Crous. In case that vocabulary's too advanced for you, it means we *don't* talk anymore. So no."

Anxious for any subject to distract from the last one, I latched onto this. "Did you know he and Mella Yarinelle are in the same cohort?"

Yulroe raised an eyebrow at me. "The *ex* part also means I don't care about where he is or what he does."

"More importantly, how'd Mella cast such an incredible animal?" Frenna asked, inspecting the fletching on an arrow.

I glowered. That was not the direction I meant for this to take.

"They're probably together now, don't you think, Yulroe?" Crous added, striding toward us with his black-and-white monitor lizard scuttling along by his boots. "I mean, with a castling like that," he shrugged. "Way more bragging rights for getting with her."

If I had to hear one more thing about how fantastic Mella Yarinelle was, I was going to lose it. Time to shed some light on that.

"Crous," I leaned on my trident, "you do realize they're both in the Wrynford cohort, right? The muckiest, saddest cohort that's never won the tournament before." Surely that would make her less desirable.

Crous shrugged, grinning at Kaido as he approached with his anaconda wrapped around his chest and shoulders. "I don't think the cohort matters much when you've got the best castling of the year! Wouldn't you say, Kaido?"

The best castling of the year, huh? My blood boiled. It wasn't fair!

"Yeah, what would you say, Kaido?" Frenna asked sweetly, her gaze full of daggers. "Do you regret taking me to the ball instead?"

"Not at all, Frenna. The look on her face when she saw us together was the best payback for...being the miserable lesser classer she is now."

He winked at Crous as Frenna inspected another arrow. The bastard. His thoughts aligned with Crous's.

"You do know her mother was a musician, don't you?"

Four sets of eyes flashed to mine.

"Nuh-uh!"

"Was she really?"

"How'd you know?"

"Not Mrs. Yarinelle—she's distantly related to my mother's side of the family." Frenna said. "None of them are musicians."

"No, not the *current* Mrs. Yarinelle. Mr. Yarinelle's first wife. That was Mella's mother."

"Really?" Yulroe's eyes widened. "Why the muck did he marry a musician?"

I shrugged. "Couldn't tell you. But that's probably why his fortunes have declined so drastically over the years. You know they're nearly lesser class by this point."

Crous frowned. "No way! I mean, who anyone's mother is doesn't make a muck of difference to me. But no money in the family..." He sent Kaido a knowing look. "Not long-term-situation material, if you know what I mean." He grinned. "But there's always the short term!"

He and Kaido cackled.

Rolling my eyes, I scrambled for anything else to put Mella down with.

"You know what else?" I asked. "You all probably missed it because you weren't as close to her, but since we dueled, I was right next to them. That avian is wobbly as skunks. And she can't fly, either. She may look impressive, but what good is a fragile castling?"

Kaido scratched his castling's scaly head. "Are you jealous of Mella or something?"

"Muck, no! Why the skunks would I be jealous of a penniless lesser classer in the poorest cohort with a weak, useless castling? I feel *bad* for her. Poor thing. She'll never have a good future with nothing going for her."

"And, ah...where's your castling?" Crous asked.

I fixed a glare on him, crossing my arms. "Making implications is cheap and cowardly, Crous. If you've got something to say, then mucking say it."

His monitor lizard looked up at him, tasting the air with his forked tongue.

Crous held up his hands in surrender. "No, not implying anything. Just curious. We're in the same cohort and I've never seen her since the ceremony. It's unusual, is all." He eyed the others.

None of them had seen her since the ceremony, either. I'd barely seen her since then.

How did we go from bad talking my enemy to commenting on my castling?

Shrugging, I brandished my trident. "The queen invests a lot of time training us herself. My castling spends all her energy there. She gets tired just like all of yours do. It's not our fault the queen thinks she and I are worth investing personal time in while the rest of you aren't. Now who am I sparring with next?"

CHAPTER 51

ACRES

M ella dodged another throwing star, still smiling like Reenalyn first thing in the morning. Which was not like her at all.

I swerved and plucked it from the tree trunk it lodged in. "You seem awfully cheerful today."

She took a deep breath, sweat sparkling on her forehead. "I have a surprise for you."

With a grunt, she lunged and I blocked with one star and sliced at her shoulder with the other. "A surprise?"

Wincing, she covered her shoulder with one hand. "Ouch. Okay, maybe I'll just take it back."

"What is it?" I deflected a blow and whirled to feint and strike at her knee.

She dodged, dancing away and into a crouch with another uncharacteristic grin. "It's more of a debt repayment than a gift really, but I'm calling it a surprise because you're not expecting it."

Frowning at her vagueness, I dove at her and tripped on the scythe's handle she aimed at my boots. I skidded on my face over the ground. "Ow."

She laughed as I rolled over.

"Sorry not sorry. You okay?" She held out a hand. I gripped it, and the forest disappeared.

The taste of tea and pelinary petals covered my tongue.

Selverine sat in front of me, scratching her nose incessantly.

Narellen offered to move me to a better cohort.

And then the trees were around me again, and Mella's hand was gone. I'd only been halfway up, and I dropped hard to the ground again.

"What did you just do?" Shaking her hand out, she stared at me, her grin gone. "It felt like you pulled energy from me again or something. What was I feeling, Acres?"

I looked at my hands, then glowered up at Mella. "The queen herself offered to move you to her granddaughter's cohort? So your whole speech last night about sticking with us—that was all a lie?"

"What?" She raised her eyebrows.

"I think I just saw your memories again."

"Well, yeah, the queen did offer to transfer me. But I didn't agree to it. I decided to stay with you all, just like I said last night."

I crossed my arms. "So you're just giving up your best chance to win the competition, get back at your parents, and secure an income for yourself."

"Maybe. I'm giving up the opportunity from the queen. If it was my best chance, it's gone now. I'm all in with the Castors of Wrynford. But how did you see that, anyway?"

"I saw your memories when our hands touched. I didn't mean to, but I saw you with the queen and Selverine and...wait. Selverine. Did she really scratch her nose so much it's red on one side?"

"What?"

"Well, did she?"

"I can't imagine how that could possibly matter, but yeah, she did."

"And did you notice her fingers twitching oddly?"

"Yeah. She almost dropped her tea."

Incessant nose scratching and finger twitching was a common sign of recent intense memory manipulation. My spectacles helped hide scars on my own nose from when I'd been affected. Maybe my grandmother's scribbled handwriting after the shattering was due to hand twitches, because someone wanted everyone to forget what happened that day.

"Maybe someone's been manipulating memories around here for a long time. And they're still at it." A horrible thought occurred to me. "Mella, tell me you didn't eat or drink anything there!"

"I drank some tea, but I'd eaten the pelinary petals you gave me, so I should be good, right?"

"How long before drinking the tea did you eat the petals?"

"I ate them on way to the palace. Maybe ten minutes?"

"Then yes. Whew."

Stretching her long sleeve over her hand, she held it out again.

I took it and she pulled me up.

"No memories that time," I said, stepping back.

"So you think the king and queen are manipulating Selverine?"

"Maybe. Or even a resourceful servant in the palace? I don't know. Just don't eat or drink anything if you don't know where it came from."

She nodded.

"I need to look at my notes on this weird thing about me seeing your thoughts. It's got to be related to a potion of some kind, but I don't know what all the ingredients are. Maybe if I can figure it out, we can use it on someone at the palace to find out what's going on."

"Oh! Brilliant!"

Stashing my throwing stars in their pouch, I sighed. "It might be easier to figure out if...well, never mind." I knew she felt bad about costing me my library pass, and I wasn't over it either. But making her feel worse wouldn't do any good.

"If you could get a book from the library?" Swiping a piece of parchment from a pocket, she held it out to me with a bow and a flourish.

"What's this?" Taking the parchment, I unfolded it and read. "Holy mucking skunks! It looks so real! How'd you forge it?"

She rolled her eyes with a grin. "It's one hundred percent real, Acres. I saved and paid for it. No one will question you with it."

I stared. "Wow." I couldn't believe it. She must have worked hard and denied herself a lot to afford this. I was touched. "Just, wow. Thank you, Mella."

She beamed. "You're welcome. Now go figure this potion thing out!"

Chapter 52

DANE

T he moment I made a point of stilling my jittery feet, they started bouncing under the table again.

I was going on a date with Mella Yarinelle. She'd finally agreed to dinner the night before the Grand Castors' Tournament.

Monkey's skunking teeth.

Maybe not a date, strictly speaking. But she *had* agreed to meet me to talk and eat. And as far as I knew, nothing between her and Kaido had started again in the weeks since he'd ditched her, despite how much attention he'd started paying her after finding out about her incredible castling.

That was good, at least. She deserved so much better.

I checked my pocket for the pelinary petals again. After the weird effects of the punch at the ball several weeks ago, Acres kept us all well stocked and we used them before every meal, even at the loaf. I'd brought extra in case Mella was out.

The bell tinkled again, and I glanced up out of habit, knowing it still wouldn't be her. I'd arrived stupidly early. And sure enough, it was just some guy.

What would she think about me once she knew about the tent peg?

The bell chimed again, and it was her. She was early, too?

I sat taller in my seat, trying to wrestle my beaming delight to a more reasonably pleased smile.

"Hey." I stood and held her chair out for her.

"Hi." She smiled, leaning her scythe against the table. "Thanks."

"You're very welcome."

Overkill, you idiot. Get over yourself!

The bartender dropped off mugs of ale for some travelers and approached our table.

"Good afternoon. What'll it be?"

I gestured to Mella.

"Black tea, please."

"Sugars?"

"No, thanks."

"And for you?" Her eyes flicked to me.

"The same for me, please, but with two sugars."

"And what would you like for dinner tonight?" The bartender looked at Mella.

"I'll take the wild mushroom, bacon, and burroot sandwich, please."

"Spiced potatoes all right with that?"

"Yes." She smiled and nodded. I imagined her smiling and nodding like that after I'd poured my heart out to her and she miraculously felt the same.

"And for you?"

"The bacon sandwich, please. And *yes* to the potatoes."

She nodded and left.

I leaned back, feeling a little foolish for ordering two whole sugars. But it was so good, and I could afford it now. At least, on occasion.

"So"—Mella leaned her elbows on the table and rested her chin over her laced fingers—"the story you promised me—why in the world does your castling weapon look like a tent peg?"

A few freckles dusted her cheeks and nose, and her ocean eyes peered into me. My stomach jumped at having her full attention on me and her being so close in a setting so different than sparring.

I took a deep breath and broke our gaze, trying to slow my heart rate enough to function. I had no claim on her. This wasn't a date. Just two friends having dinner to celebrate how far they'd come and wish good luck on the Grand Castors' Tournament.

That would have to be enough.

"Right. The tent peg for a castling weapon." I glanced at it in its makeshift sheath. "One of my jobs was to keep the tent pegs sharp to save setup time. One day I found my boss unjustly punishing my sisters for a small thing." I tapped the peg protruding from my belt. "I swiped this off a pile of freshly sharpened tent pegs and hit him in the back of the head hard enough to knock him out. And it turned out to be so useful, I've only ever fought with tent pegs since."

"Holy muck." Mella said, eyes wide. "Were your sisters okay?"

"Yeah. They were pretty shaken, but not permanently hurt."

The serving girl set steaming mugs of tea down in front of us. Taking a pelinary petal from her own pocket, Mella popped it in her mouth and then sipped her tea, licking her lips and thoroughly distracting me. "That's good. What had they done?"

Chewing on my own pelinary petal, I winced at the strong taste. "He wanted them to do something that was too hard, and they couldn't do it."

Drumming her fingers on the table, she stared at me. "Dane, are you being so vague on purpose?"

Laughing sheepishly, I glanced at the steam rising from my tea. "Well, sort of. Yes. It's just that my upbringing was really odd, and I don't want you to think I'm any weirder than you already do. I've put a lot of work into hopefully not seeming like I grew up differently." I winced. Was that too much?

Setting her mug back down, she raised an eyebrow. "I don't think you're weird. But that does just make me more curious about your past. I understand not wanting to get into it though." She met my eyes again, shooting another thrill through my chest. "Is there anything you *can* tell me about yourself you don't mind me knowing?"

I grinned and glanced down at the table. She wanted to know more about me.

"Right, well." I chuckled awkwardly, rubbing my sweaty palms on my pant legs. "I'm a little shorter than my younger brother, which he won't stop rubbing in my face. He has crazy hair. And the sisters I mentioned—they're twins. Really close twins. Adorable and sassy. And it would be cool if you could meet them someday."

Looking up, it was still a shock to find her brilliant sea-blue eyes on mine as she listened to my garbled words. Would I ever be able to tell her the whole truth? I wasn't sure. But I wouldn't make anything up, either. Everything I told her was true, if not the whole truth.

"That sounds so nice. I've always wished to have siblings. And now...well, that's complicated for me now."

"Yeah. They're a handful, but I miss them."

"So even though they move around, they're still too far away to visit? They don't ever come here?"

"No, not here, unfortunately. But once the castling year is complete, I'm planning to go see them. I might bring them here." *Especially if you wanted me to come back. Then nothing could prevent my return.*

The serving girl set down our plates, and Mella took a bite of spiced potato. "Mm. That's good."

The way she closed her eyes with just a hint of a smile punched my gut all over again.

This girl.

She cupped her tea and regarded me. "Can you tell me anything about your parents? You're pretty close to them, right? Even despite the weird upbringing stuff?"

"Yes, I am. None of that stuff was their fault, though. They've helped me as much as they could."

She raised an eyebrow, and I tried not to wince.

"I'm sorry—still too vague. What about *your* parents?" I deflected, then did wince when I realized what a sore subject that was. "Sorry, you don't have to answer that."

She shrugged. "You already know my father's in textiles. But people buy his products less often now than they used to, apparently. Hence why he can only afford one child."

"Do you miss them at all? Even though...?"

She considered, taking another sip of her tea and rubbing her lips together twice. Her mouth utterly hypnotized me, and I struggled to tear my eyes away.

"I miss who Father was when I was a young child. Mostly I miss Momma. She died when I was young. I had it pretty easy with my stepmother—she wasn't horrible, and she calmed Father down a bit. Though being kicked out and replaced by a new sibling does kind of put them in a different light. But"—she smiled like she was getting away with something, the best kind of smile—"I actually like making my own money. Earning it and then deciding how to spend it. It's kind of freeing, you know?"

Freedom. I both relished it and felt crushed by the guilt of it. But I gave her a smile. "Yeah. There's something nice about that."

Was now the time to tell her about her role in helping me get my life together here in the first place?

"So the tent pegs, all the moving around—does your family live in a caravan or something? Pitching tents to sleep in?"

Precisely and not at all.

"Kind of." I grimaced.

She rolled her eyes. "Look, Dane, you told me about the tent peg like you promised, so you don't have to reveal anything else about your past or your family if you'd rather not. That's fine. Can you tell me if there are any avian castors where you're from? Or any legends about them? It's just that I'm worried about Whisper and looking for places I can find answers, you know?"

"Oh, um..." I thought about it, but I couldn't think of anything helpful. "I don't know of any where I'm from, but maybe there's an option closer to home."

"Really? Like what?"

"Remember that guy who frequents the Loaf but always orders his sandwich without bread? The one who's an Emberlyn wood transporter to Morrenfayre who claims to see hybrid castlings. He's mentioned avian castlings, too. I don't know how trustworthy the information is because he comes up with a lot of other weird claims, but maybe it's something?"

She chewed a bite of sandwich, her eyes darting around the room without taking it in. "Maybe. What else does he say?"

I shrugged, trying to recall anything besides the usual avian, hybrid, and shattering rants. "A lot of stuff about a shattering he remembers from childhood. Anytime someone makes a joke about shatterings not being used anymore, he brings up this one he thinks he remembers from a few decades ago or something."

Her jaw dropped and her eyes locked on mine. "Did he say anything else about that?"

"About the shattering?" Why would she be interested in that? "Um, just that he thought it shouldn't have happened. That the castor and his castling were good people."

"Did he mention the man's name? The type of castling?"

I frowned. "Maybe. I don't remember though. Bermand? Or..."

"Bennet?"

"Yeah! That's the one. How'd you know?"

Suddenly she grabbed my hand on the table and squeezed it, sending surprised shocks through my arm and into my chest. "Thank you for telling me this, Dane. I'm sorry, I have to go."

She let go and slid from her chair.

I leaped up after her, grabbing her hand to delay her leaving. "Wait, Mella..."

She spun back to me, grabbing her scythe from where it leaned against the table. "I'm really sorry, Dane. But...let's do this again, okay? I was really looking forward to this date, and I hate to cut it short. Will...will you ask me out again?"

That wasn't the response I'd been expecting. "I...yes. Of course."

A gorgeous shy smile lit up her face, like she hadn't been sure I'd say yes, and then she pulled her hand from mine and flew out the door.

Did she just call this a date?

Chapter 53

MELLA

"A cres!" I called outside his window for the millionth time, using the scythe to tap on the window. "Hey! I need to talk to you. Come on!"

Finally, a half-asleep Acres appeared in the window and weakly shoved it open. "Mella?" He scrubbed a fist over one eye. "It's the middle of the night."

"Actually, it's early evening. But you won't care when you hear what I have to say. Let me in."

He stared at me with dismay before disappearing. I ran around to the locked entry door to his building and waited.

With a squeal, the rusty hinges protested as Acres opened the rickety old door. "This had better be worth it. It's the first time I've been able to sleep since the last experiment went wrong."

"It is," I said as I brushed past him.

The door slammed behind us, and his slow steps followed my energetic pace up the stairs. When the door to his room was finally closed, I whirled on him.

"We have confirmation of a shattering forty years ago."

He crossed his arms, not looking nearly as surprised as I'd expected. "What kind of confirmation?"

"A resident of Terrenthyrs who was a child at the time remembers."

"The snow leopard castor who thinks he sees hybrids on the road to Morrenfayre."

I gaped. "How the muck do you already know that?"

He shrugged. "Because I've heard him claim it."

"And you didn't think to mention this to me because...?"

"Because it's the guy who thinks he sees hybrids on the road to Morrenfayre. He's clearly not all there."

"But you know what you're missing?"

He raised an eyebrow.

"He doesn't eat bread. Something in it makes him sick. How many other people have you ever heard of who don't eat bread in Terrenthyrs, whose main export besides Emberlyn wood is wheat?"

His eyes brightened. "The only person who remembers is the only person who doesn't eat bread. Which means if there was memory floramancy involved, it must've been delivered in bread!"

"Right!" I grinned, ecstatic that I'd been the one to figure it out.

"Possibly." Acres pinched his chin in a thinking pose.

Sighing, I dropped onto his unmade bed, laying my scythe over my lap. "I know, I know. It's not a perfect theory. Could there have been anyone else allergic to bread or who didn't eat bread that day who didn't get exposed either?"

"Could be." He pulled the chair from under his desk absentmindedly and sat with his elbows resting on the desk.

"What else are you thinking?"

"I'm trying to think of what floramantic substances need to be heated like bread needs to be baked to have the suggestive powers of this memory thing we're dealing with."

"And?"

"And I can't think of any."

"What?"

"I can't think of any floramantic substance that needs to be heated or cooled. I only know about room-temperature potions." He faced me, his hands clasped in his lap, frustration on his face. "I...had a bad experience with floramancy and left before learning about the effects of temperature on potion ingredients."

"Skunking muck." I dropped onto the bed. The squeaky springs protested twice and then went quiet. "What can we do now?"

He pulled a trunk out from under his desk and opened the lid, an odd look of resignation on his face. "There might be something about it in one of these books. I'll...I'll see what I can find."

I propped myself up on my elbows, concerned at the hopelessness in his voice. "Acres, what's wrong?"

He was silent a long moment, his dark hands resting on the stack of books. "I just...this isn't what I want to be doing."

Frowning, I pushed myself into a sitting position. "Because you'd rather be reading about fossils?"

His shoulders popped up with a harsh laugh. "I guess."

"Acres, this is so much more important than a skunking hobby. Don't you get that? Think of all the other things Terrenthyrs might have forgotten? The danger everyone is in from whoever made everyone forget in the first place. We have got to find out what happened and who did it and—"

Acres slammed his fists on his desk, making me jump. "I'm aware of how important this is, Mella. I'm not an idiot, and I'm not being lazy. It's...I'm...not happy with who I am right now."

"Why not?" I asked, feeling bad for pissing him off without realizing it.

"I mean...I swore...I'm breaking a promise. I don't like doing that." He took a deep breath and sighed slowly. "And...there's something I forgot that I've been trying to remember. And I'm getting close, but the closer I get, the more I feel this...this fear. This terror that I'm not going to like what I remember. That maybe *I* took the memory away for a good reason. Maybe I shouldn't try to get it back."

I mulled over his words. "And all the experimenting just brings you closer to remembering."

"Yes."

"I'm sorry, Acres." I wanted to tell him he could just forget it. That it wasn't a big deal and I could figure it out so he didn't have to face whatever that memory was.

But I couldn't. We needed to find out, and it would take me years to get the kind of background he had in floramancy. By the time I learned a fraction of what he knew, whoever was messing with memories could mess with mine and make me forget everything I'd learned, or worse.

"Thanks, but that doesn't help much," he said.

"I know."

He turned back to the book on his desk and opened it. "Look, Mella, it's hard enough to work on this without you staring at my back. Could you give me some time, please? And you've got something between your teeth."

Frowning and rubbing a finger over my teeth, I stood, the wood floor creaking beneath me. "Yeah. I'm...good luck."

I found the herb leaf Acres had seen and flicked it to the floor, hoping Dane hadn't noticed. Then I let myself out of Acres's room, feeling sorry and grateful that he would research anyway. And feeling very tired. Tomorrow was the day we'd all been working toward for so long. And it was late. I needed to get some sleep.

I yawned as the squeaky door at the bottom of the stairs slammed behind me, and I turned toward the road and my long walk home.

Was that a footstep? I glanced behind me, thinking I must be imagining it. But no, a shadow was on the ground just behind mine.

The shadow stilled when I did.

Heart hammering, I started walking again, keeping the head of their shadow in sight at my feet. They kept pace with me, and I tightened my grip on my scythe.

Skunks, skunks, skunks!

I'd have to run right past them to get back to Acres. Should I pretend not to notice, or run for it?

Taking a last deep breath, I prepared to sprint, when a new shadow appeared in front of me.

I sidestepped them and flailed into a run, but someone knocked me over the head.

Someone yanked the scythe from my grip as I dropped to the ground, and my vision went dark.

CHAPTER 54

SELVERINE

S crubbing the sweat from my forehead, I leaned against the wall by the locked bedroom door and sighed. "That girl is a skunking pain."

Willova was already sitting on the floor with her back against the wall, hugging her knees. "We shouldn't have done that."

Sliding down the wall, I rolled my eyes. "She's a piece of muck for not telling me how she did it. She deserves it."

"But even if she *does* tell you, what good will it do? You can't cast again."

A moan came from the other side of the door.

"She must be waking up." Willova sighed.

"Finally. It's been over an hour." I examined my hands. "Must have hit her really hard to knock her out for so long."

"Hey!" Mella shouted, her voice muffled by the thick Emberlyn wood door. "What the skunking muck are you doing, Selverine? Let me the muck out right now!"

She punctuated the demand by slamming her fists against the door.

"You know how to get out," I said, feeling desperate and worried she wouldn't give in. But she'd have to today. The Grand Castors' Tournament was this morning—just a few hours away.

"I already mucking told you, Selverine, I just said my castling call and she appeared." She kicked the door this time. Just once though. She knew it was fruitless.

"Right. Want to prove that for me?"

"We don't have time, Selverine. The Grand Castors' Tournament is only a few hours away. Let me out and we can settle this later. None of us can afford to be late."

"Nope."

"Ugh!" She kicked the door again, and it sounded like it hurt.

"Give it up, Mella. The secret, or your future. Not that you'll have much of one with that slummy cohort of yours, but still."

"There's no secret to give up, Selverine, I'm telling you. Please, just let me out."

"Fine. If there's no secret, cast your castling."

"I don't have my scythe."

"Yes, you do. It's on my bed."

Willova glanced at me with a raised eyebrow, still thinking I was an idiot for letting her keep the scythe. But there was stone and Emberlyn wood between us—what could she do? Besides, this was the only way I could call her bluff and find out what her real castling weapon was.

"I'm not doing this, Selverine. This is stupid."

"Not doing it and missing the Grand Castors' Tournament would definitely be stupider than just getting it over with."

She didn't say anything.

"Well?"

She stayed silent.

For hours.

As more time passed and Mella didn't give in, dread seeped into me. I was going to the tournament without a castling. *Skunks.*

Willova's tired eyes watched me pace by the door.

Only a few hours till the Grand Castors' Tournament. Thank good fortune I'd at least taken my own weapon out before locking Mella in my room.

What if we upped the stakes a bit and let Mella think the competition was about to start in a few minutes?

I grinned at Willova and whispered, "Follow my lead."

She shoved up from the ground with one eyebrow raised, her cutlass swinging in the sheath at her side.

"The Grand Castors' Tournament will be starting soon, Willova," I said. "We should get going."

I clomped down the stairs, past a guard, and through the front door, Willova just behind me. I glanced up at my bedroom window, an idea taking shape.

"Willova, this way." I gestured to the shrubbery lining the front of the castle. "She's going to escape somehow. Let's watch and see how she'll cast when she thinks she doesn't have an audience."

Chapter 55
MELLA

T hat skunking *bitch*!

As Selverine and Willova's footsteps retreated down the stairs, I considered just how much of a mucking skunk Selverine was. They *both* were. Locking me in here on the morning of the Grand Castors' Tournament, of all things. I thought they'd at least let me out right before so I'd just have the disadvantage of no sleep.

But no, even if that had been their plan, I'd still be out of luck with just the stupid scythe and no mandolin. I glowered at it, the useless thing. Years spent crafting it just to have to lug it around all the time like it was as important as it was supposed to be.

I glanced at the window. Now that they were gone, no one could stop me from sneaking through it. Not that it would do me much good. The stone courtyard three stories below wouldn't make a nice landing.

A glance at either side showed nothing to grab to climb into an adjacent room. There was a slender stone balcony on the next floor under me, but it was so skinny I'd surely miss. And if I did, I'd likely break my neck.

But the Wrynford cohort and I had fought too hard for it to end here, and we were supposed to play our instruments one more time together before the Grand Castors' Tournament. They needed me, and whether we won or not, I was going to fight with them.

MELLA 305

With the scythe leaning against the window frame so I could grab it from outside, I shimmied one leg out the window, then the other. Easing my stomach over the rounded stone underneath, I carefully let go with one hand and reached for the scythe. If I could lay the blade over the windowsill and hold on to the handle, I could ease myself down—

My fingers brushed the scythe, pushing it a speck further away.

"No, no, no!"

Scrabbling for it, I reached as far as I could, then felt myself slipping.

"Skunks, skunks, skunks!"

My fingers closed around it, and I struggled to grip the windowsill with my other hand. I latched on to a sharp bit of stone and let go reflexively, my free arm flailing.

"No! Skunks!"

My nails chipped and tore as they tried unsuccessfully to find purchase on the stone.

As a last resort, I stretched my toes toward the balcony railing beneath me, hoping I might snag enough of a hold. Instead I found it with my face as I plummeted toward the ground.

The breath whooshed out of me as I hit hard, and for a moment I couldn't move. *Skunks.* Did I break my back?

Then pain erupted in my knee and sides and forehead. I lifted both legs and found they still worked. Sitting up slowly, I found that my ribs still worked too, though they protested with each breath. And blood dripped into my eye. Thanks to that stupid tiny balcony.

I hated balconies.

But there was the worthless scythe, lying on the stone ground next to me. The Grand Castors' Tournament would be starting any time now. How long would they wait for me? Not long, if at all.

Getting to my feet, using the scythe as a walking stick, and feeling about a hundred years old, I limped away from the skunking palace and toward my mandolin's hiding place.

I'd never get there and back in time. I'd have to go faster. Shoving myself forward, I braced my arms and tried to throw myself into a jog. A few bouncing, throbbing steps later, more blood obscured my vision. I brushed it away and wiped it on my tunic, belatedly realizing I wouldn't have time to change.

So I'd be showing up like this. But I *would* be showing up.

***

Slowing to a halt by the log, I wheezed and struggled to stay upright. I leaned the scythe against the log and pulled the mandolin from beneath it, relieved to find it safe and sound.

Taking a few deep breaths to slow my breathing enough for the castling call, I sang as loud as I could and strummed the skunk out of those strings. Whisper would need to be as strong as possible today.

"Aha!" Someone shouted from behind me.

I jumped out of my skin as Whisper's coal, snow, and chocolate dust poured from the mandolin and shimmered into her.

Selverine stepped out from the trees, her emerald earrings twinkling and a victorious gleam in her eyes. "So *that's* how you did it!"

Willova followed, her eyes wide.

"Selverine, wait—I thought you were going to the coliseum?" *Muck! Muck! Muck!*

"You were lying to me all along, Mella, I knew it! And playing illegal music, too. Oh, I'll get you for this."

"Mella!" a voice called from the other direction. "Mella?"

Skunks. It was Dane. I didn't want him to find out this way. If he was ever going to know, I wanted it to be because I'd decided to trust him. Not because someone told on me.

Selverine grinned, sensing my trepidation. "Over here!" she shouted, her bright eyes on mine.

"Mella?" Dane's footsteps disappeared, replaced by a few limbs creaking above as he leaped from branch to branch. "She's over here!" he called over his shoulder right before our eyes met.

Oh no. Would they all find out my secret this way?

A few moments later, Beldon, Trinka, Reenalyn, and Dane were all there. Everyone but Acres, who I'd left with a load of floramancy to figure out. And they all had their instruments out in the open. Skunks. Selverine had made me miss our last chance to play together before the tournament.

And now she'd seen all our instruments, too.

I glanced at Dane's confused face, my stomach sinking.

"Mella! What happened to your head? Are you all right?" he dropped from the tree and reached my side in a few breaths as the others approached.

He took my head in his hands, searching my face with such concern. Almost as if he did still have feelings for me.

"I'm all right. I just fell."

"Mella—"

"I'm taking you all to the queen." Selverine eyed each of them, then grinned at me. "You'll be disqualified before you even get to the Grand Castors' Tournament."

"What's going on—" Dane started, but Selverine interrupted.

"You *do* all know Mella was going to leave your cohort, don't you? She was only using you. The queen offered to move her up to my cohort, and that's all she's wanted the whole time. She was going to fight with mine today against you all, but once the queen finds out she's been playing music and casting from a mandolin, of all things..." Selverine tsked, shaking her head.

Reenalyn frowned. "You were going to leave us today? During the tournament?"

"No! She's lying!" I said.

"So, you weren't using us, then, right?" she asked.

I sighed. "Well, I was at first, but that changed—"

Dane's hands dropped to his sides as he frowned, still searching my eyes.

Beldon glowered. "And the badass scythe wasn't even your real castling weapon?" He crossed his arms. "Was that whole story about your grandfather even true?"

"Yes, it was! But I couldn't tell you all about casting from the mandolin, don't you see? You never would've accepted me if you'd known that secret!"

"I wish you would've given us the chance, Mella." Dane sighed, taking a step back toward the others. "What else have you been lying to us about?"

The betrayal in his eyes cut me deeply. "I wish I'd explained Whisper to you all before now, but Selverine *is* lying about today. The queen *did* offer to move me to Selverine's cohort after Wager Day, and that *was* what I'd wanted at first, but I turned her down. I chose you all instead."

If only Acres were here! He'd seen it in my memories. He could've backed me up!

Selverine tsked again. "Of course she'd say that now, wouldn't she?"

Willova piped up, "Selverine, I don't think—"

Whisper cut her off, marching in between Selverine and me. "Mella's telling the truth. I was there. The queen offered, and Mella turned her down. She chose to stay."

Selverine rolled her eyes. "Of course *her castling* backs up her lies. What else would you expect?" She pointed to the ground at her feet. "We're going to the queen. All of you, here, now."

With a clatter that made me jump, Beldon threw his drumsticks to the ground.

That's...not like him.

"I'm so sorry, Selverine. You're absolutely right. Take us in," he said, his arms at his sides.

What?

I glanced at Reenalyn with a what-the-skunk look, but she only opened her hand to drop her beautiful beloved violin on the ground as well. "You're right, Selverine. We're so sorry."

Wind whistled through the panpipes for an instant before they hit the ground behind me.

"Forgive me, Selverine," Dane said as he stepped away from me and toward Selverine.

I couldn't blame them for doubting me. I should have told them so much sooner. But why treat their instruments so badly?

Willova and Selverine looked as surprised as I felt. "Okay. Well, pick those up. I'm not going to carry them for you. Come on. We're going to see the king and queen."

Dane, Reenalyn, and Beldon stooped to retrieve their instruments and got into line behind Selverine.

"Trinka," barked Selverine. "Take that mandolin thing and the scythe from Mella and follow me."

I glanced horrified at Trinka finding her typical scowl on her face. She deliberated for a moment and then walked toward me. Facing away from Selverine, she winked.

Was *she* on my side, of all people? I would've expected her to dump me at the first whiff of betrayal faster than anyone else.

"Hand it over, Yarinelle." She held out her hand.

I shook as I handed over my precious mandolin, the anchor for Whisper's essence.

She swiped them from me and pushed me in front of her and into line with everyone else.

"Good." Selverine surveyed us with her hands on her hips. "Mella, bring your...*castling*."

My heart plummeted to my toes as my eyes met Whisper's and I saw fear in her face for the first time. The only way to save her life would be to run for it. I hated to leave the rest of them now when I needed to prove my loyalty more than ever, but they'd only lose the chance at prize money and be punished for playing music during the castling year.

Whisper—she could be shattered all over again. Killed permanently this time. I couldn't risk that.

Launching at her, I scooped her up and grasped her like a giant, heavy pillow against my chest. My knee screamed and my sides throbbed, but I booked it in the opposite direction, hoping the surprise would give me enough of a head start.

Selverine shouted something, and more footsteps crashed behind me. I pushed myself as hard as I could go, trying not to hurt Whisper as I held her.

And then iron grips latched onto my shoulders, stopping me mid-run and sending my feet flying out in front of me.

I stifled a cry as I hit the ground hard, new pain flaring in my back and shoulders as I struggled to get my feet under me. Glancing up, I met Dane's unfeeling stare and Beldon's cold eyes as they frowned at me.

My stomach dropped again. Dane and Beldon. I should have told them. Now they'd never believe me again.

I'm so sorry.

I loosened my grip on Whisper, and she slid to the ground. Shaking out her feathers, she looked at me, worry in her eyes.

"Go," I mouthed as I got to my feet. "Run. Fly."

She shook her head.

I widened my eyes, trying to show my urgency. "Run now!" I hissed.

The boys dragged me back. Whisper followed. What was she doing? She had to save herself!

But Selverine had the mandolin. Running off wouldn't have done any good. What was I thinking?

Hopelessness overwhelmed me as I met the heartless stares of my cohort. They were taking it harder than I would have thought. I was a horrible person for not trusting them all sooner. Had I lost them forever now?

The others got in line behind Selverine, Beldon and Dane in front of me, and Reenalyn and Trinka behind. Whisper struggled to keep up. I wished for the leather pad, but it was still tucked under the log where the mandolin had been. I'd have to pick her up or get her on my shoulder. Though that would hurt.

"Yarinelle," Trinka hissed, "Everyone who's not themselves—did they all drink the punch at the ball?"

"What?" I hissed as I awkwardly scooped Whisper up.

"Beldon, Reenalyn, and Acres drank the punch. I didn't. Did you or Dane?"

I thought back to the night I'd spent hours dancing with Dane. If I could pick one memory to live in for the rest of my life, it would be that one. Now he'd never even see me as a friend again, much less anything else.

"When they closed the building and made us leave, there was only enough left in the bowl for one. He scooped it into a goblet and offered it to me, but I wanted water instead and told him he could have the punch."

Whisper wheezed with my arms around her chest. I'd have to put her on my shoulder so she could breathe.

Trinka whispered sharply behind me. "So everyone who just got weird drank the punch. Those of us with brains who didn't are still ourselves."

Hope flickered in my heart as her meaning dawned on me. "You're saying the punch was floramanced?" Maybe their reactions weren't because they completely hated me now. "But that was months ago! How could it still work?"

Whisper clambered onto my shoulder and I caught my breath as she tried unsuccessfully to hold on without stabbing me with her talons. "It could be a long-lasting potion of some kind," Whisper said.

Could that be?

"You got a plan, Yarinelle?" Trinka hissed.

"No..." Between discovering epiphanies, scraping my face down a balcony, and facing my friends and enemies with my life-threatening secret, I hadn't had time to *plan* anything.

"Good. Then we'll use mine."

CHAPTER 56

SELVERINE

So the secret to casting an avian was the same thing that would get her entire cohort disqualified? That was skunking hilarious. She'd used an instrument of music instead of an instrument of war, but still, how had she made it work?

Nothing like that should even be possible.

Grandmother would be so surprised. She'd always insisted there was no way to cast other than through weapons. It was preposterous to suggest otherwise.

But she'd been *wrong*.

Though she'd been surprisingly right about how people would comply with the law if I just told them to. It was eerie how they'd cooperated. Even that Trinka person, who always glowered like she was ready to murder anyone who looked at her funny.

We reached the palace grounds, and I veered toward the palace itself.

"Aren't we going to the coliseum?" Mella growled from behind me.

"Oh no. We're going to see the queen."

"But won't she be at the Tournament?"

I grinned at the palace door as the guard nodded and opened it. "Not yet. The competition isn't for a few more hours. We just let you think it was almost time to trick you into giving up your secret. Which worked."

Glancing back at her as the door swung wide, I spotted satisfying fury on her scowling face.

Everyone marched up the stairs behind me. The king's and queen's voices rumbled from the sitting room. And mucking skunks did I have something for them to discuss now.

Tempted as I was to burst through the door with my fascinating news, I restrained myself and knocked.

"Enter," Grandmother replied.

I opened the door and directed the lawbreakers to line up in front of them.

"What's this, Selverine?" the king asked.

"I found them all playing musical instruments in the woods. Even though they've each become castors and given up music."

His bushy eyebrows rose. "Indeed?" He glanced at my grandmother.

"Yes." I eyed Mella. There was so much more to say about her.

But I wouldn't embarrass my grandmother in front of the king. I would tell her about Mella casting from a non-weapon in private so she could choose how to act without Jorros's influence. He could be so overbearing. Maybe that would put me in better standing with her despite how badly things had gone with Horizon.

The king set down his tea and stood, tall as Beldon but not quite reaching Reenalyn's height. "This is a most egregious act." He laced his fingers behind his back and looked each of them in the eye in turn. "Serious enough of an offense to warrant the shattering of your weapons."

Small gasps of shock escaped from some of them. Their odd compliance and intense anger at Mella seemed to melt away in light of that statement.

My eyebrows rose, and I struggled to keep my jaw from dropping. Surely it wasn't *that* serious? I hadn't meant for anything so drastic to happen.

"Yes, Jorros, I think you may be right." The queen joined him, eyeing each of the transgressors.

I struggled to keep my shock hidden. My grandmother *agreed* that *shattering* was a fair punishment? I just wanted them punished with something annoying to make up for being friends with Mella and her stupid castling. But I didn't want anyone's castling *dead*, just for playing an instrument.

"But perhaps it would be better not to end their castlings today. The Grand Castors' Tournament is only a few hours away. We can put these treacherous musical instruments to public shattering as a warning to remind our citizens that unauthorized musical activity is not allowed and will always be found out and punished."

The king rubbed his chin, considering. "Very well. Children, surrender your instruments immediately."

Reenalyn held out her violin and Beldon his drumsticks. Dane reached out more hesitantly, panpipes in hand, as if he considered fighting back.

The king watched Dane with narrowed eyes as a couple guards collected the instruments.

My grandmother eyed the criminals. "Jorros, hadn't they better turn in their weapons as well?"

A ripple of discomfort and stiffening went through all of them, even Reenalyn and Beldon.

"That's right." He turned toward the chaise. "Not to worry. They will be safe here and returned to you when we deem the time appropriate."

Fists tightened around handles and scabbards as the guards laid the collected instruments on the chaise and reached for the weapons.

Reenalyn's knuckles whitened around her spear. Dane placed his hand over the top of the weapon on his belt.

"Come now," the king said. "I told you they would be returned. Resistance will only mean a worse punishment. Please be compliant, and all will be well again soon."

One guard grasped Willova's cutlass.

"No, not her." I said. "She's with me. Not one of the criminals."

The guard looked at the king, who nodded, then stepped away.

One guard took hold of the chain fastening Beldon's mace to its handle. Beldon shook with fury but let go. The guard set it next to the instruments while the other reached for Reenalyn's spear. The pure scalding fire in Reenalyn's face would've made me cower. The guard hesitated but locked his jaw and took her spear.

"If anything bad befalls my castling at your hands, you will pay with your life," she hissed.

The king raised his eyebrows as the guard turned to lay her spear over the instruments. "Watch your mouth, peasant," the king said with amusement.

All Reenalyn's mouth did was twist into an even more menacing scowl.

The other guard took Mella's scythe next, then her mandolin from Trinka.

Oh, skunks. They'd decided not to shatter the others' weapons, but if they shattered Mella's mandolin...it would be a *true* shattering. The avian would be gone forever.

I eyed the strange homemade-looking mandolin as Trinka laid her spiked brass knuckles on the guard's palm with a little less scathing opposition than I would've expected.

"What kind of weapon is that, boy?" the king asked.

I looked down to see the strange metal stake held between a guard and Dane.

"It's a tent peg."

The king chuckled, shrugging. "That one wouldn't be much of a loss."

Everyone went even more stiff at his words.

Maybe I should've waited to bring them in until I could speak privately with my grandmother. I sent a concerned look to her, and she was already watching me.

"Jorros"—her eyes left mine to look at him—"why don't you let Selverine and me handle this?"

The king brightened. "Yes, of course. Excellent suggestion, Narellen."

I frowned. Why was he so excited about leaving? He'd been so into taking everyone's things from them. But I wouldn't stop him if it meant getting him out of my hair.

Wait. He'd responded to Grandmother just as Mella's friends had responded to me. Was Grandmother floramancing the king?

The king rushed from the room, and I turned to the queen. "Grandmother, may I speak to you in private before these criminals are escorted to the dungeon?"

She gestured me into the hallway. "What is it, dear?" she asked, nodding at the guard to keep an eye on the others.

"I know how Mella cast the avian," I whispered. "It was through her instrument—the mandolin! I saw her do it. She held the mandolin as if it were her weapon and said a casting call different from the one at the ceremony, and the avian manifested from the instrument."

Her eyebrows rose, and her lips pinched together. "Is that so?"

Why didn't she sound more excited? This was huge! "So let me keep her instrument and see if I can cast her avian for myself—maybe the rules are different with an instrument, you know? Maybe the eagle could be my castling instead. And if not, then I can at least interview the avian to learn what I can. We can tell the crowd that Mella's weapon—which they will think is her castling weapon—is to be shattered because she was the one leading the others in this inappropriate behavior."

I waited. Would she let me take it?

She smiled reassuringly. "Of course, dear. But first, let's have some tea."

CHAPTER 57

DANE

S o that was why Mella had always been so careful never to cast in front of anyone. Because her casting tool was a mandolin instead of a weapon. That explained why she'd failed to cast at the Castling Ceremony. Was that also why her castling was an adult? Did casting from an instrument of music instead of an instrument of war result in an adult castling, or was she just lying about when she'd cast for the first time?

No, she wasn't lying then. She'd left a lot out that I wished she'd trusted me with. But she hadn't lied.

The door opened, and Selverine returned. Instantly I straightened, reminded of how important it was to give her the best impression of myself.

Why though?

It doesn't matter. I just know I must.

She stared at us, then focused on Mella's mandolin. Hadn't I just thought of something that...something about it. Important? Something to do with Mella. Mella was nice. But of course, Selverine was the most important person in the room. Would she ever notice me? I hoped she would.

Several armed guards thumped through the door, and my eyes wandered to Mella, though I wasn't sure why. Those guards weren't here for her, right?

Selverine retrieved something I couldn't see with the guards between us, then left the room.

I missed her for a moment, and then the roiling fury in my gut reminded me how much I loathed her for putting us in this situation. Having our castling weapons taken away! Unbelievable!

What was going on? Was this like what happened to everyone who drank the punch? *Whenever Selverine's in the room, my brain gets weird. But not the same way as whenever I'm around Mella.*

Was there any way to stop that? At least they weren't serious about shattering our weapons. Just the instruments—*Monkey's teeth! Whisper's tied to the mandolin!*

Whisper fixed her fiery gaze on the door Queen Narellen had walked through moments ago, her crown feathers erect and quivering. Mella's eyes were red, and she stood awkwardly trying to balance Whisper's weight on her shoulder.

Dark stains were already spreading around Whisper's talons where they dug into Mella's shoulder without the leather pad. The sight hurt my chest. How could I help?

Stepping to her side, I passed her my last pelinary petal. If they tried anything else on us, at least she might get away.

Her eyes widened at me, then relief washed over her face as she met my eyes. Taking the crimson petal, she nodded and ate it quickly. "Thank you," she whispered.

The guards returned and bound our wrists, then pushed us toward the door we'd come through. Reenalyn's angry eyes rested on her spear, but one of the guards grabbed her shoulder and forced her from the room. With grumbles and wistful looks back at the weapon-covered chaise from each of us, we followed Reenalyn out.

All except Trinka. She got obediently in line with the rest of us, right in front of me, but determination and a bit of snark shone on her face.

She caught my eye and winked.

What?

Trinka Seranova was not the winking type. I followed her from the room, wondering what could possibly be amusing about this. I would think she of all people should be flipping tables and punching eyes out to get her castling weapon back.

As she stepped up a flight of stairs in front of me, her boots came closer to my eye level. Was that a bulge in her left boot?

I remembered the single set of spiked knuckled she'd handed Jorros and suddenly had a good guess what she was hiding. My own smile grew, and I controlled myself before one of the guards could notice. Did this mean there was a little hope?

Trinka, did you do what I think you did?

Chapter 58

MELLA

My shoulder went uncomfortably numb from Whisper's talons. But I knew she felt terrible, so I did my best to keep it to myself. The guards pushed us into the dank stone dungeon, and I wrinkled my nose as the filth and odor of unwashed bodies only grew worse the farther in they forced us.

They shoved us all into a single cell, and I sat gingerly on the floor with Whisper as close to the ground as I could, and she hopped off. I cried out, more from the shame of letting everyone down and the guilt of what was about to happen to Whisper than for the pain in my shoulder.

"Oh, Mella!" Reenalyn exclaimed, kneeling next to me.

"Reenalyn? You're still speaking to me?" I tried to calm my frantic breathing.

"Of course! There's blood running down your shoulder!"

"We didn't have the leather pad. It's my fault," Whisper said from the corner. She seemed so ashamed of it, she'd scooted as far into the shadows as she could.

"I'm so sorry for not telling you all the truth sooner. I should have—I was wrong. I'm sorry."

Reenalyn hovered, applying pressure to the punctures to slow the bleeding. "It's all right, Mella. I wish you wouldn't have felt the need to conceal so much. But I'm not angry at you any more. We've got bigger problems now."

"I'm so sorry I hurt you, Mella," Whisper said from the shadows.

"Whisper, it's fine. We didn't have another choice. It's not like you could've stopped Selverine from...everything."

"That *bitch*," Trinka said from the other corner, looking surprisingly calm for having just been parted from Mauler's weapon for the first time. Was she in shock?

"Besides, that's nothing compared to..." I forced my head up and found Whisper's eyes.

Regret for the pain she caused me, and a lot of anger. But no fear. Only strength.

"Compared to what, Mella?" Reenalyn asked.

"You might as well tell them all now." Whisper sighed.

I felt the heat of everyone's eyes landing on me, curious.

"Tell us what, Mella?" Beldon asked.

I sighed and stared at the floor, feeling wearier than ever. "Whisper...she's not a normal castling. Beyond the whole mandolin thing. Before she was my castling, she belonged to someone else."

Reenalyn cocked her head, listening as Dane waited with his arms crossed and the others frowned.

"And for her first castor, she didn't manifest as an eagle. She was a coyote. And the reason she struggles to fly so much...is because she's got some coyote body parts left over."

Whisper stuck out one leg, showing how the eagle talons and feathers of her foot morphed into a muscular, sandy-coated canine leg further up.

"Holy skunks." Beldon said. "I've heard of casting someone else's castling. But never in a different form. How'd you do that?"

"I'm not sure—"

Whisper cut me off with a sharp, desperate exclamation. "Bennet?"

I glanced around the cell, but only our cohort was in here. "Whisper? What do you mean?"

She sniffed the air and pivoted toward the wall between our cell and the next with a barred window set toward the top. "Bennet!" she screeched.

"Whisper, what are you saying?" I pushed myself up and stepped toward Whisper, confused.

"Hello?" the husky voice of an old man floated from between the bars.

"Bennet! Bennet, it's me! It's Sienna! I'm here!" she shouted.

"Sienna?" the husky voice said, full of disbelief.

Trinka was suddenly next to me. "What's that about?"

Skunking muck. No way. "I think Sienna was her name before." I offered my forearm to Whisper, who was striving unsuccessfully to climb the stone wall.

"Mella, no. I don't want to hurt you."

"It's okay. This is important!"

"What's going on?" Dane asked.

With a look of mingled regret and gratitude, Whisper stepped up onto my forearm and clung as gently as she could. I held her up to the window.

"Sienna? You're not Sienna," the man cried, his voice breaking. "Who are you?"

I peeked through the window separating our cell from his. "Bennet." My voice trembled from shock. I swallowed and spoke louder. "Did you have a coyote castling named Sienna?"

He peered at me, too many emotions on his worn face to keep up with. "Who are *you*?"

An unkempt beard and mustache twitched with his words, and his skinny shoulders showed through the thin fabric of his soiled tunic.

"And were you falsely accused of assassinating the king?" I pressed.

He gripped the bars, torchlight glowing in his eyes. "How do you know that?"

"Then this *is* Sienna. She's your castling in a different form." I glanced back to the others, who were all staring at me with varying shades of confusion and disbelief. "Something went wrong with my castling weapon, and when I played my mandolin later that day, somehow, Whisper—Sienna—came out. Right when I plucked the last string..."

And it hit me. "It was *the string*!"

"Mella, what are you talking about?" Dane asked.

But I understood now.

"Bennet, was your weapon a bow and arrow?"

"Yes. How did you know?"

"Reenalyn, the house you were cleaning right before the first Castling Ceremony months ago, do you remember who it belonged to?"

"Um." Her eyebrows drew together. "I think someone who used to take care of the coliseum—maintenance or something. Why?"

"Because on my way to the coliseum for the ceremony, I pulled some string out of the trash you threw away and used it to replace the broken string on my mandolin! It must've been Bennet's bowstring! Whisper's soul was *still* inside it, waiting to be cast!"

"Mucking skunking muck." Whisper leaned toward the window. "Bennet, it's me. I saw it all happen. You fired off an arrow to block Jorros's sword from killing King Krelwey, but he lied and told the king his sword had blocked your arrow. The last words he spoke when they separated us were: 'I'm sorry, brother.'"

"Sienna?" His voice broke again as his hand reached through the bars toward Whisper. She leaned her head into his hand, just like a dog who wants scratches behind the ears. And she smiled.

I barely felt the tug of her talons through my flesh now. We'd found her original castor. He was alive.

So this must mean that the man who couldn't eat bread was right about that shattering! And that everyone who has eaten bread has been floramanced to forget it!

"There's one man in all of Terrenthyrs who claims a man named Bennet had his weapon shattered forty years ago. But somehow, no one in the town remembers," I said. "Why would that be?"

"Narellen." Bennet wheezed. "She manipulates memories. She changed Jorros—he'd been my friend and he'd loved his father. But she twisted his mind and made him think he wanted to assassinate the king so he could rule sooner. Then she made the only witness to the assassination attempt forget so the blame went on me instead. They shattered my Sienna, rose up to become king and queen, and left me here to rot."

"How does she affect peoples' thoughts?" I asked.

"The punch!" Trinka shouted.

Everyone turned to her. Beldon asked, "What?"

"The punch! At the ball, everyone who drank the punch behaved weirdly. You all wanted to get Selverine's attention. Remember? You were all fawning over her, and you did it again today." She pointed at me. "Yarinelle, remember how Felzane dumped you for that other girl?"

I winced and nodded.

"He's a skunkass and would've done that anyway, Mella," Reenalyn announced. "Don't dump Dane! He's so much better for you!"

Dane blushed and locked eyes with me, his shocked gaze full of questions. Embarrassment warmed my face, too.

"I'm not—let's stick to the point, please?" Hopefully no one heard my voice break. Hadn't Reenalyn noticed he didn't feel that way about me anymore?

Trinka tapped her toe impatiently. "Well, Demensey's right, because he was already with some other girl, but the point is, Yarinelle and I didn't drink the punch, so we didn't get drawn to the princess like the rest of you. Yarinelle was too distracted getting lost in Velowinzinger's eyes to notice what idiots you all made of yourselves..."

"Trinka!" I shrieked.

Boots clomped over the stone floor toward us.

"But I saw it all," she continued. "What if—"

A key clicked into the lock on the door. The guards were back, their jaguar and alligator castlings glowering at us.

"Time to go," said the one with a jaguar castling.

The heavy iron door into our cell screeched over the stone floor, and the guards entered.

Backing into the shadows, my excitement over finding Bennet vanished. Whisper was about to die. She'd finally gotten to be with her castor, the true other half of her soul, after decades apart. And she was about to be shattered. Again.

No way could she survive a second shattering.

The guards started binding everyone's wrists. I had only seconds before mine would be tied, too.

I glanced up at the window. "Whisper, step up onto the windowsill."

She met my eyes, hope and fear and joy and dread all at once.

"Go on. I...I don't know how long you have." My voice cracked as a tear trailed down my cheek. "You've been an incredible castling, and I wish we could've spent more time together, but I'm truly so glad you found Bennet. Take your last minutes with him. I'll buy you as much time as I can. Hand to claw."

She squeezed herself onto the shadowed ledge that was much too small for her and ducked against the bars, sticking one foot out to bump my fist with her foot. One last time. "Hand to claw. Mella..."

"It's okay. I love—"

A guard grabbed my wrist and hauled me into line. I wanted to glance back for one more goodbye, but I didn't want them to know she was there. Better to let them think she'd fallen asleep and had her essence transported back into the weapon.

My heart wrenched. If only she could go into the weapon that would see another day instead of the instrument that was about to be shattered.

The guards pushed us outside and herded us toward the coliseum, where we should've been getting ready for the tournament. Instead, we marched toward a shattering.

Suddenly Trinka paused, and it sounded like she was whispering. Trying not to run into her, I strained to hear.

Was that her castling call?

Dust and powdered chocolate erupted from one of her boots, and moments later, Mauler appeared.

But how...

She'd handed the king the wrong set of spiked knuckles! Brilliant!

The guards jumped back and cried out in surprise as a nearly full-grown black bear erupted in their midst...with her front paw stuck down the back of Trinka's boot. Confused, Mauler jerked her paw out, slicing the boot clean through.

"Oh, sorry, Trinka. I...who *dared* tie you up!" she bellowed.

A strange expression of pride and gratitude warmed Trinka's features in a way I'd never seen before.

She beamed at her castling, then shouted, "Mauler, run!"

"But..."

"*Run! Now!*"

Mauler stumbled back, glancing from the guards to Trinka's bindings.

"Go to Acres and tell him bring *all* of the stuff! Now!" She tossed something small and shiny to Mauler, who plucked it from the air and folded her paw pads over it.

"Tell him Mella's mandolin must be saved!"

Mucking skunks. She knew about his research, too? Did she know something I didn't?

Understanding lit up Mauler's face and perked up her ears. Straightening, she gave Trinka one sharp nod, bowled over the two guards who attempted to restrain her, and roared in the faces of their alligator and jaguar castlings. A moment later she was gone, her trained muscles carrying her impossibly fast through the woods.

The remaining guard paled, then turned his wrathful gaze on Trinka.

She beamed. One of the greatest sights I'd ever seen.

Maybe there was hope for us yet.

CHAPTER 59

ACRES

T he deep blue light of morning peeked through the window as
I scrubbed my dry eyes for the thousandth time, holding the
new bit of experimental floramancy in my hands.

Somewhere in the back of my mind I knew it was ridiculous to
experiment with floramancy on the morning of the Grand Castors'
Tournament, but another part of me hoped it would give me an
excuse to sit this one out. The last public event hadn't gone well for
me, and I wasn't in any hurry to repeat that particular experience.
They would do fine without me.

With an apologetic glance at a disapproving Starstinger, I tipped
the handful of leaves and herbs into my mouth and swallowed.

Thinking of the bit of green herb leaf in Mella's teeth last night, I
ran my tongue over my own to make sure I hadn't missed any. It was
that bit of leaf that had made me realize my inexcusable oversight.
How had I obsessed over the sauce ingredients so much that I forgot
the little sprinkle of spices that accompanied every sandwich from
the Loaf? I'd brushed a few strays off my desk from last night and
mixed in a fraction of a piece of deecho fern. The dapplemint I was
already chewing completed the potion.

Shaking my head, I found Starstinger's eyes again. She raised an
eyebrow and cocked her head.

"I don't feel anything yet," I told her.

These things always took time to kick in—metabolism and all that. But I still let my shoulders droop as I stared at all the space on my desk taken up with notes on skunking floramancy books and containers of wilting ingredients.

This was not what I wanted to be doing with my life.

My life.

The concept of my life—the future—what was left of it...caused an eruption of pain in my head.

I dropped to the floor, my head in my hands and my eyes squeezed tight as I waited for the pain to clear—hoping it would end soon. Seconds oozed by, and I had no idea how much time had passed when the pain finally eased. Starstinger's front paws rested on my knee, and she peered anxiously into my face. I didn't remember her moving.

But I *did* remember I was going to die.

"Acres?

I'm dying. I've been dying since before I came to Terrenthyrs.

"Acres, can you hear me?"

This is what they'd kept from me.

"Acres?" Starstinger's high-pitched cry pulled my gaze to hers.

"Starstinger."

"Acres, what happened? Are you in pain?"

"I...a little. It's subsiding."

She slumped with relief and then jumped into my lap, peering closely into my eyes. "What happened?" she repeated.

"I remembered what I forgot."

"Oh?" she asked, her ears perking up.

"And...and I wish I hadn't." How could I tell my castling I was dying? Who would I leave her weapons with after I was gone? Castlings didn't live long after their castor's death, but they didn't die right away either. It would be terrible for her.

Her ears drooped again, and she looked so worried it hurt my chest. Would she ever stop looking like that once she knew?

"Acres, what—"

"Acres! Starstinger! Where are you?" came a little-girl voice from outside.

Starstinger's ears shot back as her head flicked to the window. With a glance at me, she slid out of my lap and jumped onto the windowsill.

I'm dying.

"It's Mauler, Trinka's castling," she told me. Grabbing the turning mechanism at the window's base, she struggled to open the window a crack. "Acres isn't feeling well today," she called down to Mauler. "We can't talk now."

I'm dying.

"You don't understand!" Mauler shouted at Starstinger. "Trinka sent me to tell you we need your help!"

"We can't help right now. We—"

Mauler cut her off. "The rest of the cohort is in the queen's custody right now, Acres. They took their weapons and instruments. King Jorros decided they're going to shatter them before starting the Grand Castors' Tournament. We've got to help them!" A sob choked the final word.

Skunks. Shattered? I pushed to my feet, a little dizzy, and hurried to the window. Mauler stood underneath, her paws braced on the brick wall, her black bear face pleading.

"They're shattering the weapons? Or the instruments?" I asked, still bleary-eyed and fuzzy in the head after remembering...*I'm going to die.*

"I don't know! She didn't have time to tell me. Guards were leading them away, and they didn't have either with them." She held something up to me, her bear lips quivering. Trinka's spiked knuckles rested in her palm, glinting in the morning sun. "She made me bring this. So I wouldn't get killed." Tears welled in her big brown eyes.

Skunks.

Weight pressed down on me at the immense wrongness of a castor parted from their castling by force. It was a relief Mauler was safe, but the others...

Would Starstinger be safe once they realized we were from the same cohort?

If music from castors was only outlawed after the shattering forty years ago, maybe someone would remember how being a musician became taboo. And I knew the potion for bringing memories back now. Would it work on memories as old as these? On older people?

I didn't know, but I had to try.

I shoved my mortality to the back of my mind and focused on scrabbling together a plan to save everyone else.

We'd never get any more dried deecho fern. That would be the limiting factor. It wouldn't be enough for everyone in the coliseum, anyway. If we could come up with a way to give it to those who were old enough to remember...

"Mauler, see all those plants at your feet? The ones with dappled leaves?"

She frowned at me and looked down. "Yes?" She raised an eyebrow.

"I think I have a way to help. We're going to make a potion, and I need every one of those multicolored leaves. Can you gather them all up for me?"

"On it!"

I turned to my desk to get something for her to put the leaves in, blinking in the dim light of my room as my eyes adjusted from the growing sunlight.

"Oh, and Acres?"

"Yes, Mauler?"

"Trinka said to tell you that Mella's mandolin must be saved."

Frowning, I leaned back over the windowsill. "Why?"

She shrugged. "I don't know, but it sounded really important."

"Okay." What was that about?

Starstinger regarded me from the desk, her tail twitching.

I knew she was still waiting for an explanation, but if I thought about that again right now, I'd lose whatever sliver of a chance I had of pulling this off for the rest of them. And to protect her.

I grabbed an empty cloth pouch and handed it to her. "Run to The Braided Loaf and fill this all the way up with their spice mix, then meet me at the coliseum. As fast as you can."

With a worried glance at me, she retrieved the pouch with her teeth and leaped from the desk to the windowsill, then through the window straight to the grass below. She disappeared around the corner, her black-tipped tail whipping behind her.

I wrenched the trunk out from under my desk and tore open the lid. Retrieving the sack of old clothes, I dumped them on the parchment covering my bed. Holding my breath, I brushed the clothes off, watching the blue-green deecho fern fibers collect on the parchments. Once I'd removed all that I could, I carefully picked up each piece of parchment and folded it into the mouth of the now-empty clothing sack to dump the fibers in.

Tripping over the trunk, I stumbled to the window and removed each remaining dapplemint leaf from the potted plants on the sill, dropping them into the sack as well. I fisted the sack closed and started shaking the ingredients together. They should work together to unlock and enhance the forgotten memories right away, like they had for me and Trinka.

Unlike Trinka and Starstinger, I wasn't going to fit through the window. I ducked out the bedroom door, stumbled down the stairs, and rounded the corner just as Mauler was looking up at the window for me, green leaves skewered up each claw.

"Oh, there you are. Here." She shoved her leaf-laden paws in my face.

I held the sack open and brushed the impaled leaves into it. Between these dapplemint leaves and the ones from inside, I should have the right ratio of dapplemint to deecho fern.

"There. Now we have to hurry!" She dropped to all fours and swung around, nearly knocking me over. "Get on!"

My still-aching head didn't love the idea of riding a bear, but it was the fastest way. So I drew the opening of the sack closed and climbed onto her back.

We were going to save some lives and unblind thousands of eyes. If this worked.

CHAPTER 60

MELLA

T hey lined us up—again—on the stage and laid our instruments at our feet, far enough out of reach that we couldn't even touch them one last time.

Guilt ate at me. I'd been so eager to save my social standing by getting better at casting Whisper, I'd helped everyone get too cavalier about playing music after casting, and now we were all paying for it. It was because of me my cohort was in trouble.

And they were going to shatter Whisper.

I watched the man distributing our instruments. He reached into his cart once more and pulled out—my scythe?

He laid it at my feet and pushed the cart away. Did that mean they were going to shatter the scythe instead of the mandolin? They thought they were doing their worst, but they were saving Whisper's life!

A ripple of relief seemed to go through all of us as each one understood what the appearance of the scythe rather than the mandolin meant.

King Jorros stood and spread his arms wide to silence the crowd. "Good people of Terrenthyrs, I come before you today with the most grievous news."

He described what horrible criminals we were for illegally playing our instruments in the woods. I struggled not to roll my eyes at his infuriating tone and leaned around Reenalyn to look at Queen Narellen. Selvenair the sea eagle perched on a stand at her side, the wind gently ruffling feathers on his neck, wings, and back. Narellen sat in her throne, her dark eyes focused on us.

The king finished addressing the crowd and gestured to the queen. She stood and spoke next.

"As you can see, because the leader of the criminals was the instigator and the one responsible for these other young people going astray, her castling weapon will be shattered in punishment. But furthermore, this instrument with which she lured them away will also be shattered. For the good of us all." Convincing false sorrow on her face.

My ears pounded.

So they were shattering both.

Whisper would die today. In just a few minutes.

I glanced frantically from my bindings to the giant boulder suspended above one side of the arena—there had to be something else I could do, something I could try.

The wind chilled the tear trails running down my face.

The eyes of everyone in the crowd and my friends weighed heavily on me.

"Shatter the scythe first," Narellen ordered the guard.

The guard picked up my scythe without looking at me and dropped it from the upper stage to the bare arena below. It clattered without breaking. It had been well-wrought.

The boulder was dropped on it then, and the sound of rocks crashing on metal and wood splintering crackled through the air.

The scythe was shattered. Irreparable.

My mandolin was next.

Metal gears squealed as someone reeled the boulder back into place. It rose slowly, speck by speck.

The queen lifted my mandolin from the ground and carried it to the edge herself.

Selverine had told her I cast Whisper from the mandolin. So why bother shattering the scythe at all?

Unless she wanted the crowd to think that shattering the scythe was to take out my castling while shattering the mandolin was to punish me for playing music after casting.

Why would she want to hide that the mandolin was how I cast Whisper?

Unless...*holy skunks*. She'd claimed that Selvenair's castling weapon was the crossbow on display in her sitting room, but what if that was a lie? The crossbow had looked dusty, and Selvenair hardly ever left his perch on that huge ancient drum. Had she cast Selvenair from *that*?

I opened my mouth to ask. Anything to delay her and buy Whisper and Bennet a few more moments. "Aren't you going to tell them all that I cast Whisper from the mandolin before you throw it over? Since you and Selverine both are determined to ruin my reputation as much as possible. Seems like you'd ensure all of Terrenthyrs knew what a *strange* person I am—not worth associating with. Unless you don't want them to know about avians and instruments."

She halted, slowly turning back to me.

"What's that, dear?"

"You've told them you're punishing me for playing music after casting, but not that doing so is how I cast my avian. Almost like you want that part to remain a secret."

Her eye twitched, and I wished I had a voice-enhancing potion so the whole crowd could hear this.

"You know, it's never made sense to any of us," I gestured to my friends on either side, "that playing music after casting is illegal. Or that a profession as skillful and challenging as a musician is reserved only for lesser classers."

Her face hardened as she strode toward me. "That's enough disrespectful speculation, Mella."

"It's almost as if someone wanted to make sure no one ever found out what can happen when you cast from an instrument of music instead of an instrument of war."

Pausing before us, her expression eased back into a smile, her arms crossed as she gripped the mandolin's arm in one hand. "Well haven't you just figured it all out, then."

"Not exactly." Glaring at her, I raised an eyebrow. "Why keep it a secret? How could other people casting avians possibly be bad?"

She smiled, the wrinkles around her eyes threatening now rather than grandmotherly looking. "Why do you think?"

The gears squealed as the boulder made it one third of the way back up.

"It could be because you're vain enough to want to be the only person in Terrenthyrs, or the whole world, with such a unique castling. But I don't think that's the answer. It's got to be something more."

"You're right about that. But you'll never guess."

"Then why don't you tell me?"

"Why would I explain myself to a child?"

Selverine cut in, tears and rage in her eyes. "Because you've been lying to all of us, even *me*, your own granddaughter. And *I* at least deserve an explanation!"

"All right, then. If answers are so important to you. I'll make you a deal. Each of you eat one of these," she pulled a little tin of wafers from a pocket in her dress, "then I'll answer every question you can ask in the next few minutes."

Ugh! Why?

Dane held up a hand. "Hang on. What's in that? Some kind of potion to make us forget everything you tell us?"

She shrugged innocently. "Only one way to find out."

If I didn't eat it, Whisper would be shattered in the next few moments and I'd never understand why. If I risked it, I'd get answers. Probably also a really bad side effect or two. I might forget what I learn. But at the very least, it would buy Whisper a few more minutes with Bennet before the end.

I reached toward the tin, but Dane grabbed my arm. "Mella, are you sure?"

The fear and concern in his eyes that the pelinary petal might have stopped working by now touched my heart. "Yes, Dane. I'll be fine. I have to know."

Nodding, he let go of my arm.

I took a bite of a wafer.

"The whole thing, Mella," the queen purred.

Hoping the petal was still working, I popped the rest in my mouth.

Dane snatched the next one, slipping his hand around mine as he chewed.

"Dane, no!"

My heart soared even as terror filled me for what I could be getting him into.

What if it was poison? Had he eaten a petal I hadn't seen?

Reenalyn swiped the next one, scowling at the queen and taking hold of my other hand. Beldon and Trinka followed suit.

"Reenalyn, you shouldn't—"

The queen cut me off, holding the tin out to Selverine and Willova, lifting an eyebrow.

"You want *me* to take some?" Selverine shrieked. "I'm your *granddaughter*!"

The queen nodded. "Even so."

Glowering, Selverine took two and handed one to Willova.

"Now none of you need to worry that you'll forget this afternoon." Closing the tin, she slid it back into her pocket. "I'm a far more accomplished floramancer than that. You'll remember. It will just be an entirely different conversation. And I know about your pelinary petals—I investigated after the tea had no effect on you, Mella—so I've used something a little stronger."

My stomach sank. And now all my friends had taken it too. None of them would have anything stronger than pelinary petals—if anything like that even existed.

With a wave of her wrist, the queen continued. "But you've got a few minutes to ask questions. So go on. Tell me what you think you've figured out so far, and I'll tell you if you're right."

The king frowned at the boulder's slow ascent, the crowd mumbling and fidgeting.

"Is the potion in the wafer the same as what was in the punch at the ball?" Trinka hissed.

"A good guess. It is similar. Only off by one ingredient."

"Why the difference?" Trinka asked.

"Because the punch was an experiment. Selverine will be ruling one day, and Terrenthyrs must be prepared to follow her when Jorros and I are gone."

Selverine made a face. "What? The king's made nothing clearer than the fact that I'm not his heir, and am not in line for the throne. Which is fine with me, because I don't want it. I've never even received any training to be queen one day! You've seen to it that all I spend any time on is preparing for the Grand Castor's Tournament. Nothing after that."

"Trust me, Selverine, all is as it should be."

"That's another thing," I said. "Has the tournament always been tradition here, or is that something you invented?"

"That was all my doing. As was Wager Day and the Castling Ceremony."

"So the ceremony," Beldon cut in, "that was to make sure you saw every new castling and could be sure no one had figured out the avian thing. But why the castling registry?"

"I frequently checked around the country for Avian castlings. Those with a registered castling I didn't have to bother with," the queen said.

"Then how'd I get away with Whisper for so long?"

"Two reasons, Mella. A particular date has been approaching for many years, and it's almost here. A stray avian castling or two won't make much difference now that we're nearly there. And secondly, because I've been too busy tutoring Selverine for the tournament to watch that as closely as I used to."

"What? Then why shatter Whisper if it doesn't even matter!"

"Might as well use caution, since you brought her right to me. Just in case."

I did have one other question. "Why doesn't anyone remember Whisper's first shattering?"

"Whisper's first shattering?" she lifted one eyebrow.

Oh, muck it all. I shouldn't have said that.

My heart plummeted to my toes as understanding lit up the queen's face. "I thought something about the glare in her eyes felt familiar. What are the odds that Sienna would return, and that you, a random child, would discover not only avian casting, but hybrid casting as well."

She regarded me for a long moment as my friends and I stayed silent. My heart raced. We all knew too much now.

"As for your question about why no one remembers Sienna's shattering—that's one of my greatest floramantic discoveries." She turned away from me. "Selverine, besides Emberlyn wood, what does Terrenthyrs produce the most of?"

She frowned. "I don't skunking know!"

"Wheat?" Willova asked.

"Indeed. What do you make with wheat that everyone likes to eat in one form or another?"

Dane raised an eyebrow. "Bread?"

"Precisely."

Holy skunks. "You've been floramancing the wheat to make people forget. And it affects everyone, because everyone eats bread. *But the snow leopard castor can't. That's why he's the only one who remembers.*

"But why?" Selverine demanded. "Why floramance your own people, prevent them from casting avians even when it's their *one and only dream*, and start the whole Castling Ceremony and Grand Castors' Tournament? What does that accomplish?"

"Ah, the Grand Castors' Tournament. One of my greatest ideas."

"It encourages the best fighters of each year to get lazy and out of shape," Trinka pointed out. "How is that one of your best ideas?"

"Because Terrenthyrs isn't the only country I rule. First and foremost, I'm the Queen of Morrenfayre."

CHAPTER 61

SELVERINE

*T*he Queen of Morrenfayre?

Were we even related at all, or was I from that country, too?

"What the muck! What do you mean, you're the Queen of Morrenfayre, Grandmother?"

The big guy, Beldon, interrupted, "So you weaken Terrenthyrs by quietly destroying their best fighters every year and use that process to distract everyone from the fact that there's no actual military in place."

But if the Castling Ceremony and the Grand Castors' Tournament were worthless, why insist I win them?

"And keeping avian casting a secret," Mella asked, "that's because you've got a bunch of them somewhere, and you're going to use them against us, isn't it?"

Then why use floramancy to prepare the people of Terrenthyrs to serve me during my surprise inevitable rule?

Grandmother smiled and nodded. "Yes, I've built up a fine Avian Army in the years I've been here."

"How long have you been here?" that tall girl, Reenalyn, asked.

"Forty-six years, eight months, and two weeks."

The squeaky gears ground to a halt as the boulder reached the top. I squinted at her. *The muck?*

"I don't know, I think we were looking for an actual day count," Beldon said. What was the idiot doing cracking a joke in this moment?

The queen rubbed her hands together. "Yes, and it will all be worth it very soon."

"So the important date you said is approaching—that's going to be a war?" Dane asked.

"Oh, no." Narellen flicked her hand at Dane as if he were being silly. "There won't be a war. Selling Emberlyn wood and other commodities to Morrenfayre at lower prices than you can get for them here was just because I could. I already control both countries, so no need for a battle."

"Then what the skunk have you been doing all of this for!" I shouted, gesturing at the crowd in the stands.

"Because someone bet I couldn't," her smile widened, "and I'm finally about to prove them wrong."

"So let me get this straight," Mella said. "You've spent forty-six years, eight months, and two weeks of your life floramancing an entire country just to prove to someone that you could?"

"That puts it very simply, but yes."

My head throbbed behind my eyes. This was too much.

Mella rubbed her forehead. How could she bully my poor grandmother like this?

No, wait, Mella wasn't bullying her. Grandmother was confessing a life of lies. What was wrong with my head?

Beldon squinted, shielding his eyes from the sun. He was the one being disrespectful. Just look at him. He looks like someone who'd be a skunk to the queen.

Now what had she just said? She was predicting that I'd win the tournament, of course.

Shaking my head, I tried to get rid of the fog in my brain. Why were these lesser classers on the stage with me? The tournament was meant to be fought up here.

Smiling at each of us, Grandmother said, "Now, the king is about to draw cohort names from the basin to select the first fighting groups. Only one basin this time, since weapons and castlings will both be used in every match. Good fortune to you and your castlings."

With an impressive motion, she pitched the instrument over the edge.

Mella smiled mildly at me. "Good fortune to you and your castling, Selverine."

Chapter 62

Acres

I'd never considered riding a bear before. I should've left it that way.

My stiff legs grew numb from Mauler's pace.

It's a good thing this happened today, and not months from now. I may not be able to hold on by then.

I shoved the thought aside. I'd have to deal with what I remembered after getting everyone else's memories back.

The streets were eerily quiet. Everyone was in the coliseum ready to spectate on the tournament. The huge doors loomed before us.

Mauler ran on at full speed.

"So, we're not stopping to open the doors?" I asked

"Why," she panted, "would we waste time doing that?"

Right.

I braced for impact as she barreled into the doors headfirst. We launched through and skidded into the arena, the sound of her smack against the doors echoing through the coliseum.

Something hit the dirt floor to the side, adding a sharper echo.

Bits of metal glinted in the dust around it.

That's not Mella's...

The queen stood at the edge of the lower stage. Her raised arm came down. A guard on the wall untied a rope.

Skunks.

They were going to shatter the mandolin.

Leaping off Mauler, I dove for the mandolin.

My fingers scrabbled for a hold.

The boulder fell toward me.

I rolled away just in time.

"Acres!" Mauler galloped to me, the bag of plant bits I'd dropped held between her teeth. "That was incredible!"

Dust from the boulder's impact settled in the air around me.

Had I really just done that?

I looked up to find the queen glowering down on me.

Better get on with this before she can stop me.

But I had to wait for Starstinger to get here with the rest of the potion. I had to buy some time.

Standing, I brushed myself off and faced the crowd.

Surely there was some way to buy time besides speaking to all of them. If there was, it didn't come to me.

Great.

"Listen, everyone." I cleared my throat and tossed a couple of locs out of my face. "Um, someone's been lying. About a lot of stuff." *Muck. What am I saying?*

"Contain this boy!" Narellen shouted. "He's trying to delay the tournament." A few guards broke away from the wall.

Skunks.

Sweating, I switched the mandolin to my other hand, gripping it and the bag together so I could pull my throwing stars from their leather pouch.

There were more guards than I had stars.

Mauler prowled in front of me, growling at them.

A dark blur shot over the railing of the lower stage and rolled across the arena. Trinka stood from the dust cloud she'd stirred up, then pelted toward us.

She skidded to a halt next to Mauler, who tossed her spiked knuckles back to her. Trinka snatched them from the air and slid them over her fingers, folding her hand into a fist.

"Is that the potion, Parrianther?"

The guards rushed us.

"Part of it," I said.

Mauler launched herself at one, tackling him to the ground.

Trinka did some kind of twirl in the air, slicing one's throat with her castling weapon and kicking another in the chest, throwing him to the ground and knocking the wind out of him.

Darting for another, Trinka shouted, "Where's the skunking rest of it!"

She dodged a sword thrust, spinning over it, and kicked that one to the ground, too. Landing on his chest, she finished him off.

"It's on the way!"

The last one aimed a dagger at her from behind, and I chucked a throwing star at him. It lodged in his skull, knocking him to the ground as well.

A black-and-yellow streak zoomed our way from the doors.

"Here it is!"

Starstinger landed at my feet, the bag of herbs between her pointy teeth.

"Thank you!" Taking it from her, I opened it and emptied it into the larger bag of drying dapplemint leaves and old deecho fern.

More guards bolted from the opposite direction. Mauler, Starstinger, and Trinka met them with roars, shrieks, and shouts as I furiously shook the bag to mix the ingredients.

Gripping the top closed, I stomped on the bag, crushing the dried ingredients together into a powder.

The crowd murmured.

Where was the rest of our cohort?

"Any day now, Parrianther!"

"It's ready!"

I opened the bag and poured some into the smaller bag.

"So we just, throw it at people?" Trinka asked, dashing sweat from her forehead.

"It's not ideal, but yes. You take that one, and I'll take this one."

Trinka shouted, "Look out!" as something hit me hard in the back of the head. I fell forward, spilling some of the green powder onto the dusty ground.

Skunks! "Go, Trinka, go!"

Rolling over, I found Beldon standing over me.

"Oh, thank good fortune!" I reached one hand up, expecting him to haul me to my feet and wondering where the guard he'd taken out was.

Kicking my arm aside, he slammed his boot against my chest.

"What the—"

Trinka screamed.

I glimpsed Selvenair's talons curling through Trinka's wrist and hand and the bag she still held.

He took to the air. With Trinka in his grip.

"Trinka!" How was he carrying her, too?

Beldon punched my head and my face slammed against the ground.

Right into the spilled green powder.

Snatching a pinch of powder and dust, I flung it into his face as he struck at me again.

Spluttering, he took a step back.

Mella launched at me next. Grabbing her arm, I pulled her down, slamming her face right into the powder.

Grabbing two more fistfuls, I shoved to my feet and threw one at Reenalyn and the other into Dane's face.

I glanced back up at Trinka. She was...punching the bag?

Thin whisps of green poured from the torn fabric and drifted on the breeze toward the crowd.

She'd torn holes with her spiked knuckles, and she was using Selvenair to disperse it.

Brilliant!

I hit the ground with my face again.

Skunks. How long had it actually taken for the powder to work on me?

I recognized Beldon's battle cry behind me and rolled to defend myself.

Glacier, the king's enormous polar bear, rose with her jaws wide open. Leaning forward, she fell toward me.

Beldon slammed into her just before she closed her teeth over my head.

Good. His must've worked.

Stumbling to my feet again, I checked on Trinka. She still fought Selvenair, throwing herself around so that he jerked back and forth through the air, tossing powder over the crowd as they went.

The crowd. They still don't know what's going on.

Oh, muck it all.

Darting for the stairs, I raced up toward the top stage to address the masses.

Someone grabbed my arm as I passed the first stage—the queen? Throwing white powder in my face, she gripped my shoulders with iron fingers, forcing my face to stay in the cloud.

Not again!

"You think you're the only one with powder potions, boy?" she hissed.

I held my breath as long as I could, but broke after only a few seconds. I inhaled whatever it was and she let go of me.

Unsure how long I'd have, I bolted up the stairs again.

Shrieking, she launched after me.

"Acres!" Starstinger yowled, scampering after me and digging her claws into the queen's calf.

With the seconds Starstinger bought me, I reached the upper stage where I'd first cast Starstinger several months ago. "Listen, everyone!" I shouted, raising my arms for their attention. "The green dust is safe. It's a potion that brings back memories."

"You can't force potions on people like this!" Someone shouted, his hand over his nose and mouth.

I winced. He was right. This was exactly the kind of thing I'd swore I'd never do. But I'd never expected these circumstances.

A girl's voice shouted, "The queen's been forcing potions on you for decades!"

Was that Mella? I peered over the edge. Beldon, Dane, and Reenalyn held Glacier and her bloody maw down as Mella addressed the crowd.

"She's been manipulating all our memories because she's really Morrenfayre's queen!"

The king chimed in from the second stage. "And would you all believe the word of these lesser-class peasants to the word of your king?"

Queen Narellen stepped next to him, blood dripping from her leg. "Is it more likely these children are confused, or that all of you—many hundreds of people—were deceived at the same time?"

That did sound unlikely. But they'd remember soon, so it shouldn't matter.

Shaking her head as if to clear a fog, Starstinger stumbled up the steps. "Are you okay?"

Selvenair's wing flaps came farther and farther apart and he lost altitude quickly. It had to be a huge strain to fly a person for so long.

They sank to the ground, and Selvenair bit Trinka's shoulder, his talons still holding her hand against the ground.

Then Mauler was there, grabbing the sea eagle with her powerful jaws and fumbling with her paws to free Trinka's hand. "I'm sorry, Trinka, I can't get them loose!" she said through a mouthful of feathers.

The sea eagle flapped again, and Mauler screamed when she snapped at her face, drawing more blood.

With a roar that shook the coliseum, Glacier threw the castors off her and dove toward them, burying her teeth in Mauler's flank. Blood dripped from Mauler's face and side as she lost her grip, and Trinka and the sea eagle soared again.

Chapter 63

MELLA

G lacier bucked Beldon, Reenalyn, Dane, and me off. I thought
she'd given up too easily before.

Beldon landed on me.

Mauler roared as Glacier took her down, letting Selvenair fly with
Trinka again.

Shoving Beldon off and ignoring his apologies, I leaped back to my
feet.

"Mauler!" Trinka shrieked, reaching with her good hand as the sea
eagle rose higher.

Bellowing, Beldon sprinted for Mauler and Glacier.

Trinka finally ripped the blood-slick talons loose and dropped ten
spans to the ground as Selvenair zoomed several feet into the air at the
sudden loss of weight.

His eagle feet flexed as he bunched up the sack, preventing the rest of
the potion from reaching the crowd.

*Skunks. Hopefully enough had poured out already to make an impact.
If Acres got it right, it should start working soon.*

A familiar eagle scream rang through the air, and Whisper blotted out
the sun for an instant before diving for Selvenair.

*Mucking skunks, she's flying! High enough for all to see she's a hybrid!
How the muck did she get out of the dungeon?*

She leveled over Selvenair and reached for the sack with her talons, but
Selvenair dropped out of her reach.

Except that Whisper's legs extended further than a normal eagle's would. Would that surprise be enough to catch Selvenair off-guard?

Her extra-long coyote legs extended far enough that her talons hooked the bag and tore through it, releasing the rest of the greenish powder on the wind.

Selvenair screamed at the same time Narellen shouted, "No!"

Selvenair went spiraling down, and Whisper thrust another long-legged kick at him.

Then she dove for Glacier, opened her beak—and her mouth opened even further to reveal sharp coyote molars—and she closed her beak and teeth over Glacier's neck.

I blinked.

Another chomp of Whisper's beak, and the polar bear stilled, red pooling from her neck.

Beldon released the now-limp polar bear he'd been trying to haul off Mauler and took a hold of Mauler's paw instead to pull her out.

Blood dripped from Trinka's single set of brass knuckles, which she'd torn Glacier's shoulder open with.

King Jorros let out a scream of shock and grief. "Glacier!"

Gore matted Mauler's shiny black coat as she heaved herself up and looked at Whisper. Mauler's eyes went wide at Whisper's height with her coyote haunches attaching her talons to her eagle body.

People in the crowd hunched with their heads in their hands, like they were overcome with splitting headaches. Was that supposed to happen?

I looked at Acres, and he nodded. "It's working."

A few at a time, people in the crowd stopped holding their heads and looked up at the king and queen with surprise. Some with anger.

"I remember the shattering. It was supposed to be young Prince Jorros losing his castling, not that other man!"

Some of the guards shook themselves as if memories returned to them, too. They all looked too young to remember Whisper's shattering, but who knew what the queen had done to their memories?

"She's the one who stole the livelihood of musicians and twisted music into a low trade!"

"It's her fault music was made illegal for castors!"

A lumberjack shouted, "You got us to sell the mucked Emberlyn wood at a high price to our own people, while we sold the best quality to Morrenfayre at a ridiculously low rate!"

They remembered.

Acres did it.

Now could we get the queen under control before she floramanced her way out of this?

CHAPTER 64

ACRES

M y head spun. I'd start forgetting any moment now.

How had I gotten myself into this again?

Mucking floramancy!

If I survived this, I'd stay away from it from now on. No matter who needed my help.

Had my grandmother felt like this when she was a girl, before the change that made her forget the things she loved and think so highly of the new queen?

"That's right!" The snow leopard castor pointed at each of the people sitting around him. "You all remember it now, too! See, I wasn't crazy!"

So he'd been right all along.

What did that mean about hybrids in Morrenfayre, then?

I might forget to protect the mandolin when the potion took effect. Was there anywhere I could hide it? I glanced down at it and blinked.

Was my memory fading already, or was this the wrong mandolin? The dark wood and smooth, shiny finish looked too normal. Mella's was more homemade-looking. Wasn't it?

"Sienna, how lovely to see you once more." The queen said. "For the record, I wasn't really going to shatter you again. You're far too interesting a specimen to waste. You'll fall asleep soon, and when you next wake up, you'll be in Morrenfayre. With the others of your kind."

Others of her kind? Other avians, or other hybrids?

I waited for my memories or thoughts to fade, but they didn't.

Starstinger hopped into view, balancing on the railing. She eyed me, brandishing a clenched paw, green dust falling from between her toe pads. "Acres! Do you know who I am?"

"Yeah," I realized, surprised it hadn't taken effect yet. "You're Starstinger, my castling," I said, the headache abating.

"Oh. Right. Good." Relief washed over her face. "Well, here's a little powder potion for you anyway, just in case." She pitched the pawful of crushed leaves in my face just as I took a breath.

I coughed and sputtered, grateful she'd been so quick to combat any memory floramancy that might have been in the powder the queen threw in my face moments ago.

I breathed in the spicy-sweet aroma of dapplemint, my memories unaffected.

Nothing had been lost. It was all still there, just as it had been before I charged into the coliseum on Mauler's back or raced up the stairs to address the crowd.

Probably because I had already breathed in some of the green dust.

It had worked. I had brought the truth back to all these people, and helped save my friends. Floramancy could do some good after all.

CHAPTER 65

SELVERINE

I inhaled as a rush of wind gusted my way catching the scent of mint and feeling the tang of copper in my mouth.

And I remembered. Narellen, standing over my father and my mother with a bloody sword after running them both through for defying her. She'd made me drink tea for the shock.

I remembered seeing her play the drum to cast Selvenair, and the fury on her face when she realized I'd seen, and the tea she'd given me right away.

I remembered the king looking on me with compassion and care, telling me he'd ensure I had the best education to take his place one day. Then the queen filling his head with lies about my incompetence and disrespect for him, and giving me more tea as she filled another cup for him as well.

I remembered sneaking through the other door in her sitting room that led to her personal greenhouse. The thrashing when she'd caught me.

More tea.

And Grandmother had been building hate for Horizon in me all along. I'd never hated my castling at all. I'd never even wanted an avian until Grandmother suggested I did. The species hadn't mattered to me—I only ever wanted a castling to love and protect me like my parents couldn't anymore. All that hate—that was Grandmother's doing. And the reason I couldn't cast her now...I clasped a hand over my mouth.

Grandmother, the one person I loved and trusted, was responsible for it all.

CHAPTER 66

MELLA

More than a week after the tournament that didn't happen, Terrenthyrs was still in an uproar.

Many older citizens remembered everything about the past, and some of the younger ones remembered things the queen had wanted them to forget. But even more people hadn't been exposed to Acres's potion because there just hadn't been enough.

My fellow Wrynford castors hauled Queen Narellen off to her very own dungeon cell as Whisper and I returned for Bennet. The queen threw her powder potion in our faces, but with Acres's potion still in our systems, it didn't work.

Bennet had been locked up so long that they'd lost the skunking key, so we couldn't get him out right away. I'd returned with a heaping plate from The Braided Loaf an hour later, and Whisper never left his side.

Selverine was furious and in shock, but Willova had seen where the queen put my real mandolin, and I retrieved it with Dane's help before the day was out.

Since then, King Jorros worked with Acres every day to get more of the antidote out to people who needed it. And Dane hadn't mentioned what Trinka and Reenalyn implied about us when we'd all been captured. I hadn't been brave enough to bring it up, either.

Sunlight dappled the brown leaf litter through the flourishing Emberlyn trees above Whisper and me as we rested against a trunk.

Whisper slid her beak over the feathers of one wing, grooming them into place. "I wonder what the king will choose to do with the queen. Did he ever really love her, or had she tricked him into everything? Will he sentence her to death?"

"I have no idea," I said. "Does he even know how to be a king, when he was under her control for decades? And now without his castling—another loss, and now he has no one he can be sure to trust."

Whisper was silent. Likely thinking about Bennet. She would finally get to see him again today, as soon as the new key cooled enough to go in the lock.

"I'm so glad Bennet is going to be freed soon."

"They better not mess up the key a *second* time," she growled. Her eyes softened. "But I don't want to leave you, though."

I smiled back. "It's okay, Whisper. You belong with Bennet. You'll both be so happy to have each other again. And thanks to all the trouble you've caused me, I've got some great new friends to keep me company."

She squinted at me. "And you'll still hang out with us old people sometimes, right? Maybe?"

"Of course! And wait—how old are you, then?"

"In my mid-forties, I guess. But I only experienced my first few years, so technically I'm still a youngling not much older than you," she teased, shaking out her crown feathers like she thought she was all that.

I returned her smile. "Yeah, I'd love to hang out with you *old people*."

She beamed. "If he gets out in time, we'll both be at the firepit tonight. Reenalyn's cooking, you know."

That sounded like a perfect way to end the evening. "I'll be there."

She smiled one more time and then took to the sky, finally able to fly now that her legs weren't a secret.

***

Dane tossed his castling tent peg in the air and caught it as it flipped, his lithe arms flexing distractingly as he balanced on a high branch. "Do you think the Grand Castors' Tournament will still happen next year? Since that was the queen's doing, too?"

I struggled to keep my balance and think of a response when all I wanted to do was watch Dane. How had I missed the lean muscles and the way his smile always made me smile? He didn't just have better hands and intelligent eyes. He was honest and considerate and real.

Infinitely more appealing than Kaido in every way.

I shifted my stance, my boots scraping over the bark. "There's no point, is there? Narellen started the whole competition just to spoil and weaken our best fighters. The winners would get paid to relax and overeat for the rest of their lives, effectively removing the best soldiers from the military if a war would ever have started between Terrenthyrs and Morrenfayre. It was a clever way to go about weakening us. But even if the tournament did happen just to see who would win—without a castling, I'd be disqualified."

He slid his castling weapon into its sheath and sat next to me, his eyes on mine. "Couldn't Whisper fight with you just once more? It's been all you wanted for so long."

Actually, Dane, it hasn't been all I've wanted for a while. "No. She would if I asked her, but that would take away from the time she deserves with Bennet."

"That's kind of you."

His voice rang through me. Why did I suddenly have to notice how nice his voice sounded?

This had to stop. He was clearly over me, and I was only hurting myself by continuing to spend so much time alone with him. I had to do something before I fell in love with him.

If it wasn't already too late.

"Thanks. Um, I've got to go, Dane. I'll see you at the bonfire tonight." I knelt to reach a lower branch, but my sweaty palms slipped. Arms flailing, I scrabbled for a hold but fell hard against the next branch and then the ground.

"Mella!" Dane was on the ground at my side in an instant. "Mella, are you okay? I'm so sorry I wasn't close enough to catch you!"

I pushed myself into a sitting position. "Yeah. I think I'm fine."

My knee hurt—I probably landed on it wrong. And my hands stung. I inspected my palms.

"Monkey's teeth, Mella, your hands are bleeding!" Dane took my hands in his, staring at the red scratches.

"It's not that bad. Just burns a little. No permanent damage." The warmth of his hands soaked into my skin. I should pull away, protect myself. But I couldn't make myself leave. "Why do you always say that?"

"What?" His eyes were frantic as he glanced over the rest of me for injuries.

"Monkey's teeth."

He blinked, his warm hands still cradling mine. "You're curious about *that* when you almost died?"

I rolled my eyes. "I did not almost die. I'm fine. Really."

"But you could've died, and it would've been my fault."

"Dane, you aren't obligated to catch me every time I fall." *Though I'm not stopping you.* "I'm still in one piece, and I'd like to know about the monkey teeth."

He peered into my eyes, his face creased with concern. "Okay. But stop me if you notice any new pain, okay?"

I nodded.

He sighed, but his hands remained around mine, and he stayed crouched next to me. Did he realize he was still holding my hands?

I wanted to glance down and see what our hands looked like together. But I didn't want to remind him if he'd forgotten. I wanted them to stay where they were.

Who am I kidding? I've completely fallen for him already.

"I had a job a while ago, with a really, *really* bad boss. Mr. Slaeryn."

His face went darker than I'd ever seen it, and it made him look older. And...sort of darkly handsome.

"Mr. Slaeryn was...bad. Dangerous. He walked with a cane he didn't need but always kept on hand in case he got the notion to strike anyone. The handle was carved into the sneering face of a capuchin monkey showing off its oversized teeth. He also kept several live capuchins, and cleaning up after them was one of my jobs. They were always biding their time to tear into anything they could get their filthy little hands on."

Dane shifted uncomfortably.

"Mr. Slaeryn liked to tear into people, too. Some of us started calling him 'the monkey's teeth' behind his back. Sometimes to warn each other when he was coming. My dad worried it was too obvious a nickname, so he said we should start using it as a common curse instead and blame its origin on the capuchins we all hated. That way if he heard anyone say it, he would just think someone was swearing."

"Why were there monkeys?"

"The capuchins were...part of the entertainment. They were tiny wild devils that pitched their muck at me while I tried to clean around them, and they bit me plenty of times, too. And if I ever let one escape, I wasn't paid again until I'd captured it. Which was never a good time."

"That sounds horrible."

"It was."

"So your father worked at the same job as you?"

"Yeah."

"How old were you when you started working there?"

"Honestly, I don't remember. Really young." His hands grew clammy against mine.

He had to be uncomfortable, crouching like that.

With a deep breath, I took a quick look at our hands, just in case. The tips of his fingers curled around my hands, a few of them brushing my wrists. His forearms were paler than mine, but so attractively shaped.

Something about this guy's hands affected me differently than even Kaido's kisses.

I opened my mouth and hesitated.

Would he pull away?

Chapter 67

DANE

"Skunks, Dane, your hands are shaking. Are you okay?" Mella's voice drew me back to the present, where my sweaty, trembling hands still clutched hers.

I jumped back and released her hands, mortified that I'd gotten sweat all over them. "I'm so sorry, Mella. Ugh. That's disgusting." I looked around for something to give her to wipe her hands off with, but there was nothing but dried leaves. "I'm so sorry."

She quirked an eyebrow. "Sorry about what? I'm the one prying into your story."

"Because I sweated all over your hands!"

"Dane, you do realize we've all sweated all over each other every day over the past several months since we joined the same cohort, right? Sort of a hazard of sparring together."

I sighed, backing against a tree trunk and crossing one leg over the other. "I guess. I just...I just don't want you to think I'm disgusting."

I couldn't meet her gaze, but the frown came through her voice. "Why would I think that?"

"Because we come from such different places."

"You mean because I'm—or I used to be—a better classer, and you're a lesser classer?"

"Yes. Sort of. I'm not really even a lesser classer though."

"Dane, first, that's silly. My family's fortune has been declining for years, and being disowned puts me beneath even that. I've been better-class in name only for a long time. That's why I tried so hard for so long to get in with Selverine and Kaido."

I scowled at the ground. Kaido, that sniveling piece of capuchin dung. "Have you seen Kaido recently?"

She scoffed. "That skunking piece of muck?"

Suddenly my spirits rose considerably, and my gut no longer roiled. "Yeah, that's the one."

"I saw him from a distance at work." She grinned mischievously.

My stomach sank. Why was she grinning mischievously about Kaido?

"That's really some scar Reenalyn gave him, isn't it?"

I sighed with relief. "Yeah, it really is." *Reenalyn, I owe you big time for that one.*

Her voice softened. "To think I ever thought the best way to get back at my parents was by marrying someone wealthy. I thought Kaido would be a good choice, if I could keep his attention until we were old enough to marry."

She winced. It was the most beautiful wince I'd ever seen.

"What an idiot. I was never anything to him."

Rage thrummed through every fiber of my being. Kaido deserved to be destroyed for treating Mella like that. He deserved...yes, even that. He deserved to have his castling shattered before his eyes.

"That was...indescribably wrong of him, Mella. You are much more—so much more than anything like that. You deserve better."

She smiled and ducked her head. Maybe I'd embarrassed her. But that was okay. She needed to know.

"That's kind of you, Dane."

She looked up at me from under her thick lashes as she said my name, and I couldn't pretend any longer. It was time to tell her that part of the story.

"Brekken Fennyl Road."

Her eyes flashed to mine. "What?"

"The street in Glenmyre where beggars gather to plead for help from the wealthy."

She stared at me, her lips parted in surprise. Had she figured it out?

"You've always been generous with beggars, haven't you?"

She quirked an eyebrow. "How did you know that?"

I sighed. This was it. "Because that's actually how you and I first met. A few months before the Castling Ceremony." There. I'd said it. There was no going back now.

"What?" Shock colored her face.

"I escaped with Sprinter from the kingdom of Zurrenbelg over the sea. Or really, he escaped with me. Mr. Slaeryn had given me a taste of the monkey's teeth, and I was in pretty rough shape. By the time we got here, I hate to say I'd mostly given up. My family sacrificed so much to help me escape, but they were stuck with Slaeryn and I was consumed with guilt. And I was sort of beaten and starving. Sprinter had to beg for us for a while, because I didn't see the point."

I shifted uncomfortably, the thick bark scraping my back through my tunic. "Where we come from, castors and castlings are myths. He didn't know anyone would believe him here. So he didn't speak, and because he looks like a wild dog, a lot of people weren't kind to him."

Her eyebrows drew together in concern. I plowed on.

"But you. You gave coins to a handful of other beggars, and they all went to the market to buy themselves food. You drew one more coin from your pocket, your last one, and bought yourself a meal, too. After, when you saw Sprinter—skin and bones by then, thanks to my terrible care of us both—you gave him your whole sandwich. Even though you couldn't buy another. He said he heard your stomach growl as he walked away with it."

My smile at the memory of her generosity melted into a frown at what came next. "That food gave me enough strength to get up from where I'd fallen. But the next day..." I took a deep breath. "The next day, I was so hungry again and angry at the better classers who ate so much food."

I paused, searching her eyes for the click of memory. Had she figured it out now? Could I skip having to say it?

She looked concerned, but not comprehending. I'd have to go on.

Staring at the ground, I continued. "Brekken Fennyl Road wasn't too far from The Braided Loaf. I followed some better classers home after they ate there and stole from them. And, having become a greedy skunk, I...I stole from some of the homeless people you'd just helped."

If only I could take it back. She'd surely hate me now. But I had to come clean. "Then I stumbled on my way back to the Loaf to buy myself a big meal, and you were there. You saw that I was cold and hungry. Of course not the coins—I'd shoved those away. And then you gave me a smile and all your coins and the cloak off your back without a second thought."

I couldn't meet her eyes. "At first I was angry at you. I was embarrassed to be caught like that. But you looked at Sprinter, patted his head, and told me to make sure I took good care of him. You smiled at us, and he wagged his tail at you, and I realized the world wasn't entirely full of horrible people. And I wanted to be worthy of your kindness and of the sacrifices my parents made to set me free. And I never wanted to feel so humiliated ever again."

I averted my eyes. I still couldn't bear to see her disgust. The girl I'd fallen in love with would certainly never want that with me now. Not knowing this about me. But she needed to know how much I owed her.

I made myself go on. "I bought food the next couple of days, and then a set of clean clothes with the better classers' money, and returned the coins I'd taken from my fellow beggars. I gave them the new coins from you, too. Wearing the clean clothes and your cloak, I informed the baker I was a friend of yours and that you recommended me for a job. He gave me a chance, and, as you know, I still work there," I laughed, but it sounded all wrong. Awkward and uncomfortable. "I guess what I'm trying to say is without your kindness, I would've died. Sprinter, too. So thank you. For saving us."

"I'm so sorry you had to go through that, Dane." Compassion filled her voice.

Here it comes. "*Sorry I can't stand to be around you anymore. Sorry I didn't realize how disgusting you are. Bye.*"

"I feel so ashamed of ever being so discontent just because Selverine had more."

Finally I let myself look at her.

There was sorrow in her face, but no disgust.

I was stunned. "That's your first thought? Not how horrible I am and how much you want me out of your sight?"

She grimaced. There it was. "Well, stealing and lying don't exactly make a nice image. But you're not a bad image, Dane." A beautiful flush bloomed on her cheeks. "I mean, you gave the money back to those who needed it, and we've got lots of other memories since then that are all good. Right?"

I stared. "So you're saying you're not disgusted by the sight of me?"

She rolled her eyes. "Of course not, Dane. You were starving and desperate and you had your castling to care for."

I blinked at her. "Yeah, I was. But you really don't think of me any differently now?"

She scrubbed her hands dramatically over her face. Pushing herself to her feet, she groaned, "Skunks, Dane, what do I have to do to prove I don't think anything is wrong with you?" Her eyes narrowed slightly. "Why would it matter if I did think you were disgusting?"

"Because my feelings about you are so completely opposite that...I couldn't stand it."

She hesitated. Deliberating? "Honestly, Dane, I think you're pretty great."

Something in my chest soared. She thought I was *great*? That wasn't what I was expecting. I stood too, in case she was getting ready to leave.

Her ocean eyes stilled as they locked on mine. "I know one way I could prove it to you." Her lips parted into a sly smile I'd never seen before—a look that didn't seem to fit in this conversation.

She couldn't mean what it looked like she meant.

"Mella?" I rasped.

She stepped closer with that sly smile. Things fluttered in my stomach. She was unbearably close now. Her body heat touched my skin through the space between us.

"What are you doing?" My voice was barely a husky whisper.

She whispered, "Close your eyes."

I did, and the scent of her skin and the sound of her breathing overwhelmed me.

Her hand touched my jaw, her fingertips brushing my neck.

My pulse hammered. Was she...?

And then she *kissed* me.

Somehow her lips were pressed against mine.

Sparks of trembling heat burst all through me. I couldn't believe this was happening.

She took up all of my mind. Mella, her gorgeous eyes, her devastating smile, her kindness that had changed my life.

And then her hand was gone and her heat was gone and her lips were gone. I opened my eyes, terrified I would wake from a daydream and find her gone, too.

But she was right there. Barely half a span away. Smiling shyly now. Tucking a strand of dark hair behind her ear. "Sorry. That wasn't really a just-friends type of thing to do, I guess."

"Mella." I stared at her, reeling. Did she have any idea what she was doing to me?

"Was that...okay?" she asked uncertainly.

The most incredible, beautiful girl I'd ever known worried that kissing me might not be okay.

I tried to catch my breath, to find words...the kiss was so incredibly perfect...but I'd barely kissed her back, she'd stunned me so completely. My arms had hung rigid at my sides. Her hair floated in the breeze, and the space between us hadn't shrunk. There was so much more to say...

It all came tumbling out.

"Mella, I haven't stopped thinking about you since the day we met. Dancing and talking with you the night of the ball was the best night of my life. And letting go of your hand that night was the hardest thing I've ever done. I said so much about being friends because I didn't want you to feel pressure for something you weren't ready for. But I can't even describe how much I don't want to be just friends."

There it was. I'd finally said it. She could easily hurt me now more than she could ever know.

But then she whispered, "Neither do I."

I gazed at her eyes, shocked but hopeful, desperate and joyful and pleading. "Mella Yarinelle. Come back."

And she stepped into my arms.

With her arms draped over my shoulders and her lips against mine, my arms wrapped around her back, her waist. I held her against my chest, and nothing had ever felt more right.

Her hair brushed against my arms, and I smiled into her lips as I slid one hand slowly up her back, over her shoulders. I weaved my fingers through her soft hair and cradled her head in my hand.

I leaned my head back just a fraction and whispered, "Nothing in the world is more precious to me than what I'm holding in my arms right now. I have loved you for a long time, Mella Yarinelle."

She made a whimpery noise, and I pulled back to see her face.

Her eyes shone as she beamed at me. I couldn't believe it. She pulled me closer and pressed her mouth to mine.

"Whoa! Get a room, people."

We both jumped, and Mella turned toward the intruder. I kept one arm around her, unwilling to let her go now that I could hold her.

"Trinka? We're busy."

Mella ran her hands through her mussed hair, and I beamed at her. Yes, we certainly were.

"Yeah, I can see that." Trinka's eyebrows stood high on her forehead. "But Berroman's been calling you for half an hour. Whisper's castor was released, and they're both at the firepit ready for dinner. And according to the Castors of Wrynford tradition, that means eating food and then playing some music—especially now that it's legal. Or, maybe less especially. But it is what it is."

She waited, but we both stood there, not willing to move out of each other's arms.

"So are you coming or what?"

"We'll be right behind you," Mella said.

"Sure." Trinka rolled her eyes but left us alone.

When I turned back to Mella, she was biting her lip, her eyes shining with joy and something else that set my pulse racing.

She wrapped her arms around my torso, running her hands over my back and shoulders. Could my body actually feel worth touching to her like that?

"I guess we shouldn't keep them waiting." The deep blue of her eyes shone at me through her thick lashes. "But a little longer surely wouldn't be so bad..."

My arms over her shoulders now, I hugged her to me, my chin against her cheek. "Are you real?"

"Maybe you should kiss me again to check."

I slid my hand over her shoulders, through her hair, under her jaw. It fit just right on the side of her neck.

With her arms around me and her fingers splayed over my shoulders, I kissed Mella Yarinelle, and she kissed me back.

Chapter 68

Mella

Firelight flickered in Bennet's bright eyes. The taming of his wild gray mane had left his chin bare and his hair a manageable length, and he looked much more human. "And when I saw Jorros aim at King Krelweyn, all the other weird things he'd been doing finally made sense."

He shook one finger knowingly at us. "So I blocked Jorros's strike. But he still pinned it on me. I never understood it, with all the witnesses. But Narellen must have floramanced everyone into saying what she wanted. I've felt so betrayed and angry at him for all these years. But maybe...maybe his life ended that day too, in a way, if Narellen was really controlling him."

"Skunks," Beldon said, leaning forward with his arms draped over his knees hanging on every word.

Whisper sprawled out in Bennet's lap, tongue lolling from her beak as she gazed at him with such love and tenderness I couldn't help being delighted for her. For them. And grateful they'd been willing to give up what could've been their last moments together for Whisper to save us all. The guards thought they'd hauled all of us out of the cell, so they didn't lock the door back.

My heart did ache at losing my castling. It seemed unfair I'd lost my one chance at a lifelong companion and comrade. But if it had saved everyone from Narellen—then it was worth it. I still couldn't believe it had been *her* all along, instead of King Jorros.

And I had real friends now. Nothing like what Yulroe and Selverine had been. And that was something I would always treasure.

I glanced at Dane, sitting on the log next to me. He'd been right about real friends. And somehow, he'd still been waiting for me. Our fingers twined together, and that was something I was looking forward to getting used to.

But I also had a question about what went down on the day of the tournament. "Trinka," I asked, turning to her, "I've been wondering, how were you not affected by the queen's floramanced wafer?"

"I never swallowed it."

"But she watched each of us eat it. How'd you pull that off?"

"A little street-style slight of hand."

I frowned. "Huh?"

She shrugged.

"So, Mella." Reenalyn leaned over and lightly knocked into my shoulder, distracting me.

I glanced up at her. "What's that face? You already freaked out about Dane and me, so what else could possibly have you grinning like that?"

"Well...I was wondering if you'd decided what you want. If it's still the same as before, or if it's changed."

I lifted an eyebrow. "I don't follow."

"For your castling!" She beamed. "I know you're not supposed to tell but...I'm so curious. And that's like the least of anyone's worries in the world right now."

"My castling? But Whisper..."

She cocked her head. "Whisper is Sienna, Bennet's castling, in an altered manifestation because you cast her from an instrument. But she's *Bennet's* castling, not yours. Not both of yours, either. You can't just share half your soul with someone else's. It doesn't work like that."

I stared at her, gaping. "You mean...I still have a chance? I haven't spent my one chance at casting?"

"Of course you do!"

Stunned, I stared at her. "I'm not sure what I want, but I won't be naming it Magnificence. That's for sure."

"That does sound like something the old Mella would've chosen." Reenalyn agreed.

Dane squeezed my hand. "Whatever you decide will be fantastic."

Squeezing Dane's hand back, I grinned at Reenalyn. Behind her, firelight glowed on the faces of each of my friends—my family.

Joy and excitement overwhelmed me.

I had all of them now.

And there was a castling in my future.

EPILOGUE

QUEEN NARELLEN

B rushing my hand over the stone floor, I swept all the dirt into a little pile. Crouching over it, I unrolled my robe sleeves three times and watched the seeds trickle from the folds.

It was only a matter of time before I'd have the plants I needed to get myself out of here.

Gripping the cool iron bars, I stared out over the buildings, past the Emberlyn Forest, toward Morrenfayre. The regent would have his work cut out for him controlling the army without my regular shipment of floramancy. But he'd find a way to manage.

The Emberlyn Forest blocked my view of Morrenfayre. Bennet, Sienna, and Mella surely celebrated their victory among those tall trees now.

But not for long. By the time I was free once again, my sources would have gotten rid of Sienna and Bennet. The king would once again be under my control. And Selverine would be almost ready.

I'd beat Slaeryn at his own game.

Smiling, I followed the beam of sunlight back down to the soil and seeds.

Just a matter of time.

ACKNOWLEDGEMENTS

Firstly, I thank God for giving me this love of writing and creating worlds (on a much smaller scale than He did!) and for working in my heart all these years so that I'm finally able to say so. I didn't acknowledge Him in my first three books, and I am so thankful to be in a healthier place now spiritually and emotionally so that I can, fearlessly and joyfully, thank Him publicly and give this book and my writing career to Him, who works all things together for the good of those who love Him.

Immediately after God, I thank my incredibly loving and supportive husband, Ben, who has believed in me and my writing career even when I didn't and devoted himself to our growing family with admirable steadfastness. You have been my greatest supporter and encourager in writing and in motherhood, and I am so grateful our daughter has the most loving and devoted father in the world. Thank you for taking care of us and for hanging out with Tessa to give me some more writing time. Without your support, this book wouldn't exist.

Thank you to Mom, who gave up her career to educate me and Tori. I remember the royal fits I pitched when you taught me how to read and write and type. I said it was a waste of time because I'd never need it. Thank you for persevering through my childhood tantrums to provide me with the skills I would, in fact, very much need to pursue my dreams. Without your inexhaustible patience and love, this book wouldn't exist.

Thank you to Missy, my wonderfully non-stereotypical mother-in-law. Thank you for your encouragement and support of my writing dreams over the years, even when they seemed much less possible. Thank you for reading several versions of this book and loving each one, for proofreading, and for taking such great care of Tessa to give me some time to work and write. Without you and your invaluable contributions, this book wouldn't exist.

Thank you to Noni and Grams, who both always speak as if it's a simple point of fact that I am awesome and have done and will continue to do great things. Everyone should be blessed with grandmothers like you two! Without your excitement and belief in me, this book wouldn't exist.

And a huge thank you to my writer friends from Dream Big Writers, Writers Business Mastermind, Snack Pack, Scribblers, NaNoWriMo, and Instagram, especially Kristin Ardis, Teresa Beasley, Holly Davis, Renee Dugan, Alicia Grumley, Michele Harper, Cam Steiman, Annie Sullivan, and Brittany Wang. I deeply treasure your manuscript critique, constant encouragement, and mutual delight in the craft of writing, and I couldn't imagine my life without you!

SAVANNAH J. GOINS is the author of multiple sweet, swoony, and spice-free YA romantic fantasy novels. While working at an exotic animal clinic, she came in contact with both tiger and dragon blood more than once. Whether she has magical abilities as a result is yet to be determined. When not writing, she hangs out with her family, draws zentangles, and helps homeless dragons find forever homes in the real world by volunteering with an exotic animal rescue.

Printed in the USA
CPSIA information can be obtained
at www.ICGtesting.com
CBHW021943080724
11298CB00016BA/54/J

9 781964 144009